高一同學的目標

1. 熟背「高中常用7000字」
2. 月期考得高分
3. 會說流利的英語

1. 「用會話背7000字①」書+ CD 280元
   以三個極短句為一組的方式，讓同學背了會話，同時快速增加單字。高一同學要從「國中常用2000字」挑戰「高中常用7000字」，加強單字是第一目標。

2. 「一分鐘背9個單字」書+ CD 280元
   利用字首、字尾的排列，讓你快速增加單字。一次背9個比背1個字簡單。

3. rival

rival⁵ ('raɪvl̩) n. 對手

arrival³ (ə'raɪvl̩) n.

festival² ('fɛstəvl̩) n.

revival⁶ (rɪ'vaɪvl̩) n. 復活

survival³ (sə'vaɪvl̩) n. 生還

carnival⁶ ('kɑrnəvl̩) n. 嘉年華

carnation⁵ (kɑr'neʃən) n. 康乃馨
donation⁶ (do'neʃən) n. 捐贈
donate⁶ ('donet) v. 捐贈
（字尾是 nation）

3. 「一口氣考試英語」書+ CD 280元
   把大學入學考試題目編成會話，背了以後，會說英語，又會考試。

   例如：
   What a nice surprise! (真令人驚喜！)【常考】
   I can't believe my eyes.
   (我無法相信我的眼睛。)
   Little did I dream of seeing you here.
   (做夢也沒想到會在這裡看到你。)【駒澤大】

4.「一口氣背文法」書+ CD 280元
英文文法範圍無限大，規則無限多，誰背得完？
劉毅老師把文法整體的概念，編成216句，背完
了會做文法題、會說英語，也會寫作文。既是一
本文法書，也是一本會話書。

1. 現在簡單式的用法

I *get up* early every day.	我每天早起。
I *understand* this rule now.	我現在了解這條規定了。
Actions *speak* louder than words.	行動勝於言辭。

【二、三句強調實踐早起】

5.「高中英語聽力測驗①」書+ MP3 280元

6.「高中英語聽力測驗進階」書+ MP3 280元
高一月期考聽力佔20%，我們根據大考中心公布的
聽力題型編輯而成。

7.「高一月期考英文試題」書 280元
收集建中、北一女、師大附中、中山、成功、景
美女中等各校試題，並聘請各校名師編寫模擬試
題。

8.「高一英文克漏字測驗」書 180元

9.「高一英文閱讀測驗」書 180元
全部取材自高一月期考試題，英雄
所見略同，重複出現的機率很高。
附有翻譯及詳解，不必查字典，對
錯答案都有明確交待，做完題目，
一看就懂。

高二同學的目標——提早準備考大學

1. 「用會話背7000字①②」
   書+CD，每冊280元

   「用會話背7000字」能夠解決所有學英文的困難。高二同學可先從第一冊開始背，第一冊和第二冊沒有程度上的差異，背得越多，單字量越多，在腦海中的短句越多。每一個極短句大多不超過5個字，1個字或2個字都可以成一個句子，如：「用會話背7000字①」p.184，每一句都2個字，好背得不得了，而且與生活息息相關，是每個人都必須知道的知識，例如：成功的祕訣是什麼？

11. What are the keys to success?

Be *ambitious*.	要有**雄心**。
Be *confident*.	要有**信心**。
Have *determination*.	要有**決心**。
Be *patient*.	要有**耐心**。
Be *persistent*.	要有**恆心**。
Show *sincerity*.	要有**誠心**。
Be *charitable*.	要有**愛心**。
Be *modest*.	要**虛心**。
Have *devotion*.	要**專心**。

當你背單字的時候，就要有「雄心」，要「決心」背好，對自己要有「信心」，一定要有「耐心」和「恆心」，背書時要「專心」。

背完後，腦中有2,160個句子，那不得了，無限多的排列組合，可以寫作文。有了單字，翻譯、閱讀測驗、克漏字都難不倒你了。高二的時候，要下定決心，把7000字背熟、背爛。雖然高中課本以7000字為範圍，編書者為了便宜行事，往往超出7000字，同學背了少用的單字，反倒忽略真正重要的單字。千萬記住，背就要背「高中常用7000字」，背完之後，天不怕、地不怕，任何考試都難不倒你。

2.「時速破百單字快速記憶」書 250元

字尾是 try，重音在倒數第三音節上

entry [3] ('ɛntrɪ) *n.* 進入【No entry. 禁止進入。】
country [1] ('kʌntrɪ) *n.* 國家；鄉下【ou 讀 /ʌ/，為例外字】
ministry [4] ('mɪnɪstrɪ) *n.* 部【mini = small】

chemistry [4] ('kɛmɪstrɪ) *n.* 化學
geometry [5] (dʒi'ɑmətrɪ) *n.* 幾何學【geo 土地，metry 測量】
industry [2] ('ɪndəstrɪ) *n.* 工業；勤勉【這個字重音常唸錯】

poetry [1] ('po‧ɪtrɪ) *n.* 詩
poultry [4] ('poltrɪ) *n.* 家禽　}字尾 y 表「集合名詞」
pastry [5] ('pestrɪ) *n.* 糕餅

3.「高二英文克漏字測驗」書 180元

4.「高二英文閱讀測驗」書 180元
全部選自各校高二月期考試題精華，英雄所見略
同，再出現的機率很高。

5.「7000字學測試題詳解」書 250元
一般模考題為了便宜行事，往往超出7000字範圍
，無論做多少份試題，仍然有大量生字，無法進
步。唯有鎖定7000字為範圍的試題，才會對準備
考試有幫助。每份試題都經「劉毅英文」同學實
際考過，效果奇佳。附有詳細解答，單字標明級
數，對錯答案都有明確交待，不需要再查字典，
做完題目，再看詳解，快樂無比。

6.「高中常用7000字解析【豪華版】」書 390元
按照「大考中心高中英文參考詞彙表」編輯而成
。難背的單字有「記憶技巧」、「同義字」及
「反義字」，關鍵的單字有「典型考題」。大學
入學考試核心單字，以紅色標記。

7.「高中7000字測驗題庫」書 180元
取材自大規模考試，解答詳盡，節省查字典的時間。

序 言

　　詞彙題是「學測」每年必考的題型。詞彙題不只是考單字，也考閱讀能力，如果你每次詞彙題都能得滿分，那其他的題型，像綜合測驗、文意選填、篇章結構、閱讀測驗、翻譯、作文，只要稍加努力，就能完全征服。

　　「高中7000字測驗題庫」以大考中心公佈的「高中常用7000字」為範圍，完全依照「學測」詞彙題的命題趨勢，精心設計40回測驗。每一回有10題詞彙測驗及5題慣用語測驗，每條題目均有中文翻譯及註釋，能節省同學查字典的時間；每個選項還附有詞類變化、同反義字、字根分析、背誦技巧、常考片語，或例句說明等補充資料，讓同學加深印象，徹底了解每個單字的用法。同學每做完一回之後，一定要徹底檢討，如此字彙實力必能在短時間內大幅提升，考起試來會更加得心應手。

　　做詞彙題，是記憶字彙最有效的輔助力量，也是厚植字彙實力最直接、最有效的方法。以前背單字，看到題目不一定會做；現在用這種方法背單字，一分耕耘、一分收穫，同學絕對不會吃虧。你試試看，先做一回，徹底了解每條題目的意思，像讀課本一樣，把每條題目，大聲地朗讀幾遍，你再做第二回時，就會發現，自己在進步。

　　本書的編審及校對，雖力求盡善盡美，但恐仍有疏漏之處，誠盼各界先進不吝指正。

編者 謹識

TEST 1

Directions: The following questions are incomplete sentences. You are to choose the one word that best completes the sentence.

1. Betty was delighted at the news that her proposal had been _____ by the student council.
   (A) adopted   (B) adjusted
   (C) advanced   (D) adapted   ( )

2. You haven't studied at all this semester. It's totally _____ to try to cram everything in for the final exams now.
   (A) dogmatic   (B) futile
   (C) isolated   (D) deliberate   ( )

3. As a teaching assistant, I need to _____ the midterm exam tomorrow, so I can't go with you.
   (A) reveal   (B) abolish
   (C) fortify   (D) monitor   ( )

4. The detective sat at the desk _____ what the witness had said.
   (A) responding   (B) wandering
   (C) stimulating   (D) pondering   ( )

5. I only have a(n) _____ recollection of going to the botanical garden as a child. I can't recall that experience clearly.
   (A) memorial   (B) evident
   (C) visual   (D) vague   ( )

6. The police were _____ of the man's alibi because someone saw him near the crime scene.
   (A) melancholy   (B) suspicious
   (C) beneficial   (D) magnificent   ( )

7. This new medicine is sure to _____ you of your toothache.
   (A) convince   (B) inform
   (C) deprive   (D) relieve   ( )

8. This soup is delicious, Jenny. You must give me the _____.
   - (A) script
   - (B) approach
   - (C) recipe
   - (D) manual
   ( )

9. The author has _____ his manuscript more than three times to make the story shorter.
   - (A) improvised
   - (B) revised
   - (C) advised
   - (D) devised
   ( )

10. It took Julia a long time to _____ the skills she needed to become a professional singer.
   - (A) acquire
   - (B) require
   - (C) inquire
   - (D) conquer
   ( )

11. The police believed that the fire was started _____. It was probably arson.
   - (A) deliberately
   - (B) elaborately
   - (C) dogmatically
   - (D) accordingly
   ( )

12. I told Jane if she passed her chemistry test, I'd take her to the French restaurant. However, she didn't seem to feel _____.
   - (A) bewildered
   - (B) depressed
   - (C) qualified
   - (D) motivated
   ( )

13. When Tina was visiting San Diego, she decided to _____ her aunt, who lived there.
   - (A) drop in on
   - (B) see off
   - (C) set out for
   - (D) live up to
   ( )

14. I had to unwrap the package because I had _____ one item I wanted to send along.
   - (A) checked out
   - (B) crossed out
   - (C) left out
   - (D) ruled out
   ( )

15. The elevator was _____, so everyone had to take the stairs.
   - (A) off and on
   - (B) up and down
   - (C) out of work
   - (D) out of order
   ( )

TEST 1 詳解

1. (**A**) Betty was delighted at the news that her proposal had been <u>adopted</u> by the student council. 貝蒂聽到她的提議被學生會<u>採用</u>的消息時，非常高興。

(A) *adopt*〔ə'dɑpt〕*v.* 採用；領養【背這個字，只要記得「孤兒」是 **o**rphan，所以字裡有 o】

(B) adjust〔ə'dʒʌst〕*v.* 調整　　adjust a clock 調整時鐘

(C) advance〔əd'væns〕*v.* 前進
Not to advance is to go back.【諺】不進則退。

(D) adapt〔ə'dæpt〕*v.* 使適應；改編【背這個字，只要記得「調整」是 **a**djust，所以字裡有 a】　　adapt *oneself* to 適應　　be adapted from 改編自
adept〔ə'dɛpt〕*adj.* 熟練的；擅長的【背這個字，只要記得「專家」是 **e**xpert，所以字裡有 e】

＊delighted〔dɪ'laɪtɪd〕*adj.* 高興的　　proposal〔prə'pozḷ〕*n.* 提議
council〔'kaʊnsḷ〕*n.* 會議　　***student council*** 學生會

2. (**B**) You haven't studied at all this semester. It's totally <u>futile</u> to try to cram everything in for the final exams now.
你這個學期都沒唸書。現在才想為期末考臨時抱佛腳，是完全<u>沒用的</u>。

(A) dogmatic〔dɔg'mætɪk〕*adj.* 武斷的
dogma〔'dɔgmə〕*n.* 教條；教義

(B) *futile*〔'fjutḷ〕*adj.* 沒用的（= *useless*）；徒勞的

(C) isolated〔'aɪsḷˌetɪd〕*adj.* 孤立的；被隔離的　　an isolated island 孤島

(D) deliberate〔dɪ'lɪbərɪt〕*adj.* 故意的（= *intentional*）　　deliberately *adv.*

＊totally〔'totḷɪ〕*adv.* 完全地　　cram〔kræm〕*v.* 填塞；臨時死記硬背（功課）
final exam 期末考

3. (**D**) As a teaching assistant, I need to <u>monitor</u> the midterm exam tomorrow, so I can't go with you.
我是助教，明天得去<u>監考</u>期中考，所以我不能和你一起去。

(A) reveal〔rɪ'vil〕*v.* 透露；顯示（= *show*）；洩露（= *disclose*）

(B) abolish〔ə'bɑlɪʃ〕*v.* 廢除（= *do away with*）
abolish slavery 廢除奴隸制度

(C) fortify〔'fɔrtəˌfaɪ〕*v.* 加強；強化（= *strengthen* = *reinforce*）

(D) *monitor*〔'mɑnətɚ〕*v.* 監視　　*n.*（電腦的）監視器；顯示器

＊assistant〔ə'sɪstənt〕*n.* 助理　　***teaching assistant*** 助教（= *TA*）
midterm exam 期中考

4. (**D**) The detective sat at the desk pondering what the witness had said.
這位警探坐在辦公桌前，思考目擊者所說的話。

    (A) respond〔rɪˈspɑnd〕v. 回答；回應；反應 < to >　　response n.

    (B) wander〔ˈwɑndɚ〕v. 徘徊；流浪　　wonder〔ˈwʌndɚ〕v. 想知道

    (C) stimulate〔ˈstɪmjəˌlet〕v. 刺激；激勵　　stimulation n.

    (D) *ponder*〔ˈpɑndɚ〕v. 考慮；沉思

    ＊detective〔dɪˈtɛktɪv〕n. 警探；偵探　　desk〔dɛsk〕n. 辦公桌
      witness〔ˈwɪtnɪs〕n. 目擊者

5. (**D**) I only have a vague recollection of going to the botanical garden as a child. I can't recall that experience clearly.
我對於小時候去植物園只有模糊的記憶。我想不起那次的經驗。

    (A) memorial〔məˈmorɪəl〕adj. 紀念的　　n. 紀念物（碑、館）
      memorable〔ˈmɛmərəbḷ〕adj. 難忘的

    (B) evident〔ˈɛvədənt〕adj. 明顯的（= obvious = apparent）
      evidence n. 證據

    (C) visual〔ˈvɪʒʊəl〕adj. 視覺的　　visual organs 視覺器官
      auditory〔ˈɔdəˌtorɪ〕adj. 聽覺的

    (D) *vague*〔veg〕adj. 模糊的　　vogue〔vog〕n. 流行；時尚

    ＊recollection〔ˌrɛkəˈlɛkʃən〕n. 記憶　　botanical〔boˈtænɪkḷ〕adj. 植物的
      botanical garden 植物園　　*as a child* 小時候　　recall〔rɪˈkɔl〕v. 記起；想起

6. (**B**) The police were suspicious of the man's alibi because someone saw him near the crime scene.
警方懷疑這個人的不在場證明，因為有人在犯罪現場附近看到他。

    (A) melancholy〔ˈmɛlənˌkɑlɪ〕adj. 憂鬱的（= sad）

    (B) *suspicious*〔səˈspɪʃəs〕adj. 懷疑的 < of >　　suspicion n.
      suspect〔səˈspɛkt〕v. 懷疑　　suspect〔ˈsʌspɛkt〕n. 嫌疑犯

    (C) beneficial〔ˌbɛnəˈfɪʃəl〕adj. 有益的　　benefit n. 利益；好處　　v. 對…有益

    (D) magnificent〔mægˈnɪfəsṇt〕adj. 華麗的；壯觀的　　magnificence n.

    ＊alibi〔ˈæləˌbaɪ〕n. 不在場證明　　*crime scene* 犯罪現場

7. (**D**) This new medicine is sure to relieve you of your toothache.
這種新藥一定可以消除你的牙痛。

    (A) convince〔kənˈvɪns〕v. 使相信　　convince sb. of sth. 使某人相信某事

    (B) inform〔ɪnˈfɔrm〕v. 通知　　inform sb. of sth. 通知某人某事

    (C) deprive〔dɪˈpraɪv〕v. 剝奪　　deprive sb. of sth. 剝奪某人的某物

    (D) *relieve*〔rɪˈliv〕v. 減輕；使解除　　*relieve sb. of sth.* 解除某人的某物

    ＊*be sure to V.* 一定～　　toothache〔ˈtuθˌek〕n. 牙痛

8. (**C**) This soup is delicious, Jenny. You must give me the recipe.
珍妮，這個湯眞好喝。妳一定要把食譜給我。

　　(A) script〔skrɪpt〕 *n.* 手稿；腳本
　　(B) approach〔ə'protʃ〕 *n.* 接近；方法　　*v.* 接近
　　(C) *recipe*〔'rɛsəpɪ〕 *n.* 烹飪法；食譜
　　(D) manual〔'mænjuəl〕 *n.* 手冊　*adj.* 手的；手動的
　　　　a teacher's manual　教師手冊
　　＊soup〔sup〕 *n.* 湯

9. (**B**) The author has revised his manuscript more than three times to make the story shorter. 這位作家已經把他的手稿修訂了三次以上，想把故事縮短。

　　(A) improvise〔'ɪmprə,vaɪz〕 *v.* 即席而作　　improvised *adj.* 即興的
　　(B) *revise*〔rɪ'vaɪz〕 *v.* 修訂　　revise a manuscript 改稿
　　(C) advise〔əd'vaɪz〕 *v.* 勸告　　advice *n.* 忠告
　　(D) devise〔dɪ'vaɪz〕 *v.* 想出 (= *think up*)；計畫；發明 (= *invent*)
　　　　device *n.* 裝置
　　＊author〔'ɔθæ〕 *n.* 作家　　manuscript〔'mænjə,skrɪpt〕 *n.* 手稿
　　　time〔taɪm〕 *n.* 次數

10. (**A**) It took Julia a long time to acquire the skills she needed to become a professional singer.
茱莉亞花了很長的時間，才學會她成爲職業歌手所需要的技巧。

　　(A) *acquire*〔ə'kwaɪr〕 *v.* 獲得；學會；養成【ac (= *to*) + quire (= *seek*)】
　　(B) require〔rɪ'kwaɪr〕 *v.* 需要 (= *need* = *call for*)
　　　　【re (= *again*) + quire (= *seek*)】
　　(C) inquire〔ɪn'kwaɪr〕 *v.* 詢問 (= *ask*)【in (= *into*) + quire (= *seek*)】
　　(D) conquer〔'kɑŋkæ〕 *v.* 征服
　　＊take〔tek〕 *v.* 花費 (時間)　　skill〔skɪl〕 *n.* 技巧
　　　professional〔prə'fɛʃənḷ〕 *adj.* 職業的

11. (**A**) The police believed that the fire was started deliberately. It was probably arson. 警方相信這場火災是有人蓄意引起的。這可能是件縱火案。

　　(A) *deliberately*〔dɪ'lɪbərɪtlɪ〕 *adv.* 故意地 (= *on purpose*)
　　(B) elaborately〔ɪ'læbərɪtlɪ〕 *adv.* 精巧地；用心地
　　(C) dogmatically〔dɔg'mætɪkḷɪ〕 *adv.* 武斷地
　　(D) accordingly〔ə'kɔrdɪŋlɪ〕 *adv.* 因此 (= *therefore*)
　　＊fire〔faɪr〕 *n.* 火災　　arson〔'ɑrsṇ〕 *n.* 縱火 (案)

12. (**D**) I told Jane if she passed her chemistry test, I'd take her to the French restaurant.　However, she didn't seem to feel <u>motivated</u>.
　　　我告訴珍，如果她的化學考試及格，我會帶她去法國餐廳。然而，她似乎不覺得<u>受到激勵</u>。
　　　(A) bewildered〔bɪ'wɪldəd〕*adj.* 困惑的
　　　　　(= *confused* = *puzzled* = *baffled* = *perplexed*)　　　bewilder *v.*
　　　(B) depressed〔dɪ'prɛst〕*adj.* 沮喪的　　　depress *v.* 使沮喪
　　　(C) qualified〔'kwɑlə,faɪd〕*adj.* 合格的　　　qualify *v.* 使合格
　　　(D) *motivated*〔'motə,vetɪd〕*adj.* 受到激勵的
　　　　　motivate *v.* 激勵；引起動機

13. (**A**) When Tina was visiting San Diego, she decided to <u>drop in on</u> her aunt, who lived there. 蒂娜去聖地牙哥時，決定要<u>順道去拜訪</u>住在那裡的阿姨。
　　　(A) *drop in on sb.* 順道拜訪某人
　　　(B) see *sb.* off 替某人送行
　　　　　see *one's* friend off at the airport 在機場替某人的朋友送行
　　　(C) set out for 前往 (= *leave for*)
　　　(D) live up to 符合 (期望)
　　　　　live up to *one's* expectations 符合某人的期望

14. (**C**) I had to unwrap the package because I had <u>left out</u> one item I wanted to send along. 我必須打開這個包裹，因為我<u>遺漏</u>了一樣要一起寄的東西。
　　　(A) check out 結帳退房 (↔ *check in*)
　　　(B) cross out 劃掉；刪除
　　　(C) *leave out* 遺漏
　　　(D) rule out 排除
　　　＊unwrap〔ʌn'ræp〕*v.* 打開　　　package〔'pækɪdʒ〕*n.* 包裹
　　　　item〔'aɪtəm〕*n.* 物品；項目　　　along〔ə'lɔŋ〕*adv.* 一起

15. (**D**) The elevator was <u>out of order</u>, so everyone had to take the stairs.
　　　電梯<u>故障</u>了，所以每個人都必須走樓梯。
　　　(A) off and on 不時地；斷斷續續地 (= *on and off* = *intermittently*)
　　　(B) up and down 上上下下；來回地；到處
　　　(C) out of work 失業 (= *jobless*)
　　　(D) *out of order* 故障
　　　＊elevator〔'ɛlə,vetə〕*n.* 電梯 (escalator *n.* 電扶梯)
　　　　take the stairs 走樓梯

TEST 2

Directions: The following questions are incomplete sentences. You are to choose the one word that best completes the sentence.

1. The lost and hungry campers were _____ to the forest rangers for finding them and taking them back home.
   - (A) destined
   - (B) indebted
   - (C) attached
   - (D) exposed   (   )

2. Steve's parents give him a weekly _____, which he can use any way he likes.
   - (A) bonus
   - (B) allowance
   - (C) donation
   - (D) reward   (   )

3. The book met with a mixed response, which meant it received both _____ and criticism.
   - (A) acclaim
   - (B) dispute
   - (C) contempt
   - (D) prospect   (   )

4. Her son being over two hours late, she was _____ by all kinds of bad thoughts.
   - (A) nurtured
   - (B) pondered
   - (C) obsessed
   - (D) bewared   (   )

5. NASA succeeded in _____ the space shuttle after its adventurous two-week voyage.
   - (A) relaying
   - (B) refunding
   - (C) retorting
   - (D) retrieving   (   )

6. The teacher looked at both students _____, not knowing which one she should believe.
   - (A) irresolutely
   - (B) inconsistently
   - (C) irresistibly
   - (D) irresponsibly   (   )

7. Michael and Rachel had _____ views on their vacation: Michael wanted to go to the beach; Rachel preferred to stay home.
   - (A) prominent
   - (B) equivalent
   - (C) benevolent
   - (D) divergent   (   )

8. Students who don't study hard _____ fail the university entrance exam.
   (A) dramatically
   (B) dejectedly
   (C) inevitably
   (D) instantly ( )

9. Our mayor has such powerful _____ that wherever he goes he is surrounded by admirers, females in particular.
   (A) anguish
   (B) charisma
   (C) disgrace
   (D) obscurity ( )

10. Mainland China's population policy is that families are _____ to having only one child.
    (A) restricted
    (B) permitted
    (C) banned
    (D) restrained ( )

11. Two days ago, David finally spoke his first word since the stroke. That's an amazing _____ for him.
    (A) crackdown
    (B) breakthrough
    (C) snapshot
    (D) checkup ( )

12. I tried to _____ a telephone call to the Director, but his line was always busy.
    (A) break through
    (B) go through
    (C) put through
    (D) run through ( )

13. To _____ for making me wait over 30 minutes for delivery, the pizza shop let me have the pizza for free.
    (A) substitute
    (B) experiment
    (C) exchange
    (D) compensate ( )

14. Before we punish a student, we should _____ whether he accidentally or purposely broke a rule.
    (A) make light of
    (B) take into account
    (C) take for granted
    (D) make a point ( )

15. We're on the wrong train! This train _____ Chicago, not St. Louis.
    (A) is dedicated to
    (B) is bound for
    (C) is absorbed in
    (D) is noted for ( )

TEST 2 詳解

1. (**B**) The lost and hungry campers were <u>indebted</u> to the forest rangers for finding them and taking them back home.
那些迷路又飢餓的露營者，很感激找到他們，並帶他們回家的森林管理員。

    (A) destined (ˈdɛstɪnd) *adj.* 命中註定的   be destined to 註定
        destiny *n.* 命運

    (B) *indebted* (ɪnˈdɛtɪd) *adj.* 感激的   be indebted to 感激

    (C) attach (əˈtætʃ) *v.* 繫上；貼上
        be attached to 貼在～上面   attack *v.* 攻擊

    (D) expose (ɪkˈspoz) *v.* 暴露；使接觸   be exposed to 暴露於～之中；接觸到

    ＊lost (lɔst) *adj.* 迷路的   camper (ˈkæmpɚ) *n.* 露營者
     ranger (ˈrendʒɚ) *n.* 森林管理員

2. (**B**) Steve's parents give him a weekly <u>allowance</u>, which he can use any way he likes. 史提夫的父母每週都給他<u>零用錢</u>，他可以自由運用這筆錢。

    (A) bonus (ˈbonəs) *n.* 紅利；特別津貼

    (B) *allowance* (əˈlaʊəns) *n.* 零用錢 (= *pocket money*)

    (C) donation (doˈneʃən) *n.* 捐贈   donate *v.*

    (D) reward (rɪˈwɔrd) *n.* 報酬；獎賞   award *v.* 頒發

    ＊weekly (ˈwiklɪ) *adj.* 每週的

3. (**A**) The book met with a mixed response, which meant it received both <u>acclaim</u> and criticism. 這本書獲得的反應不一，意思就是它獲得了<u>讚賞</u>和批評。

    (A) *acclaim* (əˈklem) *n.* 稱讚；歡呼   claim *v.* 宣稱；要求

    (B) dispute (dɪˈspjut) *n.* 爭論 (= *argument*)

    (C) contempt (kənˈtɛmpt) *n.* 輕視   attempt *n.* 企圖

    (D) prospect (ˈprɑspɛkt) *n.* 展望   prospective *adj.* 未來的；有希望的

    ＊*meet with* 遭受；獲得   mixed (mɪkst) *adj.* 混合的
     response (rɪˈspɑns) *n.* 反應   criticism (ˈkrɪtəˌsɪzəm) *n.* 批評

4. (**C**) Her son being over two hours late, she was <u>obsessed</u> by all kinds of bad thoughts. 她的兒子遲到兩個多小時了，各種不祥的念頭<u>使她心神不寧</u>。

    (A) nurture (ˈnɝtʃɚ) *v.* 滋養；培植 (= *cultivate* = *develop*)

    (B) ponder (ˈpɑndɚ) *v.* 考慮；沉思 (= *think about*)

    (C) *obsess* (əbˈsɛs) *v.* 使心神不寧；困擾

    (D) beware (bɪˈwɛr) *v.* 小心；提防 < *of* >
     Beware of pickpockets. (小心扒手。)

5. (**D**) NASA succeeded in <u>retrieving</u> the space shuttle after its adventurous two-week voyage. 美國太空總署成功地尋回太空梭，這架太空梭完成了爲期兩週驚險的太空旅行。

    (A) relay〔rɪˋle〕*v. n.* 接力；轉播   work in relays 輪班工作
        in relay 以轉播的方式

    (B) refund〔rɪˋfʌnd〕*v.* 退錢 〔ˋrifʌnd〕*n.*   fund〔fʌnd〕*n.* 資金；基金

    (C) retort〔rɪˋtɔrt〕*v.* 反駁   distort *v.* 扭曲；曲解

    (D) *retrieve*〔rɪˋtriv〕*v.* 尋回

    ＊NASA〔ˋnæsə〕*n.* 美國太空總署 (= *National Aeronautics and Space Administration*)   *succeed in* 成功地~   *space shuttle* 太空梭
    adventurous〔ədˋvɛntʃərəs〕*adj.* 危險的   voyage〔ˋvɔɪ‧ɪdʒ〕*n.* 太空旅行

6. (**A**) The teacher looked at both students <u>irresolutely</u>, not knowing which one she should believe. 老師猶豫不決地看著這兩名學生，不知道該相信哪一個。

    (A) *irresolutely*〔ɪˋrɛzə,lutlɪ〕*adv.* 猶豫不決地   resolve *v.* 決心

    (B) inconsistently〔,ɪnkənˋsɪstəntlɪ〕*adv.* 前後不一致地
        consistent *adj.* 前後一致的

    (C) irresistibly〔,ɪrɪˋzɪstəblɪ〕*adv.* 不可抗拒地   resist *v.* 抵抗

    (D) irresponsibly〔,ɪrɪˋspɑnsəblɪ〕*adv.* 不須負責任地
        responsible *adj.* 應負責任的

7. (**D**) Michael and Rachel had <u>divergent</u> views on their vacation: Michael wanted to go to the beach; Rachel preferred to stay home. 麥可和瑞秋對他們的假期有不同的看法：麥可想去海邊；瑞秋比較喜歡待在家裡。

    (A) prominent〔ˋprɑmənənt〕*adj.* 傑出的；著名的 (= *famous*)

    (B) equivalent〔ɪˋkwɪvələnt〕*adj.* 相等的 (= *equal*) < to >

    (C) benevolent〔bəˋnɛvələnt〕*adj.* 慈善的   a benevolent society 慈善團體

    (D) *divergent*〔daɪˋvɝdʒənt〕*adj.* 分歧的；不同的

    ＊view〔vju〕*n.* 看法   beach〔bitʃ〕*n.* 海邊   prefer〔prɪˋfɝ〕*v.* 比較喜歡

8. (**C**) Students who don't study hard <u>inevitably</u> fail the university entrance exam. 不用功的學生，一定無法通過大學入學考試。

    (A) dramatically〔drəˋmætɪkəlɪ〕*adv.* 戲劇性地；相當大地 (= *considerably*)
        drama *n.* 戲劇

    (B) dejectedly〔dɪˋdʒɛktɪdlɪ〕*adv.* 沮喪地   dejected *adj.*

    (C) *inevitably*〔ɪnˋɛvətəblɪ〕*adv.* 無可避免地；必然地   inevitable *adj.*

    (D) instantly〔ˋɪnstəntlɪ〕*adv.* 立即地 (= *immediately*)   instant *adj.*

    ＊fail〔fel〕*v.* (考試) 不及格   *entrance exam* 入學考試

9. (**B**) Our mayor has such powerful <u>charisma</u> that wherever he goes he is surrounded by admirers, females in particular. 我們的市長具有強大的<u>個人魅力</u>，不管他到哪裡，都被仰慕者包圍，尤其是女性。

　　(A) anguish〔'æŋgwɪʃ〕*n.*（精神上）極度的痛苦；（身體上的）劇痛

　　(B) ***charisma***〔kə'rɪzmə〕*n.* 神秘的個人魅力；一種能使大眾信服或熱烈擁護的權威或領袖氣質

　　(C) disgrace〔dɪs'gres〕*n.* 恥辱；失寵　fall into disgrace 失寵；遭罷黜 < *with* >

　　(D) obscurity〔əb'skjʊrətɪ〕*n.* 含糊；沒沒無聞　　obscure *adj.* 模糊的

　　＊mayor〔'meɚ〕*n.* 市長　　powerful〔'paʊɚfəl〕*adj.* 強大的
　　surround〔sə'raʊnd〕*v.* 包圍　　admirer〔əd'maɪrɚ〕*n.* 仰慕者
　　female〔'fimel〕*n.* 女性　　***in particular*** 尤其是

10. (**A**) Mainland China's population policy is that families are <u>restricted</u> to having only one child. 中國大陸的人口政策是，<u>限制</u>每個家庭只能生一個小孩。

　　(A) ***restrict***〔rɪ'strɪkt〕*v.* 限制；限定（= *limit* = *confine*）

　　(B) permit〔pɚ'mɪt〕*v.* 允許　　permission *n.*

　　(C) ban〔bæn〕*v.* 禁止（= *prohibit* = *forbid*）

　　(D) restrain〔rɪ'stren〕*v.* 克制；忍住

　　＊***mainland China*** 中國大陸　　population〔,pɑpjə'leʃən〕*n.* 人口
　　policy〔'pɑləsɪ〕*n.* 政策

11. (**B**) Two days ago, David finally spoke his first word since the stroke. That's an amazing <u>breakthrough</u> for him. 大衛自從中風以來，終於在兩天前說出第一句話。那對他來說是個驚人的<u>突破</u>。

　　(A) crackdown〔'kræk,daʊn〕*n.* 取締

　　(B) ***breakthrough***〔'brek,θru〕*n.* 突破

　　(C) snapshot〔'snæp,ʃat〕*n.* 快照

　　(D) checkup〔'tʃɛk,ʌp〕*n.* 健康檢查

　　＊word〔wɝd〕*n.* 字；話　　stroke〔strok〕*n.* 中風
　　amazing〔ə'mezɪŋ〕*adj.* 驚人的

12. (**C**) I tried to <u>put through</u> a telephone call to the Director, but his line was always busy. 我試著要把電話<u>轉接</u>給主任，但他總是忙線中。

　　(A) break through 突破（重圍、障礙物等）　　breakthrough *n.* 突破；重大發現

　　(B) go through 穿過；經歷（= *undergo*）

　　(C) ***put through*** 接通（電話）

　　(D) run through 衝過；瀏覽；花光

　　＊director〔də'rɛktɚ〕*n.* 主任　　busy〔'bɪzɪ〕*adj.*（電話）佔線的（= *engaged*）

13. (**D**) To <u>compensate</u> for making me wait over 30 minutes for delivery, the pizza shop let me have the pizza for free.

為了補償讓我等候外送時間超過半小時，這家披薩店免費送我這個披薩。

(A) substitute (ˈsʌbstəˌtjut) *v.* 用…代替
substitute A for B 用 A 代替 B (= *replace* B *with* A)

(B) experiment (ɪkˈspɛrəmɛnt) *v.* 實驗

(C) exchange (ɪksˈtʃendʒ) *v.* 交換

(D) *compensate* (ˈkɑmpənˌset) *v.* 補償
compensate for 補償 (= *make up for*)

＊delivery (dɪˈlɪvərɪ) *n.* 遞送；外送服務　　pizza (ˈpitsə) *n.* 披薩
for free 免費地 (= *for nothing* = *free*)

14. (**B**) Before we punish a student, we should <u>take into account</u> whether he accidentally or purposely broke a rule.

在我們處罰學生之前，應該考慮到他是不小心，或是故意違反規定。

(A) make light of 輕視；忽視；不在意 (= *make little of* = *underestimate*)

(B) *take ~ into account* 將～列入考慮 (= *take ~ into consideration*)

(C) take ~ for granted 視～為理所當然

(D) make a point of + V-ing 必定～ (= *make it a point to V.*)

＊punish (ˈpʌnɪʃ) *v.* 處罰
accidentally (ˌæksəˈdɛntl̩ɪ) *adv.* 偶然；意外地
purposely (ˈpɝpəslɪ) *adv.* 故意地　　break (brek) *v.* 違反

15. (**B**) We're on the wrong train! This train <u>is bound for</u> Chicago, not St. Louis.

我們搭錯車了！這班火車是開往芝加哥的，不是聖路易斯。

(A) be dedicated to 致力於 (= *be devoted to* = *be committed to*
= *dedicate oneself to* = *devote oneself to* = *commit oneself to*)
【注意：to 都是介系詞】

(B) *be bound for* 前往（某地）(= *be destined for* = *set out for* = *set off for*
= *head for* = *leave for* = *depart for*)

(C) be absorbed in 專心於 (= *be lost in* = *be engrossed in* = *be preoccupied with*
= *be bent on* = *concentrate on*)

(D) be noted for 以～有名 (= *be well-known for* = *be renowned for*
= *be celebrated for* = *be famous for*)

TEST 3

Directions: The following questions are incomplete sentences. You are to choose the one word that best completes the sentence.

1. By signing the lease we made a _____ to pay a rent of $150 a week.
   (A) conception
   (B) commission
   (C) commitment
   (D) confinement   (   )

2. The _____ from childhood to adulthood is always a critical time for everybody.
   (A) conversion
   (B) transition
   (C) turnover
   (D) formation   (   )

3. It is hard to tell whether we are going to have a boom in the economy or a _____.
   (A) concession
   (B) recession
   (C) submission
   (D) transmission   (   )

4. They were _____ in their scientific research, unaware of what had happened just outside their lab.
   (A) submerged
   (B) drowned
   (C) immersed
   (D) dipped   (   )

5. The author of the report is well _____ with the problems in the hospital because he has been working there for many years.
   (A) acquainted
   (B) informed
   (C) accustomed
   (D) known   (   )

6. Fortune-tellers are good at making _____ statements such as "Your sorrows will change."
   (A) philosophical
   (B) ambiguous
   (C) literal
   (D) invalid   (   )

7. For a particular reason, he wanted the information to be treated as _____.
   (A) assured
   (B) reserved
   (C) intimate
   (D) confidential   (   )

8. The automatic doors in supermarkets ———— the entry and exit of customers with shopping carts.
   (A) furnish
   (B) induce
   (C) facilitate
   (D) alleviate ( )

9. Some studies confirmed that this kind of eye disease was ———— in tropical countries.
   (A) prospective
   (B) prevalent
   (C) provocative
   (D) perpetual ( )

10. He said that they had ———— been obliged to give up the scheme for lack of support.
    (A) gravely
    (B) regrettably
    (C) forcibly
    (D) graciously ( )

11. I'm afraid that you have to alter your ———— views in light of the tragic news that has just arrived.
    (A) indifferent
    (B) distressing
    (C) optimistic
    (D) pessimistic ( )

12. The winners of the football championship ran off the field carrying the silver cup ————.
    (A) turbulently
    (B) tremendously
    (C) triumphantly
    (D) tentatively ( )

13. Attempts to persuade her to stay after she felt insulted were ————.
    (A) in no way
    (B) on the contrary
    (C) at a loss
    (D) of no avail ( )

14. The terrorists might have planted a bomb on a plane in Athens, set to ———— when it arrives in New York.
    (A) go off
    (B) get off
    (C) come off
    (D) carry off ( )

15. The younger person's attraction to smartphones cannot be explained only ———— familiarity with technology.
    (A) in quest of
    (B) by means of
    (C) in terms of
    (D) by virtue of ( )

TEST 3 詳解

1. (**C**) By signing the lease we made a <u>commitment</u> to pay a rent of $150 a week.
   我們簽了租約，承諾要每週付租金一百五十美元。
   - (A) conception〔kən'sɛpʃən〕 *n.* 觀念；概念；想法 *cf.* concept〔'kɑnsɛpt〕 *n.* 概念
   - (B) commission〔kə'mıʃən〕 *n.* 委託；佣金 【背誦技巧】com + mission（任務）
   - (C) *commitment*〔kə'mıtmənt〕 *n.* 承諾；約定
   - (D) confinement〔kən'faınmənt〕 *n.* 限制；監禁 confine *v.*
   - *sign〔saın〕 *v.* 簽署 lease〔lis〕 *n.* 租約 rent〔rɛnt〕 *n.* 房租

2. (**B**) The <u>transition</u> from childhood to adulthood is always a critical time for
   everybody. 對每個人而言，從童年時期到成年的過渡期，都是個關鍵時期。
   - (A) conversion〔kən'vɝʃən〕 *n.* 轉變；改信 convert *v.*
     Heat causes the conversion of water into steam.（熱使水轉變爲蒸氣。）
     His conversion from Hinduism to Buddhism worried his mother.
     （他從印度教改信佛教，使他的母親很擔心。）
   - (B) *transition*〔træn'zıʃən〕 *n.* 過渡時期（ = *period of transition*）
   - (C) turnover〔'tɝn,ovɚ〕 *n.*（汽車）翻覆；營業額；成交量；人事變動率
   - (D) formation〔fɔr'meʃən〕 *n.* 形成 form *v.*
   - *childhood〔'tʃaıld,hʊd〕 *n.* 童年 adulthood〔ə'dʌlt,hʊd〕 *n.* 成年（時期）
     critical〔'krıtık!〕 *adj.* 決定性的；重大的；重要的

3. (**B**) It is hard to tell whether we are going to have a boom in the economy or a
   <u>recession</u>. 很難知道我們的經濟會是繁榮或蕭條。
   - (A) concession〔kən'sɛʃən〕 *n.* 讓步 concede *v.*
   - (B) *recession*〔rı'sɛʃən〕 *n.* 蕭條；不景氣
   - (C) submission〔səb'mıʃən〕 *n.* 服從 submit *v.* 服從；甘願接受 < to >
   - (D) transmission〔træns'mıʃən〕 *n.* 傳送；傳導；傳染 transmit *v.*
   - *hard〔hɑrd〕 *adj.* 困難的 tell〔tɛl〕 *v.* 知道；看出
     boom〔bum〕 *n.* 繁榮 economy〔ı'kɑnəmı〕 *n.* 經濟

4. (**C**) They were <u>immersed</u> in their scientific research, unaware of what had happened
   just outside their lab. 他們專注於科學研究，不知道實驗室外面發生了什麼事。
   - (A) submerged〔səb'mɝdʒd〕 *adj.* 浸在水中的(= *underwater*)；淹沒的(= *flooded*)
   - (B) drowned〔draʊnd〕 *adj.* 淹死的；溺斃的
   - (C) *immersed*〔ı'mɝst〕 *adj.* 專注的；熱中的
   - (D) dip〔dıp〕 *v.* 沾；浸 dip a towel 把毛巾浸一下
   - *scientific〔,saıən'tıfık〕 *adj.* 科學的 research〔'risɝtʃ〕 *n.* 研究
     unaware〔,ʌnə'wɛr〕 *adj.* 不知道的 *be unaware of* 不知道
     lab〔læb〕 *n.* 實驗室(= *laboratory*)

5. (**A**) The author of the report is well <u>acquainted</u> with the problems in the hospital because he has been working there for many years.

這份報告的作者非常<u>了解</u>醫院的問題，因為他在那裡工作了很多年。

(A) *acquainted* ﹝ə'kwentɪd﹞*adj.* 認識的；熟悉的；了解的
acquaint *v.* 使知道；使熟悉

(B) informed ﹝ɪn'fɔrmd﹞*adj.* 見聞廣博的；消息靈通的（= *well-informed*）
inform *v.* 通知　　be well-informed about~ 熟知~

(C) accustomed ﹝ə'kʌstəmd﹞*adj.* 習慣的
be accustomed to 習慣於（= *be used to*）

(D) known ﹝non﹞*adj.* 已知的　　be well known 很有名

＊author ﹝'ɔθɚ﹞*n.* 作者　　well ﹝wɛl﹞*adv.* 相當地；十分地

6. (**B**) Fortune-tellers are good at making <u>ambiguous</u> statements such as "Your sorrows will change."

算命仙很會說些<u>模稜兩可</u>的話，像是「你的苦難會有轉機。」

(A) philosophical ﹝,fɪlə'sɑfɪkḷ﹞*adj.* 哲學的　　philosophy *n.* 哲學

(B) *ambiguous* ﹝æm'bɪgjuəs﹞*adj.* 含糊的；模稜兩可的

(C) literal ﹝'lɪtərəl﹞*adj.* 照字面的；逐字的
literally *adv.* 照字面意義地；實在地
in the literal sense of the word 按那字的字面意義
a literal translation 直譯；逐字翻譯

(D) invalid ﹝ɪn'vælɪd﹞*adj.* 無效的（↔ valid *adj.* 有效的）；﹝'ɪnvəlɪd﹞*n.* 病人

＊fortune-teller ﹝'fɔrtʃən,tɛlɚ﹞*n.* 算命者；看相的人
be good at 擅長　　statement ﹝'stetmənt﹞*n.* 陳述；聲明
sorrows ﹝'sɑroz﹞*n. pl.* 不幸；苦難

7. (**D**) For a particular reason, he wanted the information to be treated as <u>confidential</u>.

因為某個特別的原因，他希望這個資料能被視為<u>機密</u>資料。

(A) assured ﹝ə'ʃurd﹞*adj.* 有保證的；確實的；可靠的　　assure *v.* 向~保證

(B) reserved ﹝rɪ'zɜvd﹞*adj.* 預訂的；有保留的；有顧慮的
reserve *v.* 保留；預訂

(C) intimate ﹝'ɪntəmɪt﹞*adj.* 親密的　　intimate friends 密友

(D) *confidential* ﹝,kɑnfə'dɛnʃəl﹞*adj.* 機密的
a confidential secretary 機要秘書

＊particular ﹝pə'tɪkjəlɚ﹞*adj.* 特別的　　reason ﹝'rizṇ﹞*n.* 理由
information ﹝,ɪnfɚ'meʃən﹞*n.* 資訊；資料
treat ﹝trit﹞*v.* 對待；把…看成　　*be treated as* 被視為

8. (**C**) The automatic doors in supermarkets <u>facilitate</u> the entry and exit of customers with shopping carts. 超市的自動門使推購物車的顧客進出更方便。

(A) furnish ('fɜnɪʃ) v. 使配備家具　furnished *adj.* 有家具的　furniture *n.* 家具

(B) induce (ɪn'djus) v. 勸誘 (= *persuade*)；引起；導致 (= *cause* = *bring about*)
This medicine may induce drowsiness. (這種藥可能會使人想睡。)

(C) *facilitate* (fə'sɪlə,tet) v. 使便利　　facilities *n. pl.* 設備

(D) alleviate (ə'livɪ,et) v. 減輕；緩和 (= *ease*)

＊automatic (,ɔtə'mætɪk) *adj.* 自動的　　entry ('ɛntrɪ) *n.* 進入；入場
exit ('ɛgzɪt, 'ɛksɪt) *n.* 外出；出口　　cart (kɑrt) *n.* (兩輪的) 小型手推車

9. (**B**) Some studies confirmed that this kind of eye disease was <u>prevalent</u> in tropical countries. 有些研究證實，這種眼部疾病在熱帶國家很普遍。

(A) prospective (prə'spɛktɪv) *adj.* 預期的；未來的；有希望的
my prospective son-in-law 我未來的女婿
a prospective customer 可能成爲買主的人

(B) *prevalent* ('prɛvələnt) *adj.* 普遍的　　prevalence *n.*

(C) provocative (prə'vɑkətɪv) *adj.* 激怒人的；具挑逗性的　　provoke *v.*

(D) perpetual (pə'pɛtʃʊəl) *adj.* 永久的 (= *everlasting*)

＊study ('stʌdɪ) *n.* 研究　　confirm (kən'fɜm) v. 證實
disease (dɪ'ziz) *n.* 疾病　　tropical ('trɑpɪkl̩) *adj.* 熱帶的

10. (**B**) He said that they had <u>regrettably</u> been obliged to give up the scheme for lack of support. 他說由於缺乏支持，所以他們很遺憾，不得不放棄那項計畫。

(A) gravely ('grevlɪ) *adv.* 重大地；嚴肅地
grave (grev) *n.* 墳墓　　*adj.* 重大的；嚴肅的

(B) *regrettably* (rɪ'grɛtəblɪ) *adv.* 遺憾地　　regret *v.* 後悔；對…感到遺憾

(C) forcibly ('fɔrsəblɪ) *adv.* 強制性地；強有力地　　force *n.* 力量　v. 強迫

(D) graciously ('greʃəslɪ) *adv.* 親切地　　gracious *adj.*
gracefully ('gresfəlɪ) *adv.* 優雅地　　graceful *adj.*

＊*be obliged to V.* 不得不…；必須…　　*give up* 放棄
scheme (skim) *n.* 計畫；方案　　lack (læk) *n.* 缺乏
support (sə'port) *n.* 支持；支援

11. (**C**) I'm afraid that you have to alter your <u>optimistic</u> views in light of the tragic news that has just arrived. 根據剛剛傳來的不幸消息，恐怕你得改變你樂觀的看法。

(A) indifferent (ɪn'dɪfrənt) *adj.* 漠不關心的　　be indifferent to 對~漠不關心

(B) distressing (dɪ'strɛsɪŋ) *adj.* 令人苦惱的　　distress *n.* 苦惱；悲痛

(C) *optimistic* (,ɑptə'mɪstɪk) *adj.* 樂觀的 (= *upbeat*)

(D) pessimistic (,pɛsə'mɪstɪk) *adj.* 悲觀的

＊*I'm afraid that*… 恐怕…　　alter ('ɔltə) v. 改變　　view (vju) *n.* 看法
in light of 根據；有鑑於　　tragic ('trædʒɪk) *adj.* 悲慘的

12. (**C**) The winners of the football championship ran off the field carrying the silver cup <u>triumphantly</u>. 這場橄欖球錦標賽的優勝者手拿銀盃，<u>得意洋洋地</u>跑出球場。

  (A) turbulently (ˈtɝbjələntlɪ) *adv.* 激烈地；粗暴地　　turbulent *adj.*
  　turbulence *n.* 社會的動亂；（空中的）亂流

  (B) tremendously (trɪˈmɛndəslɪ) *adv.* 非常地；驚人地　tremendous *adj.* 巨大的

  (C) *triumphantly* (traɪˈʌmfəntlɪ) *adv.* 得意洋洋地　　triumph (ˈtraɪəmf) *n.* 勝利

  (D) tentatively (ˈtɛntətɪvlɪ) *adv.* 試驗性地；暫時地；猶豫地 (= *hesitantly*)

  ＊winner (ˈwɪnɚ) *n.* 優勝者　　football (ˈfʊtˌbɔl) *n.* 美式足球；橄欖球
  championship (ˈtʃæmpɪənˌʃɪp) *n.* 錦標賽；冠軍賽　　*run off* 跑離
  field (fild) *n.* （棒球、足球等的）球場　　carry (ˈkærɪ) *v.* 拿著
  silver cup 銀盃

13. (**D**) Attempts to persuade her to stay after she felt insulted were <u>of no avail</u>. 在她覺得受到侮辱之後，想說服她留下來是<u>沒有用的</u>。

  (A) in no way 絕不 (= *by no means* = *under no circumstances*)

  (B) on the contrary 相反地

  (C) at a loss 茫然；不知所措

  (D) *of no avail* 沒有用的　　avail (əˈvel) *n.* 效用

  ＊attempt (əˈtɛmpt) *n.* 企圖；嘗試　　persuade (pɚˈswed) *v.* 說服
  insult (ɪnˈsʌlt) *v.* 侮辱

14. (**A**) The terrorists might have planted a bomb on a plane in Athens, set to <u>go off</u> when it arrives in New York.
  恐怖份子可能已經在雅典的一架飛機上安裝炸彈，要讓它到達紐約時<u>爆炸</u>。

  (A) *go off* 爆炸；（鬧鐘）響

  (B) get off 下（車）

  (C) come off （鈕釦等）脫落；成功

  (D) carry off 強行帶走；（疾病）奪走（生命）

  ＊terrorist (ˈtɛrərɪst) *n.* 恐怖份子　　plant (plænt) *v.* 安裝
  bomb (bɑm) *n.* 炸彈　　Athens (ˈæθənz) *n.* 雅典　　set (sɛt) *v.* 設定

15. (**C**) The younger person's attraction to smartphones cannot be explained only <u>in terms of</u> familiarity with technology.
  較年輕的人之所以受到智慧型手機的吸引，不能只<u>從熟悉科技的角度</u>來解釋。

  (A) in quest of 尋求 (= *in pursuit of*)

  (B) by means of 藉由 (= *by*)

  (C) *in terms of* 就～而言；從～觀點

  (D) by virtue of 靠…的力量；憑藉 (= *by means of*)；由於 (= *because of*)

  ＊attraction (əˈtrækʃən) *n.* 吸引力　　smartphone (ˈmɑrtˌfon) *n.* 智慧型手機
  familiarity (fəˌmɪlɪˈærətɪ) *n.* 熟悉　　technology (tɛkˈnɑlədʒɪ) *n.* 科技

TEST 4

Directions: The following questions are incomplete sentences. You are to choose the one word that best completes the sentence.

1. Since the student complained of a headache, his teacher gave him _____ to go home.
   (A) transmission   (B) permission
   (C) admission   (D) submission   (   )

2. When she returned from her vacation, Jane noticed that her plants had _____ from lack of water.
   (A) shattered   (B) threatened
   (C) withered   (D) stimulated   (   )

3. Everyone agrees that a good result in the election is _____ to the ruling party's future in the region.
   (A) initial   (B) addictive
   (C) rational   (D) crucial   (   )

4. Janet was _____ by Tom's sudden cold attitude toward her.
   (A) enclosed   (B) violated
   (C) perplexed   (D) triggered   (   )

5. He was, _____, upset by his lover's departure, but he soon got over it.
   (A) inevitably   (B) deliberately
   (C) accidentally   (D) reluctantly   (   )

6. I've never met anyone as _____ as Robert. He can't walk into a room without bumping into something!
   (A) trustworthy   (B) graceful
   (C) stable   (D) clumsy   (   )

7. Fingerprints have been used for personal _____ for about 2,000 years.
   (A) indication   (B) illusion
   (C) instruction   (D) identification   (   )

8. To buy a ticket from the machine, first _____ coins, and then press the button.
   (A) eject
   (B) insert
   (C) enforce
   (D) intrude ( )

9. The meeting, which had already gone an hour over schedule, was _____ after a short coffee break.
   (A) assumed
   (B) presumed
   (C) resumed
   (D) consumed ( )

10. The level of pollution normally increases with population _____.
    (A) humanity
    (B) density
    (C) intensity
    (D) flexibility ( )

11. The man tried to _____ drugs through customs, but he failed.
    (A) strangle
    (B) smuggle
    (C) struggle
    (D) stumble ( )

12. The construction of a 5-million-ton iron and steel works is now under _____.
    (A) conclusion
    (B) contribution
    (C) continuation
    (D) consideration ( )

13. I live outside the city. It's a nice place to live but, _____, it takes me a long time to get to work.
    (A) so to speak
    (B) by the way
    (C) in consequence
    (D) on the other hand ( )

14. Last week, May was in the hospital, but I've heard that she's _____ now and will soon be back at work.
    (A) fair and square
    (B) up and around
    (C) back and forth
    (D) out and out ( )

15. It's hard for the abandoned child to _____ her mother after so long a time.
    (A) turn down
    (B) wear down
    (C) track down
    (D) settle down ( )

TEST 4 詳解

1. (**B**) Since the student complained of a headache, his teacher gave him <u>permission</u> to go home. 由於這位學生說他頭痛，老師<u>允許</u>他回家休養。

    (A) transmission〔træns`mɪʃən〕*n.* 傳達；傳送；傳染   transmit *v.*
        the transmission of electric power 電力的傳送
        the transmission of disease 疾病的傳染

    (B) *permission*〔pə`mɪʃən〕*n.* 允許；許可   permit *v.*

    (C) admission〔əd`mɪʃən〕*n.* (學校、場所等之) 允許進入；入學許可   admit *v.*

    (D) submission〔səb`mɪʃən〕*n.* 服從   submit *v.*

    ＊complain〔kəm`plen〕*v.* 抱怨；訴說 (病痛) *< of >*
      headache〔`hɛd͵ek〕*n.* 頭痛

2. (**C**) When she returned from her vacation, Jane noticed that her plants had <u>withered</u> from lack of water.
    當珍放假回來時，她發現她的植物都已經因為沒有澆水而<u>枯萎</u>了。

    (A) shatter〔`ʃætə〕*v.* 使破碎；使粉碎
        The explosion shattered every window in the house.
        (爆炸使屋裡的每一面玻璃窗都破碎了。)

    (B) threaten〔`θrɛtn̩〕*v.* 威脅   threat *n.*   threatening *adj.*

    (C) *wither*〔`wɪðə〕*v.* 枯萎；凋謝

    (D) stimulate〔`stɪmjə͵let〕*v.* 刺激；激勵   stimulation *n.*
        stimulating *adj.* 振奮人心的

    ＊notice〔`notɪs〕*v.* 注意到   lack〔læk〕*n.* 缺乏

3. (**D**) Everyone agrees that a good result in the election is <u>crucial</u> to the ruling party's future in the region. 每個人都認為，本次選舉獲勝，對於執政黨在這個區域的未來而言，是相當<u>重要的</u>。

    (A) initial〔ɪ`nɪʃəl〕*adj.* 起初的   initially *adv.*   initiate *v.* 創始

    (B) addictive〔ə`dɪktɪv〕*adj.* (使人) 上癮的
        additive〔`ædətɪv〕*adj.* 附加的 *n.* 添加劑

    (C) rational〔`ræʃənl̩〕*adj.* 有理性的；合理的
        Man is a rational being. (人是理性的動物。)
        a rational explanation 合理的說明

    (D) *crucial*〔`kruʃəl〕*adj.* 決定性的；極重要的
        a crucial moment 關鍵時刻；重要關頭
        Salt is a crucial ingredient in cooking. (鹽是很重要的烹飪材料。)

    ＊*ruling party* 執政黨   region〔`ridʒən〕*n.* 地區；區域

4. (**C**) Janet was <u>perplexed</u> by Tom's sudden cold attitude toward her.
珍娜對於湯姆突如其來的冷漠態度感到<u>困惑</u>。

    (A) enclose〔ɪn'kloz〕v. 隨函附寄；包圍   disclose v. 洩露

        I'm enclosing my photo.（我隨函附寄我的照片。）

    (B) violate〔'vaɪə,let〕v. 違反   violation n.

    (C) *perplex*〔pə'plɛks〕v. 使困惑

    (D) trigger〔'trɪgə〕v. 引發；扣扳機   n.（槍的）扳機

    ＊sudden〔'sʌdn̩〕adj. 突然的   cold〔kold〕adj. 冷淡的

      attitude〔'ætə,tjud〕n. 態度   toward〔tord , tə'word〕prep. 對於

5. (**A**) He was, <u>inevitably</u>, upset by his lover's departure, but he soon got over it.
<u>無可避免地</u>，愛人的離開讓他心情不好，不過他很快就克服了。

    (A) *inevitably*〔ɪn'ɛvətəblɪ〕adv. 必然地；不可避免地

    (B) deliberately〔dɪ'lɪbərɪtlɪ〕adv. 故意地（= *on purpose*）

    (C) accidentally〔,æksə'dɛntl̩ɪ〕adv. 偶然地；意外地（= *by accident*）

    (D) reluctantly〔rɪ'lʌktəntlɪ〕adv. 不情願地；勉強地（= *unwillingly*）

    ＊upset〔ʌp'sɛt〕adj. 不高興的   departure〔dɪ'pɑrtʃə〕n. 離開

    get over 克服

6. (**D**) I've never met anyone as <u>clumsy</u> as Robert. He can't walk into a room without bumping into something!
我從來都沒見過像羅柏特這麼<u>笨拙的</u>人。他每次走進房間，都撞到東西！

    (A) trustworthy〔'trʌst,wɝðɪ〕adj. 可靠的（= *reliable* = *dependable*）

    (B) graceful〔'gresfəl〕adj. 優雅的（= *elegant*）   grace n.

    (C) stable〔'stebl̩〕adj. 穩定的（= *steady*）；穩固的

      a stable foundation 穩固的基礎

    (D) *clumsy*〔'klʌmzɪ〕adj. 笨拙的

    ＊***bump into*** 撞上

7. (**D**) Fingerprints have been used for personal <u>identification</u> for about 2,000 years.
兩千年來，指紋一直被用來<u>辨別</u>個人的<u>身分</u>。

    (A) indication〔,ɪndə'keʃən〕n. 指示；標示   indicate v. 指出

    (B) illusion〔ɪ'ljuʒən〕n. 幻覺；幻象；錯覺

      optical illusion 視錯覺；視覺幻象

    (C) instruction〔ɪn'strʌkʃən〕n. 教導；指示   instruct v. 教導

    (D) *identification*〔aɪ,dɛntəfə'keʃən〕n. 身分確認   identify v.

    ＊fingerprint〔'fɪŋgə,prɪnt〕n. 指紋   personal〔'pɝsn̩l〕adj. 個人的

8. (**B**) To buy a ticket from the machine, first <u>insert</u> coins, and then press the button.
要使用這台機器買票，請先投幣，然後再按鈕。

    (A) eject〔ɪ'dʒɛkt〕v. 噴出；排出（液體、廢氣）   ejection *n.*

    (B) ***insert***〔ɪn'sɝt〕v. 將～投入；插入   insertion *n.*

    (C) enforce〔ɪn'fors〕v. 實施   enforcement *n.*

    (D) intrude〔ɪn'trud〕v. 闖入；干擾   intrusion *n.*

    ＊coin〔kɔɪn〕*n.* 硬幣   press〔prɛs〕*v.* 壓；按   button〔'bʌtn̩〕*n.* 按鈕

9. (**C**) The meeting, which had already gone an hour over schedule, was <u>resumed</u> after a short coffee break.
這場會議已經超過預定時間一個小時，經過短暫的休息後，又再繼續進行。

    (A) assume〔ə'sjum〕v. 假定；以爲；承擔；採取
        We assumed that the train would be on time.（我們以爲火車會準時到站。）
        You must also assume your share of the responsibility.
        （你也必須承擔你的一份責任。）
        assume a friendly attitude 採取友善的態度

    (B) presume〔prɪ'zum〕v. 假定；推測
        I presume that she is dead.（我推測她已經死亡。）

    (C) ***resume***〔rɪ'zum〕v. 恢復；再繼續

    (D) consume〔kən'sum〕v. 消耗；消費；吃、喝   consumer *n.* 消費者
        consumption *n.* 消耗；吃、喝

    ＊meeting〔'mitɪŋ〕*n.* 會議   ***go over*** 超過   schedule〔'skɛdʒʊl〕*n.* 時間表
    coffee break（在工作中途的）喝咖啡休息時間

10. (**B**) The level of pollution normally increases with population <u>density</u>.
污染的程度通常會隨著人口密度而增加。

    (A) humanity〔hju'mænətɪ〕*n.* 人性；人類（ = *mankind* ）   human *adj.*

    (B) ***density***〔'dɛnsətɪ〕*n.* 密度；稠密   dense *adj.*

    (C) intensity〔ɪn'tɛnsətɪ〕*n.* 強烈；強度   intense *adj.*

    (D) flexibility〔͵flɛksə'bɪlətɪ〕*n.* 彈性   flexible *adj.* 有彈性的

    ＊level〔'lɛvl̩〕*n.* 程度   normally〔'nɔrml̩ɪ〕*adv.* 通常
    increase〔ɪn'kris〕*v.* 增加   population〔͵pɑpjə'leʃən〕*n.* 人口

11. (**B**) The man tried to <u>smuggle</u> drugs through customs, but he failed.
這名男子企圖走私毒品過海關，不過他失敗了。

    (A) strangle〔'stræŋgl̩〕v. 勒死；使窒息   【背誦技巧】str + angle（角度）

    (B) ***smuggle***〔'smʌgl̩〕v. 走私

    (C) struggle〔'strʌgl̩〕v. 掙扎；奮鬥

    (D) stumble〔'stʌmbl̩〕v. 絆倒   stumble on / over a stone 被石頭絆倒

    ＊drug〔drʌg〕*n.* 藥物；毒品   customs〔'kʌstəmz〕*n.* 海關

12. (**D**) The construction of a 5-million-ton iron and steel works is now under consideration. 使用五百萬噸鋼鐵來建造的工程，目前正在被<u>考慮</u>中。

    (A) conclusion〔kən'kluʒən〕*n.* 結論；結束   conclude *v.*

    (B) contribution〔ˌkɑntrə'bjuʃən〕*n.* 捐獻；貢獻   contribute *v.*

    (C) continuation〔kənˌtɪnju'eʃən〕*n.* 連續；繼續   continue *v.*

    (D) *consideration*〔kənˌsɪdə'reʃən〕*n.* 考慮

    ＊construction〔kən'strʌkʃən〕*n.* 建造；施工

    ton〔tʌn〕*n.* 噸   iron〔'aɪən〕*n.* 鐵   steel〔stil〕*n.* 鋼

    works〔wɜks〕*n. pl.* 土木工程

13. (**D**) I live outside the city. It's a nice place to live but, <u>on the other hand</u>, it takes me a long time to get to work.

    我住在市郊。那裡的居住環境很好，不過<u>另一方面</u>，我去上班要花很多時間。

    (A) so to speak 可說是 (= *so to say* = *as it were*)

        He is, so to speak, a grown-up baby. (他可說是一個長大的嬰兒。)

    (B) by the way 順便一提 (= *incidentally*)

    (C) in consequence 因此 (= *consequently* = *therefore* = *hence* = *thus*
        = *accordingly* = *as a result*)

    (D) *on the other hand* 在另一方面

14. (**B**) Last week, May was in the hospital, but I've heard that she's <u>up and around</u> now and will soon be back at work.

    梅上禮拜住院了，不過我聽說她現在已經可以<u>起床走動</u>，而且很快就會回到工作崗位上了。

    (A) fair and square 公正的；光明正大的   fair *adj.* 公平的
        square〔skwɛr〕*adj.* 公正的

    (B) *up and around* (病人康復) 起床走動

    (C) back and forth 來回地 (= *to and fro* = *backwards and forwards*)

    (D) out and out 完全地；徹底地 (= *completely*)

15. (**C**) It's hard for the abandoned child to <u>track down</u> her mother after so long a time.

    經過這麼長的時間後，這個被遺棄的小孩要<u>查出</u>她的生母，是相當困難的。

    (A) turn down 關小聲 (↔ *turn up* 開大聲)；拒絕 (= *refuse*)

    (B) wear down 磨損；使…的力量減弱   wear〔wɛr〕*v.* 磨損

    (C) *track down* 查出；追蹤；追捕到   track〔træk〕*v.* 追蹤；追捕

    (D) settle down 定居；成家；使安靜 (= *calm down* = *relax*)

    ＊hard〔hɑrd〕*adj.* 困難的   abandoned〔ə'bændənd〕*adj.* 被遺棄的

TEST 5

Directions: The following questions are incomplete sentences. You are to choose the one word that best completes the sentence.

1. Some people opposed Charles Darwin's theory of _____ on religious grounds.
   - (A) solution
   - (B) resolution
   - (C) evolution
   - (D) revolution   (   )

2. _____ move around the sun like planets, but in a long oval course.
   - (A) Incomes
   - (B) Outcomes
   - (C) Comments
   - (D) Comets   (   )

3. He knew his arguments were _____; they were based on his intuition instead of fact.
   - (A) ambiguous
   - (B) stimulating
   - (C) subjective
   - (D) objective   (   )

4. The country has to _____ oil from abroad because it does not produce enough of its own.
   - (A) import
   - (B) export
   - (C) support
   - (D) deport   (   )

5. After she had stolen the money, her _____ was troubled.
   - (A) conscious
   - (B) conscience
   - (C) consensus
   - (D) consequence   (   )

6. We thought there would be bad weather, but on the _____, we had sunshine.
   - (A) county
   - (B) contrary
   - (C) contrast
   - (D) conflict   (   )

7. The _____ boy refused to listen to his parents' advice even though he knew they were right.
   - (A) stubborn
   - (B) nuclear
   - (C) synthetic
   - (D) primary   (   )

8. The doctor _____ on the injured man and saved his life.
   (A) acquainted
   (B) imitated
   (C) generated
   (D) operated ( )

9. She _____ her mother's good looks and her father's bad temper.
   (A) flourished
   (B) referred
   (C) inherited
   (D) compiled ( )

10. The young painter had the example of Picasso to _____ and guide him.
    (A) inspire
    (B) respire
    (C) perspire
    (D) expire ( )

11. The police caught the prisoner who _____ of jail yesterday.
    (A) dropped in
    (B) ran short
    (C) broke out
    (D) went bad ( )

12. Mary is very talkative. She never has the sense to _____ at the right time.
    (A) lose her head
    (B) keep her word
    (C) hold her tongue
    (D) catch her breath ( )

13. Our geography teacher _____ before he teaches to make sure every student is present.
    (A) calls the roll
    (B) plays it by ear
    (C) hits the ceiling
    (D) makes both ends meet ( )

14. He didn't speak to me and _____ at me yesterday. I didn't know why he was so angry.
    (A) built castles in the air
    (B) pulled a long face
    (C) took a chance
    (D) took steps ( )

15. We should _____ such evil customs.
    (A) comply with
    (B) do away with
    (C) be preoccupied with
    (D) get away with ( )

TEST 5 詳解

1. (**C**) Some people opposed Charles Darwin's theory of <u>evolution</u> on religious grounds. 有些人基於宗教的理由，反對查爾斯・達爾文的<u>進化論</u>。
   - (A) solution〔sə'luʃən〕n. 解決；解答；解決之道　　solve v.
   - (B) resolution〔,rɛzə'luʃən〕n. 決心　　resolve v.
     one's New Year resolution 新年的決心
   - (C) *evolution*〔,ɛvə'luʃən〕n. 進化；發展　　evolve v.
   - (D) revolution〔,rɛvə'luʃən〕n. 革命；公轉
     revolve v. 公轉　　rotate〔'rotet〕v. 自轉
   - * oppose〔ə'poz〕v. 反對
     Darwin〔'dɑrwɪn〕n. 達爾文【1809-1882，英國生物學家】
     theory〔'θiərɪ〕n. 理論　　religious〔rɪ'lɪdʒəs〕adj. 宗教的
     grounds〔graʊndz〕n. pl. 理由

2. (**D**) <u>Comets</u> move around the sun like planets, but in a long oval course.
   彗星像行星一樣，繞太陽運轉，然而其軌道是狹長的橢圓形。
   - (A) income〔'ɪn,kʌm〕n. 收入（↔ outgo〔'aʊt,go〕n. 支出）
   - (B) outcome〔'aʊt,kʌm〕n. 結果
   - (C) comment〔'kɑmɛnt〕n. 評論　　No comment.（不予置評。）
   - (D) *comet*〔'kɑmɪt〕n. 彗星　　Halley's Comet 哈雷彗星
     meteor〔'mitɪɚ〕n. 流星（= *shooting star*）
   - * move〔muv〕v. 移動　　planet〔'plænɪt〕n. 行星
     oval〔'ovḷ〕adj. 橢圓形的　　course〔kors〕n. 行經的路線

comet

3. (**C**) He knew his arguments were <u>subjective</u>; they were based on his intuition instead of fact.
   他知道自己的論點很<u>主觀</u>；那些論點是基於他的直覺，而非事實。
   - (A) ambiguous〔æm'bɪgjʊəs〕adj. 含糊的；模稜兩可的
     ambiguity n. 模稜兩可
   - (B) stimulating〔'stɪmjə,letɪŋ〕adj. 令人振奮的；有啓發性的
     stimulate v. 刺激
   - (C) *subjective*〔səb'dʒɛktɪv〕adj. 主觀的
   - (D) objective〔əb'dʒɛktɪv〕adj. 客觀的；公平的
   - * argument〔'ɑrgjəmənt〕n. 論點　　*be based on* 基於；以～爲基礎
     intuition〔,ɪntjʊ'ɪʃən〕n. 直覺　　*instead of* 而不是
     fact〔fækt〕n. 事實

4. (**A**) The country has to <u>import</u> oil from abroad because it does not produce enough of its own. 這個國家必須從國外<u>進口</u>石油，因為自己國內生產的不夠多。
  (A) ***import***〔 ɪmˊport 〕*v.* 進口　〔ˊɪmport 〕*n.* 進口貨；輸入品
  (B) export〔 ɪksˊport 〕*v.* 出口　〔ˊɛksport 〕*n.* 出口；輸出品
  (C) support〔 səˊport 〕*v.* 支持
  (D) deport〔 dɪˊport 〕*v.* 將…驅逐（出境）
  * abroad〔 əˊbrɔd 〕*adv.* 在國外【aboard〔 əˊbord 〕*adv.* 在船上；在飛機上】
  from abroad 來自國外　***of one's own*** 屬於自己本身的

5. (**B**) After she had stolen the money, her <u>conscience</u> was troubled.
  她偷了錢之後，覺得<u>良心</u>不安。
  (A) conscious〔ˊkɑnʃəs 〕*adj.* 知道的；察覺到的
    be conscious of 知道；察覺到（ = *be aware of* ）
  (B) ***conscience***〔ˊkɑnʃəns 〕*n.* 良心
    conscientious〔ˌkɑnʃɪˊɛnʃəs 〕*adj.* 有良心的；負責盡職的
  (C) consensus〔 kənˊsɛnsəs 〕*n.* 共識　　reach a consensus 達成共識
  (D) consequence〔ˊkɑnsəˌkwɛns 〕*n.* 後果
    in consequence 因此（ = *consequently* ）
  * troubled〔ˊtrʌbl̩d 〕*adj.* 不安的；擔心的

6. (**B**) We thought there would be bad weather, but on the <u>contrary</u>, we had sunshine.
  我們原以為天氣會很糟，但結果<u>正相反</u>，那天陽光普照。
  (A) county〔ˊkaʊntɪ 〕*n.* 郡；縣　　Taipei County 台北縣
  (B) ***contrary***〔ˊkɑntrɛrɪ 〕*n.* 正相反　　***on the contrary*** 相反地
  (C) contrast〔ˊkɑntræst 〕*n.* 對比；對照　　by contrast 對比之下
  (D) conflict〔ˊkɑnflɪkt 〕*n.* 衝突
    〔 kənˊflɪkt 〕*v.* 不相容；矛盾；（和…）衝突 < *with* >
  * weather〔ˊwɛðɚ 〕*n.* 天氣　　sunshine〔ˊsʌnˌʃaɪn 〕*n.* 陽光

7. (**A**) The <u>stubborn</u> boy refused to listen to his parents' advice even though he knew they were right. 那個<u>倔強的</u>男孩不肯聽父母的忠告，即使他知道他們是對的。
  (A) ***stubborn***〔ˊstʌbən 〕*adj.* 頑固的；倔強的（ = *obstinate* ）
  (B) nuclear〔ˊnjuklɪɚ 〕*adj.* 核子的
    nuclear power station / plant 核能發電廠
  (C) synthetic〔 sɪnˊθɛtɪk 〕*adj.* 合成的　　synthetic fiber〔ˊfaɪbɚ 〕合成纖維
  (D) primary〔ˊpraɪˌmɛrɪ 〕*adj.* 主要的（ = *main* ）；初級的
    primary school 小學
  * refuse〔 rɪˊfjuz 〕*v.* 拒絕　　advice〔 ədˊvaɪs 〕*n.* 忠告　　***even though*** 即使

8. (**D**) The doctor <u>operated</u> on the injured man and saved his life.
醫生爲那名受傷的人<u>動手術</u>，救了他一命。
(A) acquaint〔ə'kwent〕v. 使認識；使熟悉　　be acquainted with 認識；熟悉
(B) imitate〔'ɪmə,tet〕v. 模仿　　intimate〔'ɪntəmɪt〕adj. 親密的
(C) generate〔'dʒɛnə,ret〕v. 產生　　generation n. 世代；產生
(D) *operate*〔'ɑpə,ret〕v. 動手術
　　operate on sb. 爲某人動手術（= *perform an operation on sb.*）
*injured〔'ɪndʒəd〕adj. 受傷的　　save〔sev〕v. 拯救

9. (**C**) She <u>inherited</u> her mother's good looks and her father's bad temper.
她<u>遺傳</u>了母親的美貌，和父親的壞脾氣。
(A) flourish〔'flɝɪʃ〕v. 興盛；繁榮（= *thrive* = *prosper*）
(B) refer〔rɪ'fɝ〕v. 參考；提到 < to >　　refer to A as B 把 A 稱爲 B
(C) *inherit*〔ɪn'hɛrɪt〕v. 繼承；由遺傳而獲得
(D) compile〔kəm'paɪl〕v. 編輯
*looks〔lʊks〕n. pl. 容貌；相貌　　temper〔'tɛmpə〕n. 脾氣

10. (**A**) The young painter had the example of Picasso to <u>inspire</u> and guide him.
這位年輕的畫家有畢卡索爲榜樣，<u>激勵</u>並指引著他。
(A) *inspire*〔ɪn'spaɪr〕v. 激勵；給予靈感【in（= *into*）+ spire（= *breathe*）】
(B) respire〔rɪ'spaɪr〕v. 呼吸【re（= *again*）+ spire（= *breathe*）】
　　respiration n. 呼吸
(C) perspire〔pə'spaɪr〕v. 流汗【per（= *through*）+ spire（= *breathe*）透過
　　皮膚呼吸】　　perspiration n. 流汗；努力
　　Genius is one percent inspiration and ninety-nine percent perspiration.
　　（天才是百分之一的靈感和百分之九十九的努力。）
(D) expire〔ɪk'spaɪr〕v. 到期【ex（= *out*）+ spire（= *breathe*）】
　　expiration n. 期滿
　　conspire〔kən'spaɪr〕v. 密謀
　　【con（= *together*）+ spire（= *breathe*）】

Picasso

*Picasso〔pɪ'kɑso〕n. 畢卡索【（1881-1973）西班牙出生的畫家、
雕刻家，立體主義畫派的主要代表，1904 年定居巴黎，其作品對西方
現代藝術有深遠影響。】

11. (**C**) The police caught the prisoner who <u>broke out</u> of jail yesterday.
警方昨天抓到了那名越獄<u>逃走</u>的囚犯。
(A) drop in 順道拜訪（= *drop by*）
(B) run short 不足；不夠　　*cf.* run out of 用完
(C) *break out of* 從～逃走　　(D) go bad （食物）變壞
*prisoner〔'prɪzṇə〕n. 囚犯　　jail〔dʒel〕n. 監獄

12. (**C**) Mary is very talkative. She never has the sense to <u>hold her tongue</u> at the right time. 瑪麗很愛說話。她從來不知道何時該保持沉默。
　　(A) lose *one's* head 失去理智 (= *lose one's cool*)
　　　　(↔ keep *one's* head 保持冷靜)
　　(B) keep *one's* word 遵守諾言 (= *keep one's promise*)
　　(C) *hold one's tongue* 保持沉默　　tongue〔 tʌŋ 〕*n.* 舌頭
　　(D) catch *one's* breath 喘一口氣；休息一會兒
　　*talkative〔'tɔkətɪv 〕*adj.* 愛說話的　　sense〔 sɛns 〕*n.* 感覺；判斷力
　　right〔 raɪt 〕*adj.* 適當的

13. (**A**) Our geography teacher <u>calls the roll</u> before he teaches to make sure every student is present.
　　我們的地理老師上課前會先點名，以確定每位學生都有出席。
　　(A) *call the roll* 點名
　　(B) play it by ear 見機行事；隨機應變
　　(C) hit the ceiling 大發雷霆；非常生氣　　ceiling〔'silɪŋ 〕*n.* 天花板
　　　　(= *hit the roof* = *blow one's top* = *see red* = *lose one's temper* = *become angry*)
　　(D) make both ends meet 使收支相抵 (= *make ends meet*)
　　　　live from hand to mouth 生活僅夠糊口 (毫無積蓄)
　　*geography〔 dʒɪ'ɑgrəfɪ 〕*n.* 地理　　present〔'prɛznt 〕*adj.* 出席的；在場的

14. (**B**) He didn't speak to me and <u>pulled a long face</u> at me yesterday. I didn't know why he was so angry.
　　他昨天不跟我說話，而且一直對我板著臉。我不知道他為什麼那麼生氣。
　　(A) build castles in the air 建造空中樓閣；做白日夢
　　　　castle〔'kæsḷ 〕*n.* 城堡　　in the air 在空中
　　(B) *pull a long face* 板著臉　　pull〔 pʊl 〕*v.* 拉
　　(C) take a chance 冒險 (↔ play (it) safe 小心行事；不冒險)
　　(D) take steps 採取步驟；採取行動 (= *take measures* = *take action*)
　　　　step〔 stɛp 〕*n.* 步驟；措施

15. (**B**) We should <u>do away with</u> such evil customs. 我們應該廢除如此不良的習俗。
　　(A) comply with 遵守 (= *conform to* = *stick to* = *adhere to* = *abide by*
　　　　 = *follow* = *obey*)
　　(B) *do away with* 廢除 (= *abolish*)
　　(C) be preoccupied with 專心於 (= *be lost in* = *be absorbed in* = *be bent on*
　　　　 = *concentrate on*)
　　(D) get away with 逃避懲罰
　　*evil〔'ivḷ 〕*adj.* 壞的；邪惡的　　custom〔'kʌstəm 〕*n.* 習俗

TEST 6

Directions: The following questions are incomplete sentences. You are to choose the one word that best completes the sentence.

1. Put on dark glasses, or the sun will _____ you and you won't be able to see.
   - (A) discern
   - (B) distort
   - (C) distract
   - (D) dazzle　　　　　　　　　　　　( )

2. What the correspondent sent us is an _____ news report. We can depend on it.
   - (A) evident
   - (B) authentic
   - (C) ultimate
   - (D) inevitable　　　　　　　　　　( )

3. No one imagined that the apparently _____ businessman was really a criminal.
   - (A) respective
   - (B) respectable
   - (C) respectful
   - (D) realistic　　　　　　　　　　　( )

4. After several nuclear disasters, a _____ has raged over the safety of nuclear energy.
   - (A) quarrel
   - (B) suspicion
   - (C) verdict
   - (D) controversy　　　　　　　　　( )

5. If nothing is done to protect the environment, millions of species that are alive today will become _____.
   - (A) deteriorated
   - (B) nauseous
   - (C) suppressed
   - (D) extinct　　　　　　　　　　　( )

6. The international situation has been growing _____ difficult for the last few years.
   - (A) invariably
   - (B) presumably
   - (C) increasingly
   - (D) dominantly　　　　　　　　　( )

7. The manager gave her his _____ that her complaint would be investigated.
   - (A) assurance
   - (B) assumption
   - (C) sanction
   - (D) insurance　　　　　　　　　　( )

8. Small farms and the lack of modern technology have _____ agricultural production.
   (A) blundered   (B) tangled
   (C) bewildered   (D) hampered   ( )

9. The cars were _____ because the lack of visibility made it impossible to go any further in the fog.
   (A) sacrificed   (B) transported
   (C) abandoned   (D) removed   ( )

10. All the students have to _____ to the rules and regulations of the school.
    (A) confirm   (B) confront
    (C) confine   (D) conform   ( )

11. Please do not get _____ by his offensive remarks since he is merely trying to attract attention.
    (A) distinguished   (B) disregarded
    (C) irritated   (D) intervened   ( )

12. The helicopter _____ a light plane and both pilots were killed.
    (A) coincided with   (B) stumbled on
    (C) tumbled to   (D) collided with   ( )

13. Although the model looks good on the surface, it will not bear close _____.
    (A) temperament   (B) contamination
    (C) scrutiny   (D) symmetry   ( )

14. Body paint or face paint is used mostly by men in preliterate societies in order to ensure good health or to _____ disease.
    (A) set aside   (B) ward off
    (C) shrug off   (D) give away   ( )

15. Though her parents _____ her musical ability, Judy's piano playing is really terrific.
    (A) pour scorn on   (B) heap praise upon
    (C) give vent to   (D) cast light upon   ( )

TEST 6 詳解

1. (**D**) Put on dark glasses, or the sun will <u>dazzle</u> you and you won't be able to see.
要戴上墨鏡，否則陽光會<u>使你目眩</u>，然後你就會看不見。

    (A) discern〔dɪ'sɝn〕v. 看出；辨別 (= *distinguish*)

        discern good and evil 辨別善惡 (= *discern good from evil* = *discern between good and evil*)

    (B) distort〔dɪs'tɔrt〕v. 扭曲；曲解

        You have distorted what I said. (你曲解了我說的話。)

    (C) distract〔dɪ'strækt〕v. 使分心   distraction n. 分心；使人分心的事物

    (D) *dazzle*〔'dæzl〕v. 使目眩；使眼花   dazzling *adj.* 令人目眩的；耀眼的

        drizzle〔'drɪzl〕n. 毛毛雨   v. 下毛毛雨

    * *put on* 戴上   *dark glasses* 墨鏡 (= *sunglasses*)

     the sun 陽光   *be able to* 能夠

2. (**B**) What the correspondent sent us is an <u>authentic</u> news report. We can depend
on it. 通訊記者寄給我們的是<u>眞實</u>的新聞報導。我們可以相信它。

    (A) evident〔'ɛvədənt〕*adj.* 明顯的 (= *obvious* = *apparent*)   evidence n. 證據

    (B) *authentic*〔ɔ'θɛntɪk〕*adj.* 可信的；可靠的；眞正的

    (C) ultimate〔'ʌltəmɪt〕*adj.* 最終的 (= *final*)；最高的 (= *supreme*)；

        最大的 (= *greatest*)

    (D) inevitable〔ɪn'ɛvətəbl〕*adj.* 無法避免的 (= *unavoidable*)

    * correspondent〔ˌkɔrə'spandənt〕n. (新聞、廣播等的) 通訊員；特派員；

     通訊記者   *depend on* 依賴；信任；相信

3. (**B**) No one imagined that the apparently <u>respectable</u> businessman was really a
criminal. 大家都想不到，那位看似<u>正當的</u>商人，其實是個罪犯。

    (A) respective〔rɪ'spɛktɪv〕*adj.* 個別的；各自的   respect n. 方面

        The tourists went back to their respective countries.

        (那些觀光客回到各自的國家。)

    (B) *respectable*〔rɪ'spɛktəbl〕*adj.* 可敬的；正當的   respect *v. n.* 尊敬

    (C) respectful〔rɪ'spɛktfəl〕*adj.* 尊敬的；恭敬的【背這個字，只要背respect + ful

        (充滿…的)】

    (D) realistic〔ˌriə'lɪstɪk〕*adj.* 現實的；實際的

        It isn't a realistic plan. (那是個不切實際的計畫。)

    * imagine〔ɪ'mædʒɪn〕v. 想像   apparently〔ə'pɛrəntlɪ〕*adv.* 表面上看來；似乎

     criminal〔'krɪmənl〕n. 罪犯

4. (**D**) After several nuclear disasters, a <u>controversy</u> has raged over the safety of nuclear energy.

在發生好幾起核能意外事故後，關於核能是否安全的<u>爭論</u>，在全國蔓延開來。

(A) quarrel (ˈkwɔrəl) *n. v.* 吵架；爭吵　　have a quarrel with 與…爭吵

(B) suspicion (səˈspɪʃən) *n.* 懷疑

suspect (səˈspɛkt) *v.* 懷疑　(ˈsʌspɛkt) *n.* 嫌疑犯

(C) verdict (ˈvɝdɪkt) *n.* 判決

<u>bring in / return</u> a verdict of <u>guilty / not guilty</u> （陪審團）判決有罪 / 無罪

(D) *controversy* (ˈkɑntrəˌvɝsɪ) *n.* 爭論

* nuclear (ˈnjuklɪə) *adj.* 核子的；核能的

disaster (dɪzˈæstə) *n.* 災害；災難；不幸

rage (redʒ) *v.* （暴風雨、戰爭、疾病、熱情等）肆虐；猖獗；蔓延；澎湃

nuclear energy 核能

5. (**D**) If nothing is done to protect the environment, millions of species that are alive today will become <u>extinct</u>.

如果不想辦法保護環境，那麼現在還活著的好幾百萬種動物就會<u>絕種</u>。

(A) deteriorate (dɪˈtɪrɪəˌret) *v.* 惡化 (= *degenerate* = *worsen*)

(B) nauseous (ˈnɔʃəs , ˈnɔʒəs) *adj.* 噁心的；想吐的 (= *sick*)

nausea (ˈnɔʒə , ˈnɔzɪə) *n.*

(C) suppress (səˈprɛs) *v.* 鎮壓 (= *repress*)；抑制 (= *hold back* = *restrain*)

(D) *extinct* (ɪkˈstɪŋkt) *adj.* 絕種的　　distinct (dɪˈstɪŋkt) *adj.* 不同的；明確的

* protect (prəˈtɛkt) *v.* 保護　　environment (ɪnˈvaɪrənmənt) *n.* 環境

millions of 好幾百萬的　　species (ˈspiʃɪz) *n.* 種；物種

alive (əˈlaɪv) *adj.* 活的　　today (təˈde) *adv.* 現在

6. (**C**) The international situation has been growing <u>increasingly</u> difficult for the last few years. 最近幾年，國際局勢變得<u>越來越</u>複雜。

(A) invariably (ɪnˈvɛrɪəblɪ) *adv.* 不變地；必定；常常 (= *always*)

vary (ˈvɛrɪ) *v.* 改變

(B) presumably (prɪˈzuməblɪ) *adv.* 可能；大概 (= *probably*)

presume *v.* 假定；推測

(C) *increasingly* (ɪnˈkrisɪŋlɪ) *adv.* 越來越 (= *more and more*)

(D) dominantly (ˈdɑmənəntlɪ) *adv.* 佔優勢地；主要地 (= *primarily*)

dominant *adj.*

* international (ˌɪntəˈnæʃənl) *adj.* 國際的

situation (ˌsɪtʃuˈeʃən) *n.* 狀態；情勢　　grow (gro) *v.* 變成

difficult (ˈdɪfəˌkʌlt) *adj.* 艱難的；難對付的；複雜的

7. (**A**)　The manager gave her his <u>assurance</u> that her complaint would be investigated.
經理向她<u>保證</u>，會調查她所投訴的事。

(A) *assurance*〔ə'ʃʊrəns〕*n.* 保證　　assure *v.* 向~保證
(B) assumption〔ə'sʌmpʃən〕*n.* 假定；臆測（= *supposition* = *guess* ）
assume *v.*
(C) sanction〔'sæŋkʃən〕*n.* 批准；認可；制裁；處罰
give sanction to 批准；認可
apply economic sanctions against 對…實施經濟制裁
(D) insurance〔ɪn'ʃʊrəns〕*n.* 保險　　insure *v.*
＊manager〔'mænɪdʒɚ〕*n.* 經理
complaint〔kəm'plent〕*n.* 抱怨；不滿
investigate〔ɪn'vɛstə,get〕*v.* 調查

8. (**D**)　Small farms and the lack of modern technology have <u>hampered</u> agricultural production.
小型農場以及缺乏現代科技，已經<u>阻礙</u>了農業生產。

(A) blunder〔'blʌndɚ〕*v.* 犯（愚蠢的）錯（= *make a mistake* ）
n.（愚蠢的）錯誤
(B) tangle〔'tæŋgl̩〕*v.* 使糾纏；使捲入
His foot became tangled in the rope.（他的一隻腳被繩子纏住。）
(C) bewilder〔bɪ'wɪldɚ〕*v.* 使困惑（= *confuse* = *baffle* = *puzzle* = *perplex* ）
(D) *hamper*〔'hæmpɚ〕*v.* 妨礙；阻礙（= *hinder* ）
＊lack〔læk〕*n.* 缺乏　　technology〔tɛk'nɑlədʒɪ〕*n.* 科技
agricultural〔,ægrɪ'kʌltʃərəl〕*adj.* 農業的
production〔prə'dʌkʃən〕*n.* 生產

9. (**C**)　The cars were <u>abandoned</u> because the lack of visibility made it impossible to go any further in the fog.
因爲能見度很差，無法在霧中繼續前進，因此這些車子就被棄置了。

(A) sacrifice〔'sækrə,faɪs〕*v. n.* 犧牲　　at the sacrifice of… 犧牲…
(B) transport〔træns'port〕*v.* 運送　　transportation *n.* 運輸系統
(C) *abandon*〔ə'bændən〕*v.* 拋棄
(D) remove〔rɪ'muv〕*v.* 除去（= *get rid of* ）
＊lack〔læk〕*n.* 缺乏　　visibility〔,vɪzə'bɪlətɪ〕*n.* 能見度
further〔'fɝðɚ〕*adv.* 更遠地　　fog〔fɔg, fɑg〕*n.* 霧

10. (**D**) All the students have to <u>conform</u> to the rules and regulations of the school.
所有的學生都必須遵守學校的規定。

    (A) confirm〔kən'fɝm〕*v.* 證實;確認

    (B) confront〔kən'frʌnt〕*v.* 面對 (= *be confronted with*);使面對;勇敢對抗

    (C) confine〔kən'faɪn〕*v.* 限制 (= *restrict* = *limit*)

    (D) *conform*〔kən'fɔrm〕*v.* 遵守

      conform to 遵守 (= *follow* = *obey* = *observe* = *abide by*)

    ＊rule〔rul〕*n.* 規則;規定   regulation〔ˌrɛgjə'leʃən〕*n.* 規定

11. (**C**) Please do not get <u>irritated</u> by his offensive remarks since he is merely trying to attract attention.
請不要對他無禮的話生氣,因為他只是想要吸引注意力。

    (A) distinguished *adj.* 著名的

      distinguish〔dɪ'stɪŋgwɪʃ〕*v.* 分辨

    (B) disregard〔ˌdɪsrɪ'gɑrd〕*v.* 忽視 (= *ignore*)

    (C) *irritated*〔'ɪrəˌtetɪd〕*adj.* 生氣的   irritate *v.* 激怒

    (D) intervene〔ˌɪntɚ'vin〕*v.* 介入 (= *interfere*);調停 (= *arbitrate*)

    ＊offensive〔ə'fɛnsɪv〕*adj.* 觸怒人的;無禮的

     remark〔rɪ'mɑrk〕*n.* 話;評論

     merely〔'mɪrlɪ〕*adv.* 僅僅   attract〔ə'trækt〕*v.* 吸引

     attention〔ə'tɛnʃən〕*n.* 注意力

12. (**D**) The helicopter <u>collided with</u> a light plane and both pilots were killed.
直昇機和輕型飛機相撞,兩名飛行員都因而喪生。

    (A) coincide with 和⋯同時發生;和⋯一致

      coincide〔ˌko·ɪn'saɪd〕*v.* (和⋯) 同時發生

    (B) stumble on 被⋯絆倒;偶然發現

      stumble〔'stʌmbl̩〕*v.* 絆倒;偶然發現

    (C) tumble to 忽然注意到;忽然想起

      tumble〔'tʌmbl̩〕*v.* 跌倒;忽然注意到

    (D) *collide with* 和⋯相撞   collide〔kə'laɪd〕*v.* 相撞;衝突

    ＊helicopter〔'hɛlɪˌkɑptɚ〕*n.* 直昇機   light〔laɪt〕*adj.* 輕的

    light plane 輕型飛機   pilot〔'paɪlət〕*n.* 飛行員

    be killed (因意外而) 死亡

13. (**C**) Although the model looks good on the surface, it will not bear close <u>scrutiny</u>.
雖然這個模型表面上看起來很好，但卻經不起<u>細看</u>。

    (A) temperament〔ˈtɛmpərəmənt〕*n.* 性情；氣質

        temper〔ˈtɛmpɚ〕*n.* 脾氣

    (B) contamination〔kənˌtæməˈneʃən〕*n.* 污染   contaminate *v.*

        radioactive contamination 放射線污染

    (C) *scrutiny*〔ˈskrutn̩ɪ〕*n.* 細看；仔細觀察   scrutinize *v.*

    (D) symmetry〔ˈsɪmɪtrɪ〕*n.* （左右的）對稱

    * model〔ˈmɑdl̩〕*n.* 模型   surface〔ˈsɝfɪs〕*n.* 表面

      bear〔bɛr〕*v.* 忍耐；忍受；經得起   close〔klos〕*adj.* 仔細的

14. (**B**) Body paint or face paint is used mostly by men in preliterate societies in order
to ensure good health or to <u>ward off</u> disease.
史前社會的男人大多會將顏料塗在身體或臉部，以確保健康，或是<u>避免生病</u>。

    (A) set aside 保留（= *reserve*）；儲存（金錢、時間等）（= *save*）

    (B) *ward off* 躲避；避開；防備

    (C) shrug off （認為微不足道而）不理會（= *ignore* = *disregard*）

        shrug〔ʃrʌg〕*v.* 聳肩   shrug off a protest 不理會抗議

    (D) give away 贈送；洩露（= *disclose*）

    * paint〔pent〕*n.* 油漆；顏料   mostly〔ˈmostlɪ〕*adv.* 大多

      preliterate〔priˈlɪtərɪt〕*adj.* 使用文字之前的   ensure〔ɪnˈʃʊr〕*v.* 確保

15. (**A**) Though her parents <u>pour scorn on</u> her musical ability, Judy's piano playing is
really terrific.
雖然茱蒂的父母<u>輕視</u>她的音樂才能，但她鋼琴真的彈得很棒。

    (A) *pour scorn on* 輕視   pour〔por〕*v.* 傾倒

        scorn〔skɔrn〕*n.* 輕視

    (B) heap praise upon 一再地對…加以稱讚

        heap〔hip〕*v.* 一再地（對某人）加以…

    (C) give vent to 發洩（= *unleash* = *release*）

        vent〔vɛnt〕*n.* 通風口

    (D) cast light upon 使人了解；闡明（= *clarify* = *explain*）

    * musical〔ˈmjuzɪkl̩〕*adj.* 音樂的   terrific〔təˈrɪfɪk〕*adj.* 很棒的

TEST 7

Directions: The following questions are incomplete sentences. You are to choose the one word that best completes the sentence.

1. It's not likely that Lillian's conservative father will _____ of her marrying a foreigner, especially an African American.
   (A) accept
   (B) adopt
   (C) approve
   (D) assure   (   )

2. Since his graduation from college, my brother has filled out half a dozen _____ for jobs but hasn't gotten a single reply.
   (A) applications
   (B) condolences
   (C) introductions
   (D) transcripts   (   )

3. The villagers looked at the stranger _____, curious to know what he was going to do.
   (A) inevitably
   (B) inquiringly
   (C) inspiringly
   (D) insistently   (   )

4. I was happy to see my old classmate Kevin, and he said the feeling was _____.
   (A) passive
   (B) hostile
   (C) tempting
   (D) mutual   (   )

5. Nothing _____ a person's vocabulary like reading good literature.
   (A) enables
   (B) declines
   (C) enriches
   (D) restricts   (   )

6. Passing exams requires knowledge, skill and _____ as well as a little luck.
   (A) competition
   (B) communication
   (C) contribution
   (D) concentration   (   )

7. Danny is very _____; he never thinks before he acts.
   (A) reserved
   (B) impulsive
   (C) motivated
   (D) composed   (   )

8. The structure of the DNA was completely _____ after exposure to excessive radiation.
   - (A) transmitted
   - (B) transformed
   - (C) transcended
   - (D) transcribed   (   )

9. He is quite sure that it's _____ impossible for him to finish the task within two days.
   - (A) drastically
   - (B) significantly
   - (C) accidentally
   - (D) absolutely   (   )

10. The _____ of time hasn't left much sign on her face; she really looks young for her age.
   - (A) consumption
   - (B) demonstration
   - (C) passage
   - (D) voyage   (   )

11. He _____ his father both in his appearance and in his character; they are both tall and serious.
   - (A) looks after
   - (B) takes after
   - (C) names after
   - (D) ever after   (   )

12. The idea seems good, but it needs to be _____ before we can approve it.
   - (A) broken into
   - (B) turned down
   - (C) run over
   - (D) tried out   (   )

13. The topic he chose for his talk was designed to allow him to _____ his expertise in machinery.
   - (A) show off
   - (B) cut off
   - (C) bite off
   - (D) shut off   (   )

14. The alarm clock _____ at six o'clock and woke Father in time to catch the early train.
   - (A) went around
   - (B) went off
   - (C) went over
   - (D) went without   (   )

15. That man looks suspicious. _____ him and make sure he doesn't steal anything.
   - (A) Keep an eye on
   - (B) Turn a deaf ear to
   - (C) Turn your back on
   - (D) Make the best of   (   )

TEST 7 詳解

1. (**C**) It's not likely that Lillian's conservative father will <u>approve</u> of her marrying a foreigner, especially an African American.

莉莉安的父親很保守,他不可能贊成她嫁給外國人,尤其是黑人。

(A) accept〔ək'sɛpt〕v. 接受【為及物動詞,不加 of】

(B) adopt〔ə'dɑpt〕v. 採用;領養

adapt〔ə'dæpt〕v. 使適應;改編　　adapt *oneself* to 適應

adept〔ə'dɛpt〕*adj.* 精通的　　be adept in/at 擅長於

(C) *approve*〔ə'pruv〕v. 贊成 < *of* >

(D) assure〔ə'ʃur〕v. 向~保證 < *of* >　　assure *sb.* of~ 向某人保證~

＊likely〔'laɪklɪ〕*adj.* 可能的　　conservative〔kən'sɝvətɪv〕*adj.* 保守的

marry〔'mærɪ〕v. 和…結婚　　foreigner〔'fɔrɪnə〕*n.* 外國人

African American 非裔美國人;黑人

2. (**A**) Since his graduation from college, my brother has filled out half a dozen <u>applications</u> for jobs but hasn't gotten a single reply. 自從我哥哥大學畢業之後,他已經寫了六封求職信了,可是卻連一個回應也沒有。

(A) *application*〔,æplə'keʃən〕*n.* 申請書;應徵 < *for* >

applicant〔'æpləkənt〕*n.* 應徵者

(B) condolence〔kən'doləns〕*n.* 弔慰;哀悼　　a letter of condolence 弔慰信

(C) introduction〔,ɪntrə'dʌkʃən〕*n.* 介紹;引進　　introduce *v.*

(D) transcript〔'træn,skrɪpt〕*n.* 成績單 (= *report card*)

＊graduation〔,grædʒu'eʃən〕*n.* 畢業　　*fill out* 填寫

dozen〔'dʌzn̩〕*n.* 一打　　single〔'sɪŋgl̩〕*adj.* 單一的;連一個 (也沒有) 的

reply〔rɪ'plaɪ〕*n.* 答覆;回答

3. (**B**) The villagers looked at the stranger <u>inquiringly</u>, curious to know what he was going to do.

村民以探詢的眼光看著這個陌生人,很好奇地想知道他要做什麼。

(A) inevitably〔ɪn'ɛvətəblɪ〕*adv.* 不可避免地　　inevitable *adj.*

(B) *inquiringly*〔ɪn'kwaɪrɪŋlɪ〕*adv.* 探詢地

inquisitive〔ɪn'kwɪzətɪv〕*adj.* 好問的

(C) inspiringly〔ɪn'spaɪrɪŋlɪ〕*adv.* 使人振奮地　　inspire *v.* 激勵;給予靈感

inspiration *n.*

(D) insistently〔ɪn'sɪstəntlɪ〕*adv.* 堅持地　　insist *v.* 堅持

4. (**D**) I was happy to see my old classmate Kevin, and he said the feeling was <u>mutual</u>.
我很高興見到我的老同學凱文，他說他也有<u>同樣的</u>感覺。

(A) passive〔'pæsɪv〕*adj.* 被動的；消極的（↔ *active*)
(B) hostile〔'hɑstḷ, 'hɑstɪl〕*adj.* 有敵意的　　hostility *n.* 敵意
(C) tempting〔'tɛmptɪŋ〕*adj.* 誘人的　　temptation *n.* 誘惑
(D) ***mutual***〔'mjutʃʊəl〕*adj.* 共同的；互相的

5. (**C**) Nothing <u>enriches</u> a person's vocabulary like reading good literature.
閱讀好的文學作品最能<u>增加</u>一個人的字彙量。

(A) enable〔ɪn'ebḷ〕*v.* 使能夠　　enable *sb.* to V. 使某人能夠～
(B) decline〔dɪ'klaɪn〕*v.* 拒絕（ = *refuse* = *turn down*)；衰退
(C) ***enrich***〔ɪn'rɪtʃ〕*v.* 使豐富
(D) restrict〔rɪ'strɪkt〕*v.* 限制（ = *limit* = *confine*)

*vocabulary〔və'kæbjə,lɛrɪ〕*n.* 字彙　　literature〔'lɪtərətʃɚ〕*n.* 文學作品

6. (**D**) Passing exams requires knowledge, skill and <u>concentration</u> as well as a little
luck. 想要通過考試，需要知識、技巧、<u>專心</u>，以及一點運氣。

(A) competition〔,kɑmpə'tɪʃən〕*n.* 競爭　　compete *v.*　　competitive *adj.*
competitor *n.*　　keen competition 激烈的競爭
in competition with 和～競爭
(B) communication〔kə,mjunə'keʃən〕*n.* 溝通　　communicate *v.*
(C) contribution〔,kɑntrə'bjuʃən〕*n.* 貢獻；捐贈　　contribute *v.*
(D) ***concentration***〔,kɑnsṇ'treʃən〕*n.* 專心；集中
concentration camp 集中營
concentrate *v.*（ = *focus*)　　concentrated *adj.* 濃縮的

*require〔rɪ'kwaɪr〕*v.* 需要　　***as well as*** 以及　　luck〔lʌk〕*n.* 運氣

7. (**B**) Danny is very <u>impulsive</u>; he never thinks before he acts.
丹尼非常<u>衝動</u>；他從不三思而後行。

(A) reserved〔rɪ'zɝvd〕*adj.* 保留的；有所顧慮的　　reserve *v.* 保留；預訂
(B) ***impulsive***〔ɪm'pʌlsɪv〕*adj.* 衝動的
(C) motivated〔'motə,vetɪd〕*adj.* 受激勵的；受鼓舞的　　motivate *v.*
motivation *n.* 激勵
(D) composed〔kəm'pozd〕*adj.* 鎮定的；冷靜的（ = *calm*)
composure *n.* 鎮靜；冷靜
compose *v.* 組成；作（詩、曲、文章）；使鎮定

*act〔ækt〕*v.* 行動

8. (**B**) The structure of the DNA was completely <u>transformed</u> after exposure to excessive radiation.

接觸過量的輻射線後，這個 DNA 的結構就完全改變了。

(A) transmit〔træns'mɪt〕v. 傳送；傳染；傳導【trans (= *across*) + mit (*send*)】

(B) *transform*〔træns'fɔrm〕v. 轉變【trans (= *across*) + form (形態)】

(C) transcend〔træn'sɛnd〕v. 超越【tran(s) (= *across*) + scend (= *climb*)】

(D) transcribe〔træn'skraɪb〕v. 抄寫【tran(s) (= *across*) + scribe (= *write*)】

　　transcript *n.*

＊structure〔'strʌktʃɚ〕*n.* 結構　　**DNA** 去氧核糖核酸

　exposure〔ɪk'spoʒɚ〕*n.* 暴露；接觸 < *to* >

　excessive〔ɪk'sɛsɪv〕*adj.* 過度的　　radiation〔ˌredɪ'eʃən〕*n.* 輻射線

9. (**D**) He is quite sure that it's <u>absolutely</u> impossible for him to finish the task within two days.

他確信他絕對不可能在兩天內，把這件工作完成。

(A) drastically〔'dræstɪkəlɪ〕*adv.* 激烈地 (= *radically*)；徹底地

(B) significantly〔sɪg'nɪfəkəntlɪ〕*adv.* 顯著地；意義重大地

(C) accidentally〔ˌæksə'dɛntlɪ〕*adv.* 偶然地；意外地 (= *by accident*)

　　incidentally *adv.* 順便一提 (= *by the way*)

(D) *absolutely*〔'æbsəˌlutlɪ , ˌæbsə'lutlɪ〕*adv.* 完全地；絕對地

＊task〔tæsk〕*n.* 任務；工作

10. (**C**) The <u>passage</u> of time hasn't left much sign on her face; she really looks young for her age.

時間的流逝並未在她臉上留下太多痕跡；以她這個年紀來看，她真的很年輕。

(A) consumption〔kən'sʌmpʃən〕*n.* 消費；消耗；吃、喝　　consume *v.*

(B) demonstration〔ˌdɛmən'streʃən〕*n.* 示威；證明；示範說明　　demonstrate *v.*

(C) *passage*〔'pæsɪdʒ〕*n.* 通道；經過；一段 (文章)　　pass *v.*

　　The city has changed a great deal with the passage of time.

　　（隨著時間的過去，這座城市已經改變了很多。）

　　Although he still missed his wife occasionally, the passage of time had eased his grief.

　　（雖然他偶爾還會思念他的太太，但是隨著時間的過去，他已經沒那麼悲傷了。）

(D) voyage〔'vɔɪ‧ɪdʒ , 'vɔjɪdʒ〕*n.* 航行；旅行　　Bon voyage! 祝一路順風！

＊sign〔saɪn〕*n.* 跡象；痕跡

11. (**B**) He <u>takes after</u> his father both in his appearance and in his character; they are
both tall and serious.

他的外表和性格都<u>像</u>他的父親；他們兩個都很高，而且很嚴肅。

(A) look after　照顧 (= *take care of* = *care for*)

(B) *take after*　像 (= *resemble*)

(C) name A after B　以 B 的名字替 A 命名

(D) ever after　從此以後一直

　　They lived happily ever after. (從此以後他們就過著幸福快樂的日子。)

＊appearance〔ə'pɪrəns〕*n.* 外表　　character〔'kærɪktə〕*n.* 性格

　serious〔'sɪrɪəs〕*adj.* 嚴肅的

12. (**D**) The idea seems good, but it needs to be <u>tried out</u> before we can approve it.

這個想法似乎很不錯，但必須經過<u>徹底的試驗</u>，我們才能同意。

(A) break into　闖入

　　Some burglars broke into the shop last night.

　　(昨晚有幾個竊賊潛入店裡。)

(B) turn down　關小聲 (↔ *turn up*)；拒絕 (= *decline* = *refuse*)

(C) run over　輾過　　The car ran over some glass. (那輛車輾過一些玻璃。)

(D) *try out*　徹底試驗；試用

＊seem〔sim〕*v.* 似乎　　approve〔ə'pruv〕*v.* 贊成；同意

13. (**A**) The topic he chose for his talk was designed to allow him to <u>show off</u> his
expertise in machinery.

他選這個演講主題，目的是為了要讓他能<u>展現</u>自己在機器方面的專門知識。

(A) *show off*　展示；炫耀 (= *boast of* = *brag about*)

(B) cut off　切斷

　　Our electricity has been cut off. (我們的供電被切斷了。)

(C) bite off　咬下

　　Don't bite off more than you can chew.

　　(【諺】貪多嚼不爛；不要自不量力。)

(D) shut off　關掉 (瓦斯、自來水、收音機等)

　　shut off the gas　關掉瓦斯　　shut off the electricity　關掉電源

＊topic〔'tɑpɪk〕*n.* 主題　　talk〔tɔk〕*n.* (非正式的) 演講；談話

　be designed to　目的是為了　　allow〔ə'lau〕*v.* 讓；允許

　expertise〔,ɛkspə'tiz〕*n.* 專門知識

　machinery〔mə'ʃinərɪ〕*n.* 機器 (集合名詞)

14. (**B**) The alarm clock <u>went off</u> at six o'clock and woke Father in time to catch the early train.

鬧鐘在六點鐘響，叫醒了我爸爸，讓他及時趕上早班的火車。

(A) go around 足夠分配；（謠言）流傳；（疾病）流行

　　There aren't enough to go around.（不夠分配給大家。）

(B) *go off* （鬧鐘）響；（炸彈）爆炸（＝ *explode*）

(C) go over 復習（＝ *review*）；檢查（＝ *examine*）

　　The pupil went over the lesson before the exam.

　　（學生在考試前復習功課。）

　　The prospective buyer went over the house very carefully.

　　（那位可能成爲買主的人很仔細地察看房子。）

(D) go without 沒有；沒有…而將就度過

　　（＝ *not have* ＝ *do without* ＝ *be without*）

　　She got up late and had to go without breakfast.

　　（她起得太晚，因此沒吃早餐。）

　　There is no butter left, so we have to go without.

　　（奶油沒了，所以我們必須將就一下。）

　　＊*alarm clock* 鬧鐘　　wake〔wek〕*v.* 叫醒

　　in time 及時　　catch〔kætʃ〕*v.* 趕上

15. (**A**) That man looks suspicious. <u>Keep an eye on</u> him and make sure he doesn't steal anything.

那個人看起來很可疑。要<u>密切注意</u>他，確定他沒偷任何東西。

(A) *keep an eye on* 密切注意；盯著

(B) turn a deaf ear to 不聽　　turn a blind eye to 忽視

　　deaf〔dɛf〕*adj.* 聾的　　blind〔blaɪnd〕*adj.* 瞎的

(C) turn *one's* back on 不理睬；背棄

(D) make the best of 善用；儘量利用（＝ *make the most of*）

　　＊suspicious〔səˈspɪʃəs〕*adj.* 可疑的　　*make sure* 確定

　　steal〔stil〕*v.* 偷

TEST 8

Directions: The following questions are incomplete sentences. You are to choose the one word that best completes the sentence.

1. All the newspapers _____ articles about the pop singer's marriage.
   - (A) lifted
   - (B) carried
   - (C) held
   - (D) rented   (   )

2. Because of his _____ situation, he does not have to pay tuition.
   - (A) positive
   - (B) ordinary
   - (C) accurate
   - (D) particular   (   )

3. Organic foods are foods grown without the use of anything _____.
   - (A) nutritious
   - (B) superstitious
   - (C) artificial
   - (D) explicit   (   )

4. The strikers were at first peaceful, but when the government refused to listen to their demands, they started _____ in the streets.
   - (A) rioting
   - (B) consisting
   - (C) arresting
   - (D) predicting   (   )

5. As was predicted from the very _____, the plan turned out to be a failure eventually.
   - (A) outcome
   - (B) outbreak
   - (C) outskirts
   - (D) outset   (   )

6. The offices in this building are not heated _____ but are jointly warmed by a central heating system.
   - (A) independently
   - (B) involuntarily
   - (C) indispensably
   - (D) indifferently   (   )

7. The girl did not want to take sides in the argument between her two friends, but her _____ only made them angry with her.
   - (A) implication
   - (B) impartiality
   - (C) indignation
   - (D) immortality   (   )

8. When a climber reaches the top of a mountain, he has reached the
   _____.
   (A) summary   (B) consensus
   (C) concession   (D) summit   (　　)

9. She is a very _____ student. She's always talking about traveling
   to outer space.
   (A) imaginary   (B) imaginative
   (C) imaginable   (D) imagining   (　　)

10. Advertisers _____ credibility when they make exaggerated
    claims for the products they promote.
    (A) interfere   (B) appreciate
    (C) sacrifice   (D) dominate   (　　)

11. The early pioneers had to _____ many hardships to settle in the
    new land.
    (A) go after   (B) go into
    (C) go without   (D) go through   (　　)

12. _____ the enemy's stubborn resistance, our army occupied the
    town as originally scheduled.
    (A) To say nothing of   (B) With regard to
    (C) In spite of   (D) In case of   (　　)

13. The public _____ and listened to the announcement.
    (A) held their breath   (B) wasted their breath
    (C) took their breath away   (D) gave up their breath   (　　)

14. The first brain tissue transplant operation in Taiwan was _____
    on May 30, 1996.
    (A) dropped out   (B) carried out
    (C) worn out   (D) followed out   (　　)

15. No matter how extensive our vocabulary is, we will frequently face
    words that _____ us.
    (A) are bound to   (B) are accustomed to
    (C) are becoming to   (D) are foreign to   (　　)

TEST 8 詳解

1. (**B**) All the newspapers <u>carried</u> articles about the pop singer's marriage.
所有的報紙都<u>刊登</u>了關於這位流行歌手結婚的文章。
(A) lift〔lɪft〕*v.* 舉起；抬起 (= *raise*)
(B) *carry*〔'kærɪ〕*v.* (報紙) 刊登 (新聞、消息)
(C) hold〔hold〕*v.* 握住；舉行；保持
(D) rent〔rɛnt〕*v.* 出租；租用　　*n.* 租金
＊article〔'ɑrtɪkl̩〕*n.* 文章　　***pop singer*** 流行歌手
marriage〔'mærɪdʒ〕*n.* 婚姻；結婚

2. (**D**) Because of his <u>particular</u> situation, he does not have to pay tuition.
因為他的情況<u>特殊</u>，所以他不用付學費。
(A) positive〔'pɑzətɪv〕*adj.* 正面的；積極的 (↔ negative *adj.* 負面的；消極的)
(B) ordinary〔'ɔrdn̩͵ɛrɪ〕*adj.* 一般的；普通的；平常的
　　(↔ extraordinary *adj.* 不尋常的)
(C) accurate〔'ækjərɪt〕*adj.* 正確的；準確的 (= *correct*)
(D) *particular*〔pə'tɪkjələ〕*adj.* 特殊的
＊tuition〔tju'ɪʃən〕*n.* 學費

3. (**C**) Organic foods are foods grown without the use of anything <u>artificial</u>.
有機食品就是不用任何<u>人工</u>物質培植出來的食品。
(A) nutritious〔nju'trɪʃəs〕*adj.* 營養的　　nutrition *n.*
(B) superstitious〔͵supə'stɪʃəs〕*adj.* 迷信的　　superstition *n.*
(C) *artificial*〔͵ɑrtə'fɪʃəl〕*adj.* 人造的；人工的
　　artificial flowers 人造花　　artificial intelligence 人工智慧
(D) explicit〔ɪk'splɪsɪt〕*adj.* 明確的 (↔ implicit *adj.* 暗示的)
＊organic〔ɔr'gænɪk〕*adj.* 有機的　　grow〔gro〕*v.* 種植；栽培

4. (**A**) The strikers were at first peaceful, but when the government refused to listen to their demands, they started <u>rioting</u> in the streets. 起初這些罷工者很平和，
不過當政府拒絕聽從他們的要求時，他們就開始在街頭<u>暴動</u>。
(A) *riot*〔'raɪət〕*v. n.* 暴動　　riot squad 鎮暴警察 (= *riot police*)
(B) consist〔kən'sɪst〕*v.* 組成
　　consist of 由…組成 (= *be made up of* = *be composed of*)
(C) arrest〔ə'rɛst〕*v. n.* 逮捕　　be under arrest 被逮捕
(D) predict〔prɪ'dɪkt〕*v.* 預測　　prediction *n.*
＊striker〔'straɪkə〕*n.* 罷工者　　***at first*** 起初　　peaceful〔'pisfəl〕*adj.* 溫和的
refuse〔rɪ'fjuz〕*v.* 拒絕　　demand〔dɪ'mænd〕*n.* 要求

5. (**D**) As was predicted from the very <u>outset,</u> the plan turned out to be a failure eventually. 正如一<u>開始</u>所預料的，這個計劃最後失敗了。

   (A) outcome（'aʊt,kʌm）*n.* 結果（= *result*）　　　*cf.* income *n.* 收入

   (B) outbreak（'aʊt,brek）*n.* 爆發；（突然）發生

   　　break out （戰爭、疾病、火災）爆發

   (C) outskirts（'aʊt,skɝts）*n. pl.* 郊區（= *suburbs*）

   　　on the outskirts of Taipei 在台北的郊區（= **in** the suburbs of Taipei）

   (D) *outset*（'aʊt,sɛt）*n.* 開始　　　*from / at the* (*very*) *outset* 從一開始

   ＊turn out 結果　　failure（'feljɚ）*n.* 失敗

   　　eventually（ɪ'vɛntʃʊəlɪ）*adv.* 最後

6. (**A**) The offices in this building are not heated <u>independently</u> but are jointly warmed by a central heating system.

   這棟大樓的辦公室沒有<u>獨立</u>暖氣系統，而是一起由中央暖氣系統供應暖氣。

   (A) *independently*（,ɪndɪ'pɛndəntlɪ）*adv.* 獨立地；個別地

   (B) involuntarily（ɪn'vɑlən,tɛrəlɪ）*adv.* 不由自主地；非出於本意地；無心地

   　　voluntary（'vɑlən,tɛrɪ）*adj.* 自願的

   　　volunteer（,vɑlən'tɪr）*n.* 自願者；志工

   (C) indispensably（,ɪndɪ'spɛnsəblɪ）*adv.* 不可或缺地

   　　indispensable *adj.* 不可或缺的

   (D) indifferently（ɪn'dɪfərəntlɪ）*adv.* 漠不關心地

   　　indifferent *adj.* 漠不關心的

   *＊heat（hit）*v.* 使變熱　　jointly（'dʒɔɪntlɪ）*adv.* 共同地

   　　warm（wɔrm）*v.* 使暖和　　*central heating* (*system*) 中央暖氣系統

7. (**B**) The girl did not want to take sides in the argument between her two friends, but her <u>impartiality</u> only made them angry with her. 這個女孩子不想在兩位朋友的爭論中偏袒任何一方，但是她的<u>中立</u>卻使他們很生氣。

   (A) implication（,ɪmplɪ'keʃən）*n.* 暗示；涵義　　　imply *v.*

   (B) *impartiality*（,ɪmpɑrʃɪ'æ\ətɪ）*n.* 不偏不倚；中立

   　　impartial *adj.* 不偏不倚的；沒有偏見的

   　　（↔ partial *adj.* 不公平的；偏袒的）

   (C) indignation（,ɪndɪg'neʃən）*n.* 憤怒；憤慨　　　indignant *adj.*

   (D) immortality（,ɪmɔr'tælətɪ）*n.* 不死；不朽

   　　immortal *adj.* 不朽的（↔ mortal *adj.* 必死的）

   　　immorality（,ɪmə'rælətɪ）*n.* 不道德　　immoral *adj.* 不道德的

   ＊take sides 偏袒　　argument（'ɑrgjəmənt）*n.* 爭論

8. (**D**) When a climber reaches the top of a mountain, he has reached the summit.
當登山者到達山頂時，他就登上頂峰了。

(A) summary ('sʌmərɪ) *n.* 摘要；總結　in summary 總之
give a summary 做總結

(B) consensus (kən'sɛnsəs) *n.* 共識　reach a consensus 達成共識

(C) concession (kən'sɛʃən) *n.* 讓步
make a concession to 對~讓步 (= *yield to*)

(D) *summit* ('sʌmɪt) *n.* 山頂；巔峰
reach the summit of *one's* career 到達事業的巔峰

＊climber ('klaɪmə) *n.* 登山者

9. (**B**) She is a very imaginative student. She's always talking about traveling to
outer space.
她是一個非常富有想像力的學生。她總是在談論有關到外太空旅行的事。

(A) imaginary (ɪ'mædʒə,nɛrɪ) *adj.* 想像的；虛構的 (↔ *real*)
an imaginary enemy 假想敵

(B) *imaginative* (ɪ'mædʒə,netɪv) *adj.* 富有想像力的

(C) imaginable (ɪ'mædʒɪnəbḷ) *adj.* 想像得到的
every imaginable means 一切可能的方法

(D) imagine (ɪ'mædʒɪn) *v.* 想像　imagination *n.* 想像力

＊*outer space* 外太空

10. (**C**) Advertisers sacrifice credibility when they make exaggerated claims for the
products they promote.
當刊登廣告者對他們所促銷的商品做出誇大的宣傳時，他們就犧牲了可信度。

(A) interfere (,ɪntə'fɪr) *v.* 妨礙＜ with ＞；干涉＜ in ＞　interference *n.*

(B) appreciate (ə'priʃɪ,et) *v.* 欣賞；感激　appreciation *n.*

(C) *sacrifice* ('sækrə,faɪs) *v. n.* 犧牲
make sacrifices for *sb.* 為某人犧牲

(D) dominate ('dɑmə,net) *v.* 支配；控制
dominant *adj.* 支配的；佔優勢的

＊advertiser ('ædvə,taɪzə) *n.* 刊登廣告者；廣告客戶
credibility (,krɛdə'bɪlətɪ) *n.* 可信度
exaggerated (ɪg'zædʒə,retɪd) *adj.* 誇大的
claim (klem) *n.* 宣稱　promote (prə'mot) *v.* 促銷

11. (**D**) The early pioneers had to <u>go through</u> many hardships to settle in the new land.
早期的拓荒者為了在新的土地上定居，必須歷經千辛萬苦。

    (A) go after 追求   He went after wealth and fame. (他追求名利。)

    (B) go into 進入   go into a coma 陷入昏迷

    (C) go without 沒有… (也就算了)；將就 (= *do without*)

       There's no more coffee, so you'll have to go without.

       (沒咖啡了，所以你必須將就一下。)

    (D) *go through* 通過；經歷 (苦難)；仔細檢查

    *pioneer〔͵paɪə'nɪr〕*n.* 拓荒者；先鋒；先驅

     hardship〔'hardʃɪp〕*n.* 艱難；辛苦   settle〔'sɛtḷ〕*v.* 定居

12. (**C**) <u>In spite of</u> the enemy's stubborn resistance, our army occupied the town as originally scheduled.
儘管敵軍頑強抵抗，我軍還是按原定計劃佔領這個城鎮。

    (A) to say nothing of 更不用說

       (= *not to speak of* = *not to mention* = *let alone*)

    (B) with regard to 關於 (= *in regard to* = *as to* = *as for* = *with respect to*

       = *regarding* = *respecting* = *concerning* = *about*)

    (C) *in spite of* 儘管 (= *despite*)

    (D) in case of 如果發生   in case of fire 如果發生火災

    *enemy〔'ɛnəmɪ〕*n.* 敵人   stubborn〔'stʌbən〕*adj.* 頑固的；頑強的

     resistance〔rɪ'zɪstəns〕*n.* 抵抗

     army〔'armɪ〕*n.* 軍隊   occupy〔'akjə͵paɪ〕*v.* 佔領

     originally〔ə'rɪdʒənḷɪ〕*adv.* 原本；本來

     schedule〔'skɛdʒul〕*v.* 排定；預定

13. (**A**) The public <u>held their breath</u> and listened to the announcement.
民眾都屏氣凝神要聆聽宣佈。

    (A) *hold one's breath* 屏氣凝神   hold〔hold〕*v.* 保持

     breath〔brɛθ〕*n.* 呼吸

    (B) waste *one's* breath 白費唇舌 (↔ save *one's* breath 不白費唇舌)

    (C) take *one's* breath away 使某人大為驚訝；使某人非常感動

    (D) give up *one's* breath 斷氣；死亡

     catch *one's* breath (在運動過後) 喘一口氣

    *the public 民眾   announcement〔ə'naʊnsmənt〕*n.* 宣佈

14. (**B**) The first brain tissue transplant operation in Taiwan was <u>carried out</u> on May 30, 1996.

台灣第一次腦部組織移植手術,是在一九九六年五月三十日進行的。

(A) drop out 退出;中途輟學

One runner twisted his foot and dropped out.

(有位跑者扭傷了腳,因而退出比賽。)

She got a scholarship to Harvard but dropped out six months later.

(她獲得一筆哈佛大學的獎學金,但六個月後就輟學了。)

(B) *carry out* 執行   carry out an operation 動手術

undergo an operation 接受手術

(C) wear out 使筋疲力盡;磨損

I really feel worn out. (我真的覺得筋疲力盡。)

Cheap shoes wear out quickly. (便宜的鞋子很快就磨破了。)

(D) follow out 徹底實行;貫徹

＊brain〔bren〕*n.* 腦   tissue〔'tıʃʊ〕*n.* 組織

transplant〔'trænsplænt〕*n.* 移植

operation〔ˌɑpə'reʃən〕*n.* 手術 (= *surgery*)

15. (**D**) No matter how extensive our vocabulary is, we will frequently face words that <u>are foreign to</u> us.

無論我們的字彙量有多大,我們還是時常會遇到不認識的生字。

(A) be bound to (+ *V.*) 必須 (= *be required to* = *be obliged to* = *be supposed to* = *have (got) to* = *ought to* = *should*)

be bound for 前往 (= *leave for*)

(B) be accustomed to (+ *N. / V-ing*) 習慣於 (= *be used to*)

(C) be becoming to (+ *N.*) 適合 (= *be suitable for*)

Such conduct is not becoming to a lady.

(這樣的行為是不適合一個淑女做的。)

(D) *be foreign to* (+ *N.*) 對～而言是陌生的

foreign〔'fɔrın〕*adj.* 外國的;性質不同的;外來的;異質的

a foreign substance in the eye 眼中的異物

Flattery is foreign to his nature. (諂媚不是他的本性。)

＊extensive〔ık'stɛnsıv〕*adj.* 大量的;廣泛的

vocabulary〔və'kæbjəˌlɛrı〕*n.* 字彙

frequently〔'frikwəntlı〕*adv.* 經常   face〔fes〕*v.* 面對;面臨

TEST 9

Directions: The following questions are incomplete sentences. You are to choose the one word that best completes the sentence.

1. Danny complained that he couldn't afford much on such a tight _____.
   (A) rehearsal   (B) security
   (C) budget   (D) dilemma   (   )

2. Ray has a(n) _____ against Korean soap operas. He believes that they are only for people who have no taste.
   (A) prejudice   (B) compromise
   (C) negotiation   (D) alternative   (   )

3. Make certain that your passport is _____ if you plan to go overseas this summer.
   (A) valid   (B) blank
   (C) comprehensive   (D) extensive   (   )

4. The restaurant _____ hot, spicy food. Everything you have there is guaranteed to burn your mouth!
   (A) overlooks   (B) prohibits
   (C) excludes   (D) features   (   )

5. I have read Shakespeare's Romeo and Juliet, but just the translation, not the _____ version.
   (A) commercial   (B) current
   (C) original   (D) individual   (   )

6. It was generous of the billionaire to _____ all his assets to charity.
   (A) withdraw   (B) donate
   (C) launch   (D) suspend   (   )

7. The judo class is aimed at teaching women the basics of _____ themselves against attacks.
   (A) convincing   (B) motivating
   (C) defending   (D) inheriting   (   )

8. Brenda's secret to making a great-tasting salad is choosing the finest and freshest _____.
   - (A) souvenirs
   - (B) targets
   - (C) accents
   - (D) ingredients   (   )

9. Visitors were fascinated by the variety of fish in the zoo's new _____.
   - (A) stadium
   - (B) aquarium
   - (C) escalator
   - (D) territory   (   )

10. Karen _____ admitted to her friends that she was seeing someone. Obviously, she hadn't meant to let them know.
    - (A) exclusively
    - (B) bluntly
    - (C) absolutely
    - (D) reluctantly   (   )

11. The boy _____ a cry of pain when the nurse stuck a needle in his arm.
    - (A) figured out
    - (B) gave away
    - (C) let out
    - (D) called for   (   )

12. After battling lung cancer for several months, he finally _____ at the age of 63.
    - (A) worked out
    - (B) passed away
    - (C) caught on
    - (D) turned up   (   )

13. The company is losing money, so they had to _____ 1,000 workers.
    - (A) lay off
    - (B) sharpen up
    - (C) let down
    - (D) miss out on   (   )

14. The computer company is planning to _____ a new notebook computer in the spring.
    - (A) break down
    - (B) bring out
    - (C) pick up
    - (D) settle down   (   )

15. Eve is so protective of her children that she won't allow them to _____ their schoolmates after school.
    - (A) cope with
    - (B) hang out with
    - (C) comply with
    - (D) dispense with   (   )

TEST 9 詳解

1. (**C**) Danny complained that he couldn't afford much on such a tight <u>budget</u>.
丹尼抱怨說，因為預算很緊，所以他付不起很多錢。
   - (A) rehearsal〔rɪ'hɜsḷ〕 *n.* 預演；排練　　rehearse *v.*
   - (B) security〔sɪ'kjʊrətɪ〕 *n.* 安全　　secure *adj.*
   - (C) *budget*〔'bʌdʒɪt〕 *n.* 預算　*adj.* 便宜的（= *cheap*）
   - (D) dilemma〔də'lɛmə〕 *n.* 困境；進退兩難
      be in a dilemma　進退兩難；左右爲難
   - *complain〔kəm'plen〕 *v.* 抱怨　　afford〔ə'fɔrd〕 *v.* 負擔得起
      tight〔taɪt〕 *adj.* 緊的

2. (**A**) Ray has a <u>prejudice</u> against Korean soap operas. He believes that they are only for people who have no taste.
雷對韓國的連續劇有偏見。他認爲那些連續劇是沒有品味的人才會看的。
   - (A) *prejudice*〔'prɛdʒədɪs〕 *n.* 偏見 < *against* >
   - (B) compromise〔'kɑmprə,maɪz〕 *n. v.* 妥協
   - (C) negotiation〔nɪ,goʃɪ'eʃən〕 *n.* 交涉；協商；談判　　negotiate *v.*
   - (D) alternative〔ɔl'tɜnətɪv〕 *n.* 可選擇的事物；另一個選擇
      You have the alternative of going to college or finding a job.
      （你可以選擇上大學或就業。）
   - *Korean〔ko'riən〕 *adj.* 韓國的　　*soap opera*　（電視的）連續劇
      taste〔test〕 *n.* 品味

3. (**A**) Make certain that your passport is <u>valid</u> if you plan to go overseas this summer.
如果你打算今年夏天出國的話，就要確定你的護照是有效的。
   - (A) *valid*〔'vælɪd〕 *adj.* 有效的（↔ *invalid*）
   - (B) blank〔blæŋk〕 *adj.* 空白的　 *n.* 空格
      go blank　（腦中）變得一片空白
   - (C) comprehensive〔,kɑmprɪ'hɛnsɪv〕 *adj.* 全面的；有理解力的
      comprehension *n.* 理解（力）　　reading comprehension test　閱讀測驗
   - (D) extensive〔ɪk'stɛnsɪv〕 *adj.* 廣泛的　　extend *v.* 延伸
      extension *n.*（電話）分機
   - *make certain　確定　　passport〔'pæs,port〕 *n.* 護照
      overseas〔'ovɚ'siz〕 *adv.* 到國外
      go overseas　出國（= *go abroad*）

4. (**D**) The restaurant <u>features</u> hot, spicy food. Everything you have there is guaranteed to burn your mouth!

這家餐廳<u>以香辣的食物爲其特色</u>。你在那裡吃到的所有食物，保證會使你的嘴裡火辣辣的！

(A) overlook〔͵ovə'lʊk〕*v.* 忽視 (= *ignore*)；俯瞰 (= *command*)

(B) prohibit〔pro'hɪbɪt〕*v.* 禁止 (= *forbid* = *ban*)

(C) exclude〔ɪk'sklud〕*v.* 不包括 (↔ include *v.* 包括)

(D) *feature*〔'fitʃɚ〕*v.* 以～爲特色

＊hot〔hɑt〕*adj.* 辣的　　spicy〔'spaɪsɪ〕*adj.* 加香料的；火辣的

　have〔hæv〕*v.* 吃　　guarantee〔͵gærən'ti〕*v.* 保證

　burn〔bɝn〕*v.* 使有火辣感　　mouth〔maʊθ〕*n.* 嘴巴

5. (**C**) I have read Shakespeare's *Romeo and Juliet*, but just the translation, not the <u>original</u> version.

我讀過莎士比亞的「羅密歐與茱麗葉」，但只是譯本，不是<u>原文</u>版。

(A) commercial〔kə'mɝʃəl〕*adj.* 商業的　*n.* (電視或廣播的) 商業廣告

(B) current〔'kɝənt〕*adj.* 目前的；現今的　　current events 時事

　currently *adv.* 目前

(C) *original*〔ə'rɪdʒənḷ〕*adj.* 原來的；最初的　　originally *adv.*

(D) individual〔͵ɪndə'vɪdʒʊəl〕*adj.* 個別的　*n.* 個人

＊Shakespeare〔'ʃek͵spɪr〕*n.* 莎士比亞

　【1514-1616，英國劇作家、詩人】

　translation〔træns'leʃən〕*n.* 譯本

　version〔'vɝʒən〕*n.* 版本

Shakespeare

6. (**B**) It was generous of the billionaire to <u>donate</u> all his assets to charity.

那位億萬富翁很慷慨，他將所有的財產，都<u>捐</u>給慈善機構。

(A) withdraw〔wɪθ'drɔ〕*v.* 撤退；提 (款)【↔ deposit〔dɪ'pɑzɪt〕*v.* 存 (款)】

(B) *donate*〔'donet〕*v.* 捐贈　　donate blood 捐血

(C) launch〔lɔntʃ〕*v.* 發射；發動　　launch a space shuttle 發射太空梭

　launch an attack 發動攻擊

(D) suspend〔sə'spɛnd〕*v.* 暫停　　suspend payment 止付

　All flights were suspended because of a typhoon.

　（因爲有颱風，所以所有的班機都暫時停飛。）

＊generous〔'dʒɛnərəs〕*adj.* 慷慨的；大方的

　billionaire〔͵bɪljən'ɛr〕*n.* 億萬富翁

　assets〔'æsɛts〕*n. pl.* 財產　　charity〔'tʃærətɪ〕*n.* 慈善機構

7. (**C**) The judo class is aimed at teaching women the basics of <u>defending</u> themselves against attacks.

這堂柔道課的目的，是要教導婦女一<u>些</u>保護自己不受攻擊的基本技巧。

(A) convince (kən'vɪns) v. 使相信　　convince *sb.* of *sth.* 使某人相信某事

(B) motivate ('motə,vet) v. 給予動機；激勵　　motivation n. 動機；動力

(C) **defend** (dɪ'fɛnd) v. 保護；防禦　　defense n. 防禦

defendant n. 被告 (↔ plaintiff ('plentɪf) n. 原告)

(D) inherit (ɪn'hɛrɪt) v. 繼承　　heritage ('hɛrətɪdʒ) n. 遺產

hereditary (hə'rɛdə,tɛrɪ) *adj.* 遺傳的

*judo ('dʒudo) n. 柔道　　***be aimed at*** 目的是在於

basics ('besɪks) n. pl. 基礎；基本原理　　attack (ə'tæk) n. 攻擊

8. (**D**) Brenda's secret to making a great-tasting salad is choosing the finest and freshest <u>ingredients</u>.

布蘭達會做非常好吃的沙拉，她的秘訣就是選擇最好而且最新鮮的<u>材料</u>。

(A) souvenir ('suvə,nɪr) n. (能使人回憶旅行、地點、事情等的) 紀念品；

特產【注意發音】

(B) target ('tɑrgɪt) n. 目標　v. 將…定作目標

be targeted at 以…為目標 (= be aimed at = be directed at)

(C) accent ('æksɛnt) n. 口音；腔調；【語音】重音

primary accent 主重音　　secondary accent 次重音

speak English with a strong accent 說英語帶著一種很重的口音

(D) **ingredient** (ɪn'gridɪənt) n. 原料；成分

*secret ('sikrɪt) n. 秘訣　　***a secret to doing*** *sth.* 做某事的秘訣

salad ('sæləd) n. 沙拉　　fine (faɪn) *adj.* 好的

fresh (frɛʃ) *adj.* 新鮮的

9. (**B**) Visitors were fascinated by the variety of fish in the zoo's new <u>aquarium</u>.

動物園的新<u>水族館</u>裡，有各式各樣的魚，令遊客十分著迷。

(A) stadium ('stedɪəm) n. (周圍有看台的) 體育場

(B) **aquarium** (ə'kwɛrɪəm) n. 水族館；水族箱【拉丁文 aqua = water】

(C) escalator ('ɛskə,letə) n. 電扶梯

elevator ('ɛlə,vetə) n. 升降機；電梯

(D) territory ('tɛrə,torɪ) n. 領土；領域

*visitor ('vɪzɪtə) n. 遊客　　fascinate ('fæsn,et) v. 使著迷

be fascinated by 對～著迷　　variety (və'raɪətɪ) n. 各式各樣；多樣性

10. (**D**) Karen <u>reluctantly</u> admitted to her friends that she was seeing someone. Obviously, she hadn't meant to let them know.

凱倫很<u>不情願地</u>向她的朋友承認，她正在和某人交往。很顯然地，她原本不打算讓他們知道。

(A) exclusively〔ɪk'sklusɪvlɪ〕*adv.* 僅僅；限於⋯；專門地

(B) bluntly〔'blʌntlɪ〕*adv.* 直率地；不拐彎抹角地

　　(= *honestly* = *frankly* = *straightforwardly*)

(C) absolutely〔'æbsə,lutlɪ〕*adv.* 絕對地 (= *definitely*)

(D) *reluctantly*〔rɪ'lʌktəntlɪ〕*adv.* 不情願地；勉強地

＊admit〔əd'mɪt〕*v.* 承認　　see〔si〕*v.* 與⋯交往；和⋯約會

　obviously〔'ɑbvɪəslɪ〕*adv.* 明顯地　　mean〔min〕*v.* 打算

11. (**C**) The boy <u>let out</u> a cry of pain when the nurse stuck a needle in his arm.

當護士在那男孩的手臂上扎了一針時，他<u>大聲</u>喊疼。

(A) figure out 了解 (= *work out* = *understand*)；算出

(B) give away 贈送 (= *give* = *give out* = *donate*)

(C) *let out* 大聲地表達

(D) call for 需要 (= *need* = *require*)

＊cry〔kraɪ〕*n.* 大叫　　pain〔pen〕*n.* 疼痛

　stick〔stɪk〕*v.* 刺　　needle〔'nidl̩〕*n.* 針

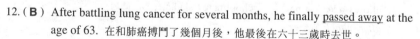

12. (**B**) After battling lung cancer for several months, he finally <u>passed away</u> at the age of 63. 在和肺癌搏鬥了幾個月後，他最後在六十三歲時<u>去世</u>。

(A) work out 解決；(順利) 進行；運動

(B) *pass away* 去世 (= *die*)

(C) catch on 受歡迎；流行 (= *become popular*)；了解 (= *understand*)

　　The song caught on quickly. (那首歌很快就受到歡迎。)

(D) turn up 開大聲 (↔ turn down 關小聲)；出現 (= *show up*)

＊battle〔'bætl̩〕*v.* 與⋯作戰　　lung〔lʌŋ〕*n.* 肺

　cancer〔'kænsɚ〕*n.* 癌症

13. (**A**) The company is losing money, so they had to <u>lay off</u> 1,000 workers.

這家公司正在賠錢，所以他們必須<u>暫時解僱</u>一千名員工。

(A) *lay off* 暫時解僱　　　　　(B) sharpen up 使更敏銳；使更強烈

(C) let down 放下；使失望　　(D) miss out on 錯過⋯的機會

＊lose〔luz〕*v.* 損失

14. (**B**) The computer company is planning to <u>bring out</u> a new notebook computer
in the spring.

這家電腦公司打算在春天推出一款新的筆記型電腦。

(A) break down 故障（= *stop working*）；（精神）崩潰

(B) *bring out* 推出（新產品）；出版（書籍）

(C) pick up 撿起；開車接（某人）；（中斷之後）再繼續

(D) settle down 安頓下來；定居；適應新環境

＊notebook〔'notˌbʊk〕*n.* 筆記本

　notebook computer 筆記型電腦（= *notebook* = *laptop*）

15. (**B**) Eve is so protective of her children that she won't allow them to <u>hang out</u>
<u>with</u> their schoolmates after school.

伊芙十分保護她的子女，她不准他們在放學後，<u>和</u>其他的同學<u>在一起</u>。

(A) cope with 應付（= *deal with* = *handle*）

(B) *hang out with* 和～在一起

(C) comply with 遵守（= *obey* = *observe* = *follow* = *abide by*）

(D) dispense with 免除；省去；不用

　　dispense with ceremony 免除儀式

　　Robots dispense with much labor.（機器人可省去很多勞力。）

＊protective〔prə'tɛktɪv〕*adj.* 保護的；過分愛護的

　allow〔ə'laʊ〕*v.* 允許　　schoolmate〔'skulˌmet〕*n.* 同學

　after school 放學後

TEST 10

Directions: The following questions are incomplete sentences. You are to choose the one word that best completes the sentence.

1. To arrest the suspects in the murder case, the police have issued a detailed _____ of each suspect.
   (A) description   (B) prescription
   (C) subscription   (D) inscription   (   )

2. Although there is only one month left, I still see a _____ of hope if you open your books and study hard.
   (A) remedy   (B) melody
   (C) shift   (D) glimmer   (   )

3. The big diamond is _____ and I could not afford to buy it if I worked my entire life.
   (A) priceless   (B) costless
   (C) worthless   (D) valueless   (   )

4. The car accident was _____ to the driver's violation of the traffic regulations.
   (A) assigned   (B) contributed
   (C) attributed   (D) transferred   (   )

5. _____, the youngest and shortest student won the championship in the swimming competition.
   (A) Unfortunately   (B) Incredibly
   (C) Inevitably   (D) Invariably   . (   )

6. The sound of your voice was completely _____ out by the roar of the machinery.
   (A) reduced   (B) scattered
   (C) altered   (D) drowned   (   )

7. The students lack motivation and won't study on their own unless _____ by heavy pressure.
   (A) propelled   (B) repelled
   (C) expelled   (D) dispelled   (   )

8. The civil servant brought the scandal to light in an _____ interview with the journalist.

(A) enclosing
(B) exclusive
(C) inaudible
(D) inclusive
( )

9. He made an important discovery, which caused a great _____.

(A) sensation
(B) sensitivity
(C) sentiment
(D) sensor
( )

10. Chimpanzees in the wild use simple objects as tools, but in laboratory situations they can use more _____ items.

(A) anonymous
(B) sarcastic
(C) deliberate
(D) sophisticated
( )

11. John was very nervous because this time there was no one around to get him _____.

(A) on the rocks
(B) in the pink
(C) off the hook
(D) on the blink
( )

12. My father is a serious man but, _____, he is funny.

(A) on call
(B) on board
(C) on occasion
(D) on schedule
( )

13. Kenny seemed to have _____ the flu, which stopped him from scuba diving.

(A) kept up with
(B) put up with
(C) come up with
(D) come down with
( )

14. We _____ a new road back to town while we were out for a ride Sunday.

(A) came upon
(B) looked after
(C) turned out
(D) called off
( )

15. The results of the examination _____ the teacher's expectations.

(A) ran out of
(B) fell short of
(C) made much of
(D) took hold of
( )

TEST 10 詳解

1. (**A**) To arrest the suspects in the murder case, the police have issued a detailed <u>description</u> of each suspect.
   爲了逮捕謀殺案的嫌疑犯，警方已經發布每個嫌犯詳細的<u>相貌描述</u>。
   (A) *description* ﹝dɪˋskrɪpʃən﹞ *n.* 描述；相貌描述
      describe *v.* 【 de (= *down*) + scribe (= *write*)】
   (B) prescription ﹝prɪˋskrɪpʃən﹞ *n.* 處方
      prescribe *v.* 【 pre (= *before*) + scribe (= *write*)】
   (C) subscription ﹝səbˋskrɪpʃən﹞ *n.* 訂閱 < *to* >
      subscribe *v.* 【 sub (= *under*) + scribe (= *write*)】
   (D) inscription ﹝ɪnˋskrɪpʃən﹞ *n.* 銘刻
      inscribe *v.* 【 in (= *upon*) + scribe (= *write*)】
   * arrest ﹝əˋrɛst﹞ *v.* 逮捕　　suspect ﹝ˋsʌspɛkt﹞ *n.* 嫌疑犯
     murder ﹝ˋmɝdɚ﹞ *n.* 謀殺　　case ﹝kes﹞ *n.* 案件
     issue ﹝ˋɪʃju﹞ *v.* 發佈　　detailed ﹝ˋditeld, dɪˋteld﹞ *adj.* 詳細的

2. (**D**) Although there is only one month left, I still see a <u>glimmer</u> of hope if you open your books and study hard.
   雖然只剩下一個月，我認爲如果你打開書本用功讀書，仍然是有一<u>線</u>希望的。
   (A) remedy ﹝ˋrɛmədɪ﹞ *n.* 治療法 < *for* >　　beyond remedy 無可救藥
   (B) melody ﹝ˋmɛlədɪ﹞ *n.* 旋律 (= *tune*)
   (C) shift ﹝ʃɪft﹞ *n. v.* 改變；變換；輪班　　a shift in policy 政策的改變
      an eight-hour shift 八小時輪班　　shift gears （開車時）換檔
   (D) *glimmer* ﹝ˋglɪmɚ﹞ *n.* 微光；（希望、關心等）輕微的表露；跡象
   * left ﹝lɛft﹞ *adj.* 剩下的

3. (**A**) The big diamond is <u>priceless</u> and I could not afford to buy it if I worked my entire life. 這顆大鑽石是<u>無價</u>之寶，我就算工作一輩子也買不起。
   (A) *priceless* ﹝ˋpraɪslɪs﹞ *adj.* 無價的；極爲貴重的
   (B) costless ﹝ˋkɔstlɪs﹞ *adj.* 不花錢的；免費的
   (C) worthless ﹝ˋwɝθlɪs﹞ *adj.* 無價值的；無用的
   (D) valueless ﹝ˋvæljulɪs﹞ *adj.* 無價值的 (= *worthless* = *of no value* = *of little worth*)
   * diamond ﹝ˋdaɪ(ə)mənd﹞ *n.* 鑽石　　afford ﹝əˋford﹞ *v.* 負擔得起
     entire ﹝ɪnˋtaɪr﹞ *adj.* 整個的

4. (**C**) The car accident was <u>attributed</u> to the driver's violation of the traffic regulations.

這場車禍要<u>歸因於</u>駕駛人違反交通規則。

(A) assign〔ə'saɪn〕*v.* 指派　　assignment *n.* 作業

(B) contribute〔kən'trɪbjʊt〕*v.* 貢獻 < *to* >
contribute to 促成　　contribution *n.*

(C) *attribute*〔ə'trɪbjʊt〕*v.* 歸因於 < *to* >

(D) transfer〔træns'fɝ〕*v.* 轉移；調職；轉車；轉學

* *car accident* 車禍　　violation〔,vaɪə'leʃən〕*n.* 違反
regulation〔,rɛgjə'leʃən〕*n.* 規則

5. (**B**) <u>Incredibly</u>, the youngest and shortest student won the championship in the swimming competition.

<u>令人難以置信的是</u>，那個最年輕而且最矮的學生，贏得了游泳比賽的冠軍。

(A) unfortunately〔ʌn'fɔrtʃənɪtlɪ〕*adv.* 不幸地；遺憾地

(B) *incredibly*〔ɪn'krɛdəblɪ〕*adv.* 令人難以置信地

(C) inevitably〔ɪn'ɛvətəblɪ〕*adv.* 不可避免地 (= *unavoidably*)

(D) invariably〔ɪn'vɛrɪəblɪ〕*adv.* 不變地；必然地
vary〔'vɛrɪ〕*v.* 改變；變化

* championship〔'tʃæmpɪən,ʃɪp〕*n.* 冠軍（資格）
competition〔,kɑmpə'tɪʃən〕*n.* 比賽

6. (**D**) The sound of your voice was completely <u>drowned</u> out by the roar of the machinery.

你們的聲音完全被機器轟隆轟隆的聲音給<u>淹沒</u>了。

(A) reduce〔rɪ'djus〕*v.* 減少；減低　　reduce expenses 減少開銷

(B) scatter〔'skætɚ〕*v.* 散播；把~亂放　　scatter seeds 播種
scatter toys around 亂放玩具

(C) alter〔'ɔltɚ〕*v.* 改變 (= *change*)　　alter opinions 改變意見

(D) *drown*〔draʊn〕*v.* 淹死；（噪音）淹沒（小聲）；（噪音）蓋住（小聲）

* completely〔kəm'plitlɪ〕*adv.* 完全地　　roar〔ror〕*n.* 轟隆聲
machinery〔mə'ʃinərɪ〕*n.* 機器

7. (**A**) The students lack motivation and won't study on their own unless <u>propelled</u> by heavy pressure.

這些學生缺乏動機，除非受到沉重壓力的驅策，不然他們不會自己唸書。

(A) ***propel*** 〔 prə'pɛl 〕 v. 推進；驅策【pro (= *forward*) + pel (= *drive*)】
The ship is propelled by nuclear power.
（這艘船是以核子動力來推動的。）

(B) repel 〔 rɪ'pɛl 〕 v. 逐退；擊退；不透（水）【re (= *back*) + pel (= *drive*)】
This cloth repels water very well. (這種布不透水。)
rebel 〔 rɪ'bɛl 〕 v. 反叛；反抗

(C) expel 〔 ɪk'spɛl 〕 v. 驅逐；開除【ex (= *out*) + pel (= *drive*)】
The boy was expelled from school. (那個男生被學校開除了。)

(D) dispel 〔 dɪ'spɛl 〕 v. 驅散；消除（煩惱）【dis (= *away*) + pel (= *drive*)】
Change can dispel boredom. (改變可以消除厭倦。)

＊lack 〔 læk 〕 v. 缺乏　　　motivation 〔ˌmotə'veʃən 〕 n. 動機
on *one's* ***own*** 靠自己；獨自　　　heavy 〔 'hɛvɪ 〕 *adj.* 沉重的；重大的
pressure 〔 'prɛʃ✗ 〕 n. 壓力

8. (**B**) The civil servant brought the scandal to light in an <u>exclusive</u> interview with the journalist.

這個公務員在與記者的<u>獨家</u>專訪中，揭露了一件醜聞。

(A) enclose 〔 ɪn'kloz 〕 v. 包圍；（隨函）附寄
enclose a check with a letter 隨函附寄一張支票

(B) ***exclusive*** 〔 ɪk'sklusɪv 〕 *adj.* 獨有的；獨家的　　　exclude v. 不包括
exclusively *adv.* 專有地；單獨地
This room is exclusively for women. (這間房間是婦女專用的。)

(C) inaudible 〔 ɪn'ɔdəbḷ 〕 *adj.* 聽不見的；無法聽到的

(D) inclusive 〔 ɪn'klusɪv 〕 *adj.* 包含的 < *of* >　　　include v. 包括

There were 216 people on the plane, $\left\{\begin{array}{l} \text{inclusive of the crew.} \\ \text{including the crew.} \\ \text{the crew included.} \end{array}\right.$

（飛機上共有兩百一十六人，包括機組員在內。）

＊civil 〔 'sɪvḷ 〕 *adj.* 公民的；國民的　　　servant 〔 's✗vənt 〕 n. 僕人；佣人
civil servant 公僕；公務員　　　scandal 〔 'skændḷ 〕 n. 醜聞
bring *…* ***to light*** 將…公諸於世
interview 〔 'ɪnt✗ˌvju 〕 n. (記者的) 採訪；面談
journalist 〔 'dʒȝnḷɪst 〕 n. 記者 (= *reporter*)

9. (**A**) He made an important discovery, which caused a great <u>sensation</u>.

　　他有了重要的發現，因而引起了很大的<u>轟動</u>。

 (A) ***sensation*** 〔 sɛn'seʃən 〕 *n.* 轟動；激動；感覺 (= *feeling*)

  sensational 〔 sɛn'seʃənḷ 〕 *adj.* 煽情的；聳動的；引起轟動的；聳人聽聞的

  a sensational murder trial 轟動一時的謀殺案審判

  sensational headlines 聳動的標題

 (B) sensitivity 〔 ˌsɛnsə'tɪvətɪ 〕 *n.* 敏感 (度) sensitive *adj.* < *to* >

 (C) sentiment 〔 'sɛntəmənt 〕 *n.* 情緒；情操

  sentimental 〔 ˌsɛntə'mɛntḷ 〕 *adj.* 多愁善感的

 (D) sensor 〔 'sɛnsɚ 〕 *n.* 感應器

10. (**D**) Chimpanzees in the wild use simple objects as tools, but in laboratory situations they can use more <u>sophisticated</u> items.

　　野外的黑猩猩會使用簡單的物品來當作工具，但在實驗情況中，牠們會使用更<u>複雜</u>的物品。

 (A) anonymous 〔 ə'nɑnəməs 〕 *adj.* 匿名的

  【an (= *without*) + onym (= *name*) + ous (*adj.*)】

  unanimous 〔 ju'nænəməs 〕 *adj.* 全體一致的

  【un (= *one*) + anim (= *mind*) + ous (*adj.*)】

  synonymous 〔 sɪn'ɑnəməs 〕 *adj.* 同義的

  【syn (= *same*) + onym (= *name*) + ous (*adj.*)】

  monotonous 〔 mə'nɑtn̩əs 〕 *adj.* 單調的

  【mono (= *one*) + ton (= *tone*) + ous (*adj.*)】

 (B) sarcastic 〔 sɑr'kæstɪk 〕 *adj.* 諷刺的 a sarcastic comment 諷刺的話

 (C) deliberate 〔 dɪ'lɪbərɪt 〕 *adj.* 故意的；蓄意的

  deliberate murder 蓄意謀殺

 (D) ***sophisticated*** 〔 sə'fɪstɪˌketɪd 〕 *adj.* 複雜的；精巧的；世故的；老練的

  a sophisticated computer 精巧的電腦

 *chimpanzee 〔 ˌtʃɪmpæn'zi 〕 *n.* 黑猩猩

 in the wild 在野外 object 〔 'ɑbdʒɪkt 〕 *n.* 東西

 tool 〔 tul 〕 *n.* 工具

 laboratory 〔 'læbrəˌtorɪ 〕 *n.* 實驗室

 item 〔 'aɪtəm 〕 *n.* 物品

chimpanzee

11. (**C**) John was very nervous because this time there was no one around to get him
<u>off the hook</u>.

約翰很緊張，因為這次沒有人可以幫他<u>脫離困境</u>了。

(A) on the rocks （船）觸礁的；（威士忌等酒類）加冰塊的

(B) in the pink (of health) 很健康；精神飽滿

pink〔pɪŋk〕*n.* 最佳狀態；高點

(C) *off the hook* 脫離困境　　hook〔huk〕*n.* 鉤子；陷阱

(D) on the blink 壞的；需要修理的　　blink〔blɪŋk〕*n.* 閃光；一瞥

The washing machine is on the blink again. （洗衣機又壞了。）

* nervous〔ˈnɜvəs〕*adj.* 緊張的　　around〔əˈraund〕*adv.* 在附近

12. (**C**) My father is a serious man but, <u>on occasion</u>, he is funny.

我爸爸很嚴肅，不過他<u>有時</u>也很好笑。

(A) on call 隨叫隨到的；隨時待命的

A company's car is always on call. （公司的車子總是隨叫隨到。）

Which doctor is on call tonight? （今天晚上是哪一位醫生在值班？）

(B) on board 在船（或火車、飛機）上

(C) *on occasion* 偶爾；有時候　　occasion〔əˈkeʒən〕*n.* 場合；時候

(D) on schedule 按照預定；按照時間表

behind schedule 比預定的時間慢；進度落後

ahead of schedule 比預定的時間快；進度超前

* serious〔ˈsɪrɪəs〕*adj.* 嚴肅的　　funny〔ˈfʌnɪ〕*adj.* 好笑的；有趣的

13. (**D**) Kenny seemed to have <u>come down with</u> the flu, which stopped him from
scuba diving.

肯尼似乎<u>罹患</u>了流行性感冒，因此他不能去潛水。

(A) keep up with 與～並駕齊驅（ = *keep step with* = *keep abreast with* / *of* ）

(B) put up with 忍耐；忍受（ = *stand* = *tolerate* = *endure* = *bear* ）

(C) come up with 想出；提出

He came up with an answer to our problem.

（他為我們的問題找出了答案。）

(D) *come down with* 因…而病倒；罹患

* seem〔sim〕*v.* 似乎　　*stop sb. from V-ing* 阻止某人…

scuba〔ˈskubə〕*n.* 水肺　　*scuba diving* （水肺）潛水

14. (**A**) We <u>came upon</u> a new road back to town while we were out for a ride Sunday.
星期天我們出去兜風時，<u>偶然發現</u>了這條回鎮上的新路。

(A) *come upon* 偶然發現；偶然遇到

(B) look after 照顧 (= *take care of* = *care for*)

(C) turn out 結果

The plan turned out to have no effect. (這個計畫結果沒什麼效果。)

(D) call off 取消 (= *cancel*)

＊ride〔raɪd〕 *n.* 乘車兜風

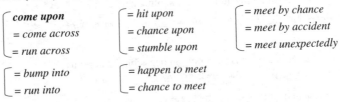

15. (**B**) The results of the examination <u>fell short of</u> the teacher's expectations.
考試的成績<u>沒有達到</u>老師的期望。

(A) run out of 用完 (= *use up*)

We have run out of our fuel and food.

(我們的燃料和糧食用完了。)

(B) *fall short of* 未達到；不足

fall short of one's expectations 辜負某人的期望

fall〔fɔl〕 *v.* 變成 (…的狀態)　　short〔ʃɔrt〕 *adj.* 缺乏的；不足的

(C) make much of 重視；充分利用；很了解…的話

I cannot make much of his argument. (我不太懂他的論點。)

(D) take hold of 抓住 (= *catch hold of* = *grasp*)

＊results〔rɪ'zʌlts〕 *n. pl.* (考試) 成績

expectations〔͵ɛkspɛk'teʃənz〕 *n. pl.* 期望

TEST 11

Directions: The following questions are incomplete sentences. You are to choose the one word that best completes the sentence.

1. The representatives from both parties have entered into _____, hoping to reach an agreement on this issue.
   - (A) permissions
   - (B) objections
   - (C) negotiations
   - (D) combinations   (   )

2. The sight of the lion _____ hunting down the deer was appalling.
   - (A) internally
   - (B) previously
   - (C) densely
   - (D) brutally   (   )

3. The notorious king and his dynasty were finally _____ by rebels.
   - (A) overflowed
   - (B) overseen
   - (C) overthrown
   - (D) overlooked   (   )

4. If you are not happy with what I've just said, I'm sorry. I didn't mean to _____ you.
   - (A) offend
   - (B) nourish
   - (C) capture
   - (D) relate   (   )

5. The jury seemed to have been _____ against the accused, and their verdict was unfavorable to him.
   - (A) intense
   - (B) biased
   - (C) panicked
   - (D) elastic   (   )

6. As the proverb goes, "There is no _____ road to learning." The more and harder you study, the more knowledge and wisdom you will acquire.
   - (A) rough
   - (B) tough
   - (C) royal
   - (D) loyal   (   )

7. Her outward friendliness toward him was only a _____ for her hate.
   - (A) disgust
   - (B) disguise
   - (C) disposal
   - (D) disgrace   (   )

8. Mr. Lee felt extremely flattered when the village received him most _____.
   - (A) vaguely
   - (B) composedly
   - (C) invaluably
   - (D) hospitably (　)

9. Mr. Williamson displayed marvelous leadership in our section, and this _____ the way for his promotion to general manager.
   - (A) paved
   - (B) blocked
   - (C) led
   - (D) showed (　)

10. Her _____ of this character got a complimentary review, and she was nominated for best actress in a motion picture drama in the Golden Globe Awards.
    - (A) interaction
    - (B) interpretation
    - (C) interruption
    - (D) intonation (　)

11. Peter got _____ by his father because he broke one of his grandfather's favorite vases.
    - (A) called on
    - (B) called off
    - (C) called down
    - (D) called for (　)

12. Don't _____ your welcome by dropping in on her too frequently.
    - (A) wear out
    - (B) hold out
    - (C) make out
    - (D) drop out (　)

13. He promised that he would never _____, and that he would be my best friend forever.
    - (A) rub me the wrong way
    - (B) stand out against me
    - (C) meet me halfway
    - (D) turn his back on me (　)

14. She has been looking after her four young kids all day long, and she is really _____ now.
    - (A) at her own pace
    - (B) at her best
    - (C) at the end of her rope
    - (D) at her disposal (　)

15. The patient was kept _____ by his family about the news that his illness was terminal.
    - (A) in the black
    - (B) in the dark
    - (C) in the air
    - (D) in the clouds (　)

TEST 11 詳解

1. (**C**) The representatives from both parties have entered into <u>negotiations</u>, hoping to reach an agreement on this issue.
雙方代表已經進入協商，希望能在此議題上達成共識。

    (A) permission〔pəˈmɪʃən〕*n.* 允許　　permit *v.*
    (B) objection〔əbˈdʒɛkʃən〕*n.* 反對；異議　　object to *v.*
    (C) *negotiation*〔nɪˌgoʃɪˈeʃən〕*n.* 協商；談判　　negotiate *v.*
    (D) combination〔ˌkɑmbəˈneʃən〕*n.* 結合　　combine *v.*

    * representative〔ˌrɛprɪˈzɛntətɪv〕*n.* 代表　　party〔ˈpɑrtɪ〕*n.* 一方
    　reach an agreement 達成共識　　issue〔ˈɪʃjʊ〕*n.* 議題

2. (**D**) The sight of the lion <u>brutally</u> hunting down the deer was appalling.
獅子殘忍獵鹿的景象真是駭人。

    (A) internally〔ɪnˈtɜnlɪ〕*adv.* 內在地（= *on the inside*）
    (B) previously〔ˈprivɪəslɪ〕*adv.* 之前地（= *before*；*formerly*）
    (C) densely〔ˈdɛnslɪ〕*adv.* 濃密地；密集地（= *thickly*）
    (D) *brutally*〔ˈbrutlɪ〕*adv.* 殘忍地；冷酷地（= *cruelly*）
    　brute *n.* 動物；野獸（= *animal*；*beast*）

    * appalling〔əˈpɔlɪŋ〕*adj.* 駭人的；可怕的（= *shocking*；*dreadful*；*horrifying*）

3. (**C**) The notorious king and his dynasty were finally <u>overthrown</u> by rebels.
惡名昭彰的國王和他的王朝終於被叛軍推翻。

    (A) overflow〔ˌovəˈflo〕*v.* 溢出；氾濫（= *spill over*；*flood*）〔ˈovəˌflo〕*n.*
    (B) oversee〔ˌovəˈsi〕*v.* 監督（= *supervise*）
    (C) *overthrow*〔ˌovəˈθro〕*v.* 打翻；推翻
    (D) overlook〔ˌovəˈlʊk〕*v.* 俯瞰（= *look down at*）；忽略（= *neglect*；*pass by*）

    * notorious〔noˈtorɪəs〕*adj.* 惡名昭彰的（= *infamous*）
    　dynasty〔ˈdaɪnəstɪ〕*n.* 朝代；王朝　　rebel〔ˈrɛbl̩〕*n.* 叛徒；反抗者

4. (**A**) If you are not happy with what I've just said, I'm sorry. I did't mean to <u>offend</u> you.
如果你因為我剛才所說的話而不高興，我很抱歉。我不是有意冒犯你的。

    (A) *offend*〔əˈfɛnd〕*v.* 冒犯；傷感情　　offense *n.*
    (B) nourish〔ˈnɝɪʃ〕*v.* 滋養（= *nurture*）；培養（= *cultivate*）
    (C) capture〔ˈkæptʃə〕*v.* 捕捉；俘虜（= *catch*）
    (D) relate〔rɪˈlet〕*v.* 與～有關（= *connect*）；敘述（= *tell*）

    * *mean to* + *V.* 有意；故意

5. (**B**) The jury seemed to have been <u>biased</u> against the accused, and their verdict was unfavorable to him.

陪審團似乎對被告<u>有偏見</u>，他們的判決對他不利。

    (A) intense〔ɪn'tɛns〕*adj.* 強烈的（= *strong*；*extreme*）

    (B) ***biased*** 〔'baɪəst〕*adj.* 有偏見的（= *prejudiced*）   **bias** *n.* 偏見（= *prejudice*）

    (C) panicked〔'pænɪkt〕*adj.* 驚慌的（= *frightened*；*alarmed*）

        panic *v. n.* 驚恐；恐慌

    (D) elastic〔ɪ'læstɪk〕*adj.* 有彈性的；靈活的（= *flexible*）

    * jury〔'dʒʊrɪ〕*n.* 陪審團   accuse〔ə'kjuz〕*v.* 控告   **the accused** 被告

      verdict〔'vɝdɪkt〕*n.* 判決   unfavorable〔ʌn'fevərəbl̩〕*adj.* 不利的

6. (**C**) As the proverb goes, "There is no <u>royal</u> road to learning." The more and harder you study, the more knowledge and wisdom you will acquire.

諺語說：「學問<u>無捷徑</u>。」你讀越多書、越努力用功，你就會獲得越多知識和智慧。

    (A) rough〔rʌf〕*adj.* 粗劣的；粗暴的（= *violent*）；崎嶇的（= *uneven*）

    (B) tough〔tʌf〕*adj.* 堅硬的（= *hard*）；頑強的；困難的（= *difficult*）

    (C) ***royal*** 〔'rɔɪəl〕*adj.* 皇室的   ***royal road*** 捷徑

    (D) loyal〔'lɔɪəl〕*adj.* 忠實的；忠誠的（= *faithful*）

    * acquire〔ə'kwaɪr〕*v.* 獲得（= *obtain*）

7. (**B**) Her outward friendliness toward him was only a <u>disguise</u> for her hate.

她表面上對他非常友善，只是為了<u>偽裝</u>她的憎恨。

    (A) disgust〔dɪs'gʌst〕*n. v.* 厭惡；嫌惡

    (B) ***disguise*** 〔dɪs'gaɪz〕*n. v.* 偽裝

    (C) disposal〔dɪ'spozl̩〕*n.* 處理；處置

        dispose of *v.* 處置（= *get rid of*；*throw away*）

    (D) disgrace〔dɪs'gres〕*n. v.* 恥辱；丟臉（= *shame*）

    * outward〔'aʊtwəd〕*adj.* 外表的；外在的（= *external*）

8. (**D**) Mr. Lee felt extremely flattered when the village received him most <u>hospitably</u>.

村民們非常<u>殷勤地</u>款待李先生，使他感到十分受寵若驚。

    (A) vaguely〔'veglɪ〕*adv.* 模糊地（= *unclearly*；*dimly*）

    (B) composedly〔kəm'pozɪdlɪ〕*adv.* 冷靜地；沉著地（= *calmly*；*coolly*）

    (C) invaluably〔ɪn'væljəblɪ〕*adv.* 無價地；非常珍貴地

    (D) ***hospitably*** 〔'hɑspɪtəblɪ〕*adv.* 好客地；殷勤地   hospitality *n.* 好客

    * flatter〔'flætə〕*v.* 奉承；諂媚   flattered〔'flætəd〕*adj.* 受寵若驚的；高興的

      village〔'vɪlɪdʒ〕*n.* 村莊；村民   receive〔rɪ'siv〕*v.* 接待；款待

9. (**A**) Mr. Williamson displayed marvelous leadership in our section, and this <u>paved</u> the way for his promotion to general manager. 威廉森先生在我們部門裡展現了絕佳的領導能力，這為他<u>鋪</u>下了晉升總經理之路。

(A) *pave* 〔pev〕*v.* 鋪（路）　　***pave the way for*~** 為~鋪路；為~做好準備

(B) block 〔blɑk〕*v.* 阻擋 (= *jam* ; *obstruct*)

(C) lead 〔lid〕*v.* 領導　　lead the way 開路；創始 (= *set a trend* ; *originate*)

(D) show 〔ʃo〕*v.* 給~看

show the way 帶路；指路 (= *direct* ; *guide* ; *give directions*)

* display 〔dɪ'sple〕*v.* 展現 (= *show*)　　marvelous 〔'mɑrvḷəs〕*adj.* 絕佳的

leadership 〔'lidɚˌʃɪp〕*n.* 領導能力　　section 〔'sɛkʃən〕*n.* 部門

promotion 〔prə'moʃən〕*n.* 升職　　***general manager*** 總經理

10. (**B**) Her <u>interpretation</u> of this character got a complimentary review, and she was nominated for best actress in a motion picture drama in the Golden Globe Awards. 她對這個角色的<u>詮釋</u>得到了影評的讚許，並且獲得金球獎電影戲劇類最佳女演員的提名。

(A) interaction 〔ˌɪntɚ'ækʃən〕*n.* 互動；交互作用　　interact *v.*

(B) *interpretation* 〔ɪnˌtɜprɪ'teʃən〕*n.* 解釋；詮釋

interpret 〔ɪn'tɜprɪt〕*v.* 解釋；詮釋；口譯

(C) interruption 〔ˌɪntə'rʌpʃən〕*n.* 中斷；阻礙　　interrupt *v.*

(D) intonation 〔ˌɪntə'neʃən〕*n.* 語調

* character 〔'kærɪktɚ〕*n.* 角色

complimentary 〔ˌkɑmplə'mɛntərɪ〕*adj.* 稱讚的

review 〔rɪ'vju〕*n.* 評論　　nominate 〔'nɑməˌnet〕*v.* 提名

actress 〔'æktrɪs〕*n.* 女演員　　***motion picture*** 電影

drama 〔'dræmə〕*n.* 戲劇　　award 〔ə'wɔrd〕*n.* 獎

the Golden Globe Award 金球獎

11. (**C**) Peter got <u>called down</u> by his father because he broke one of his grandfather's favorite vases.

彼得被他爸爸嚴厲斥責，因為他把爺爺最心愛的一支花瓶打破了。

(A) call on 拜訪（某人）(= *visit*)；要求 (= *request*)

(B) call off 取消 (= *cancel*)

(C) *call down* 嚴厲斥責 (= *scold*)

(D) call for 要求 (= *request*)；去取、接、拿 (= *arrive and pick up*)

12. (**A**) Don't <u>wear out</u> your welcome by dropping in on her too frequently.

你不要太經常去拜訪她，才不會不受歡迎。

(A) ***wear out*** 磨損；耗損 (= *use up* ; *exhaust*)

(B) hold out 伸出；提供 (= *extend* ; *offer*)；堅持；維持 (= *endure* ; *withstand*)

(C) make out 辨認 (= *recognize*)；列出（清單等）；了解 (= *understand*)

(D) drop out 漏掉；退出；輟學 (= *leave* ; *quit* ; *abandon*)

dropout *n.* 退出者；中輟生

＊***drop in on*** *sb.* 順道拜訪某人 (= *call on sb.* ; *visit sb.*)

frequently (ˈfrikwəntlɪ) *adv.* 經常地

13. (**D**) He promised that he would never <u>turn his back on me</u>, and that he would be my best friend forever.

他承諾他永遠不會背棄我，他永遠都會是我最好的朋友。

(A) rub *sb.* the wrong way 激怒某人 (= *irritate sb.* ; *annoy sb.*)

(B) stand out against *sth.* 突出；顯眼 (= *be easily seen*)；

堅持抵抗 (= *refuse to accept*)

(C) meet *sb.* halfway 對某人讓步、妥協 (= *compromise with sb.*)

(D) ***turn*** *one's* ***back on*** *sb.* 背棄某人；不理會某人 (= *abandon sb.*)

14. (**C**) She has been looking after her four young kids all day long, and she is really <u>at the end of her rope</u> now.

她照顧她四個年幼的小孩已經一整天，現在她已經力氣、耐性用盡了。

(A) at *one's* own pace 以某人自己的步調　　pace *n.* 步伐；步調 (= *speed*)

(B) at *one's* best 在某人最佳、最顛峰狀態

(C) ***at the end of*** *one's* ***rope*** 技窮；（力量、智慧、忍耐）已到極限

(D) at *one's* disposal 任某人任意處置

＊***look after*** 照顧 (= *take care of*)

15. (**B**) The patient was kept <u>in the dark</u> by his family about the news that his illness was terminal.

這名病人被他的家人蒙在鼓裡，完全不知道自己的病已經是末期了。

(A) in the black 有盈餘的；賺錢 (↔ in the red 有虧損；賠錢)

(B) ***in the dark*** 在黑暗中；全然不知 (= *ignorant*)

(C) in the air 在空中；瀰漫著；散布著；未決定 (= *undecided*)

(D) in the clouds 心不在焉；虛構的

＊terminal (ˈtɜmənl̩) *adj.* （疾病、病人）末期的

TEST 12

Directions: The following questions are incomplete sentences. You are to choose the one word that best completes the sentence.

1. We visited the aboriginal village and watched their _____ dance of the celebration.
   (A) irritable
   (B) militant
   (C) chronic
   (D) ritual   (   )

2. After her engagement, Jenny often showed off the _____ diamond ring that her fiancé gave her.
   (A) purifying
   (B) dazzling
   (C) methodical
   (D) intensive   (   )

3. When the waiter served us soup, David _____ his with some pepper.
   (A) sprinkled
   (B) captured
   (C) liberated
   (D) preserved   (   )

4. The little girl was _____ by all the gifts she received on her birthday.
   (A) enchanted
   (B) circulated
   (C) penetrated
   (D) denounced   (   )

5. Mr. Brown has an inferiority complex about his short _____. Be careful not to mention the subject of height to his face.
   (A) statue
   (B) status
   (C) stature
   (D) statute   (   )

6. While Susan was reading the book, she wrote some comments in the _____ of the pages.
   (A) phases
   (B) margins
   (C) notions
   (D) brigades   (   )

7. The interest rate of the bank is likely to change _____, and we'll keep you informed.
   (A) devotedly
   (B) solemnly
   (C) quarterly
   (D) serially   (   )

8. An _____ trivial thing may some day develop into a new invention.
   (A) approvingly
   (B) apparently
   (C) evenly
   (D) uniformly ( )

9. Although Dina was a foreigner in this little town, she overcame the language and cultural _____ and blended in very well.
   (A) diversities
   (B) majorities
   (C) successions
   (D) barriers ( )

10. In some corporations and administrations, it is still the male that _____ in managerial positions.
    (A) reveals
    (B) compels
    (C) dominates
    (D) migrates ( )

11. He tried to say something humorous to break the ice, but his joke _____.
    (A) fell behind
    (B) fell away
    (C) fell off
    (D) fell flat ( )

12. It appears that nothing has gone wrong, but he still _____. There must be something we haven't noticed.
    (A) smells a rat
    (B) comes to himself
    (C) goes down the drain
    (D) takes for granted ( )

13. He came out of prison hoping to start life again with _____, but things were not as good as he had expected.
    (A) a big shot
    (B) a clean slate
    (C) a bed of roses
    (D) a ball of fire ( )

14. Their work left something to be desired, but, _____, they did quite a good job.
    (A) for dear life
    (B) for a song
    (C) by and large
    (D) at large ( )

15. The little boy really _____ by completing such a complicated and tough job.
    (A) took to his heels
    (B) took our breath away
    (C) took our word for it
    (D) took his stand on this ( )

TEST 12 詳解

1. (**D**) We visited the aboriginal village and watched their <u>ritual</u> dance of the celebration. 我們去參觀原住民的村落，並觀賞他們慶典<u>儀式的</u>舞蹈。

   (A) irritable〔ˈɪrətəbḷ〕*adj.* 易怒的；暴躁的 (= *short-tempered*)
   irritate *v.* 使生氣
   (B) militant〔ˈmɪlətənt〕*adj.* 好戰的 (= *aggressive*)　　military *adj.* 軍事的
   (C) chronic〔ˈkrɑnɪk〕*adj.* (病) 慢性的 (↔ acute〔əˈkjut〕*adj.* 急性的)；長期的
   (D) *ritual*〔ˈrɪtʃʊəl〕*adj. n.* 儀式 (的)
   * aboriginal〔͵æbəˈrɪdʒənḷ〕*adj.* 原住民的　　village〔ˈvɪlɪdʒ〕*n.* 村落

2. (**B**) After her engagement, Jenny often showed off the <u>dazzling</u> diamond ring that her fiancé gave her.
   珍妮訂婚後，就常常炫耀她未婚夫送給她的那只<u>燦爛炫目的</u>鑽戒。

   (A) purifying〔ˈpjʊrə͵faɪɪŋ〕*adj.* 淨化的 (= *cleansing*)
   purify *v.* (= *clean*；*cleanse*)
   (B) *dazzling*〔ˈdæzlɪŋ〕*adj.* 燦爛炫目的 (= *bright*)　　dazzle *v.* 使目眩；使迷惑
   (C) methodical〔məˈθɑdɪkḷ〕*adj.* 有系統的；有組織的 (= *systematic*)
   (D) intensive〔ɪnˈtɛnsɪv〕*adj.* 密集的；徹底的 (= *concentrated*；*thorough*)
   * engagement〔ɪnˈgedʒmənt〕*n.* 訂婚　　*show off* 炫耀
   fiancé〔͵fiɑnˈse〕*n.* 未婚夫 (未婚妻為 fiancée，字尾多一個 e，發音相同)

3. (**A**) When the waiter served us soup, David <u>sprinkled</u> his (soup) with some pepper.
   當服務生幫我們送上湯時，大衛在他的湯裡<u>撒了</u>一點胡椒。

   (A) *sprinkle*〔ˈsprɪŋkḷ〕*v.* 撒/灑 (粉末、液體等) (= *scatter*)
   (B) capture〔ˈkæptʃɚ〕*v.* 捕捉；俘虜；擄獲 (= *seize*；*catch*；*arrest*)
   (C) liberate〔ˈlɪbə͵ret〕*v.* 解放；使自由 (= *free*；*set free*；*release*)
   (D) preserve〔prɪˈzɝv〕*v.* 保存；維持 (= *maintain*；*keep*)
   * serve〔sɝv〕*v.* 端上 (菜餚等)　　pepper〔ˈpɛpɚ〕*n.* 胡椒

4. (**A**) The little girl was <u>enchanted</u> by all the gifts she received on her birthday.
   生日當天所收到的一切禮物，令這個小女孩為之<u>著迷</u>。

   (A) *enchant*〔ɪnˈtʃænt〕*v.* 施以魔法；使著迷 (= *fascinate*)
   enchanting *adj.* 迷人的
   (B) circulate〔ˈsɝkjə͵let〕*v.* 循環；流通 (= *move around*)　　circulation *n.*
   (C) penetrate〔ˈpɛnə͵tret〕*v.* 貫穿；穿透 (= *pass through*；*pierce*)
   (D) denounce〔dɪˈnaʊns〕*v.* (公開) 譴責 (= *condemn*；*criticize publicly and harshly*)

5. (**C**) Mr. Brown has an inferiority complex about his short <u>stature</u>. Be careful not to mention the subject of height to his face.

布朗先生對他的<u>身高</u>不高有自卑感。你要小心，別當著他的面提起身高的話題。

(A) statue〔'stætʃʊ〕*n.* 雕像

(B) status〔'stetəs〕*n.* 地位；身份

(C) *stature*〔'stætʃ♂〕*n.* 身高（= *height*）

(D) statute〔'stætʃʊt〕*n.* 法令；法規（= *law*）

* inferiority〔ɪn,fɪrɪ'ɔrətɪ〕*n.* 低劣（↔ superiority〔sə,pɪrɪ'ɔrətɪ〕優越）
complex〔'kɑmplɛks〕*n.*【精神分析】情結
inferiority complex 自卑感（↔ superiority complex 優越感）
subject〔'sʌbdʒɪkt〕*n.* 話題　　*to one's face* 當著某人的面

6. (**B**) While Susan was reading the book, she wrote some comments in the <u>margins</u> of the pages. 當蘇珊在閱讀這本書時，她把一些評論寫在頁邊的<u>空白之處</u>。

(A) phase〔fez〕*n.* 階段；時期　*v.* 分階段、逐步地進行
phase in 分階段、逐步地採用　　phase out 分階段、逐步地廢除

(B) *margin*〔'mɑrdʒɪn〕*n.* 邊緣；（書籍的）頁邊空白

(C) notion〔'noʃən〕*n.* 觀念；概念（= *idea*；*concept*）

(D) brigade〔brɪ'ged〕*n.* 隊；組
例：fire brigade 消防隊（= *fire department*）

* comment〔'kɑmɛnt〕*n.* 評論；意見（= *remark*）

7. (**C**) The interest rate of the bank is likely to change <u>quarterly</u>, and we'll keep you informed. 銀行的利率可能<u>每一季</u>會更動，我們會通知你的。

(A) devotedly〔dɪ'votɪdlɪ〕*adv.* 忠誠地（= *loyally*）；熱中地（= *enthusiastically*）

(B) solemnly〔'sɑləmlɪ〕*adv.* 莊嚴地；隆重地（= *seriously*；*formally*）

(C) *quarterly*〔'kwɔrtəlɪ〕*adv. adj.* 每季地（的）　*n.*（雜誌）季刊

(D) serially〔'sɪrɪəlɪ〕*adv.* 連續地（= *successively*；*in succession*；*in a row*）

* interest〔'ɪnt(ə)rɪst〕*n.* 利息　　rate〔ret〕*n.* 比率　　*interest rate* 利率
be likely to + V. 可能　　informed〔ɪn'fɔrmd〕*adj.* 知道的；消息靈通的

8. (**B**) An <u>apparently</u> trivial thing may some day develop into a new invention.
<u>表面上</u>微不足道的東西，也許有一天會發展成一項新發明。

(A) approvingly〔ə'pruvɪŋlɪ〕*adv.* 贊同地；認可地（= *favorably*）　　approve *v.*

(B) *apparently*〔ə'pærəntlɪ〕*adv.* 表面上；似乎（= *seemingly*）

(C) evenly〔'ivənlɪ〕*adv.* 平坦地（= *levelly*；*flatly*）；公平地（= *equally*）

(D) uniformly〔'junə,fɔrmlɪ〕*adv.* 統一地；一律（= *consistently*）

* trivial〔'trɪvjəl〕*adj.* 瑣碎的；不重要的

9. (**D**) Although Dina was a foreigner in this little town, she overcame the language and cultural <u>barriers</u> and blended in very well.
雖然迪娜是這個小鎮上的外國人，她克服了語言和文化上的<u>障礙</u>，非常能夠融入。

    (A) diversity〔də'vɜsətɪ, daɪ-〕n. 多樣；變化（= *variety*）

    (B) majority〔mə'dʒɔrətɪ〕n. 大多數；大部分

        （↔ minority〔mə'nɔrətɪ, maɪ-〕n. 少數）

    (C) succession〔sək'sɛʃən〕n. 連續（的事物）（= *series*）；繼承

    (D) ***barrier***〔'bærɪə〕n. 障礙（= *obstacle*）

    ＊overcome〔ˌovə'kʌm〕v. 克服   blend〔blɛnd〕v. 混合；融合

10. (**C**) In some corporations and administrations, it is still the male that <u>dominates</u> in managerial positions. 在有些公司和機關裡，管理階層仍然是男性<u>佔優勢</u>。

    (A) reveal〔rɪ'vil〕v. 透露；揭發（= *make public*；*disclose*；*uncover*）

    (B) compel〔kəm'pɛl〕v. 強迫（= *force*；*coerce*）

    (C) ***dominate***〔'dɑməˌnet〕v. 支配；佔優勢（= *lead*）

    (D) migrate〔'maɪgret〕v. 遷移   migration n.

    ＊corporation〔ˌkɔrpə'reʃən〕n. 公司（= *company*；*business*；*firm*）

    administration〔ədˌmɪnə'streʃən〕n. 局；政府機關

    managerial〔ˌmænə'dʒɪrɪəl〕adj. 管理的；經理的   position〔pə'zɪʃən〕n. 職位

11. (**D**) He tried to say something humorous to break the ice, but his joke <u>fell flat</u>.
他試著想說點幽默的話來緩和一下氣氛，但是他的笑話<u>一點都不好笑</u>。

    (A) fall behind 落後（= *drop back*；*lag behind*）；延遲（= *be late*；*be delayed*）

    (B) fall away 離開；減少；消失（= *leave*；*decrease*；*disappear*）

    (C) fall off 減少；衰退（= *decline*；*decrease*；*drop*）

    (D) ***fall flat*** 倒下；失敗；毫無效果（= *fail*）   flat adj. 平伏的；洩氣的；枯燥的

    ＊***break the ice*** 打破僵局；緩和氣氛

12. (**A**) It appears that nothing has gone wrong, but he still <u>smells a rat</u>. There must be something we haven't noticed.
表面上似乎一切順利，但他還是<u>覺得可疑</u>。一定有什麼事情我們沒有注意到。

    (A) ***smell a rat*** 覺得可疑；覺得不對勁（= *feel suspicious*）   rat n. 老鼠

    (B) come to *oneself* 恢復正常；甦醒（= *regain consciousness*；*come to*）

    (C) go down the drain 白費；化為烏有（= *go to waste*；*be wasted*）

        drain n. 下水道

    (D) take *sth*. for granted 視某事為理所當然

    ＊appear〔ə'pɪr〕v. 表面上；似乎；好像（= *seem*；*look as if*）

    go wrong 出錯（= *fail*；*be unsuccessful*；*be a mistake*）

    notice〔'notɪs〕v. 注意

13. (**B**) He came out of prison hoping to start life again with a clean slate, but things were not as good as he had expected.

他出獄後想要洗心革面、重新做人，但事情並沒有他預期中好。

(A) a big shot　重要人物（= *important person*；*VIP*）

(B) *a clean slate*　清白的經歷；無過失記錄　　slate　*n.* 石板
　　start (*again*) *with a clean slate*　重新開始

(C) a bed of roses　安樂的生活（= *life of ease*；*good life*）

(D) a ball of fire　精力充沛的人（= *a person full of energy*）

＊prison〔'prɪzn̩〕*n.* 監獄

14. (**C**) Their work left something to be desired, but, by and large, they did quite a good job.

他們的工作仍有待改進，但大致上他們還算做得不錯。

(A) for dear life　拼命地；全力地（= *desperately*）

(B) for a song　非常便宜地；低價地（= *at a very low price*；*very cheaply*）

(C) *by and large*　一般說來；大致上（= *generally speaking*；*in general*）

(D) at large　（犯人、動物等）未被捕獲；逍遙法外（= *free*；*on the loose*）

＊desire〔dɪ'zaɪr〕*v.* 渴望；想要
　　leave something to be desired　有待改進

15. (**B**) The little boy really took our breath away by completing such a complicated and tough job.

這個小男孩竟然能完成這樣複雜並困難的工作，真是使我們大為驚訝。

(A) take to *one's* heels　逃走（= *run away*）

(B) *take sb.'s breath away*　使某人大為驚訝、感動（= *surprise*；*impress*）

(C) take *sb.'s* word for it　相信某人的話（= *believe what sb. says*）

(D) take *one's* stand on this　表明立場、態度等（= *declare one's position or opinion on sth.*）

＊complete〔kəm'plit〕*v.* 完成
　　complicated〔'kɑmplə,ketɪd〕*adj.* 複雜的

TEST 13

Directions: The following questions are incomplete sentences. You are to choose the one word that best completes the sentence.

1. The candles _____ a dim light on the dinner table, which created a romantic atmosphere.
   - (A) browsed
   - (B) splashed
   - (C) cast
   - (D) loaned   ( )

2. The old man didn't _____ change easily, and refused to move from his home when he became sick.
   - (A) embrace
   - (B) rotate
   - (C) seclude
   - (D) deplete   ( )

3. It took a lot of _____ for Arthur to tell his boss that he disagreed with his ideas.
   - (A) myth
   - (B) deed
   - (C) veil
   - (D) nerve   ( )

4. The doctor wasn't sure if it would be _____ to help his suffering patient die.
   - (A) filial
   - (B) ethical
   - (C) ominous
   - (D) massive   ( )

5. Danny and Carrie broke up because they had _____ ideas about their future.
   - (A) repetitive
   - (B) comprehensive
   - (C) momentary
   - (D) contradictory   ( )

6. In _____ of his dream to travel around the world, Mario worked three jobs in order to save up his money.
   - (A) decree
   - (B) award
   - (C) pursuit
   - (D) attempt   ( )

7. He was speaking with such _____ that I couldn't find any words to rebut his argument.
   - (A) eloquence
   - (B) monologue
   - (C) suspension
   - (D) autonomy   ( )

8. While the chairman was delivering his speech in German, there was also an interpreter interpreting what he was saying into English _____.

(A) deafeningly   (B) sarcastically
(C) simultaneously   (D) monotonously   ( )

9. Leading such a busy and stressful life, you really need some diversion to _____.

(A) unwind   (B) unarm
(C) uncover   (D) undo   ( )

10. This question was easy and nearly every student could answer it _____ without difficulty.

(A) cordially   (B) evenly
(C) strictly   (D) promptly   ( )

11. With the coming of spring, the hillside is _____ flowers. What a gorgeous view!

(A) a sort of   (B) a bit of
(C) a mass of   (D) a matter of   ( )

12. Sorry, I have some business to take care of tonight. Can I _____ on your invitation?

(A) take a powder   (B) take a bow
(C) take a back seat   (D) take a rain check   ( )

13. She looked very familiar to me, but I _____ and still couldn't recall who on earth she was.

(A) had money to burn   (B) made ends meet
(C) packed my bags   (D) racked my brains   ( )

14. I feel _____ to warn you that you should be more careful with that guy. He doesn't have a good reputation.

(A) called on   (B) called off
(C) called down   (D) called away   ( )

15. Take my advice no matter what. _____, you will understand I mean well to you.

(A) By all means   (B) By and by
(C) By halves   (D) By stealth   ( )

TEST 13 詳解

1. (**C**) The candles <u>cast</u> a dim light on the dinner table, which created a romantic atmosphere. 蠟燭<u>投射</u>朦朧的燈光在餐桌上，營造出很
羅曼蒂克的氣氛。

  (A) browse〔braʊz〕*v.* 瀏覽（= *read casually*）；
   隨意看看（= *look round casually*）

  (B) splash〔splæʃ〕*v. n.* 潑濺（水等）（= *splatter*）

  (C) ***cast***〔kæst〕*v.* 投擲（= *throw*；*toss*）；投射

  (D) loan〔lon〕*v.* 借貸（= *lend*） *n.* 借出；貸款

  ＊dim〔dɪm〕*adj.* 微弱的；朦朧的（= *soft*；*faint*）

   atmosphere〔'ætməˌsfɪr〕*n.* 氣氛

2. (**A**) The old man didn't <u>embrace</u> change easily, and refused to move from his home when he became sick.
這位老先生不輕易<u>接受</u>改變，生病時還拒絕搬離自己的家。

  (A) ***embrace***〔ɪm'bres〕*v.* 擁抱（= *hug*）；包含（= *contain*）；欣然接受（= *accept*）

  (B) rotate〔'rotet〕*v.* 旋轉（= *revolve*）

  (C) seclude〔sɪ'klud〕*v.* 隔絕（= *isolate*；*keep away/apart*）

  (D) deplete〔dɪ'plit〕*v.* 用盡；使枯竭（= *use up*；*drain*）

3. (**D**) It took a lot of <u>nerve</u> for Arthur to tell his boss that he disagreed with his ideas.
亞瑟提起了很大的<u>勇氣</u>，告訴他的老闆說他不同意他的想法。

  (A) myth〔mɪθ〕*n.* 神話；迷思（= *illusion*）

  (B) deed〔did〕*n.* 行為（= *action*；*act*）

  (C) veil〔vel〕*n.* 面紗　*v.* 以面紗覆蓋（= *cover*）；遮蔽（= *conceal*；*hide*）

  (D) ***nerve***〔nɝv〕*n.* 神經；勇氣（= *courage*）；膽量；厚顏無恥（= *boldness*）

  ＊disagree〔ˌdɪsə'gri〕*v.* 不同意

4. (**B**) The doctor wasn't sure if it would be <u>ethical</u> to help his suffering patient die.
這位醫生不確定，幫助飽受病魔摧殘的病人安樂死是否<u>合乎道德</u>。

  (A) filial〔'fɪlɪəl〕*adj.* 子女的（↔ parental 父母的）

   filial piety 孝道　　piety〔'paɪətɪ〕*n.* 虔敬；孝順

  (B) ***ethical***〔'ɛθɪkl̩〕*adj.* 道德的；倫理的（= *moral*）　　ethics *n.* 倫理道德；倫常

  (C) ominous〔'ɑmənəs〕*adj.* 不祥的；惡兆的（= *ill-omened*）

   omen *n.* 預兆（= *sign*）

  (D) massive〔'mæsɪv〕*adj.* 大量的；大的（= *huge*；*vast*；*enormous*）

5. (**D**) Danny and Carrie broke up because they had <u>contradictory</u> ideas about their future. 丹尼和凱莉因爲對未來的意見<u>相左</u>而分手了。

    (A) repetitive〔rɪ'pɛtətɪv〕*adj.* 重複的（= *repetitious*）

        repeat *v.*   repetition *n.*

    (B) comprehensive〔,kɑmprɪ'hɛnsɪv〕*adj.* 廣泛的；全面的

        （= *wide-ranging* ; *all-inclusive*）；理解的

        comprehend *v.* 理解；包含   comprehension *n.* 理解；包含

    (C) momentary〔'momən,tɛrɪ〕*adj.* 瞬間的；短暫的（= *brief* ; *temporary*）

        moment *n.* 片刻；瞬間（= *instant*）

    (D) *contradictory*〔,kɑntrə'dɪktərɪ〕*adj.* 矛盾的；對立的

    * *break up* 分手（↔ *make up* 和好）

6. (**C**) In <u>pursuit</u> of his dream to travel around the world, Mario worked three jobs in order to save up his money.

    爲了<u>追尋</u>環遊世界的夢想，馬里歐兼了三份工作來存錢。

    (A) decree〔dɪ'kri〕*n.* 法令（= *law* ; *order*） *v.* 頒佈法令（= *declare*）

    (B) award〔ə'wɔrd〕*n.* 獎（獎品、獎金、獎盃等） *v.* 頒發（= *give* ; *present*）

    (C) *pursuit*〔pɚ'sut〕*n.* 追求   pursue *v.*（= *chase* ; *follow*）

    (D) attempt〔ə'tɛmpt〕*n.* 嘗試；企圖 *v.* 嘗試（= *try* ; *make an attempt*）

        in an attempt to + V. 試著要～；爲了要～（= *in an effort to* + *V.* ; *in a bid to* + *V.*）

7. (**A**) He was speaking with such <u>eloquence</u> that I couldn't find any words to rebut his argument. 他的<u>口才</u>如此之好，我找不到任何來反駁他的論點。

    (A) *eloquence*〔'ɛləkwəns〕*n.* 雄辯；口才   eloquent *adj.*

    (B) monologue〔'manḷ,ɔg〕*n.* 獨白【mono = one ; logue = speech】

    (C) suspension〔sə'spɛnʃən〕*n.* 懸掛；中止（= *interruption* ; *pause* ; *temporary stop*）   比較：suspense *n.* 懸而未決；懸疑；緊張（= *uncertainty* ; *nervousness*）

    (D) autonomy〔ɔ'tanəmɪ〕*n.* 自治（= *self-rule* ; *self-government* ; *independence*）【auto = self ; nomy = law】

    * rebut〔rɪ'bʌt〕*v.* 反駁（= *contradict*）

    argument〔'ɑrgjəmənt〕*n.* 論點

suspension bridge 吊橋

8. (**C**) While the chairman was delivering his speech in German, there was also an interpreter interpreting what he was saying into English simultaneously.

當主席用德文發表演說時，有位口譯人員將他所說的<u>同步</u>翻譯成英文。

(A) deafeningly〔'dɛfənɪŋlɪ〕*adv.* 震耳欲聾地 (= *very loudly* ; *noisily*)

deafen　*v.* 使耳聾

(B) sarcastically〔sɑr'kæstɪkəlɪ〕*adv.* 諷刺地 (= *ironically*)　　　sarcasm　*n.*

(C) *simultaneously*〔ˌsaɪmḷ'tenjəslɪ〕*adv.* 同步地；同時地 (= *at the same time*)

(D) monotonously〔mə'nɑtṇəslɪ〕*adv.* 單調地；無聊地 (= *dully* ; *tediously*)

【mono = one ; ton = tone ; ous 形容詞字尾】

＊chairman〔'tʃɛrmən〕*n.* 主席　　　deliver〔dɪ'lɪvə〕*v.* 發表（演說）

interpreter〔ɪn'tɜprɪtə〕*n.* 口譯者

interpret〔ɪn'tɜprɪt〕*v.* 翻譯；口譯

9. (**A**) Leading such a busy and stressful life, you really need some diversion to unwind.

過著如此忙碌又充滿壓力的生活，你實在需要一些消遣來<u>放鬆一下</u>。

(A) *unwind*〔ʌn'waɪnd〕*v.* 鬆開；放鬆 (= *relax*)

wind　*v.* 纏繞；上緊發條

(B) unarm〔ʌn'ɑrm〕*v.* 解除武裝；繳械 (= *disarm*)　　　arm　*v.* 武裝

(C) uncover〔ʌn'kʌvə〕*v.* 揭開；揭發 (= *expose* ; *disclose*)

(D) undo〔ʌn'du〕*v.* 恢復；解開 (= *untie* ; *unfasten* ; *loosen*)

＊*lead/live a ~ life* 過著～的生活

stressful〔'strɛsfəl〕*adj.* 充滿壓力的

diversion〔də'vɜʒən , daɪ-〕*n.* 轉換；消遣；娛樂 (= *recreation*)

10. (**D**) This question was easy and nearly every student could answer it promptly without difficulty.

這個問題很簡單，幾乎每一個學生都能輕鬆地<u>迅速</u>回答出來。

(A) cordially〔'kɔrdʒəlɪ〕*adv.* 誠摯地；由衷地 (= *sincerely* ; *warmly*)

(B) evenly〔'ivənlɪ〕*adv.* 平坦地 (= *levelly* ; *flatly*)；公平地 (= *equally*)

(C) strictly〔'strɪktlɪ〕*adv.* 嚴格地 (= *severely* ; *sternly*)

(D) *promptly*〔'prɑmptlɪ〕*adv.* 迅速地 (= *quickly* ; *rapidly*)；

準時地 (= *punctually* ; *on time*)

＊*without difficulty* 沒有困難地；輕鬆地 (= *effortlessly* ; *easily*)

11. (**C**) With the coming of spring, the hillside is <u>a mass of</u> flowers. What a gorgeous view!

隨著春天的到來，整個山坡上滿是花朵。風景真是太美了！

(A) a sort of~　一種~；可以說是~（= *a kind of*）

比較：sort of　有點（= *kind of*）（副詞用法）

例：He was *sort of* angry. 他有點生氣了。

(B) a bit of~　一小片~；一點點~（= *a small piece of*；*a small amount of*）

比較：a bit of a~　有點；有幾分像（= *rather a*；*somewhat of a*）

（後接單數可數名詞）

例：He knows *a bit of* literature. He is *a bit of a* poet.

他懂一點文學。他有幾分像詩人。

(C) *a mass of*~　盡是~；滿是~；充滿~　　　mass *n.* 團；大量；大眾

(D) a matter of~　~的事情；大約~（= *about*）

例：*a matter of* opinion　看法不同的問題

a matter of life and death　攸關生死的事情

* gorgeous〔'gɔrdʒəs〕*adj.* 美麗的（= *beautiful*；*stunning*；*striking*）

12. (**D**) Sorry, I have some business to take care of tonight. Can I <u>take a rain check</u> on your invitation?

很抱歉，我今晚有事情要處理。你可以改天再邀請我嗎？

(A) take a powder　服用藥粉；逃之夭夭（源自女士假裝到洗手間補妝，藉機

逃離討厭的男士）

powder〔'paudə〕*n.* 粉末；（化妝用的）粉

(B) take a bow　鞠躬謝幕　　　bow〔bau〕*n.* 鞠躬

(C) take a back seat　坐後座；扮演不重要的角色（= *play a less important part*）

take a back seat to *sb.*　對某人禮讓；屈居於某人之下

例：He won't *take a back seat to* anyone. 他不願意屈居於任何人之下。

(D) *take a rain check*　改天再邀請

rain check　因雨延期的憑證；改天再邀請

* *take care of*　處理（= *deal with*；*handle*）

take a bow

13. (**D**) She looked very familiar to me, but I <u>racked my brains</u> and still couldn't recall who on earth she was.

她看起來很面熟，但是我<u>絞盡腦汁</u>也想不起來她到底是誰。

(A) have money to burn　有的是錢

(B) make (both) ends meet　使收支平衡；收支相抵

(C) pack *one's* bags　（準備）離開；捲鋪蓋辭職（ = *prepare to leave*；
leave/give up a job ）

(D) *rack one's brains*　絞盡腦汁　　　rack〔ræk〕*v.* 拷問；折磨；壓榨

＊familiar〔fəˈmɪljɚ〕*adj.* 熟悉的

recall〔rɪˈkɔl〕*v.* 記得；想起（ = *remember* ）

on earth　到底；究竟（ = *in the world* ）（置於疑問詞之後，加強語氣）

14. (**A**) I feel <u>called on</u> to warn you that you should be more careful with that guy. He doesn't have a good reputation.

我覺得我<u>應該</u>警告你，你和那個傢伙在一起要更小心一點。他的名聲不好。

(A) *call on*　要求；請求；需要（ = *ask*；*require*；*request*；*appeal to* ）

call on *sb.* 拜訪某人/call at *sb.'s* place　拜訪某人的家（ = *visit* ）

例：He will *call on* Mr. Smith to make a speech.

他將會請史密斯先生發表演說。

(B) call off　取消；放棄（ = *cancel*；*abandon* ）

(C) call down　嚴厲斥責（ = *scold severely* ）

(D) call away　叫走

＊reputation〔ˌrɛpjəˈteʃən〕*n.* 名聲

15. (**B**) Take my advice no matter what. <u>By and by</u>, you will understand I mean well to you. 你無論如何要聽我的勸。你<u>很快</u>就會了解我是為你好。

(A) by all means　必定；當然（ = *certainly*；*of course* ）

(B) *by and by*　不久；很快（ = *soon*；*before long* ）

(C) by halves　半途而廢地；不完全地（通常用於否定句）

例：It's not my way to do things *by halves*.

做事情半途而廢不是我的作風。

(D) by stealth　秘密地；暗中地（ = *secretly* ）

stealth〔stɛlθ〕*n.* 秘密行動

＊*take/follow sb.'s advice*　聽從某人的勸告

no matter what　無論如何（ = *anyway* ）

TEST 14

Directions: The following questions are incomplete sentences. You are to choose the one word that best completes the sentence.

1. There came such a large _____ of locusts that it looked like a huge dark cloud had blotted out the sky.
   - (A) flock
   - (B) swarm
   - (C) pack
   - (D) herd
   (　　)

2. Under her mother's scrupulous care, her health improved by _____ and bounds.
   - (A) fits
   - (B) degrees
   - (C) leaps
   - (D) odds
   (　　)

3. The leading role in this comedy required a _____ performance but Willy was far too serious.
   - (A) vibrant
   - (B) admirable
   - (C) transient
   - (D) captive
   (　　)

4. Even though she was _____ born, she aimed high and strove for the best and finally made it.
   - (A) mildly
   - (B) markedly
   - (C) rigidly
   - (D) humbly
   (　　)

5. With the train still so far away, the house was only _____ visible.
   - (A) warily
   - (B) cozily
   - (C) vaguely
   - (D) gravely
   (　　)

6. We arrived here too early. The Prague-_____ train will depart in another hour.
   - (A) seated
   - (B) proof
   - (C) bound
   - (D) based
   (　　)

7. Although he didn't say anything, his eagerness to go was _____ in his eyes.
   - (A) mirrored
   - (B) confined
   - (C) flattened
   - (D) enhanced
   (　　)

8. Her excellent performance of her job had been _____ by her
   superiors; therefore, she felt very discouraged and decided to quit.
   (A) overflowed   (B) overcome
   (C) overrated   (D) overlooked   (   )

9. He is such a troublemaker that everyone avoids him like the _____.
   (A) plague   (B) pirate
   (C) stall   (D) taboo   (   )

10. His _____ remark against the government made him a suspect in
    the assassination of the president.
    (A) glowing   (B) fleeting
    (C) scorching   (D) flattering   (   )

11. The typewriter has certainly _____ to the computer. That is, the
    computer has almost completely taken the place of the typewriter.
    (A) given ground   (B) gained ground
    (C) broken ground   (D) covered ground   (   )

12. They told him that he would never succeed in anything, but he
    made them _____.
    (A) play on words   (B) keep their word
    (C) weigh their words   (D) eat their words   (   )

13. The winning numbers are drawn _____, so whoever picked them
    is really fortunate.
    (A) at large   (B) at random
    (C) at ease   (D) at length   (   )

14. On our trip from Los Angeles to New York, we _____ one night
    in Chicago.
    (A) stopped over   (B) stopped out
    (C) made over   (D) made out   (   )

15. Considered a legacy of his family, the oil painting has been _____
    from generation to generation.
    (A) handed in   (B) handed down
    (C) handed out   (D) handed over   (   )

TEST 14 詳解

1. (**B**) There came such a large <u>swarm</u> of locusts that it looked like a huge dark cloud had blotted out the sky.

那裡來了好大一<u>群</u>蝗蟲，看起來像一大片烏雲遮蔽了天空。

(A) flock〔flɑk〕*n.*（羊、鳥）群

(B) *swarm*〔swɔrm〕*n.*（昆蟲）群（如螞蟻、蜜蜂等）

(C) pack〔pæk〕*n.*（狗、狼）群

(D) herd〔hɝd〕*n.*（獸）群（如牛、羊、馬等）

＊locust〔'lokəst〕*n.* 蝗蟲　　***blot out*** 遮蔽

2. (**C**) Under her mother's scrupulous care, her health improved by <u>leaps</u> and bounds.

在她母親細心照料之下，她的健康<u>快速地</u>好轉。

(A) fit〔fɪt〕*n.* 一陣　　by fits (and starts) 一陣一陣地

(B) degree〔dɪ'gri〕*n.* 程度　　by degrees 逐漸地（= *little by little* ; *bit by bit* ; *gradually*）

(C) *leap*〔lip〕*v. n.* 跳躍（= *jump*）　　***by leaps and bounds*** 快速地

(D) odd〔ɑd〕*n.* 勝算；可能性　　by (all) odds 顯然；確實（修飾比較級、最高級）

＊scrupulous〔'skrupjələs〕*adj.* 細心的　　bound〔baʊnd〕*n.* 反彈；跳躍

3. (**A**) The leading role in this comedy required a <u>vibrant</u> performance but Willy was far too serious. 這齣喜劇中的主角需要<u>充滿活力的</u>演出，但威利實在太嚴肅了。

(A) *vibrant*〔'vaɪbrənt〕*adj.* 震動的；充滿活力的（= *lively*）

vibrate *v.* 震動　　vibration *n.*

(B) admirable〔'ædmərəbḷ〕*adj.* 值得欽佩的；極佳的（= *excellent* ; *remarkable*）

admire *v.* 欽佩；稱讚　　admiration *n.*

(C) transient〔'trænʃənt〕*adj.* 短暫的；瞬間的（= *fleeting* ; *brief*）

(D) captive〔'kæptɪv〕*adj.* 被俘的（= *imprisoned*）；被迷住的　　*n.* 俘虜

capture *v.* 俘虜；捕捉；抓住

＊comedy〔'kɑmədɪ〕*n.* 喜劇　　***leading role*** 主角　　require〔rɪ'kwaɪr〕*v.* 需要

4. (**D**) Even though she was <u>humbly</u> born, she aimed high and strove for the best and finally made it. 即使出身<u>卑微</u>，但她胸懷大志、力爭上游，終於成功了。

(A) mildly〔'maɪldlɪ〕*adv.* 溫和地（= *gently*）；稍微（= *slightly*）

(B) markedly〔'mɑrkɪdlɪ〕*adv.* 顯著地；引人注目地（= *noticeably*）

(C) rigidly〔'rɪdʒɪdlɪ〕*adv.* 嚴格地（= *strictly*）

(D) *humbly*〔'hʌmblɪ〕*adv.* 卑微地（= *lowly*）

＊*aim high* 目標定得高；胸懷大志　　strive〔straɪv〕*v.* 努力　　***make it*** 成功

5. (**C**) With the train still so far away, the house was only <u>vaguely</u> visible.
火車距離還很遠，那棟房子也只是模糊難見。
  (A) warily〔'wɛrəlɪ〕*adv.* 小心謹慎地（= *carefully* ; *cautiously* ）　　wary *adj.*
  (B) cozily〔'kozɪlɪ〕*adv.* 舒適地（= *comfortably* ; *snugly* ）　　cozy *adj.*
  (C) ***vaguely***〔'veglɪ〕*adv.* 模糊地（= *dimly* ）　　vague *adj.*
  (D) gravely〔'grevlɪ〕*adv.* 嚴肅地；重大地（= *seriously* ）
  * visible〔'vɪzəbl̩〕*adj.* 看得見的

6. (**C**) We arrived here too early. The Prague-<u>bound</u> train will depart in another hour.
我們太早到這兒了。前往布拉格的火車再過一小時才會出發。
  (A) seated〔'sitɪd〕*adj.* 有…座位/坐墊的；固定的
    例：a two-*seated* motorbike 雙座摩托車　　a soft-*seated* chair 軟墊座椅
    deeply-*seated* prejudices 根深蒂固的偏見
  (B) proof〔pruf〕*adj.* 防…的；隔絕…的　　例：water*proof* 防水的
    fire*proof* 防火的　　bullet*proof* 防彈的　　sound*proof* 隔音的
  (C) ***bound***〔baʊnd〕*adj.* 前往…的　　例：east(west)*bound* 東（西）行的
    north(south)*bound* 北上（南下）的
  (D) based〔best〕*adj.* 位於…的；以…為基礎的
    例：London-based office 駐倫敦辦事處
  * Prague〔preg〕*n.* 布拉格（捷克首都）　depart〔dɪ'part〕*v.* 離開；出發（= *leave* ）

7. (**A**) Although he didn't say anything, his eagerness to go was <u>mirrored</u> in his eyes.
雖然他什麼也沒說，但他想去的熱切之情反映在他的眼神裡。
  (A) ***mirror***〔'mɪrɚ〕*v.* 反映；反射（= *reflect* ）　　*n.* 鏡子
  (B) confine〔kən'faɪn〕*v.* 限制（= *limit* ; *restrict* ）
  (C) flatten〔'flætn̩〕*v.* 使變平；使洩氣　　flat *adj.* 平的；洩氣的
  (D) enhance〔ɪn'hæns〕*v.* 提高；增進（= *increase* ; *improve* ; *boost* ）
  * eagerness〔'igɚnɪs〕*n.* 熱切；渴望（= *keenness* ; *desire* ）

8. (**D**) Her excellent performance of her job had been <u>overlooked</u> by her superiors;
therefore, she felt very discouraged and decided to quit.
她工作上優秀的表現一直被上司忽略；因此她覺得很氣餒，決定要辭職。
  (A) overflow〔,ovɚ'flo〕*v.* 氾濫；溢出　〔'ovɚ,flo〕*n.*
  (B) overcome〔,ovɚ'kʌm〕*v.* 克服；打敗（= *defeat* ; *beat* ）
  (C) overrate〔,ovɚ'ret〕*v.* 高估（= *overestimate* ）
  (D) ***overlook***〔,ovɚ'lʊk〕*v.* 俯瞰（= *look down at* ）；監視；監督（= *supervise* ）；
    忽略（= *neglect* ; *ignore* ）
  * excellent〔'ɛkslənt〕*adj.* 優秀的　　performance〔pɚ'fɔrməns〕*n.* 表現
  superior〔sə'pɪrɪɚ〕*n.* 上司；長官　　discouraged〔dɪs'kɝɪdʒd〕*adj.* 氣餒的
  quit〔kwɪt〕*v.* 辭職；放棄

9.(**A**) He is such a troublemaker that everyone avoids him like the <u>plague</u>.

他實在是個麻煩製造機，所以每個人都躲著他像躲<u>瘟疫</u>一樣。

(A) *plague* 〔 pleg 〕 *n.* 瘟疫；黑死病　*v.* 困擾；使痛苦（ = *bother* ; *torture* ）

(B) pirate 〔'paɪrət 〕 *n.* 海盜；盜印者　*v.* 掠奪；盜印

　　piracy *n.* 海盜行為；盜印

(C) stall 〔 stɔl 〕 *n.* 攤子（ = *stand* ; *booth* ）

(D) taboo 〔 tə'bu 〕 *n.* 禁忌　*adj.* 禁忌的　*v.* 禁用；使成為禁忌

　　* troublemaker 〔'trʌbḷ,mekə 〕 *n.* 麻煩製造者（ ↔ troubleshooter 解決問題者）

10.(**C**) His <u>scorching</u> remark against the government made him a suspect in the assassination of the president.

他對政府嚴厲的批評，使他成為行刺總統事件的嫌疑犯。

(A) glowing 〔'gloɪŋ 〕 *adj.* 灼熱的；熱情的　　glow *v.* 燒得通紅；發光；發熱

(B) fleeting 〔'flitɪŋ 〕 *adj.* 飛逝的；瞬間的　　fleet *v.* 疾馳；飛逝

(C) *scorching* 〔'skɔrtʃɪŋ 〕 *adj.* 灼熱的；嚴厲的（ = *severe* ）　　scorch *v.* 燒焦

　　例： *glowing/scorching/*burning/boiling hot

　　　　灼熱；熾熱（動名詞當副詞，加強熱的語氣）

(D) flattering 〔'flætərɪŋ 〕 *adj.* 阿諛的；諂媚的　　flatter *v.*

　　* remark 〔 rɪ'mɑrk 〕 *n.* 評論　　suspect 〔'sʌspɛkt 〕 *n.* 嫌疑犯

　　assassination 〔 ə,sæsṇ'eʃən 〕 *n.* 暗殺；行刺

11.(**A**) The typewriter has certainly <u>given ground</u> to the computer.　That is, the computer has almost completely taken the place of the typewriter.

打字機確實已<u>被電腦迎頭趕上</u>。也就是說，電腦已經幾乎全面取代了打字機。

(A) *give/lose ground* 撤退（ = *retreat* ）；被追趕上

(B) gain ground 佔領陣地；前進（ = *progress* ; *advance* ）

(C) break ground 破土

　　break new/fresh ground 開創新局面；改革（ = *innovate* ）

(D) cover ground 走/前進（一段距離）；（報告、演說等）涵蓋～範圍

　　例： *cover* a lot of *ground* 走了很多路；涵蓋很大的範圍

　　* *take the place of* 取代（ = *replace* ）

12.(**D**) They told him that he would never succeed in anything, but he made them <u>eat their words</u>.　他們對他說，他將會一事無成，但他使他們<u>承認說錯了話</u>。

(A) play on words *v.* 用雙關語；說俏皮話　*n.* 雙關語；俏皮話

(B) keep *one's* word 信守承諾　　word 〔 wɜd 〕 *n.* 承諾（ = *promise* ）

(C) weigh *one's* words 斟酌用字　　weigh 〔 we 〕 *v.* 秤重量；斟酌

(D) *eat one's words* 承認說錯話；收回前言

13. (**B**) The winning numbers are drawn <u>at random</u>, so whoever picked them is really fortunate. 得獎號碼是<u>隨機</u>抽取的,所以抽中的人真是太幸運了。

(A) at large (動物、嫌犯)自由地;未被捕獲 (= *free* ; *on the loose*)

　　例 : The murderer is still *at large*. 兇手仍然逍遙法外。

(B) *at random* 隨機地;隨便地　　random ('rændəm) *adj.* 隨便的

　　例 : a *random* guess 隨便亂猜　　*random* sampling 隨機取樣

(C) at ease 輕鬆自在 (= *comfortable* ; *relaxed*)

　　比較 : ill at ease 不安;心神不寧

(D) at length 最後;終於 (= *at last* ; *in the end* ; *eventually*)

　　length 〔 lɛŋθ 〕 *n.* 長度

　 * draw 〔 drɔ 〕 *v.* 抽取;抽(籤)　　pick 〔 pɪk 〕 *v.* 挑選;抽取

14. (**A**) On our trip from Los Angeles to New York, we <u>stopped over</u> one night in Chicago. 在我們由洛杉磯到紐約的旅途中,我們在芝加哥<u>短暫停留</u>一晚。

(A) *stop over* 中途下車;短暫停留

(B) stop out 在外過夜 (= *stay out*);中途休學

(C) make over 修改 (= *alter* ; *change*)

　　例 : They *made* part of their garden *over* into a garage.

　　　　他們把他們庭園的一部分改成車庫。

(D) make out 了解 (= *comprehend* ; *figure out*);看出;寫出;

　　進展 (= *get along*)

　　例 : I can't *make out* his writing. 我無法辨認他的字跡。

　　　　make out a list 列表

　 * Chicago 〔 ʃɪ'kɑgo 〕 *n.* 芝加哥 (美國伊利諾州東北部,臨密西根湖,全美第三大都市)

15. (**B**) Considered a legacy of his family, the oil painting has been <u>handed down</u> from generation to generation. 這幅油畫被視為是他的家族遺產而代代相<u>傳</u>。

(A) hand in 繳交 (= *turn in* ; *submit*)　　例 : *hand in* one's homework 交作業

(B) *hand down* 傳遞 (= *pass down* ; *pass on*)

(C) hand out 分發 (= *give out* ; *distribute*)

　　例 : The teacher is *handing out* test papers to the students.

　　　　老師正在發考卷給學生。

(D) hand over 移交;轉交 (= *turn over*)

　　例 : The father *handed over* his business to his son.

　　　　這位父親將生意交給他的兒子。

　 * legacy 〔'lɛgəsɪ 〕 *n.* 遺產　　***oil painting*** 油畫

　　generation 〔,dʒɛnə'reʃən 〕 *n.* 世代

TEST 15

Directions: The following questions are incomplete sentences. You are to choose the one word that best completes the sentence.

1. Owing to the economic recession, the company doesn't plan to _____ many new employees this year.
   - (A) regulate
   - (B) recruit
   - (C) relay
   - (D) register
   ( )

2. Record every payment you make during your business trip, and the company will _____ you for all the expenses.
   - (A) revoke
   - (B) restore
   - (C) reimburse
   - (D) reinforce
   ( )

3. The company cannot market the new drug until it receives _____ from the government.
   - (A) approval
   - (B) reproof
   - (C) reputation
   - (D) apprehension
   ( )

4. Because of his reputation for fairness, honesty, and _____, Judge Brighten is highly respected.
   - (A) segregation
   - (B) nuisance
   - (C) piracy
   - (D) integrity
   ( )

5. The election _____ was not very good due to the cold, rainy weather. Only about 60 percent of voters went to the polls.
   - (A) takeout
   - (B) lookout
   - (C) breakout
   - (D) turnout
   ( )

6. The quality of the company's products produced overseas is _____ to that of those made in its home country.
   - (A) impartial
   - (B) desperate
   - (C) comparable
   - (D) reparable
   ( )

7. They hadn't noticed such a slight change at all, not even Mark, who was normally so _____.
   - (A) reserved
   - (B) observant
   - (C) obscure
   - (D) piercing
   ( )

8. The scientists are _____ making progress in the development of a new weather satellite.
   (A) abruptly
   (B) accurately
   (C) extensively
   (D) gradually   ( )

9. We can _____ renew your magazine subscription if you desire it.
   (A) psychologically
   (B) reluctantly
   (C) negligently
   (D) automatically   ( )

10. On hearing the siren of the police car, the thief _____ over the wall and ran away.
    (A) scrambled
    (B) scribbled
    (C) sculptured
    (D) scratched   ( )

11. No matter what career you choose in the future, it is _____ to have a good command of English.
    (A) against the tide
    (B) to your advantage
    (C) in the spotlight
    (D) up in smoke   ( )

12. The college football game made it hard to find a place to eat that _____ students.
    (A) was patterned after
    (B) was extracted from
    (C) was swarmed with
    (D) wasn't packed with   ( )

13. Market penetration depends _____ on the ability of a company to establish a good sales network.
    (A) on no account
    (B) on the verge of
    (C) to a great extent
    (D) to the point of   ( )

14. A total of thirty teams from 10 countries joined in the tournament _____ the championship.
    (A) in competition for
    (B) in return for
    (C) in remembrance of
    (D) in favor of   ( )

15. I was almost frightened to death when the plane suddenly _____ a sharp nose dive.
    (A) brought into
    (B) went into
    (C) put into
    (D) made into   ( )

TEST 15 詳解

1. (**B**) Owing to the economic recession, the company doesn't plan to <u>recruit</u> many new employees this year.
   由於經濟不景氣，這家公司今年不打算<u>招募</u>太多新進員工。
   (A) regulate〔ˈrɛgjəˌlet〕v. 管理；整頓；調整　regulation n.
   (B) *recruit*〔rɪˈkrut〕v. 招募 (新人、新兵)　n. 新人；新兵
   (C) relay〔rɪˈle〕v. 轉播；傳達
   (D) register〔ˈrɛdʒɪstə〕v. 登記；註冊；掛號
   　　例：*registered* trademark 註冊商標　　*registered* mail 掛號郵件
   * recession〔rɪˈsɛʃən〕n. 不景氣

2. (**C**) Record every payment you make during your business trip, and the company will <u>reimburse</u> you for all the expenses.
   記下你出差時付出的每筆款項，公司會<u>支付</u>你所有的開銷。
   (A) revoke〔rɪˈvok〕v. 廢除；撤銷；吊銷 (執照)　　revocation n.
   (B) restore〔rɪˈstor〕v. 恢復；修復　　restoration n.
   (C) *reimburse*〔ˌriɪmˈbɜs〕v. 償還；付還 (= *repay* ; *pay back*)
   　　reimbursement n.
   (D) reinforce〔ˌriɪnˈfors〕v. 增強；強化　　reinforcement n.
   * *make a payment* 支付款項　　expense〔ɪkˈspɛns〕n. 費用

3. (**A**) The company cannot market the new drug until it receives <u>approval</u> from the government. 直到這種新的藥物得到政府的<u>批准</u>，該公司才能將它推出市場。
   (A) *approval*〔əˈpruvḷ〕n. 批准；贊成 (= *permission*)　　approve v. < of >
   (B) reproof〔rɪˈpruf〕n. 譴責；斥責　　reprove v.
   (C) reputation〔ˌrɛpjəˈteʃən〕n. 名聲
   (D) apprehension〔ˌæprɪˈhɛnʃən〕n. 憂慮；恐懼　　apprehend v.
   * market〔ˈmɑrkɪt〕v. 推出市場；銷售

4. (**D**) Because of his reputation for fairness, honesty, and <u>integrity</u>, Judge Brighten is highly respected. 由於以公正、誠實，及<u>正直</u>著稱，布萊登法官備受尊重。
   (A) segregation〔ˌsɛgrɪˈgeʃən〕n. 隔離；種族隔離　　segregate v.
   (B) nuisance〔ˈnjusns〕n. 令人討厭的人、事、物
   (C) piracy〔ˈpaɪrəsɪ〕n. 海盜行為；侵犯著作權、專利權等
   　　pirate〔ˈpaɪrət〕n. 海盜；侵權者　v. 當海盜；侵權
   (D) *integrity*〔ɪnˈtɛgrətɪ〕n. 正直；廉潔
   * judge〔dʒʌdʒ〕n. 法官
   　　reputation〔ˌrɛpjəˈteʃən〕n. 名聲

5. (**D**) The election <u>turnout</u> was not very good due to the cold, rainy weather. Only about 60 percent of voters went to the polls.

由於天氣寒冷又下雨，此次選舉<u>投票人數</u>並不多。只有大約六成的選民去投票。

(A) takeout〔'tek,aʊt〕*n.* 取出；外賣餐館　*adj.* 外賣的 (= *takeaway*)

　　take out　取出；外帶

　　例：a pizza *takeout* 披薩外賣店　　a *takeout* counter　外賣櫃台

(B) lookout〔'lʊk,aʊt〕*n.* 警戒；提防　　look out 向外看；小心；注意 < *for* >

(C) breakout〔'brek,aʊt〕*n.* 越獄；突破　　break out 爆發；突然發生；逃走

(D) *turnout*〔'tɜn,aʊt〕*n.* 出席、投票、集會人數

　　turn out　產生～結果；把～趕出去

＊voter〔'votɚ〕*n.* 選民　　polls〔polz〕*n. pl.* 投票所　　***go to the polls*** 去投票

6. (**C**) The quality of the company's products produced overseas is <u>comparable</u> to that of those made in its home country.

該公司在國外生產的產品品質，可<u>比得上</u>在國內生產的產品。

(A) impartial〔ɪm'parʃəl〕*adj.* 公平的；不偏袒的 (= *fair*)

(B) desperate〔'dɛspərɪt〕*adj.* 拼命的；絕望的；極渴望的

(C) *comparable*〔'kampərəbḷ〕*adj.* 類似的 < *to, with* >；可比擬的 < *to* >

　　例：A heart is *comparable* with a pump. 心臟類似幫浦。

(D) reparable〔'rɛpərəbḷ〕*adj.* 可修理的；可補救的

＊overseas〔,ovɚ'siz〕*adv.* 在國外 (= *abroad*)

7. (**B**) They hadn't noticed such a slight change at all, not even Mark, who was normally so <u>observant</u>. 他們完全沒有注意到如此輕微的變化，甚至連平常觀察非常<u>入微</u>的馬克也沒有注意到。

(A) reserved〔rɪ'zɜvd〕*adj.* 謹慎的；矜持的；預約的；保留的　　reserve *v.*

(B) *observant*〔əb'zɜvənt〕*adj.* 觀察力敏銳的　　observe *v.*

(C) obscure〔əb'skjʊr〕*adj.* 模糊的；朦朧的

(D) piercing〔'pɪrsɪŋ〕*adj.* (寒冷) 刺骨的；(聲音) 刺耳的；刺痛的

　　pierce *v.* 刺穿；穿透

＊slight〔slaɪt〕*adj.* 輕微的　　normally〔'nɔrmḷɪ〕*adv.* 通常；一般 (= *usually*)

8. (**D**) The scientists are <u>gradually</u> making progress in the development of a new weather satellite. 科學家正在發展一枚新的氣象衛星，<u>並且</u>漸進步。

(A) abruptly〔ə'brʌptlɪ〕*adv.* 突然地 (比 suddenly 意外程度更強)

　　abrupt *adj.* (= *sudden*)

(B) accurately〔'ækjərɪtlɪ〕*adv.* 正確地；精密地　　accurate *adj.*　　accuracy *n.*

(C) extensively〔ɪk'stɛnsɪvlɪ〕*adv.* 廣泛地　　extensive *adj.*

(D) *gradually*〔'grædʒʊəlɪ〕*adv.* 逐漸地　　gradual *adj.*

＊***make progress*** 有進步　　satellite〔'sætḷ,aɪt〕*n.* 衛星

9. (**D**) We can <u>automatically</u> renew your magazine subscription if you desire it.
如果您想要的話，我們可以<u>自動</u>為您續訂雜誌。

    (A) psychologically〔͵saɪkəˋlɑdʒɪkəlɪ〕*adv.* 心理上　　psychological *adj.*
        psychology *n.*

    (B) reluctantly〔rɪˋlʌktəntlɪ〕*adv.* 不願意地；勉強地（= *unwillingly*）
        reluctant *adj.*

    (C) negligently〔ˋnɛglədʒəntlɪ〕*adv.* 怠慢地；不注意地　　negligent *adj.*

    (D) ***automatically***〔͵ɔtəˋmætɪkəlɪ〕*adv.* 自動地　　automatic *adj.*

    ＊renew〔rɪˋnju〕*v.* 更新；續訂　　subscription〔səbˋskrɪpʃən〕*n.* 訂閱
     desire〔dɪˋzaɪr〕*v.* 希望；渴望（比 want 更正式）

10. (**A**) On hearing the siren of the police car, the thief <u>scrambled</u> over the wall and
ran away. 一聽到警車的警笛聲，小偷就<u>翻</u>過圍牆跑掉了。

    (A) ***scramble***〔ˋskræmbl̩〕*v.* 攀爬（= *climb*）；炒（蛋）
        例：*scrambled* eggs 炒蛋

    (B) scribble〔ˋskrɪbl̩〕*v. n.* 潦草書寫；亂寫亂塗
        scribbler *n.* 書寫潦草的人；拙劣的作家

    (C) sculpture〔ˋskʌlptʃə〕*v. n.* 雕刻　　sculptor *n.* 雕刻家

    (D) scratch〔skrætʃ〕*v.* 抓；搔　*n.* 抓；搔；（賽跑的）出發點
        例：start from *scratch* 從零開始；從頭做起；白手起家

    ＊siren〔ˋsaɪrən〕*n.* 警笛；警報器

11. (**B**) No matter what career you choose in the future, it is <u>to your advantage</u> to have
a good command of English. 無論未來你選擇什麼職業，精通英文都<u>對你有利</u>。

    (A) go/swim against the tide/stream 逆流；反抗潮流

    (B) ***to sb.'s advantage*** 對某人有利

    (C) in the spotlight 在聚光燈下；成為眾人注目的焦點
        spotlight〔ˋspɑt͵laɪt〕*n.* 聚光燈

    (D) end/go up in smoke 成泡影；化為烏有

    ＊command〔kəˋmænd〕*n.*（對語言）運用自如的能力
    have a good command of 精通

12. (**D**) The college football game made it hard to find a place to eat that <u>wasn't packed</u>
<u>with</u> students. 由於舉行大學足球賽，要找個<u>沒有擠滿</u>學生的地方吃飯很困難。

    (A) pattern〔ˋpætən〕*v.* 仿造；模仿 < *after* >

    (B) extract〔ɪkˋstrækt〕*v.* 抽出；得到；選取 < *from* >

    (C) swarm〔swɔrm〕*v.* 群集；蜂擁；擠滿 < *with* >（應用否定）

    (D) ***pack***〔pæk〕*v.* 擠滿 < *with* >
    be packed with 擠滿（= *be crowded with*；*be swarmed with*）

13. (**C**) Market penetration depends <u>to a great extent</u> on the ability of a company to establish a good sales network.

市場普及率<u>非常</u>仰賴一家公司能否建立良好的銷售網路。

(A) on no account 絕不 (= *by no means* ; *under no circumstances*)

(B) on the verge of 瀕臨；將近 (通常用於不好的情形)   verge〔vɝdʒ〕*n.* 邊緣

(C) *to a great extent* 大大地；大部分 (= *greatly*)   extent〔ɪk'stɛnt〕*n.* 程度

(D) to the point of 到達～程度 (= *to the extent of*)

    例：He admired his uncle, almost *to the point of* hero worship.

        他非常敬仰他的叔叔，幾乎到了英雄崇拜的地步。

    * penetration〔,pɛnə'treʃən〕*n.* 滲透；貫穿；普及   network〔'nɛt,wɝk〕*n.* 網路

14. (**A**) A total of thirty teams from 10 countries joined in the tournament <u>in competition for</u> the championship.

總共有來自十個國家三十支隊伍，參加這次比賽<u>角逐冠軍</u>。

(A) *in competition for* 互相競爭角逐、爭奪～

(B) in return for 作爲～的回報

(C) in remembrance of 爲了紀念～ (= *in honor of* ; *in memory of*)

    remembrance〔rɪ'mɛmbrəns〕*n.* 記憶；紀念

    例：The monument was erected *in remembrance of* the hero.

        豎立這座紀念碑是爲了紀念那位英雄。

(D) in favor of 支持；贊成；有利於～

    例：The referee's decision was *in favor of* our team.   裁判的決定對我隊有利。

    * tournament〔'tʊrnəmənt , 'tɝ-〕*n.* 比賽；錦標賽

    championship〔'tʃæmpɪən,ʃɪp〕*n.* 冠軍 (資格、頭銜) (不可數名詞)

    cf. champion *n.* 冠軍者 (人或隊伍) (可數名詞)

15. (**B**) I was almost frightened to death when the plane suddenly <u>went into</u> a sharp nose dive. 當飛機突然急速俯衝時，我幾乎快嚇死了。

(A) bring～into… 使～成爲… (及物動詞)

    例：*bring* the new law *into* effect 開始實施新法

    (= *put the new law into effect*)

(B) *go/come into* 進入；成爲 (某種狀態) (不及物動詞)

    例：The new law will *go/come into* effect on July 1.

        新法將在七月一日開始實施。

(C) put into 流入；駛入   例：The river *puts into* a lake. 這條河流入一個湖。

(D) make A into B 把 A 製成 B

    例：Mother *made* her skirt *into* my coat. 媽媽把她的裙子改成外套給我穿。

    * sharp〔ʃɑrp〕*adj.* 急速的；陡峭的   *nose dive* (飛機) 俯衝

TEST 16

Directions: The following questions are incomplete sentences. You are to choose the one word that best completes the sentence.

1. So much construction _____ was stacked along the road that there was only one lane left free.
   (A) deposit
   (B) equipment
   (C) contagion
   (D) withdrawal
   ( )

2. Even though the economy was in _____, the company was opening new stores.
   (A) resistance
   (B) reception
   (C) retrieval
   (D) recession
   ( )

3. Mark won a silver _____ in the 400-meter dash, so his parents were very proud of him.
   (A) metal
   (B) pedal
   (C) medal
   (D) petal
   ( )

4. I am against building nuclear power plants; I think they should be _____ as soon as possible.
   (A) abolished
   (B) accomplished
   (C) approached
   (D) accelerated
   ( )

5. The number of crimes is on the rise since more guns are being _____ into the country.
   (A) condemned
   (B) smuggled
   (C) perceived
   (D) purchased
   ( )

6. A leading mediator was sent by the court to _____ the labor dispute in the corporation.
   (A) settle
   (B) contaminate
   (C) accommodate
   (D) aggravate
   ( )

7. In order to prepare students for the future, schools are trying to create more _____ programs of study.
   (A) invalid
   (B) innovative
   (C) interior
   (D) intentional
   ( )

8. All of the _____ luggage is stored in a special room for three months.
   (A) unclassified　　　　　(B) undefined
   (C) unclaimed　　　　　　(D) undecided　　　　　　( )

9. The construction of the building will take _____ nine months to complete.
   (A) simultaneously　　　(B) approximately
   (C) accordingly　　　　　(D) relatively　　　　　　( )

10. The executives of the organization were _____ criticized for not apologizing for their actions.
    (A) lawfully　　　　　　(B) doubtfully
    (C) regretfully　　　　　(D) severely　　　　　　( )

11. I sent my resume to over twenty companies, but unfortunately I was _____ by every one of them.
    (A) traced back　　　　(B) given off
    (C) made out　　　　　(D) turned down　　　　( )

12. The machine _____ because the maintenance people did not service it on a regular basis.
    (A) worked out　　　　(B) broke down
    (C) took over　　　　　(D) pulled ahead　　　　( )

13. To save money and energy, the parents of the three families decided to form _____ to take their kids to school.
    (A) a dark horse　　　　(B) a car pool
    (C) a dead end　　　　　(D) a hard line　　　　( )

14. The mountains _____ are bathed in the glow of the setting sun, looking most enchanting.
    (A) in the distance　　　(B) at sea
    (C) below the horizon　　(D) on the rocks　　　　( )

15. Only _____ the roof is repaired will we agree to rent the house.
    (A) on occasion　　　　(B) on account of
    (C) on condition that　　(D) in case of　　　　( )

TEST 16 詳解

1. (**B**) So much construction <u>equipment</u> was stacked along the road that there was only one lane left free.
太多建築器材沿著馬路堆放，結果只剩一線車道可行。
   (A) deposit〔dɪ'pɑzɪt〕*n.* 存款；訂金；保證金　*v.* 存款；付訂金
   (B) ***equipment***〔ɪ'kwɪpmənt〕*n.* 裝備　　equip *v.* 裝備；使具有 < *with* >
   (C) contagion〔kən'tedʒən〕*n.* 傳染（病）　　contagious *adj.* 傳染性的
   (D) withdrawal〔wɪð'drɔəl〕*n.* 取款；撤退　　withdraw *v.*
   * stack〔stæk〕*v.* 堆積　　lane〔len〕*n.* 車道
   free〔fri〕*adj.*（道路）可自由通行的

2. (**D**) Even though the economy was in <u>recession</u>, the company was opening new stores. 即使經濟不景氣，該公司仍然開設新店面。
   (A) resistance〔rɪ'zɪstəns〕*n.* 抵抗 < *to* >　　resist *v.*
   (B) reception〔rɪ'sɛpʃən〕*n.* 接待
   (C) retrieval〔rɪ'trivl〕*n.* 取回；恢復　　retrieve *v.*
   (D) ***recession***〔rɪ'sɛʃən〕*n.* 不景氣（= *depression* ）

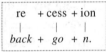

3. (**C**) Mark won a silver <u>medal</u> in the 400-meter dash, so his parents were very proud of him.
馬克在四百公尺短跑中贏得銀牌，所以他的父母非常以他為榮。
   (A) metal〔'mɛtl〕*n.* 金屬
   (B) pedal〔'pɛdl〕*n.* 踏板
   (C) ***medal***〔'mɛdl〕*n.* 獎牌
   (D) petal〔'pɛtl〕*n.* 花瓣
   * dash〔dæʃ〕*n.* 短跑

   > gold medal 金牌；第一名（= *first place* ）
   > silver medal 銀牌；第二名（= *second place* ）
   > bronze medal 銅牌；第三名（= *third place* ）

4. (**A**) I am against building nuclear power plants; I think they should be <u>abolished</u> as soon as possible.
我反對興建核能發電廠；我認為它們應該儘快被廢除。
   (A) ***abolish***〔ə'bɑlɪʃ〕*v.* 廢除（= *do away with* ）
   (B) accomplish〔ə'kɑmplɪʃ〕*v.* 達到（= *achieve* ）
   (C) approach〔ə'protʃ〕*v.* 接近
   (D) accelerate〔æk'sɛlə,ret〕*v.* 加速
   * against〔ə'gɛnst〕*prep.* 反對（↔ *for* ）
   nuclear power plant 核能發電廠

   > *be against* 反對
   > = oppose
   > = be opposed to
   > = object to

5. (**B**) The number of crimes is on the rise since more guns are being <u>smuggled</u> into the country. 犯罪的數目一直在增加，因為有更多槍枝走私進口。

    (A) condemn〔kənˈdɛm〕*v.* 譴責

    (B) *smuggle*〔ˈsmʌgl〕*v.* 走私

    (C) perceive〔pɚˈsiv〕*v.* 察覺

       (*= become aware of*)

    (D) purchase〔ˈpɝtʃəs〕*v.* 購買 (*= buy*)

   * *on the rise* 增加中

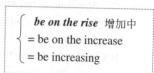

```
be on the rise  增加中
= be on the increase
= be increasing
```

6. (**A**) A leading mediator was sent by the court to <u>settle</u> the labor dispute in the corporation. 法院派遣一位一流的調停者，去解決該公司勞方的爭論。

    (A) *settle*〔ˈsɛtl〕*v.* 解決 (*= solve*)；安置；移居；決定

    (B) contaminate〔kənˈtæməˌnet〕*v.* 污染 (*= pollute*)

    (C) accommodate〔əˈkɑməˌdet〕*v.* 容納

    (D) aggravate〔ˈægrəˌvet〕*v.* 惡化 (*= make worse*)

   * leading〔ˈlidɪŋ〕*adj.* 主要的；一流的　　mediator〔ˈmidɪˌetɚ〕*n.* 調停者

    dispute〔dɪˈspjut〕*n.* 爭論

    corporation〔ˌkɔrpəˈreʃən〕*n.* 公司 (*= company*)

7. (**B**) In order to prepare students for the future, schools are trying to create more <u>innovative</u> programs of study.

    為培養學生為未來做好準備，學校要努力開設更多創新的學習課程。

    (A) invalid〔ɪnˈvælɪd〕*adj.* 無效的　〔ˈɪnvəlɪd〕*n.* 病人

    (B) *innovative*〔ˈɪnəˌvetɪv〕*adj.* 創新的 (*= new*)

    (C) interior〔ɪnˈtɪrɪɚ〕*adj.* 內部的 (*= internal*)

    (D) intentional〔ɪnˈtɛnʃənl〕*adj.* 故意的 (*= deliberate*)

8. (**C**) All of the <u>unclaimed</u> luggage is stored in a special room for three months.

    所有無人認領的行李，會被放置在一個特別的房間裡，存放三個月。

    (A) unclassified〔ʌnˈklæsəˌfaɪd〕*adj.* 未分類的　　classify *v.* 分類

    (B) undefined〔ˌʌndɪˈfaɪnd〕*adj.* 未下定義的；不明確的　　define *v.* 下定義

    (C) *unclaimed*〔ʌnˈklemd〕*adj.* 無人認領的　　claim *v.* 宣稱；認領

    (D) undecided〔ˌʌndɪˈsaɪdɪd〕*adj.* 未決定的；優柔寡斷的

   * luggage〔ˈlʌgɪdʒ〕*n.* 行李 (*= baggage*)

    store〔stor〕*v.* 儲存；存放

9. (**B**) The construction of the building will take <u>approximately</u> nine months to
complete. 這棟大樓的興建大約需要九個月才能完成。

    (A) simultaneously〔ˌsaɪml'tenɪəslɪ〕*adv.* 同時（= *at the same time*）

    (B) *approximately*〔ə'prɑksəmɪtlɪ〕*adv.* 大約（= *roughly*; *about*）

    (C) accordingly〔ə'kɔrdɪŋlɪ〕*adv.* 因此（= *consequently*; *therefore*）

    (D) relatively〔'rɛlətɪvlɪ〕*adv.* 相對地；相當地

10. (**D**) The executives of the organization were <u>severely</u> criticized for not apologizing
for their actions.
該組織的主管，因不爲自己的行爲道歉，受到嚴厲批評。

    (A) lawfully〔'lɔfəlɪ〕*adv.* 合法地（= *legally*）

    (B) doubtfully〔'dautfəlɪ〕*adv.* 懷疑地（= *suspiciously*）

    (C) regretfully〔rɪ'grɛtfəlɪ〕*adv.* 後悔地

    (D) *severely*〔sə'vɪrlɪ〕*adv.* 嚴厲地（= *harshly*）

    * executive〔ɪg'zɛkjutɪv〕*n.* 主管   organization〔ˌɔrgənə'zeʃən〕*n.* 組織

      criticize〔'krɪtəˌsaɪz〕*v.* 批評   apologize〔ə'pɑləˌdʒaɪz〕*v.* 道歉

11. (**D**) I sent my resume to over twenty companies, but unfortunately I was
<u>turned down</u> by every one of them.
我將履歷寄到二十多家公司應徵工作，但不幸全被拒絕。

    (A) trace back 追溯

        例：The origin of the custom can be *traced back* to 50 years ago.

            這個習俗的由來可以追溯到五十年前。

    (B) give off 發出；放出（光、煙、味道等）

    (C) make out 辨認（= *distinguish*）；理解（= *understand*）

    (D) *turn down* 拒絕（= *reject*; *refuse*）

    * resume〔ˌrɛzu'me〕*n.* 履歷表

12. (**B**) The machine <u>broke down</u> because the maintenance people did not service it on
a regular basis.
這台機器故障了，因爲維修人員沒有定期做保養。

    (A) work out 解決；擬定（計劃等）；運動（= *exercise*）

    (B) *break down* 故障（= *fail*; *crash*）；崩潰（= *collapse*）；（神經）衰弱

    (C) take over 接管（工作、事業等）

    (D) pull ahead 領先（= *get ahead*）；追過（= *overtake*）

    * maintenance〔'mentənəns〕*n.* 維修   service〔'sɝvɪs〕*v.* 修護；保養

      on a regular basis 定期地（= *regularly*）

13. (**B**) To save money and energy, the parents of the three families decided to form
a car pool to take their kids to school.
為了節省金錢和體力，這三個家庭的父母決定，利用<u>汽車共乘</u>的方式輪流送小
孩上學。

(A) a dark horse　黑馬　　*cf.* a black sheep　害群之馬
(B) *a car pool*　汽車共乘
(C) a dead end　死巷；絕境
(D) a hard line　強硬立場
　　例：take *a hard line*　採取強硬手段

14. (**A**) The mountains <u>in the distance</u> are bathed in the glow of the setting sun,
looking most enchanting.
<u>遠方</u>群山籠罩在落日餘暉中，看起來非常迷人。

(A) *in the distance*　在遠方　　*cf.* at a distance　隔一段距離
(B) at sea　航行中；困惑　　*cf.* at the sea　在海邊
(C) below the horizon　地平面以下　　horizon〔həˋraɪzn〕*n.* 地平面
(D) on the rocks　觸礁；（婚姻）瀕臨破裂；（威士忌）加冰塊
* bathe〔beð〕*v.* 沐浴；籠罩　　glow〔glo〕*n.* 光輝
　enchanting〔ɪnˋtʃæntɪŋ〕*adj.* 迷人的

15. (**C**) Only <u>on condition that</u> the roof is repaired will we agree to rent the house.
唯有<u>在屋頂修好的條件下</u>，我們才會同意承租這間房子。

(A) on occasion　偶爾；有時
(B) on account of　因為
(C) *on condition that* + 子句　在～條件下
* Only 引導條件子句 on condition that the roof is repaired 置於句首，主要子句
　will we agree to rent the house 為倒裝句。
(D) in case of + N.　萬一發生
　　cf. in case + 子句　萬一；以防
　　例：Call 119 *in case of* fire. = Call 119 *in case* a fire happens.
　　　（萬一發生火災，請打 119。）

> **on account of** 因為；由於
> = because of
> = as a result of
> = due to
> = owing to

> **on occasion** 偶爾；有時
> = occasionally
> = once in a while
> = now and then
> = sometimes
> = at times
> = from time to time

TEST 17

Directions: The following questions are incomplete sentences. You are to choose the one word that best completes the sentence.

1. A body of volunteers was organized to aid the helpless people in their _____ for survival.
   - (A) portion
   - (B) restraint
   - (C) defense
   - (D) struggle   (   )

2. Sarah put in a special _____ for an extra day's holiday so that she could attend her friend's wedding.
   - (A) inquiry
   - (B) proposal
   - (C) request
   - (D) ambition   (   )

3. The custom of keeping the dead bodies in their homes for three days before burial still _____ in this mountain area.
   - (A) advances
   - (B) insures
   - (C) bargains
   - (D) prevails   (   )

4. Postal _____ are determined primarily by the class and weight of the parcel mailed.
   - (A) prizes
   - (B) fees
   - (C) fares
   - (D) tolls   (   )

5. Honor cannot be _____ in inches or counted like money.
   - (A) measured
   - (B) divided
   - (C) compared
   - (D) revised   (   )

6. All night, the wind _____ through the tiny crack in the window.
   - (A) ground
   - (B) grumbled
   - (C) roared
   - (D) whistled   (   )

7. John's outstanding performance in the competition proved that he was a _____ winner.
   - (A) worthwhile
   - (B) worthy
   - (C) worth
   - (D) worthless   (   )

8. Paul was so _____ about his baldness that he wore a hat, whether it was winter or summer.
   (A) self-composed
   (B) self-centered
   (C) self-conscious
   (D) self-confident   (   )

9. John Smith and Peter White were, _____, the silver and bronze medal winners in this race.
   (A) repeatedly
   (B) respectively
   (C) respectably
   (D) respectfully   (   )

10. Henry told me to lock the door and I acted _____.
    (A) accordingly
    (B) likewise
    (C) gratefully
    (D) typically   (   )

11. Our team was not in good form. _____, the best player had broken his leg in a car accident. It was no wonder that we lost the game.
    (A) To say nothing of
    (B) To have two strikes against one
    (C) Once in a blue moon
    (D) To make matters worse (   )

12. Robert _____ a cold when he went to Italy on business.
    (A) came up with
    (B) came down with
    (C) came away with
    (D) came out with   (   )

13. It's _____ in the regulations that you can take 20 kilos of luggage with you.
    (A) laid aside
    (B) laid off
    (C) laid down
    (D) laid up   (   )

14. I have several plans in mind, and one _____ seems good and feasible.
    (A) in general
    (B) in part
    (C) in particular
    (D) in person   (   )

15. Mr. White is over eighty, but he still _____ his position as chairman of the board and will not retire.
    (A) goes in for
    (B) gets on with
    (C) falls back on
    (D) holds on to   (   )

TEST 17 詳解

1. (**D**) A body of volunteers was organized to aid the helpless people in their <u>struggle</u> for survival.

有一批義工組織起來，幫助那些無助的人<u>努力</u>生存下去。

(A) portion ('porʃən) *n.* 部分 (= *part*)

(B) restraint (rɪ'strent) *n.* 抑制　　restrain *v.* 抑制；克制 < *from* >

(C) defense (dɪ'fɛns) *n.* 防衛　　defend *v.*

(D) *struggle* ('strʌgl̩) *n. v.* 努力；奮鬥；掙扎

* *a body of* 一批　　organize ('ɔrgən,aɪz) *v.* 組織

aid (ed) *v.* 幫助 (= *help*)　　survival (sə'vaɪvl̩) *n.* 生存

2. (**C**) Sarah put in a special <u>request</u> for an extra day's holiday so that she could attend her friend's wedding.

莎拉提出特別<u>要求</u>，希望能多休一天假，好去參加她朋友的婚禮。

(A) inquiry ('ɪnkwərɪ , ɪn'kwaɪrɪ) *n.* 詢問

inquire *v.*

(B) proposal (prə'pozl̩) *n.* 提議；求婚

propose *v.*

(C) *request* (rɪ'kwɛst) *n. v.* 要求

(D) ambition (æm'bɪʃən) *n.* 抱負；志願　　ambitious *adj.* 有抱負的

* *put in* 提出 (文件、要求等)　　attend (ə'tɛnd) *v.* 參加

> acquire (ə'kwaɪr) *v.* 獲得
> inquire (ɪn'kwaɪr) *v.* 詢問
> require (rɪ'kwaɪr) *v.* 需要

> pose (poz) *v.* 擺姿勢　　impose (ɪm'poz) *v.* 加於　　propose (prə'poz) *v.* 提議；求婚
> oppose (ə'poz) *v.* 反對　　expose (ɪk'spoz) *v.* 暴露　　dispose (dɪ'spoz) *v.* 配置
> suppose (sə'poz) *v.* 認為　　compose (kəm'poz) *v.* 組成　　repose (rɪ'poz) *v.* 休息

3. (**D**) The custom of keeping the dead bodies in their homes for three days before burial still <u>prevails</u> in this mountain area.

葬禮前要把過世者的遺體放在家裡三天，這個習俗在此山區仍然很<u>盛行</u>。

(A) advance (əd'væns) *v. n.* 前進；進步

(B) insure (ɪn'ʃur) *v.* 保險　　insurance *n.*　　*cf.* assure *v.* 確保；保證

(C) bargain ('bɑrgɪn) *v.* 討價還價 (= *haggle*)　　*n.* 交易；便宜貨

(D) *prevail* (prɪ'vel) *v.* 盛行；普及

* burial ('bɛrɪəl) *n.* 葬禮

4. (**B**) Postal <u>fees</u> are determined primarily by the class and weight of the parcel (which is) mailed.
郵資的決定主要在於郵寄包裹的類別和重量。
　　(A) prize〔praɪz〕*n.* 獎；獎金；獎品　　例：win the first *prize* 得第一名
　　(B) *fee*〔fi〕*n.* 費用
　　　　例：admission / membership / a doctor's *fee* 入場費/會費/出診費
　　(C) fare〔fɛr〕*n.* (交通工具的) 運費；票價　　例：bus *fare* 公車票價
　　(D) toll〔tol〕*n.* (道路、橋樑、長途電話) 過路費；通行費
　　* postal〔'postḷ〕*adj.* 郵件的
　　　primarily〔'praɪ,mɛrəlɪ〕*adv.* 主要地
　　　class〔klæs〕*n.* 類別　　　parcel〔'pɑrsḷ〕*n.* 包裹

5. (**A**) Honor cannot be <u>measured</u> in inches or counted like money.
榮譽是不能用英吋<u>衡量</u>，或是像錢一樣用數的。
　　(A) *measure*〔'mɛʒɚ〕*v.* 衡量；測量　　*n.* 措施　　take measures 採取措施
　　(B) divide〔də'vaɪd〕*v.* 分開　　division *n.* 分開；除法
　　(C) compare〔kəm'pɛr〕*v.* 比較　　comparison *n.*
　　(D) revise〔rɪ'vaɪz〕*v.* 修訂　　revision *n.*

6. (**D**) All night, the wind <u>whistled</u> through the tiny crack in the window.
整個晚上，風穿過窗戶微小的縫隙<u>颼颼作響</u>。
　　(A) grind〔graɪnd〕*v.* 磨碎【三態變化為：grind-ground-ground】
　　(B) grumble〔'grʌmbḷ〕*v.* 抱怨 (= *complain*)
　　(C) roar〔ror〕*v.* 吼叫；(海、風、火、大砲等) 轟鳴
　　(D) *whistle*〔'hwɪsḷ〕*v.* 吹口哨；鳴笛；(風) 颼颼作響
　　* tiny〔'taɪnɪ〕*adj.* 微小的　　　crack〔kræk〕*n.* 縫隙

7. (**B**) John's outstanding performance in the competition proved that he was a <u>worthy</u> winner. 約翰在比賽中的傑出表現，證明了他得獎是<u>當之無愧</u>。
　　(A) worthwhile〔'wɝθ,hwaɪl〕*adj.* 值得花時間、精力的
　　　　例：a *worthwhile* task 值得做的工作
　　(B) *worthy*〔'wɝðɪ〕*adj.* 值得的；值得尊敬/考慮的 (= *respectable*)
　　　　例：a *worthy* gentleman 令人敬仰的紳士
　　(C) worth〔wɝθ〕*adj.* 值得的 (不可置於名詞前)
　　(D) worthless〔'wɝθlɪs〕*adj.* 沒有價值的 (↔ priceless 無價的；非常珍貴的)
　　* outstanding〔aʊt'stændɪŋ〕*adj.* 傑出的　　performance〔pɚ'fɔrməns〕*n.* 表現
　　　competition〔,kɑmpə'tɪʃən〕*n.* 競爭；比賽

8. (**C**) Paul was so <u>self-conscious</u> about his baldness that he wore a hat, whether it was winter or summer.

保羅非常<u>在意</u>自己的禿頭，所以無論多天、夏天他都戴著帽子。

(A) self-composed〔ˌsɛlfkəm'pozd〕 *adj.* 鎮靜的；沉著的 (= *composed* ; *calm*)

(B) self-centered〔'sɛlf'sɛntəd〕 *adj.* 以自我為中心的；自私的 (= *selfish*)

(C) *self-conscious*〔'sɛlf'kɑnʃəs〕 *adj.* 自覺的；不自然的

(D) self-confident〔'sɛlf'kɑnfədənt〕 *adj.* 有自信的

＊baldness〔'bɔldnɪs〕 *n.* 禿頭

9. (**B**) John Smith and Peter White were, <u>respectively</u>, the silver and bronze medal winners in this race.

約翰‧史密斯和彼得‧懷特，<u>分別</u>是此次賽跑的銀牌和銅牌得主。

(A) repeatedly〔rɪ'pitɪdlɪ〕 *adv.* 反覆地；一再地 (= *again and again*)

(B) *respectively*〔rɪ'spɛktɪvlɪ〕 *adv.* 分別地；各自地 (= *individually*)

(C) respectably〔rɪ'spɛktəblɪ〕 *adv.* 高尚地 (= *decently*)

(D) respectfully〔rɪ'spɛktfəlɪ〕 *adv.* 有禮貌地；恭敬地 (= *politely*)

＊bronze〔brɑnz〕 *adj.* 青銅的　　medal〔'mɛdl̩〕 *n.* 獎牌

race〔res〕 *n.* 賽跑

10. (**A**) Henry told me to lock the door and I acted <u>accordingly</u>.

亨利叫我去把門鎖上，我便<u>照辦</u>。

(A) *accordingly*〔ə'kɔrdɪŋlɪ〕 *adv.* 依照；照著

(B) likewise〔'laɪk,waɪz〕 *adv.* 同樣地 (= *similarly* ; *in the same way*)

(C) gratefully〔'gretfəlɪ〕 *adv.* 感激地 (= *with gratitude* ; *thankfully*)

(D) typically〔'tɪpɪklɪ〕 *adv.* 典型地 (= *characteristically*)；通常 (= *normally*)

11. (**D**) Our team was not in good form. <u>To make matters worse</u>, the best player had broken his leg in a car accident. It was no wonder that we lost the game.

我們隊上狀況不是很好。<u>更糟的是</u>，全隊最好的選手又在車禍中摔斷了腿。難怪我們比賽會輸。

(A) to say nothing of 更別提 (= *not to mention* ; *not to speak of*)

(B) have two strikes against one 處於不利地位【此片語源於棒球，

如果一個球員已經得到兩好球，再一次好球就要被三振出局了】

strike〔straɪk〕 *n.* 好球

(C) once in a blue moon 罕見地 (= *rarely* ; *seldom*)

(D) *to make matters worse* 更糟的是 (= *what is worse* ; *worse yet*)

＊*in good form* 狀況良好　　*no wonder* 難怪

12. (**B**) Robert <u>came down with</u> a cold when he went to Italy on business.
羅伯特到義大利出差時<u>得了</u>感冒。

 (A) come up with　想到（構想、計劃）

 (B) *come down with*　感染（疾病）；因～病倒

 (C) come away with　懷著（某種感情、印象）離開

  例：She *came away with* a sad feeling.　她帶著悲傷的心情離開了。

 (D) come out with　發表（= *make known*）；說出（= *say*; *utter*）

  例：The newspaper *came out with* the story on the front page.

   該家報紙把這則報導刊登在頭版。

   He rarely *came out with* such clever remarks.　他難得說出這麼聰明的話。

 ＊*on business*　出差（↔ *for pleasure*　遊玩）

13. (**C**) It's <u>laid down</u> in the regulations that you can take 20 kilos of luggage with you.
規則裡有<u>訂定</u>，你可以隨身攜帶二十公斤的行李。

 (A) lay aside　放置一旁；擱置（= *give up*）；儲蓄（= *save*）

 (B) lay off　暫時解雇（= *dismiss*; *discharge*）

 (C) *lay down*　放下；訂定（規則、計劃等）

 (D) lay up　貯存；保留（= *store for future*）

 ＊regulation (ˌrɛgjəˈleʃən) *n.* 規則（= *rule*）

 luggage (ˈlʌgɪdʒ) *n.* 行李（= *baggage*）

14. (**C**) I have several plans in mind, and one <u>in particular</u> seems good and feasible.
我心裡有幾個計劃，<u>特別</u>是其中一個似乎很不錯、蠻可行的。

 (A) in general　大略地（= *generally*）

 (B) in part　部分地（= *partly*）

 (C) *in particular*　尤其；特別是（= *particularly*）

 (D) in person　親自（= *personally*）

 ＊feasible (ˈfizəbl̩) *adj.* 可行的

15. (**D**) Mr. White is over eighty, but he still <u>holds on to</u> his position as chairman of the board and will not retire.
懷特先生已經八十多歲了，但他仍然<u>霸</u>著董事會主席的位子，不肯退休。

 (A) go in for　喜歡；愛好（= *like*; *take to*）

 (B) get on with　與～和睦相處（= *get along with*）

 (C) fall back on　依靠（= *rely on*; *turn to*）

 (D) *hold on to*　抓住（= *grasp*; *seize*）

 ＊position (pəˈzɪʃən) *n.* 職位　　chairman (ˈtʃɛrmən) *n.* 主席

 board (bord) *n.* 董事會

TEST 18

Directions: The following questions are incomplete sentences. You are to choose the one word that best completes the sentence.

1. The author was a _____ in modern literature, and his free style of writing was once severely criticized by traditional writers.
   - (A) trainee
   - (B) pioneer
   - (C) spectator
   - (D) comedian
   (　)

2. I couldn't resist his _____ in pressing the invitation and finally agreed to go to his party.
   - (A) assistance
   - (B) existence
   - (C) distance
   - (D) persistence
   (　)

3. The scandal concerning the minister hit the _____ and became widely known to everyone.
   - (A) headlines
   - (B) deadlines
   - (C) outlines
   - (D) underlines
   (　)

4. The morning dew soon _____ under the bright sun.
   - (A) evaluated
   - (B) evacuated
   - (C) evaporated
   - (D) eradicated
   (　)

5. To start the new language course, the teacher _____ the students with the alphabet using flash cards.
   - (A) acquainted
   - (B) isolated
   - (C) motivated
   - (D) submitted
   (　)

6. A big storm struck this small town last night. There was heavy rain and thunder _____ by lightning.
   - (A) vomited
   - (B) counteracted
   - (C) broadcasted
   - (D) accompanied
   (　)

7. I can't stand your _____ comments any more. Tell me directly what you are dissatisfied with.
   - (A) sarcastic
   - (B) complimentary
   - (C) agreeable
   - (D) humorous
   (　)

8. I think we will be unable to finish the project by this Friday. We will need an _____ week to get it done.
   (A) occasional
   (B) elementary
   (C) additional
   (D) inaccessible   ( )

9. Stewart tends to do everything _____. He can't tolerate disorder in any way.
   (A) potentially
   (B) systematically
   (C) confidentially
   (D) graciously   ( )

10. _____ speaking, the construction is estimated to cost one billion dollars and take about a year.
   (A) Repeatedly
   (B) Fairly
   (C) Conversely
   (D) Roughly   ( )

11. As he is still single, he always hangs out in pubs, drinking and chatting with his friends when _____.
   (A) on occasion
   (B) on call
   (C) off balance
   (D) off duty   ( )

12. Jessie always thinks of everything _____ money. She thinks money is power.
   (A) in terms of
   (B) in case of
   (C) at the cost of
   (D) in excess of   ( )

13. As a trustworthy man, he is the last to _____ his friends.
   (A) turn his back on
   (B) take the place of
   (C) keep track of
   (D) think the world of   ( )

14. Management is weak and morale is low. When the workers are treated unreasonably, the firm is definitely _____.
   (A) losing no time
   (B) playing its part
   (C) getting nowhere
   (D) keeping off   ( )

15. The host and hostess cordially welcomed their guests and told them to _____ whatever they liked.
   (A) concern themselves with
   (B) devote themselves to
   (C) help themselves to
   (D) accustom themselves to   ( )

TEST 18 詳解

1. (**B**) The author was a <u>pioneer</u> in modern literature, and his free style of writing was once severely criticized by traditional writers.
   這位作家是現代文學的<u>先驅</u>，他自由的寫作風格，曾經受到傳統作家嚴厲的批評。

   (A) trainee〔tren'i〕*n.* 受訓者（↔ trainer 訓練者）
   (B) *pioneer*〔͵paɪə'nɪr〕*n.* 先驅；先鋒
   (C) spectator〔'spɛktetə〕*n.* 觀衆（= *viewer*）
   (D) comedian〔kə'midɪən〕*n.* 喜劇演員

   * author〔'ɔθə〕*n.* 作者；作家（= writer）　　literature〔'lɪtərətʃə〕*n.* 文學
     severely〔sə'vɪrlɪ〕*adv.* 嚴厲地　　criticize〔'krɪtə͵saɪz〕*v.* 批評

2. (**D**) I couldn't resist his <u>persistence</u> in pressing the invitation and finally agreed to go to his party.
   我禁不起他一再<u>堅持</u>強迫邀請，終於同意去參加他的舞會。

   (A) assistance〔ə'sɪstəns〕*n.* 協助；輔助（= *help*）　　assist *v.* 協助
   (B) existence〔ɪg'zɪstəns〕*n.* 存在　　exist *v.* 存在
   (C) distance〔'dɪstəns〕*n.* 距離　　insist *v.* < *on* >
   (D) *persistence*〔pə'sɪstəns〕*n.* 堅持；持久 < *in* >　　persist *v.* < *in* >

   * resist〔rɪ'zɪst〕*v.* 抵抗；抗拒　　press〔prɛs〕*v.* 壓迫；強迫；催促

   > **-sist** 為表示「站」的字根　　<u>assist</u>〔ə'sɪst〕*v.* 幫助　　　<u>exist</u>〔ɪg'zɪst〕*v.* 存在
   > <u>insist</u>〔ɪn'sɪst〕*v.* 堅持　　　　<u>subsist</u>〔səb'sɪst〕*v.* 生存　　<u>desist</u>〔dɪ'zɪst〕*v.* 停止
   > <u>persist</u>〔pə'sɪst〕*v.* 堅持；持久　<u>consist</u>〔kən'sɪst〕*v.* 組成　　<u>resist</u>〔rɪ'zɪst〕*v.* 抵抗

3. (**A**) The scandal concerning the minister hit the <u>headlines</u> and became widely known to everyone.
   關於該部長的醜聞被媒體大肆報導，變成報紙<u>頭條</u>，衆所皆知。

   (A) *headline*〔'hɛd͵laɪn〕*n.*（報紙）標題　　***hit the headlines*** 變成報紙頭條
   (B) deadline〔'dɛd͵laɪn〕*n.* 最後期限　　meet a deadline 趕上最後期限
   (C) outline〔'aʊt͵laɪn〕*n.* 輪廓；綱要
   (D) underline〔'ʌndə͵laɪn〕*n.* 底線　　draw a line under 劃底線

   * scandal〔'skændl〕*n.* 醜聞
     concerning〔kən'sɜnɪŋ〕*prep.* 關於（= *about*）
     minister〔'mɪnɪstə〕*n.* 部長

4. (**C**) The morning dew soon <u>evaporated</u> under the bright sun.
　　早晨的露珠在耀眼的陽光下很快就<u>蒸發</u>了。

　　　(A) evaluate〔ɪ'væljʊ,et〕*v.* 評估
　　　　　value *n.* 價值
　　　(B) evacuate〔ɪ'vækjʊ,et〕*v.* 撤離；疏散
　　　(C) *evaporate*〔ɪ'væpə,ret〕*v.* 蒸發（= *vaporize*）
　　　(D) eradicate〔ɪ'rædɪ,ket〕*v.* 消滅；撲滅
　　　* dew〔dju〕*n.* 露珠

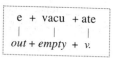

```
e  +  vacu  + ate
|        |       |
out + empty  +  v.
```

```
e  +  radic + ate
|        |       |
out +  root  +  v.
```

5. (**A**) To start the new language course, the teacher <u>acquainted</u> the students with the alphabet using flash cards.
　　開始新的語言課程時，老師用閃視卡片，讓同學<u>熟悉</u>整組字母。

　　　(A) *acquaint*〔ə'kwent〕*v.* 使熟悉 < *with* >　　acquaintance *n.*
　　　(B) isolate〔'aɪsḷ,et〕*v.* 孤立；隔離　　isolation *n.*
　　　(C) motivate〔'motə,vet〕*v.* 激勵；給予動機　　motivation *n.*
　　　(D) submit〔səb'mɪt〕*v.* 屈服 < *to* >；提出
　　　* alphabet〔'ælfə,bɛt〕*n.*（整組）字母（*cf.* letter 單一個字母）
　　　　flash card 閃視卡片（寫著字母或圖畫的卡片，給初學者辨認）

6. (**D**) A big storm struck this small town last night. There was heavy rain and thunder <u>accompanied</u> by lightning.
　　昨晚一陣狂風暴雨侵襲這個小鎮，豪雨、打雷<u>夾雜</u>著閃電。

　　　(A) vomit〔'vɑmɪt〕*v.* 嘔吐（= *throw up*）
　　　(B) counteract〔,kaʊntə'ækt〕*v.* 抵消；中和（*counter* ⇒ *against*）
　　　(C) broadcast〔'brɔd,kæst〕*v. n.* 廣播
　　　(D) *accompany*〔ə'kʌmpənɪ〕*v.* 陪伴；伴隨（= *go with*）
　　　* strike〔straɪk〕*v.* 侵襲　　thunder〔'θʌndə〕*n.* 雷
　　　　lightning〔'laɪtnɪŋ〕*n.* 閃電

7. (**A**) I can't stand your <u>sarcastic</u> comments any more. Tell me directly what you are dissatisfied with.
　　我再也無法忍受你<u>諷刺</u>的評論了。請你直接告訴我你哪裡不滿意。

　　　(A) *sarcastic*〔sɑr'kæstɪk〕*adj.* 諷刺的（= *ironic*）
　　　(B) complimentary〔,kɑmplə'mɛntərɪ〕*adj.* 稱讚的（= *admiring*）；
　　　　　免費贈送的（= *free*）
　　　(C) agreeable〔ə'griəbḷ〕*adj.* 宜人的；令人愉快的
　　　(D) humorous〔'hjumərəs〕*adj.* 幽默的
　　　* stand〔stænd〕*v.* 忍受（= *put up with*）　　*not ~ any more* 不再 ~
　　　　comment〔'kɑmɛnt〕*n.* 評論（= *remark*）

8. (**C**) I think we will be unable to finish the project by this Friday. We will need an underline{additional} week to get it done. 我想我們在這個星期五前，是無法完成這個計劃的。我們將需要再一週的時間才能完成。

(A) occasional〔ə'keʒənl〕*adj.* 偶爾的
(B) elementary〔͵ɛlə'mɛntərɪ〕*adj.* 基本的（= *basic*；*fundamental*）
(C) *additional*〔ə'dɪʃənl〕*adj.* 額外的（= *extra*）
(D) inaccessible〔͵ɪnək'sɛsəbl〕*adj.* 難接近的；難到達的

＊project〔'prɑdʒɛkt〕*n.* 計劃

9. (**B**) Stewart tends to do everything systematically. He can't tolerate disorder in any way. 斯圖亞特習慣每件事都做得有條不紊。他無法忍受任何方面的混亂。

(A) potentially〔pə'tɛnʃəlɪ〕*adv.* 潛在地（= *possibly*）
(B) *systematically*〔͵sɪstə'mætɪklɪ〕*adv.* 有系統地；有條不紊地（= *methodically*）
(C) confidentially〔͵kɑnfə'dɛnʃəlɪ〕*adv.* 機密地
(D) graciously〔'greʃəslɪ〕*adv.* 和藹地；仁慈地（= *kindly*）

＊tolerate〔'tɑlə͵ret〕*v.* 忍受（= *stand*；*bear*）
　disorder〔dɪs'ɔrdə〕*n.* 混亂；無秩序

10. (**D**) Roughly speaking, the construction is estimated to cost one billion dollars and take about a year.
大致說來，這項建築根據估計，需要十億的經費，和一年的時間。

(A) repeatedly〔rɪ'pitɪdlɪ〕*adv.* 不斷地（= *again and again*）
(B) fairly〔'fɛrlɪ〕*adv.* 公平地（= *justly*）；相當地（= *rather*）
　　fairly speaking 平心而論
(C) conversely〔kən'vɜslɪ〕*adv.* 相反地　　conversely speaking 反過來說
(D) *roughly*〔'rʌflɪ〕*adv.* 大約地　　*roughly speaking* 大致說來

＊construction〔kən'strʌkʃən〕*n.* 建築　　estimate〔'ɛstə͵met〕*v.* 估計
　billion〔'bɪljən〕*n.* 十億

11. (**D**) As he is still single, he always hangs out in pubs, drinking and chatting with his friends when off duty.
由於他仍單身，他下班時總是常常到酒吧，和朋友喝酒聊天。

(A) on occasion 偶爾；有時（= *occasionally*；*once in a while*；*now and then*）
(B) on call 隨時聽候召喚的；隨傳隨到的
(C) off balance 失去平衡
(D) *off duty* 下班（↔ *on duty* 上班；執勤中）

＊single〔'sɪŋgl〕*adj.* 單身的　　*hang out* 常去

12. (**A**) Jessie always thinks of everything <u>in terms of</u> money.　She thinks money is
power.　傑西總是<u>以</u>錢的<u>觀點</u>來看事物。她認為金錢就是力量。
(A) *in terms of*　以～觀點、角度；關於
(B) in case of～　萬一～發生（= *if～happens*）
(C) at the cost of　付出～代價（= *at the expense/price of*）
(D) in excess of　超過（= *more than*；*greater than*；*exceeding*）

13. (**A**) As a trustworthy man, he is the last to <u>turn his back on</u> his friends.
身為一個值得信任的人，他是最不可能<u>背棄</u>朋友的人。
(A) *turn one's back on*　背棄（= *abandon*）
(B) take the place of　取代（= *replace*）
(C) keep track of　追蹤（= *follow*）；注意（= *pay attention to*）
(D) think the world of　非常重視、尊敬、賞識
* trustworthy〔'trʌst,wɝðɪ〕*adj.* 值得信任的　　**the last** 最不可能的

14. (**C**) Management is weak and morale is low.　When the workers are treated
unreasonably, the firm is definitely <u>getting nowhere</u>.　管理薄弱，士氣低
落。當員工受到不合理的對待時，這家公司一定是<u>無法成功</u>的。
(A) lose no time　不浪費時間
(B) play *one's* part　盡自己的本分（= *do one's part*）
(C) *get nowhere*　無進展；不能成功（↔ *get somewhere* 有點進展；有成果）
(D) keep off　讓開；不接近
* management〔'mænɪdʒmənt〕*n.* 管理　　morale〔mə'ræl〕*n.* 士氣
unreasonably〔ʌn'riznəblɪ〕*adv.* 不合理地
definitely〔'dɛfənɪtlɪ〕*adv.* 一定

15. (**C**) The host and hostess cordially welcomed their guests and told them to
<u>help themselves to</u> whatever they liked.
男主人和女主人熱誠地歡迎他們的賓客，並告訴他們，喜歡吃什麼<u>自己拿</u>。
(A) concern *oneself* with　有關；干涉；參與（= *be concerned with*）
(B) devote *oneself* to　致力於；獻身於（= *dedicate oneself to*；
be devoted/dedicated to）
(C) *help oneself to*　自行取用（食物）
(D) accustom *oneself* to　習慣於（= *be accustomed/used to*）
* host〔host〕*n.* 男主人　　hostess〔'hostɪs〕*n.* 女主人
cordially〔'kɔrdʒəlɪ〕*adv.* 熱誠地

TEST 19

Directions: The following questions are incomplete sentences. You are to choose the one word that best completes the sentence.

1. International disputes are often settled through diplomatic _____.
   - (A) specimens
   - (B) channels
   - (C) flavors
   - (D) features   ( )

2. The mayor expressed strong opposition because his municipal budget was _____ reduced by the central government.
   - (A) favorably
   - (B) drastically
   - (C) necessarily
   - (D) universally   ( )

3. Wherever she goes, the girl enchants everyone she meets. She really is a _____.
   - (A) globe-trotter
   - (B) takeoff
   - (C) strike-out
   - (D) knockout   ( )

4. The police suspected that he had been involved in the kidnapping and _____ all of his phone calls.
   - (A) monitored
   - (B) revised
   - (C) constituted
   - (D) convicted   ( )

5. The party is too crowded and noisy and annoying. I feel _____ to leave early.
   - (A) stirred
   - (B) slapped
   - (C) tempted
   - (D) bathed   ( )

6. His life was miserable; he was _____ by poverty and illness.
   - (A) crawled
   - (B) aided
   - (C) plagued
   - (D) scratched   ( )

7. Thousands of people went to the concert hall to listen to the performance of the famous _____.
   - (A) orchestra
   - (B) tunnel
   - (C) newlyweds
   - (D) personnel   ( )

8. The Spanish thought their fleet was so strong that it was _____.
   However, it was defeated by the British navy in 1588.
   (A) understated   (B) defective
   (C) invincible   (D) distinctive   (   )

9. Man is _____. What really counts is not how long one lives but
   how well one lives.
   (A) loyal   (B) royal
   (C) moral   (D) mortal   (   )

10. Jessica is always _____ dressed. In other words, she always
    dresses in the latest fashion.
    (A) briefly   (B) rigidly
    (C) trendily   (D) vaguely   (   )

11. Before a man's wedding, his male friends often hold a stag party
    for him where they drink and dance and _____.
    (A) take the night shift (B) take a night off
    (C) have an early night   (D) make a night of it   (   )

12. We will have to _____ if we don't want to be late for the movie.
    (A) step down   (B) step back
    (C) step aside   (D) step on it   (   )

13. He is _____ bruises because he accidentally fell down the stairs.
    (A) a mass of   (B) a series of
    (C) a matter of   (D) a nice bit of   (   )

14. Clothing made of denim has _____ in the past few years. You
    can see denim clothes, bags, and even shoes.
    (A) caught on   (B) caught up
    (C) taken on   (D) taken up   (   )

15. I don't feel like going out tonight. I feel a little _____.
    (A) out of bloom   (B) out of common
    (C) out of sorts   (D) out of hand   (   )

TEST 19 詳解

1. (**B**) International disputes are often settled through diplomatic <u>channels</u>.
國際間的爭議通常透過外交<u>途徑</u>來解決。

    (A) specimen〔'spɛsəmən〕*n.* 樣品；標本

    (B) *channel*〔'tʃænl〕*n.* 海峽；途徑；頻道

    (C) flavor〔'flevɚ〕*n.* 味道；風味

    (D) feature〔'fitʃɚ〕*n.* 特色

    * international〔,ɪntɚ'næʃənl〕*adj.* 國際的   dispute〔dɪ'spjut〕*n.* 爭議

    settle〔'sɛtl〕*v.* 解決   diplomatic〔,dɪplə'mætɪk〕*adj.* 外交的

2. (**B**) The mayor expressed strong opposition because his municipal budget was
<u>drastically</u> reduced by the central government.
市長表達出強烈的不滿，因爲他的市政預算被中央政府<u>大幅</u>刪減。

    (A) favorably〔'fevərəblɪ〕*adv.* 贊成地；有利地

    (B) *drastically*〔'dræstɪkəlɪ〕*adv.* 激烈地；大幅地（= *radically*）

    (C) necessarily〔'nɛsə,sɛrəlɪ〕*adv.* 必定；必然（= *certainly*）

    (D) universally〔,junə'vɝslɪ〕*adv.* 普遍地；一般地（= *generally*）

    * mayor〔'meɚ, mɛr〕*n.* 市長   opposition〔,apə'zɪʃən〕*n.* 反對；異議

    municipal〔mju'nɪsəpl〕*adj.* 市的   budget〔'bʌdʒɪt〕*n.* 預算

3. (**D**) Wherever she goes, the girl enchants everyone she meets. She really is a
<u>knockout</u>. 那個女孩所到之處，人人爲她著迷。她真是<u>令人傾倒</u>。

    (A) globe-trotter〔'glob,tratɚ〕*n.* 環遊世界者   trot〔trat〕*v.* 快步走

    (B) takeoff〔'tek,ɔf〕*n.*（飛機）起飛（↔ landing ; touchdown 降落）

        take off *v.* 起飛   land *v.* 降落（= *touch down*）

    (C) strike-out〔'straɪk,aʊt〕*n.*（棒球）三振   strike〔straɪk〕*n.*（棒球）好球

        strike out *v.* 使（打者）三振出局

    (D) *knockout*〔'nak,aʊt〕*n.*（拳擊）擊倒（簡稱爲 KO）；有吸引力的人或物

        knock out *v.* 擊倒；使潰敗；使吃驚

    * enchant〔ɪn'tʃænt〕*v.* 使著迷（= *fascinate*）

4. (**A**) The police suspected that he had been involved in the kidnapping and <u>monitored</u> all of his phone calls.

警方懷疑他涉及這件綁架案，而<u>監聽</u>他所有的電話。

(A) ***monitor*** 〔ˈmɑnətɚ〕 *v.* 監視；監聽　　*n.* 監視器；（電腦）螢幕

(B) revise 〔rɪˈvaɪz〕 *v.* 修訂；改正　　　revision 〔rɪˈvɪʒən〕 *n.*

(C) constitute 〔ˈkɑnstəˌtjut〕 *v.* 組成

　　constitution 〔ˌkɑnstəˈtjuʃən〕 *n.* 構成；體格；憲法

　　例：Seven days *constitute* a week. 一週有七天。（部分<u>組成</u>整體）

　　　　= Seven days *make up* a week.

　　　　= A week *is constituted of* seven days.（整體由部分<u>組成</u>）

　　　　= A week *is made up of* seven days.

　　　　= A week *consists of* seven days.（只有主動用法）

　　　　= A week *is composed of* seven days.（只有被動用法）

(D) convict 〔kənˈvɪkt〕 *v.* 判決 < *of* ～罪 >　〔ˈkɑnvɪkt〕 *n.* 罪犯

＊suspect 〔səˈspɛkt〕 *v.* 懷疑　　involve 〔ɪnˈvɑlv〕 *v.* 牽涉；捲入

　 kidnapping 〔ˈkɪdnæpɪŋ〕 *n.* 綁架

5. (**C**) The party is too crowded and noisy and annoying. I feel <u>tempted</u> to leave early.

這個舞會太擠、太吵，令人心煩。我<u>想要</u>早點兒離開。

(A) stir 〔stɝ〕 *v.* 攪拌；使激動

(B) slap 〔slæp〕 *v. n.* 打耳光

(C) ***tempt*** 〔tɛmpt〕 *v.* 引誘　　***be/feel tempted to + V.*** 想要～

(D) bathe 〔beð〕 *v.* 洗澡；沐浴；籠罩　　bath 〔bæθ〕 *n.* 洗澡；浴缸

＊annoying 〔əˈnɔɪɪŋ〕 *adj.* 令人生厭的；使人心煩的

6. (**C**) His life was miserable; he was <u>plagued</u> by poverty and illness.

他的生活非常悲慘，貧病交<u>迫</u>。

(A) crawl 〔krɔl〕 *v.* 爬行（= *creep* ）

(B) aid 〔ed〕 *v. n.* 幫助（= *help* ）

(C) ***plague*** 〔pleg〕 *n.* 瘟疫；黑死病　*v.* 煩擾；折磨（= *trouble* ）

(D) scratch 〔skrætʃ〕 *v. n.* 搔癢；抓傷

＊miserable 〔ˈmɪzərəbl̩〕 *adj.* 悲慘的　　poverty 〔ˈpɑvɚtɪ〕 *n.* 貧窮

7. (**A**) Thousands of people went to the concert hall to listen to the performance of the famous <u>orchestra</u>.

數千人來到音樂廳，聆聽這個知名<u>管弦樂團</u>的表演。

(A) ***orchestra*** (ˈɔrkɪstrə) *n.* 管弦樂團

(B) tunnel (ˈtʌnḷ) *n.* 隧道

(C) newlyweds (ˈnjulɪˌwɛdz) *n. pl.* 新婚夫婦

(D) personnel (ˌpɝsṇˈɛl) *n.* 全體職員（集合名詞）(= *staff*)

8. (**C**) The Spanish thought their fleet was so strong that it was <u>invincible</u>. However, it was defeated by the British navy in 1588.

西班牙人認為他們的艦隊非常強，是<u>無敵的</u>。然而，他們卻在一五八八年被英國海軍擊敗。

(A) understated (ˌʌndɚˈstetɪd) *adj.* 低調的　　understate *v.* 輕描淡寫

(B) defective (dɪˈfɛktɪv) *adj.* 有缺點的；不完美的 (= *faulty* ; *imperfect*)

(C) ***invincible*** (ɪnˈvɪnsəbḷ) *adj.* 不敗的；無敵的 (= *unbeatable* ; *unconquerable*)

(D) distinctive (dɪˈstɪŋktɪv) *adj.* 獨特的 (= *unique* ; *characteristic*)

＊fleet (flit) *n.* 艦隊　　defeat (dɪˈfit) *v.* 擊敗　　navy (ˈnevɪ) *n.* 海軍

9. (**D**) Man is <u>mortal</u>. What really counts is not how long one lives but how well one lives.

人<u>難免一死</u>。真正重要的不是活多久，而是活得多有意義。

(A) loyal (ˈlɔɪəl) *adj.* 忠實的 (= *faithful*)

(B) royal (ˈrɔɪəl) *adj.* 皇家的　　royal family 皇室

(C) moral (ˈmɔrəl) *adj.* 道德的　*n.* 道德教訓

(D) ***mortal*** (ˈmɔrtḷ) *adj.* 會死的　　immortal *adj.* 不朽的

＊count (kaʊnt) *v.* 重要 (= *matter*)

10. (**C**) Jessica is always <u>trendily</u> dressed. In other words, she always dresses in the latest fashion.

潔西卡總是打扮得很<u>時髦</u>。換句話說，她總是穿著最新流行的服裝款式。

(A) briefly (ˈbriflɪ) *adv.* 簡短地 (= *for a short time*)

(B) rigidly (ˈrɪdʒɪdlɪ) *adv.* 嚴格地 (= *strictly* ; *severely* ; *harshly*)

(C) ***trendily*** (ˈtrɛndɪlɪ) *adv.* 時髦地 (= *fashionably* ; *stylishly*)

(D) vaguely (ˈveglɪ) *adv.* 模糊地 (= *unclearly* ; *dimly*)

＊***in other words*** 換句話說　　fashion (ˈfæʃən) *n.* 流行 (= *vogue*)

11. (**D**) Before a man's wedding, his male friends often hold a stag party for him where they drink and dance and <u>make a night of it</u>.

在男人結婚前，他的男性朋友常會爲他舉行單身漢派對，他們喝酒、跳舞，<u>狂歡一夜</u>。

(A) take the night shift 值夜班　　shift〔ʃɪft〕*n.* 輪値

(B) take/get/have a night off 休息一晚

(C) have an early night 早睡

(D) *make a night of it* 痛快玩一晚；狂歡一夜

＊wedding〔'wɛdɪŋ〕*n.* 婚禮

　 stag〔stæg〕*n.* 成熟的雄鹿；（宴會中）不帶女伴的男士

　 stag party 單身漢派對（不帶女伴，只限男士參加）

12. (**D**) We will have to <u>step on it</u> if we don't want to be late for the movie.

如果不想看電影遲到的話，我們得<u>趕快走了</u>。

(A) step down 走下來；辭職；下台（ = *resign* ）

(B) step back 後退；退出

(C) step aside 靠邊；讓路；退出

(D) *step on it* 踩油門；趕快（ = *hurry up* ）

13. (**A**) He is <u>a mass of</u> bruises because he accidentally fell down the stairs.

他<u>全身都是</u>瘀傷，因爲他不小心從樓梯上摔下來。

(A) *a mass of* 全是；遍佈著

　　例：The streets are *a mass of* confusion. *街道一片混亂。*

(B) a series of 一連串；一系列

　　例：*a series of* victories *一連串勝利*

　　　　a series of bird stamps *一整套、一系列的鳥類郵票*

(C) a matter of ～的事情、問題；大約（ = *about* ）

　　例：*a matter of* life and death *攸關生死的事情*

(D) a nice bit of 相當多的

　　例：have *a nice bit of* money *有相當多的錢*

　　比較：a bit of 一點點；一小塊

　　例：*a bit of* hope 一點點希望　　*a bit of* land 一小塊地

＊bruise〔bruz〕*n.* 瘀傷　　stair〔stɛr〕*n.* 樓梯

14. (**A**) Clothing made of denim has <u>caught on</u> in the past few years. You can see denim clothes, bags, and even shoes.

丹寧布製成的服飾近幾年來很<u>流行</u>。你可以看到
牛仔布的衣服、包包，甚至還有鞋子。

(A) *catch on* 受歡迎；流行（= *become popular*）

(B) catch up 趕上 < *with* >

(C) take on 呈現（情況、性質）（= *show*）；
雇用（= *hire*；*employ*）；從事（= *undertake*）

(D) take up 佔用（時間、空間）（= *occupy*）；開始（= *start*；*begin*）

＊be made of 由～（原料）製成

denim〔ˊdɛnəm〕*n.* 丹寧布；丁尼布（做牛仔褲的斜紋粗棉布）

15. (**C**) I don't feel like going out tonight. I feel a little <u>out of sorts</u>.

我今晚不想出門。我覺得<u>身體</u>有點兒<u>不舒服</u>。

(A) out of bloom 花已凋謝；顛峰期已過
（↔ *in bloom* 開花中；正值顛峰）

(B) out of (the) common 非凡的；不尋常的（= *unusual*；*extraordinary*）

(C) *out of sorts* 身體不舒服（= *unwell*；*under the weather*）；
心情不佳（= *not in a good mood*）

(D) out of hand 即時（= *immediately*）；失去控制（= *out of control*）
【↔ in hand 掌握中（= *under control*）】

＊feel like + V-ing 想要～

TEST 20

Directions: The following questions are incomplete sentences. You are to choose the one word that best completes the sentence.

1. The doctor tried _____ to save the patient's life, but in vain. She died anyway at last.
   - (A) smoothly
   - (B) desperately
   - (C) enormously
   - (D) conventionally   (   )

2. The engineers spared no effort in working toward the _____ of the latest design of the machine.
   - (A) infection
   - (B)) perfection
   - (C) affection
   - (D) affectation   (   )

3. His accomplishments far _____ his parents' expectations. They were so proud of him.
   - (A) exceeded
   - (B) proceeded
   - (C) preceded
   - (D) receded   (   )

4. Professor Wilson has the _____ of a born leader. Many of his students love him very much.
   - (A) chamber
   - (B) champion
   - (C) challenge
   - (D) charisma   (   )

5. I'm so sorry to have caused you so much inconvenience. Please accept my _____ apology.
   - (A) humane
   - (B) heated
   - (C) heartfelt
   - (D) hostile   (   )

6. I like winter better than summer. For me, cold is _____ to heat.
   - (A) prejudiced
   - (B) preferable
   - (C) honorable
   - (D) honorary   (   )

7. Leave it to me. I promise your suggestion will be _____ noted.
   - (A) duly
   - (B) gently
   - (C) radically
   - (D) namely   (   )

8. Communication satellites _____ messages and signals from country to country.

   (A) rehearse   (B) recite

   (C) refer   (D) relay   (   )

9. The memorial stamps were _____ to celebrate the 25th anniversary of the organization.

   (A) departed   (B) patented

   (C) enrolled   (D) issued   (   )

10. Maggie is such a superstitious girl that she does everything according to her _____. She never leaves home without consulting it.

   (A) horoscope   (B) intellect

   (C) instinct   (D) sensitivity   (   )

11. Look at the water bill for last month. Did we really consume that huge quantity of water? Perhaps we need to call a _____.

   (A) flatterer   (B) fastener

   (C) porter   (D) plumber   (   )

12. The boss decided to _____ the minor mistakes she had made because she was, by and large, an excellent and hard-working employee.

   (A) overcome   (B) overlook

   (C) overtake   (D) oversee   (   )

13. Dr. Jones is a _____ speaker who never makes his audience feel bored.

   (A) literary   (B) brutal

   (C) ridiculous   (D) dynamic   (   )

14. After the seminar, she did improve and has become _____ more confident in herself.

   (A) noticeably   (B) inevitably

   (C) scarcely   (D) tensely   (   )

15. A French "chateau" is the _____ of a "castle" in English.

   (A) illustration   (B) avenue

   (C) obedience   (D) equivalent   (   )

TEST 20 詳解

1. (**B**) The doctor tried <u>desperately</u> to save the patient's life, but in vain. She died anyway at last.

醫生拼命地試著要解救病人的生命，但徒勞無功。她最後還是死了。

(A) smoothly (ˈsmuðlɪ) *adv.* 平滑地；順利地 (= *easily* ; *effortlessly* ; *without difficulty*)

(B) *desperately* (ˈdɛspərɪtlɪ) *adv.* 拼命地；猛烈地；絕望地

(C) enormously (ɪˈnɔrməslɪ) *adv.* 龐大地；非常地 (= *hugely* ; *immensely* ; *extremely*)

(D) conventionally (kənˈvɛnʃənḷɪ) *adv.* 傳統地；千篇一律地 (= *traditionally* ; *conservatively*)

　＊*in vain* 徒勞地　　anyway (ˈɛnɪˌwe) *adv.* 還是；無論如何　　*at last* 最後

2. (**B**) The engineers spared no effort in working toward the <u>perfection</u> of the latest design of the machine.

工程師們不遺餘力，設計這部機器的最新款，到最<u>完美</u>的境界。

(A) infection (ɪnˈfɛkʃən) *n.* 傳染　　infect *v.*

(B) *perfection* (pɚˈfɛkʃən) *n.* 完美

　　perfect (pɚˈfɛkt) *v.* 使完美　 (ˈpɝfɪkt) *adj.* 完美的

(C) affection (əˈfɛkʃən) *n.* 情愛；感情 (= *love* ; *fondness*)

　　affect *v.* 影響；喜歡；假裝

(D) affectation (ˌæfɪkˈteʃən) *n.* 假裝；做作；裝模作樣 (= *pretension*)

　　＊spare (spɛr) *v.* 吝惜　　*spare no effort* 不遺餘力

　　latest (ˈletɪst) *adj.* 最新的　　design (dɪˈzaɪn) *n.* 設計

3. (**A**) His accomplishments far <u>exceeded</u> his parents' expectations. They were so proud of him. 他的成就遠遠<u>超過</u>他父母的期望。他們非常以他為榮。

(A) *exceed* (ɪkˈsid) *v.* 超過 (= *surpass* ; *go beyond*) 【ex = out ; ceed = go 】

(B) proceed (proˈsid) *v.* 前進；繼續進行 【pro = forward ; ceed = go 】

(C) precede (prɪˈsid) *v.* 在～之前；比～優先 【pre = before ; cede = go 】

(D) recede (rɪˈsid) *v.* 後退 【re = back ; cede = go 】

　　＊accomplishment (əˈkamplɪʃmənt) *n.* 成就

　　expectation (ˌɛkspɛkˈteʃən) *n.* 期望　　*be proud of* 以～為榮

【 -cede, -ceed, -cess = go 】

concede (kənˈsid) *v.* 讓步；承認

intercede (ˌɪntɚˈsid) *v.* 居中調停

excess (ɪkˈsɛs) *n.* 過多；超過

access (ˈæksɛs) *n.* 接近；進入

recess (rɪˈsɛs) *n.* 休息；休會

process (ˈprɑsɛs) *n.* 過程

success (səkˈsɛs) *n.* 成功

succeed (səkˈsid) *v.* 成功

4. (**D**) Professor Wilson has the <u>charisma</u> of a born leader. Many of his students love him very much.

威爾森教授具有天生的<u>領袖氣質</u>。他的許多學生都非常喜歡他。

(A) chamber〔'tʃembɚ〕*n.* 房間　　例：*chamber* music 室內樂

(B) champion〔'tʃæmpɪən〕*n.* 冠軍（指人或隊伍）

　　比較：championship〔'tʃæmpɪən,ʃɪp〕*n.* 冠軍（指頭銜或資格）；冠軍賽

(C) challenge〔'tʃælɪndʒ〕*n.* 挑戰

(D) *charisma*〔kə'rɪzmə〕*n.* 個人魅力；領袖氣質

∗ born〔bɔrn〕*adj.* 天生的

5. (**C**) I'm so sorry to have caused you so much inconvenience. Please accept my <u>heartfelt</u> apology.

非常對不起，造成你如此大的不便。請接受我<u>衷心的</u>道歉。

(A) humane〔hju'men〕*adj.* 人道的；仁愛的

　　比較：human〔'hjumən〕*adj.* 人類的

(B) heated〔'hitɪd〕*adj.* 加熱的；激烈的　　heat *n.* 熱　*v.* 加熱

(C) *heartfelt*〔'hɑrt,fɛlt〕*adj.* 衷心的（= *sincere* ）

(D) hostile〔'hɑstl̩〕*adj.* 敵對的；有敵意的　　hostility〔hɑs'tɪlətɪ〕*n.*

∗ apology〔ə'pɑlədʒɪ〕*n.* 道歉

6. (**B**) I like winter better than summer. For me, cold is <u>preferable</u> to heat.

我喜歡冬天勝過夏天。對我而言，冷<u>比熱好</u>。

(A) prejudiced〔'prɛdʒədɪst〕*adj.* 有偏見的 < *against* > (= *biased*)

(B) *preferable*〔'prɛfrəbl̩〕*adj.* 較好的；較受歡迎的 < *to* > (= *better*)

(C) honorable〔'ɑnərəbl̩〕*adj.* 光榮的；令人尊敬的 (= *admirable*)

(D) honorary〔'ɑnə,rɛrɪ〕*adj.* 榮譽的；名譽上的

　　例：*honorary* degree 榮譽學位

∗ *like* A *better than* B 喜歡 A 勝過 B (= *prefer* A *to* B)

7. (**A**) Leave it to me. I promise your suggestion will be <u>duly</u> noted.

這件事交給我來辦。我保證，你的提議會得到<u>充分的</u>注意。

(A) *duly*〔'djulɪ〕*adv.* 適當地；充分地；適時地 (= *properly*)

(B) gently〔'dʒɛntlɪ〕*adv.* 溫和地 (= *tenderly*；*softly*)

(C) radically〔'rædɪkl̩ɪ〕*adv.* 徹底地；激烈地 (= *drastically*；*thoroughly*)

(D) namely〔'nemlɪ〕*adv.* 也就是 (= *that is*)

∗ promise〔'prɑmɪs〕*v.* 承諾；保證　　note〔not〕*v.* 注意

8. (**D**) Communication satellites <u>relay</u> messages and signals from country to country.
　　 通訊衛星可以<u>轉播</u>國際之間的訊息和信號。

　　(A) rehearse〔rɪ'hɜs〕*v.* 預演；彩排　　rehearsal〔rɪ'hɜsḷ〕*n.*

　　(B) recite〔rɪ'saɪt〕*v.* 背誦　　recital〔rɪ'saɪtḷ〕*n.* 獨奏會；獨唱會

　　(C) refer〔rɪ'fɜ〕*v.* 參考；指示；提及 <*to*>　　reference〔'rɛfərəns〕*n.*

　　(D) *relay*〔rɪ'le〕*v.* 轉播；接力　　例：*relay* race 接力賽跑

　　* satellite〔'sætḷˌaɪt〕*n.* 衛星　　signal〔'sɪgnḷ〕*n.* 信號

9. (**D**) The memorial stamps were <u>issued</u> to celebrate the 25th anniversary of the
　　 organization. 這組紀念郵票的<u>發行</u>，是爲了慶祝該組織成立二十五週年。

　　(A) depart〔dɪ'part〕*v.* 出發；離開（= *leave*）　　departure *n.* (↔ *arrival*)

　　(B) patent〔'pætṇt〕*v.* 取得專利　　*n.* 專利（權）

　　(C) enroll〔ɪn'rol〕*v.* 登記（入會）；入學；入伍　　enrollment *n.*

　　(D) *issue*〔'ɪʃjʊ〕*v.* 發行；發布　　*n.* 發行；發布；（刊物的）一期

　　* memorial〔mə'morɪəl〕*adj.* 紀念的
　　　anniversary〔ˌænə'vɜsərɪ〕*n.* 週年紀念
　　　organization〔ˌɔrgənə'zeʃən〕*n.* 組織；團體

10. (**A**) Maggie is such a superstitious girl that she does everything according to her
　　 <u>horoscope</u>. She never leaves home without consulting it. 瑪姬是個非常迷信
　　的女孩，她做每件事都要參照<u>星象運勢</u>。她出門一定要查詢一下。

　　(A) *horoscope*〔'hɔrəˌskop〕*n.* 星象

　　(B) intellect〔'ɪntḷˌɛkt〕*n.* 智力；理解力

horo + scope
  | |
hour + *look*

　　(C) instinct〔'ɪnstɪŋkt〕*n.* 本能

　　(D) sensitivity〔ˌsɛnsə'tɪvətɪ〕*n.* 敏感度

　　* superstitious〔ˌsupə'stɪʃəs〕*adj.* 迷信的　　consult〔kən'sʌlt〕*v.* 查詢

11. (**D**) Look at the water bill for last month. Did we really consume that huge
　　 quantity of water? Perhaps we need to call a <u>plumber</u>. 看看上個月的水費。
　　我們眞的有用掉那麼多的水嗎？也許我們得找個<u>水管工人</u>了。

　　(A) flatterer〔'flætərə〕*n.* 奉承者；馬屁精　　flatter *v.* 諂媚；奉承

　　(B) fastener〔'fæsṇə〕*n.* 繫緊、固定的東西（如釦子、拉鍊、夾子等）
　　　fasten *v.* 繫緊

　　(C) porter〔'portə〕*n.*（車站、機場、飯店的）搬運工

　　(D) *plumber*〔'plʌmə〕*n.* 水管工人　　plumbing *n.* 水管工程

　　* bill〔bɪl〕*n.* 帳單　　consume〔kən'sum〕*v.* 消耗；使用
　　　quantity〔'kwɑntətɪ〕*n.* 量（= *amount*）

12. (**B**) The boss decided to <u>overlook</u> the minor mistakes she had made because she was, by and large, an excellent and hard-working employee. 老闆決定原諒她所犯的小錯誤，因為整體而言，她是個優秀且工作認眞的員工。

    (A) overcome (ˏovɚˋkʌm) v. 克服；打敗 (= *conquer*；*defeat*)

    (B) ***overlook*** (ˏovɚˋluk) v. 原諒 (= *excuse*；*forgive*)；忽略 (= *ignore*)；俯瞰；監督

    (C) overtake (ˏovɚˋtek) v. 趕上；超過；超車 (= *pass*)

    (D) oversee (ˏovɚˋsi) v. 監督 (= *overlook*；*supervise*)

    * minor (ˋmaɪnɚ) *adj.* 輕微的；較不重要的

    by and large 整體而言 (= *in general*)

    employee (ˏɛmplɔɪˋi) *n.* 員工【employ *v.* 雇用，-ee 表示「被動者」】

13. (**D**) Dr. Jones is a <u>dynamic</u> speaker who never makes his audience feel bored. 瓊斯博士演講時非常<u>有活力</u>，他從不會讓他的聽衆感到無聊。

    (A) literary (ˋlɪtəˏrɛrɪ) *adj.* 文學的　　literature *n.* 文學

    (B) brutal (ˋbrutḷ) *adj.* 殘忍的；無情的 (= *cruel*；*ruthless*)

    (C) ridiculous (rɪˋdɪkjələs) *adj.* 荒謬的；可笑的 (= *absurd*)

    (D) ***dynamic*** (daɪˋnæmɪk) *adj.* 有活力的 (= *energetic*；*vigorous*)

    * audience (ˋɔdɪəns) *n.* 聽衆；觀衆　　bored (bord) *adj.* 無聊的

14. (**A**) After the seminar, she did improve and has become <u>noticeably</u> more confident in herself. 在座談會之後，她眞的有改善，而且變得<u>明顯地</u>對自己比較有信心了。

    (A) ***noticeably*** (ˋnotɪsəblɪ) *adv.* 明顯地 (= *clearly*)

    (B) inevitably (ɪnˋɛvətəblɪ) *adv.* 無法避免地 (= *unavoidably*)

    (C) scarcely (ˋskɛrslɪ) *adv.* 幾乎不 (= *hardly*；*barely*)

    (D) tensely (ˋtɛnslɪ) *adv.* 緊張地；生硬地 (= *nervously*；*anxiously*)

    * seminar (ˋsɛməˏnɑr) *n.* 座談會；研討會

    confident (ˋkɑnfədənt) *adj.* 有信心的

15. (**D**) A French "chateau" is the <u>equivalent</u> of a "castle" in English. 法文中的 "chateau" <u>等於</u>英文中的 "castle" (城堡) 。

    (A) illustration (ˏɪlʌsˋtreʃən) *n.* 插圖；實例 (= *example*)

        illustrate *v.* 舉例說明；畫插圖

    (B) avenue (ˋævəˏnju) *n.* (林蔭) 大道；途徑

    (C) obedience (əˋbidɪəns) *n.* 服從；順從　　obey *v.*

    (D) ***equivalent*** (ɪˋkwɪvələnt) *n.* 同等物；同義語

        adj. 相等的；等值的 (= *equal*) < *to* >

    * chateau (ʃæˋto) *n.* 城堡　　castle (ˋkæsḷ) *n.* 城堡

equi + val + ent
| | |
equal + value + n., adj.

TEST 21

Directions: The following questions are incomplete sentences. You are to choose the one word that best completes the sentence.

1. The _____ of a mouse set her screaming at the top of her lungs.
   (A) phantom   (B) fancy
   (C) sight   (D) imagination   (　)

2. The speaker was scarcely _____ in the banquet hall because he spoke too softly.
   (A) negligible   (B) accessible
   (C) audible   (D) visible   (　)

3. Many countries continue to maintain unofficial but _____ ties with Taiwan.
   (A) flawless   (B) appreciative
   (C) radiant   (D) substantial   (　)

4. The government recently _____ a license for a new kind of lottery. Many people are leaping at the chance to win big bucks.
   (A) illustrated   (B) issued
   (C) integrated   (D) inquired   (　)

5. Since cyber scams are everywhere, the government is planning ways to crack down on _____ on the Internet.
   (A) fraud   (B) extortion
   (C) burglar   (D) infringement   (　)

6. You are _____ invited to a luncheon at the Grand Hyatt Hotel next Friday.
   (A) hospitably   (B) gratefully
   (C) cordially   (D) intimately   (　)

7. If you fall forward, remember to slide on your palms and forearms with your _____ bent to prevent a broken arm.
   (A) knees   (B) elbows
   (C) chins   (D) hips   (　)

8. There's a sign on the bus that reads, "_____ of pickpockets."
   (A) Aware   (B) Unaware
   (C) Beware   (D) Ware   ( )

9. When confronted with such questions, my mind goes _____, and I can hardly remember my own date of birth.
   (A) dim   (B) blank
   (C) faint   (D) vain   ( )

10. More than 150 nations agreed to begin formal talks on mandatory post-2012 reductions in _____ gases.
    (A) white-book   (B) greenhouse
    (C) blue-collar   (D) red-carpet   ( )

11. How many people _____ for the soccer game yesterday?
    (A) showed off   (B) turned out
    (C) came to   (D) lost ground   ( )

12. The driver's carelessness has caused a crash of ten cars. It is a _____.
    (A) show-up   (B) crush-up
    (C) pile-up   (D) turn-around   ( )

13. "It's not our policy to _____ the demands of terrorists," a government spokesman stressed.
    (A) give up   (B) give off
    (C) give back   (D) give in to   ( )

14. Come what may, I must have that house. I intend to get it _____.
    (A) by no means   (B) by the way
    (C) by and by   (D) by hook or by crook   ( )

15. I can't answer your questions; go see the supervisor and _____.
    (A) keep them in mind   (B) take them up with him
    (C) make the best of him   (D) go over with him   ( )

TEST 21 詳解

1. (**C**) The <u>sight</u> of a mouse set her screaming at the top of her lungs.
   她一<u>看見</u>老鼠，就大聲尖叫。
   (A) phantom (ˈfæntəm) *n.* 幽靈；幻影　　a phantom ship 鬼船
   　　a phantom company 空頭公司
   (B) fancy (ˈfænsɪ) *n.* 幻想；喜好　　have a fancy for 喜好
   (C) *sight* (saɪt) *n.* 看見 <*of*>；視力；風景　　the sight of 一看見
   (D) imagination (ɪ,mædʒəˈneʃən) *n.* 想像（力）　　imagine *v.* 想像
   ＊set (sɛt) *v.* 使；讓　　scream (skrim) *v.* 尖叫
   　　at the top of one's *lungs* 音量大到極限地

2. (**C**) The speaker was scarcely <u>audible</u> in the banquet hall because he spoke too
   softly. 演講者的聲音在宴會廳裡幾乎無法<u>聽得見</u>，因為他講話的聲音太輕了。
   (A) negligible (ˈnɛglədʒəbḷ) *adj.* 微不足道的；可以忽視的　　neglect *v.* 忽視
   (B) accessible (ækˈsɛsəbḷ) *adj.* 易接近的；容易到達的
   　　access (ˈæksɛs) *n.* 接近或使用權
   (C) *audible* (ˈɔdəbḷ) *adj.* 聽得見的
   (D) visible (ˈvɪzəbḷ) *adj.* 看得見的（vis 這個字根代表 see 的意思）
   ＊scarcely (ˈskɛrslɪ) *adv.* 幾乎不　　banquet (ˈbæŋkwɪt) *n.* 宴會
   　　hall (hɔl) *n.* 大廳

3. (**D**) Many countries continue to maintain unofficial but <u>substantial</u> ties with
   Taiwan. 許多國家繼續與台灣維持非官方但<u>實質</u>的關係。
   (A) flawless (ˈflɔlɪs) *adj.* 毫無瑕疵的　　flaw *n.* 瑕疵；缺點
   (B) appreciative (əˈpriʃɪ,etɪv) *adj.* 感激的；鑑賞的　　appreciate *v.* 感激；鑑賞
   　　be appreciative of~ = appreciate~ 感激~
   (C) radiant (ˈredɪənt) *adj.* 明亮的；輻射的　　radiate *v.* 發光；輻射
   (D) *substantial* (səbˈstænʃəl) *adj.* 實質的；相當大的　　substance *n.* 物質
   ＊unofficial (,ʌnəˈfɪʃəl) *adj.* 非官方的　　tie (taɪ) *n.* 關係（常用複數形）

4. (**B**) The government recently <u>issued</u> a license for a new kind of lottery. Many
   people are leaping at the chance to win big bucks.
   政府最近<u>發行</u>了一種新的彩券的執照。許多人躍躍欲試，想贏得很多錢。
   (A) illustrate (ɪˈlʌstret) *v.* （以實例、比較）說明　　illustration *n.*
   (B) *issue* (ˈɪʃʊ) *v. n.* 發行（獎券、鈔票、郵票等）；發出（命令、公告等）
   (C) integrate (ˈɪntə,gret) *v.* 統合；結合　　integrate A into B 把 A 結合到 B 當中
   (D) inquire (ɪnˈkwaɪr) *v.* 詢問　　inquiry *n.*
   ＊lottery (ˈlɑtərɪ) *n.* 彩券　　license (ˈlaɪsṇs) *n.* 執照
   　　leap at 對~躍躍欲試　　buck (bʌk) *n.* 錢　　*big bucks* 很多錢

5. (**A**) Since cyber scams are everywhere, the government is planning ways to crack down on <u>fraud</u> on the Internet.

因爲網路詐財非常氾濫，政府正在研擬方案，要嚴加取締網際網路詐欺。

(A) *fraud* 〔frɔd〕 *n.* 詐欺（不可數名詞）；騙局（可數名詞）

　　obtain ~ by fraud 詐騙取得 ~　　　　commit a fraud 欺騙；舞弊

(B) extortion 〔ɪk'stɔrʃən〕 *n.* 勒索　　extort *v.*

(C) burglar 〔'bɝglə〕 *n.* （侵入住家的）盜賊

(D) infringement 〔ɪn'frɪndʒmənt〕 *n.* （權利）侵犯（ = *encroachment* ）

　　infringe *v.*　　copyright infringement 侵犯著作權

　　patent infringement 侵犯專利

＊cyber 〔'saɪbə〕 *n.* 網路；電腦　　scam 〔skæm〕 *n.* 詐欺

　government 〔'gʌvənmənt〕 *n.* 政府　　***crack down on*** 嚴加取締

　the Internet 網際網路

6. (**C**) You are <u>cordially</u> invited to a luncheon at the Grand Hyatt Hotel next Friday.

誠摯地邀請您參加下週五於君悅飯店舉辦的午宴。

(A) hospitably 〔'hɑspɪtəblɪ〕 *adv.* （人、行爲）慇勤地　　*cf.* hospital *n.* 醫院

(B) gratefully 〔'gretfəlɪ〕 *adv.* 感謝地

　　be grateful to *sb.* for *sth.* 爲某事而感謝某人

(C) *cordially* 〔'kɔrdʒəlɪ〕 *adv.* 誠心地；由衷地

　　a cordial welcome 誠心的歡迎　　a cordial dislike for ~ 打從心裡討厭 ~

　　Cordially yours （信最後）敬上

(D) intimately 〔'ɪntəmɪtlɪ〕 *adv.* 親密地；個人地　　an intimate friend 密友

＊luncheon 〔'lʌntʃən〕 *n.* 午餐（比 lunch 更正式的用法）

7. (**B**) If you fall forward, remember to slide on your palms and forearms with your <u>elbows</u> bent to prevent a broken arm.

如果向前跌倒時，記得用手掌和前臂（在地上）滑行，並且將<u>手肘</u>彎曲，

以免摔斷了手。

(A) knee 〔ni〕 *n.* 膝蓋　　fall on *one's* knees 跪下來；屈膝哀求

(B) *elbow* 〔'ɛlbo〕 *n.* 手肘　　*v.* 用手肘推開

　　elbow *one's* way through ~ （用手肘）擠過 ~

(C) chin 〔tʃɪn〕 *n.* 下巴　　keep *one's* chin up 打起精神

(D) hip 〔hɪp〕 *n.* 臀部（通常用複數形，因爲臀部是兩邊對稱的，但是若用

　　bottom, ass 等字，指的是整個臀部，則用單數形）

＊forward 〔'fɔrwəd〕 *adv.* 向前地　　slide 〔slaɪd〕 *v.* 滑行

　palm 〔pɑm〕 *n.* 手掌　　forearm 〔'for,ɑrm〕 *n.* 前臂

　bend 〔bɛnd〕 *v.* 彎曲　　prevent 〔prɪ'vɛnt〕 *v.* 避免

8. (**C**) There's a sign on the bus that reads, "<u>Beware</u> of pickpockets."
公車上有個牌子，上頭寫著：「<u>小心扒手。</u>」
(A) aware〔ə'wɛr〕*adj.* 察覺到的；知道的　　be aware of 察覺到
(B) unaware〔͵ʌnə'wɛr〕*adj.* 未察覺到的　　be unaware of 未察覺到
【注意】aware 與 unaware 都是形容詞，且都不能放在名詞之前修飾名詞。
(C) *beware*〔bɪ'wɛr〕*v.* 小心；注意　　beware of 小心
(D) ware〔wɛr〕*n.* 商品 (常用在複合名詞當中，如：glassware「玻璃製品」；
tableware「餐具」)
＊sign〔saɪn〕*n.* 牌子　　read〔rid〕*v.* (牌子、公告) 寫著
pickpocket〔'pɪk͵pɑkɪt〕*n.* 扒手

9. (**B**) When (*I am*) confronted with such questions, my mind goes <u>blank</u>, and I can
hardly remember my own date of birth.
碰到這種問題時，我腦中一片<u>空白</u>，幾乎連自己的生日都記不得了。
(A) dim〔dɪm〕*adj.* 微弱的；模糊的　　a dim light 微弱的燈光
dim memory 記憶模糊
(B) *blank*〔blæŋk〕*adj.* 空白的　*n.* 空白處
mind goes blank 腦中一片空白
(C) faint〔fent〕*adj.* 頭暈的；微弱的　*v.* 昏倒 (= *pass out*)
(D) vain〔ven〕*adj.* 無效的　　in vain 徒勞無功地
＊*be confronted with* 面對　　date〔det〕*n.* 日期

10. (**B**) More than 150 nations agreed to begin formal talks on mandatory post-2012
reductions in <u>greenhouse</u> gases. 超過一百五十個國家，同意針對 2012 年之
後，如何強制減少<u>溫室效應</u>製造的氣體，開始展開協商。
(A) white-book〔'(h)waɪt'buk〕*n.* 白皮書 (政府所發表的國情報告)
(B) *greenhouse*〔'grin'haus〕*n.* 溫室；溫室效應
(C) blue-collar〔'blu'kɑlɚ〕*n. adj.* 藍領階級 (的)【↔ white-collar 白領階級 (的)】
(D) red-carpet〔'rɛd'kɑrpɪt〕*n.* 紅地毯；隆重歡迎
roll out the red-carpet for *sb.* 隆重歡迎某人
＊formal〔'fɔrml̩〕*adj.* 正式的　　talks〔tɔks〕*n. pl.* 協商
mandatory〔'mændə͵torɪ〕*adj.* 強制的
post-～　～之後　　reduction〔rɪ'dʌkʃən〕*n.* 減少

11. (**B**) How many people <u>turned out</u> for the soccer game yesterday?
有多少人<u>出現</u>參加昨天的足球賽？
(A) show off 炫耀 (應改成 show up，見答案 B)
(B) *turn out* 出現 (= *turn up* = *show up* = *make an appearance*)
(C) come to 甦醒 (= *come to oneself* = *come to one's senses* = *revive*)
(D) lose ground 失勢；節節敗退 (↔ gain ground 進步；有進展)
＊soccer〔'sɑkɚ〕*n.* 足球

12. (**C**) The driver's carelessness has caused a crash of ten cars. It is a <u>pile-up</u>.
   駕駛員的疏忽造成十輛車連續追撞。這是一個連環車禍。
   - (A) show-up *n.* 出現 (= *appearance*)　　show up *v.* 出現
   - (B) crush-up *n.* 打碎　　crush〔krʌʃ〕*v.* 壓扁；弄碎
   - (C) *pile-up* *n.* 連環車禍 (此字是形容發生連環車禍時，車輛都 "pile"「堆積」成一堆)
   - (D) turn-around *n.* 轉變；轉身 (= *turn-round*)
     the turn-around in public opinion　輿論的轉變
   ＊carelessness〔'kɛrlɪsnɪs〕*n.* 疏忽　　crash〔kræʃ〕*n.* 相撞

13. (**D**) "It's not our policy to <u>give in to</u> the demands of terrorists," a government
   spokesman stressed.
   「<u>屈服於</u>恐怖分子的要求，絕非我們的策略。」政府發言人如此強調。
   - (A) give up 放棄 (= *surrender* = *abandon*)
   - (B) give off 散發 (光、煙、氣味)
     The public restroom gave off a bad smell. 公廁發出惡臭。
   - (C) give back 歸還 < *to* > (= *return*)
   - (D) *give in to* 屈服於
   ＊policy〔'pɑləsɪ〕*n.* 策略　　demand〔dɪ'mænd〕*n.* 要求
   terrorist〔'tɛrərɪst〕*n.* 恐怖分子　　spokesman〔'spoksmən〕*n.* 發言人
   stress〔strɛs〕*v.* 強調

14. (**D**) Come what may, I must have that house. I intend to get it <u>by hook or by crook</u>.
   無論發生什麼事，我一定要擁有那棟房子。我打算<u>不擇手段</u>把它拿到手。
   - (A) by no means 絕不 (= *on no account*)
   - (B) by the way 順便一提 (= *by the by*)
   - (C) by and by 不久 (= *before long*)；過一會兒 (= *later on*)
   - (D) *by hook or (by) crook* 不擇手段　　hook〔hʊk〕*n.* 鉤子
     crook〔krʊk〕*n.* 騙子
   ＊*come what may* 無論發生什麼事 (= *no matter what may come*)

15. (**B**) I can't answer your questions; go see the supervisor and <u>take them up with him</u>.
   我無法回答你的問題；去見督導<u>跟他討論這些問題</u>。
   - (A) keep ~ in mind 牢記住 (= *bear* ~ *in mind* = *have* ~ *in mind*)
   - (B) *take* ~ *up with sb.* 跟某人討論 ~ (= *discuss* ~ *with sb.*)
   - (C) make the best of 充分利用 (= *make the most of*)
   - (D) go over with *sb.* 受某人好評
     Did his lecture go over with the audience?
     他的演講受到觀眾的好評嗎？
   ＊supervisor〔ˌsupɚ'vaɪzɚ〕*n.* 督導；督學

TEST 22

Directions: The following questions are incomplete sentences. You are to choose the one word that best completes the sentence.

1. To enhance the efficiency of the government agencies, _____ criticism is welcome.
   - (A) negative
   - (B) constructive
   - (C) conscientious
   - (D) democratic   (   )

2. People from all walks of life should be held in high esteem regardless of _____, religion, or wealth.
   - (A) technology
   - (B) profession
   - (C) integration
   - (D) racial   (   )

3. Henry is not a person whose words can be taken _____. Remember every word he said.
   - (A) light
   - (B) lightly
   - (C) easy
   - (D) easily   (   )

4. Visitors never fail to _____ at the greatness of the Egyptian pyramids.
   - (A) enchant
   - (B) frighten
   - (C) marvel
   - (D) whistle   (   )

5. The EPA _____ a public education campaign on the garbage separation policy, which was set to go into effect in 2006.
   - (A) reshuffled
   - (B) launched
   - (C) revived
   - (D) probed   (   )

6. AIDS is _____ through blood transfusion. People may be infected through injections.
   - (A) exchangeable
   - (B) favorable
   - (C) communicable
   - (D) transitional   (   )

7. Even though no one was seriously injured, the plane crash was a terrible _____ for the passengers.
   - (A) order
   - (B) ordeal
   - (C) orphan
   - (D) orangeade   (   )

8. During the island-wide blackout, all the business operations were
_____.
   (A) suspended   (B) comprehended
   (C) oppressed   (D) suppressed   ( )

9. Once a lighthouse is built, no ship of any nationality can be
effectively _____ from the utilization of the lighthouse for
navigational purposes.
   (A) isolated   (B) dismissed
   (C) distracted   (D) excluded   ( )

10. After the setback in the election, the party leaders _____ to
reform their platform.
   (A) vowed   (B) cursed
   (C) seized   (D) mounted   ( )

11. Craig assured his boss that he would _____ all his skills and
knowledge in doing this new job.
   (A) call in   (B) call at
   (C) call on   (D) call off   ( )

12. More than two hundred years ago the United States _____ from
the British Empire and became an independent country.
   (A) got off   (B) pulled down
   (C) broke away   (D) dropped off   ( )

13. Care should be taken to decrease the length of time that one is
_____ loud continuous noise.
   (A) subjected to   (B) filled with
   (C) associated with   (D) attached to   ( )

14. Without the friction between their feet and the ground, people
would _____ be able to walk.
   (A) in no time   (B) by all means
   (C) in no way   (D) on any account   ( )

15. If any man here does not agree with me, he should _____ his
own plan.
   (A) put on   (B) put out
   (C) put in   (D) put forward   ( )

TEST 22 詳解

1. (**B**) To enhance the efficiency of the government agencies, <u>constructive</u> criticism is welcome. 為提高政府機關的效率，我們歡迎建設性的批評。
   (A) negative〔'nɛgətɪv〕*adj.* 負面的；消極的 (↔ positive 正面的；積極的)
   (B) *constructive*〔kən'strʌktɪv〕*adj.* 建設性的 (↔ destructive 破壞性的)
   (C) conscientious〔,kɑnʃɪ'ɛnʃəs〕*adj.* 有良心的　　conscience *n.* 良心
   (D) democratic〔,dɛmə'krætɪk〕*adj.* 民主的　　democracy *n.* 民主
   *enhance〔ɪn'hæns〕*v.* 提高　　efficiency〔ɪ'fɪʃənsɪ〕*n.* 效率
   agency〔'edʒənsɪ〕*n.* 機關　　criticism〔'krɪtə,sɪzəm〕*n.* 批評

2. (**B**) People from all walks of life should be held in high esteem regardless of <u>profession</u>, religion, or wealth.
   各行各業的人都應該被充分尊重，不管他們的職業、宗教信仰或是財力。
   (A) technology〔tɛk'nɑlədʒɪ〕*n.* 科技　　technological *adj.* 科技的
   (B) *profession*〔prə'fɛʃən〕*n.* 職業；專業
   　　professional *adj.* 職業的；專業的
   　　He is a doctor by profession. 他的職業是醫生。
   (C) integration〔,ɪntə'greʃən〕*n.* 整合；(數學) 積分　　integrate *v.* 整合
   (D) racial〔'reʃəl〕*adj.* 種族的 (應改成名詞 race，才正確)
   　　racial discrimination 種族歧視
   **walk of life* 行業　　*hold sb. in esteem* 尊重某人
   　regardless of 不管；無論　　religion〔rɪ'lɪdʒən〕*n.* 宗教 (信仰)

3. (**B**) Henry is not a person whose words can be taken <u>lightly</u>. Remember every word he said. 千萬不能輕忽亨利所說的話。牢記住他說過的每一個字。
   (A) light〔laɪt〕*adj.* 淡的；輕的；輕忽的　　make light of 輕視
   (B) *lightly*〔'laɪtlɪ〕*adv.* 輕忽地；不注意地
   　　take~lightly 輕忽~；把~當耳邊風
   (C) easy〔'izɪ〕*adj.* 容易的　*adv.* 輕鬆地；安逸地　take it easy 放輕鬆；不緊張
   (D) easily〔'izɪlɪ〕*adv.* 容易地；無疑地 (= without (a) doubt)

4. (**C**) Visitors never fail to <u>marvel</u> at the greatness of the Egyptian pyramids.
   旅客一定會對埃及金字塔的壯觀讚嘆不已。
   (A) enchant〔ɪn'tʃænt〕*v.* 使著迷　　be enchanted with/by 著迷於
   (B) frighten〔'fraɪtn̩〕*v.* 驚嚇　　be frightened at/by 受~驚嚇
   (C) *marvel*〔'mɑrvl̩〕*v.* 讚嘆　　marvel at 讚嘆於
   (D) whistle〔'hwɪsl̩〕*v.* 吹口哨　*n.* 哨子　　blow a whistle 吹哨子
   **fail to* 無法　　Egyptian〔ɪ'dʒɪpʃən〕*adj.* 埃及的
   　pyramid〔'pɪrəmɪd〕*n.* 金字塔

5. (**B**) The EPA <u>launched</u> a public education campaign on the garbage separation policy, which was set to go into effect in 2006.

環保署<u>開始</u>垃圾分類的公眾教育活動，此政策預定從 2006 年起開始生效。

(A) reshuffle〔rɪ'ʃʌfḷ〕*v. n.* 重新洗牌；改組（內閣、人事等）

reshuffled Cabinet = a Cabinet reshuffle 內閣改組

(B) *launch*〔lɔntʃ〕*v. n.* 開始（= *start*）；著手；發射（火箭等）（= *send off*）

(C) revive〔rɪ'vaɪv〕*v.* 使復活；使恢復精神【re-（= *back*）+ vive（= *live*）】

(D) probe〔prob〕*v. n.* 探索；細查

probe into *one's* private life 調查某人的私生活

＊EPA 環保署（= *Environmental Protection Administration*）

public〔'pʌblɪk〕*adj.* 公共的；公眾的　　　education〔ˌɛdʒə'keʃən〕*n.* 教育

campaign〔kæm'pen〕*n.* 活動　　　separation〔ˌsɛpə'reʃən〕*n.* 分開

policy〔'paləsɪ〕*n.* 政策　　　*be set to* 預定　　　*go into effect* 生效

6. (**C**) AIDS is <u>communicable</u> through blood transfusion. People may be infected through injections.

愛滋病會透過輸血<u>傳染</u>。人們會經由注射被感染。

(A) exchangeable〔ɪks'tʃendʒəbḷ〕*adj.* 可交換的　　　exchange *v.* 交換

(B) favorable〔'fevərəbḷ〕*adj.* 贊成的；有利的　　　favor *v. n.* 贊成；喜愛

(C) *communicable*〔kə'mjunɪkəbḷ〕*adj.*（疾病）會傳染的

communicate *v.* 傳染；溝通

(D) transitional〔træn'zɪʃənḷ〕*adj.* 過渡（時期）的

transition *n.* 過渡；轉變

＊ transfusion〔træns'fjuʒən〕*n.* 輸血　　　infect〔ɪn'fɛkt〕*v.* 感染

injection〔ɪn'dʒɛkʃən〕*n.* 注射

7. (**B**) Even though no one was seriously injured, the plane crash was a terrible <u>ordeal</u> for the passengers.

即使沒人受重傷，這場空難對於機上的乘客而言，仍是可怕的<u>折磨</u>。

(A) order〔'ɔrdɚ〕*n.* 秩序；命令；訂購

law and order 法治　　　place an order 下訂單

(B) *ordeal*〔ɔr'dil〕*n.* 折磨；嚴峻的考驗

(C) orphan〔'ɔrfən〕*n.* 孤兒　　　orphanage〔'ɔrfənɪdʒ〕*n.* 孤兒院

(D) orangeade〔ˌɔrɪndʒ'ed〕*n.* 橘子水

【比較】lemonade〔ˌlɛmən'ed〕*n.* 檸檬汁

＊ injure〔'ɪndʒɚ〕*v.* 使受傷　　　crash〔kræʃ〕*n.* 墜毀

passenger〔'pæsndʒɚ〕*n.* 乘客

8. (**A**) During the island-wide blackout, all the business operations were <u>suspended</u>.
在全島大停電期間，所有的商業運作都告<u>暫停</u>。

    (A) ***suspend*** 〔 səˋspɛnd 〕*v.* 暫停　　suspension *n.*

    (B) comprehend 〔ˌkɑmprɪˋhɛnd 〕*v.* 理解【com- (= *with*) + prehend (= *seize*)】

    (C) oppress 〔 əˋprɛs 〕*v.* 壓迫【op- (= *against*) + press (= *press*)】

    (D) suppress 〔 səˋprɛs 〕*v.* 抑制；鎮壓【sup- (= *under*) + press (= *press*)】

    ＊island-wide 〔ˋaɪləndˋwaɪd 〕*adj.* 全島的
     blackout 〔ˋblækˌaʊt 〕*n.* 停電 (= *power failure*)
     operation 〔ˌɑpəˋreʃən 〕*n.* 運作

9. (**D**) Once a lighthouse is built, no ship of any nationality can be effectively
<u>excluded</u> from the utilization of the lighthouse for navigational purposes.
一座燈塔一旦蓋好之後，實際上就無法<u>排除</u>任何國籍的船隻，不讓其使用燈塔
來航行。

    (A) isolate 〔ˋaɪsḷˌet 〕*v.* 孤立；隔絕 (= *segregate* = *set apart*)　　isolation *n.*

    (B) dismiss 〔 dɪsˋmɪs 〕*v.* 遣散；解雇　　Class (*is*) dismissed. 下課。

    (C) distract 〔 dɪˋstrækt 〕*v.* 分散；轉移 (↔ attract 吸引)　　distraction *n.*

    (D) ***exclude*** 〔 ɪkˋsklud 〕*v.* 排除 (在外) (↔ include 包括在內)　　exclusion *n.*

    ＊lighthouse 〔ˋlaɪtˌhaʊs 〕*n.* 燈塔　　nationality 〔ˌnæʃənˋælətɪ 〕*n.* 國籍
     effectively 〔 ɪˋfɛktɪvlɪ 〕*adv.* 實際上　　utilization 〔ˌjutḷəˋzeʃən 〕*n.* 利用
     navigational 〔ˌnævəˋgeʃənḷ 〕*adj.* 航行的　　purpose 〔ˋpɝpəs 〕*n.* 目的

10. (**A**) After the setback in the election, the party leaders <u>vowed</u> to reform their
platform. 在選舉挫敗之後，政黨的領導者<u>發誓</u>要改革政黨的綱領。

    (A) ***vow*** 〔 vaʊ 〕*v. n.* 發誓 (= *swear*)

    (B) curse 〔 kɝs 〕*v. n.* 詛咒　　curse ~ = put/lay a curse on/upon ~ 詛咒 ~

    (C) seize 〔 siz 〕*v.* 抓住 (= *hold*)；把握 (= *grasp*)；了解 (= *understand*)

    (D) mount 〔 maʊnt 〕*v.* 登上 (= *climb*)；騎上 (= *get up on*)；鑲上 (珠寶等)

    ＊setback 〔ˋsɛtˌbæk 〕*n.* 挫敗　　election 〔 ɪˋlɛkʃən 〕*n.* 選舉
     party 〔ˋpɑrtɪ 〕*n.* 政黨　　reform 〔 rɪˋfɔrm 〕*n.* 改革
     platform 〔ˋplætˌfɔrm 〕*n.* (政黨的) 政綱；綱領

11. (**C**) Craig assured his boss that he would <u>call on</u> all his skills and knowledge in doing
this new job. 克瑞格向老闆保證，他會<u>使出</u>全部的技能和知識來做新工作。

    (A) call in 延請 (醫生)；回收 (產品)

    (B) call at 訪問 (某地)

    (C) ***call on*** 鼓起 (力氣)；訪問 (某人) (= *visit*)；呼籲

    (D) call off 取消 (= *cancel*)

    ＊assure 〔 əˋʃʊr 〕*v.* 向…保證　　skill 〔 skɪl 〕*n.* 技能；技術

12. (**C**) More than two hundred years ago the United States <u>broke away</u> from the British Empire and became an independent country.
兩百多年前，美國從大英帝國<u>脫離</u>，變成一個獨立的國家。
(A) get off 下車；出發
(B) pull down 拆除
(C) *break away* 脫離　　*break away from* ~　自~脫離
(D) drop off 減少；打瞌睡
例：Business has dropped off drastically during this season.
（這一季生意劇減。）
＊ British〔'brɪtɪʃ〕*adj.* 英國的　　empire〔'ɛmpaɪr〕*n.* 帝國
independent〔ˌɪndɪ'pɛndənt〕*adj.* 獨立的

13. (**A**) Care should be taken to decrease the length of time that one is <u>subjected to</u> loud continuous noise. 我們要小心，減少<u>暴露在</u>連續大聲噪音下的時間。
(A) *be subjected to* 遭受；暴露在
(B) be filled with 充滿（＝*be full of*）
(C) be associated with~　跟~聯想在一起
例：Spain is always associated with bull-fighting.
（西班牙常被人跟鬥牛聯想在一起。）
(D) be attached to 附著於；深愛著
例：He has been attached to his mother.（他深愛著母親。）
＊ *take care* 小心　　loud〔laʊd〕*adj.* 音量大的
continuous〔kən'tɪnjʊəs〕*adj.* 連續的

14. (**C**) Without the friction between their feet and the ground, people would <u>in no way</u> be able to walk. 如果沒有腳掌與地面之間的摩擦力，我們<u>絕對無法</u>行走。
【注意】此句為假設語氣，可將其改寫為：If there *were* no friction between their feet and the ground, people *would* in no way be able to walk.
(A) in no time 立即（＝*at once* ＝*right away* ＝*immediately*）
(B) by all means 無論如何；千方百計
(C) *in no way* 絕對無法（＝*by no means* ＝*on no account* ＝*not at all* ＝*never*）
(D) on any account 不計一切代價（＝*in any case* ＝*at any rate*）
＊ friction〔'frɪkʃən〕*n.* 摩擦力

15. (**D**) If any man here does not agree with me, he should <u>put forward</u> his own plan.
如果現在有人看法與我不同，就得<u>提出</u>自己的計劃。
(A) put on 穿（衣服）；增加（體重）　　put on weight 增加體重
(B) put out 熄滅（＝*blow out* ＝*extinguish*）
(C) put in 伸進；插嘴（＝*cut in*）；任命（＝*appoint*）
(D) *put forward* 提出（計劃；看法）（＝*propose*）
＊ *agree with* (*sb.*) 同意（某人）

TEST 23

Directions: The following questions are incomplete sentences. You are to choose the one word that best completes the sentence.

1. In this trade, you should learn the ropes by _____ yourself with the company regulations.
   - (A) acquainting
   - (B) packing
   - (C) connecting
   - (D) replacing   (   )

2. She seemed to notice everything at only a single _____.
   - (A) expression
   - (B) looks
   - (C) view
   - (D) glance   (   )

3. "Card slaves," people who regularly use their credit cards to get a cash advance, formed a self-help club in Taipei to prevent each other from turning to crime to get out of their _____.
   - (A) reprimand
   - (B) mockery
   - (C) predicament
   - (D) essence   (   )

4. Come with us to the concert. _____, meet us at the concert hall.
   - (A) Presumably
   - (B) Alternatively
   - (C) Superbly
   - (D) Supposedly   (   )

5. On sunny days you can see many people _____ on the beach in their swimsuits.
   - (A) crawling
   - (B) crouching
   - (C) marching
   - (D) sprawling   (   )

6. John was too much _____ with the thought of passing the bar exam.
   - (A) indebted
   - (B) impressed
   - (C) withdrawn
   - (D) preoccupied   (   )

7. I _____ a piece of purple ribbon to my hair to match my new purple cocktail dress.
   - (A) attacked
   - (B) attached
   - (C) attained
   - (D) adjourned   (   )

8. The mountain climbers sought _____ from the storm when it came up unexpectedly.
   (A) refuse
   (B) refugee
   (C) refrain
   (D) refuge   (   )

9. Microsoft seems to _____ the computer software market. It has been successfully ruling out any other possible players in this field.
   (A) monopolize
   (B) intensify
   (C) justify
   (D) authorize   (   )

10. The mailman just brought your _____ delivery letter to our house.
    (A) pungent
    (B) punctual
    (C) express
    (D) proficient   (   )

11. It is true that _____ something to excess, for example reading too much, can turn it into a vice.
    (A) indulging in
    (B) converging on
    (C) making a fuss about
    (D) teaming up with   (   )

12. This is exactly what happened. _____ for it.
    (A) Take my word
    (B) Hold true
    (C) Turn a deaf ear
    (D) Stick to the point   (   )

13. Janet can't wear that hat; it will not _____ her pink dress.
    (A) come into contact with
    (B) do with
    (C) be through with
    (D) go with   (   )

14. A _____ is a group of experts who serve as consultants on strategy.
    (A) brainstorming
    (B) brain trust
    (C) brain drain
    (D) brainwashing   (   )

15. The police plan to _____ the selling of liquor to minors.
    (A) have a word with
    (B) crack down on
    (C) hunt down
    (D) pull a face at   (   )

TEST 23 詳解

1. (**A**) In this trade, you should learn the ropes by <u>acquainting</u> yourself with the company regulations.

在這個行業中,你必須熟悉公司的規定,才能得心應手。

(A) *acquaint* 〔əˋkwent〕 *v.* 使熟悉　　acquaint *sb.* with *sth.* 使某人熟悉某事

(B) pack 〔pæk〕 *v.* 打包;裝進　　pack A with B 把 B 裝進 A 中

(C) connect 〔kəˋnɛkt〕 *v.* 連接　　connect A with B 連接 A 與 B

(D) replace 〔rıˋples〕 *v.* 取代　　replace A with B 用 B 取代 A

* trade 〔tred〕 *n.* 行業　　*learn the ropes* 熟悉訣竅;得心應手

regulation 〔ˌrɛgjəˋleʃən〕 *n.* 規定

2. (**D**) She seemed to notice everything at only a single <u>glance</u>.

她似乎只看一眼,就注意到每件事。

(A) expression 〔ɪkˋsprɛʃən〕 *n.* (言語) 表達;(臉上) 表情

beyond expression 言語無法表達

(B) looks 〔luks〕 *n. pl.* 樣子;外貌　　good/fair looks 容貌美麗

【比較】look (臉上) 表情

a serious/puzzled/worried look 嚴肅的/困惑的/擔心的表情

(C) view 〔vju〕 *n.* 觀看;景色 (= *scene*);視力 (= *vision*)

(D) *glance* 〔glæns〕 *n.* 看一眼;一瞥　　at a glance 看一眼

* notice 〔ˋnotɪs〕 *v.* 注意到　　single 〔ˋsɪŋgl〕 *adj.* 單一的

3. (**C**) "Card slaves," people who regularly use their credit cards to get a cash advance, formed a self-help club in Taipei to prevent each other from turning to crime to get out of their <u>predicament</u>.

「卡奴」,即經常會使用信用卡來預借現金者,在台北成立一個自助會,以預防彼此會為了脫離困境而以身試法。

(A) reprimand 〔ˋrɛprəˌmænd〕 *n.* (嚴厲的) 斥責;訓誡 (= *rebuke*)

(B) mockery 〔ˋmɑkərı〕 *n.* 嘲笑;愚弄;嘲笑的對象　　mock *v.*

(C) *predicament* 〔prıˋdɪkəmənt〕 *n.* 困境;苦境

be in a predicament 身處困境

(D) essence 〔ˋɛsn̩s〕 *n.* 本質;精華　　the essence of~ ~的本質

chicken essence 雞精

* slave 〔slev〕 *n.* 奴隸　　regularly 〔ˋrɛgjələlı〕 *adv.* 定期地;經常地

cash advance 預借現金　　self-help 〔ˋsɛlfˋhɛlp〕 *n.* 自助

turn to 訴諸於　　crime 〔kraɪm〕 *n.* 犯罪

4. (**B**) Come with us to the concert. <u>Alternatively</u>, meet us at the concert hall.
跟我們去音樂會。<u>或者</u>，在音樂廳跟我們見面。

    (A) presumably〔prɪˈzuməblɪ〕*adv.* 或許地；可能地
        presume〔prɪˈzum〕*v.* 假定；推測

    (B) *alternatively*〔ɔlˈtɝnətɪvlɪ〕*adv.* 二選一地；替代地；或者
        alternative *n. adj.* 二選一（的）

    (C) superbly〔suˈpɝblɪ〕*adv.* 極好地；超群地（注意發音）

    (D) supposedly〔səˈpozɪdlɪ〕*adv.* 推測上是；傳聞是

    ＊concert〔ˈkɑnsɝt〕*n.* 音樂會　　***concert hall*** 音樂廳

5. (**D**) On sunny days you can see many people <u>sprawling</u> on the beach in their swimsuits. 天氣晴朗時，你會看到很多人身著泳裝<u>伸開四肢躺</u>在海灘上。

    (A) crawl〔krɔl〕*v.*（四肢落地）爬（ = *go on all fours* ）；緩慢進行

    (B) crouch〔kraʊtʃ〕*v.* 蹲　【比較】stoop 彎腰　　kneel 跪下

    (C) march〔mɑrtʃ〕*v.* 大步走；行軍

    (D) *sprawl*〔sprɔl〕*v.* 大字攤開而躺；伸開四肢而躺

    ＊beach〔bitʃ〕*n.* 海灘　　swimsuit〔ˈswɪm,sut〕*n.* 泳裝

6. (**D**) John was too much <u>preoccupied</u> with the thought of passing the bar exam.
約翰太過<u>沈迷</u>於通過律師資格考試的念頭。

    (A) indebted〔ɪnˈdɛtɪd〕*adj.* 感激的
        be indebted to *sb.* for *sth.* 因某事而感激某人

    (B) impressed〔ɪmˈprɛst〕*adj.* 印象深刻的　　be impressed with 對…印象深刻

    (C) withdrawn〔wɪðˈdrɔn〕*adj.*（人、態度）內向的；退縮的　withdraw *v.* 退縮

    (D) *preoccupied*〔priˈɑkjə,paɪd〕*adj.* 沈迷的
        be preoccupied with~ 沈迷於~

    ＊thought〔θɔt〕*n.* 想法　　***bar exam*** 律師資格考試

7. (**B**) I <u>attached</u> a piece of purple ribbon to my hair to match my new purple cocktail dress. 我在頭髮上<u>繫</u>一條紫色緞帶，以搭配我新的紫色小禮服。

    (A) attack〔əˈtæk〕*v. n.* 攻擊（敵人）；抨擊（行為）
        make/begin an attack 攻擊

    (B) *attach*〔əˈtætʃ〕*v.* 繫；貼；附加 < *to* >　　attach A to B 把 A 貼附在 B 上

    (C) attain〔əˈten〕*v.* 達到　　attain *one's* goal/hope 達到目的/希望

    (D) adjourn〔əˈdʒɝn〕*v.* 休會；延期（ = *put off* = *postpone* ）
        We adjourned the meeting until next Monday. 我們休會至下週一。

    ＊purple〔ˈpɝpl̩〕*adj.* 紫色的　　ribbon〔ˈrɪbən〕*n.* 緞帶
    cocktail dress 雞尾酒禮服；半正式的小禮服

8. (**D**) The mountain climbers sought <u>refuge</u> from the storm when it came up
unexpectedly. 當暴雨突如其來逼近時，登山者趕緊<u>躲避</u>。

 (A) refuse〔'rɛfjus〕*n.* 垃圾　〔rɪ'fjuz〕*v.* 拒絕

 (B) refugee〔,rɛfjʊ'dʒi〕*n.* 難民　　a refugee camp 難民營

 (C) refrain〔rɪ'fren〕*v.* 忍住（= *abstain*）< *from* >

 (D) *refuge*〔'rɛfjudʒ〕*n.* 避難；逃避；避難所　　*seek refuge from* 躲避

 ＊*mountain climber* 登山者　　seek〔sik〕*v.* 尋求（三態變化 seek-sought-sought）
come up 逼近；前來　　unexpectedly〔,ʌnɪk'spɛktɪdlɪ〕*adv.* 意料外地

9. (**A**) Microsoft seems to <u>monopolize</u> the computer software market. It has been
successfully ruling out any other possible players in this field. 微軟似乎已
<u>壟斷</u>電腦軟體市場。它已成功地把這個領域內可能的競爭者都排除出去。

 (A) *monopolize*〔mə'nɑpḷ,aɪz〕*v.* 壟斷　　monopoly *n.*

 (B) intensify〔ɪn'tɛnsə,faɪ〕*v.* 加強　　intensification *n.*

 (C) justify〔'dʒʌstə,faɪ〕*v.* 使正當化　　justification *n.*

 (D) authorize〔'ɔθə,raɪz〕*v.* 授權；認可　　authorization *n.*

 ＊software〔'sɔft,wɛr〕*n.* 軟體　　*rule out* 排除　　player〔'pleɚ〕*n.* 競爭者
field〔fild〕*n.* 領域

10. (**C**) The mailman just brought your <u>express</u> delivery letter to our house.
郵差剛把你的<u>限時</u>專送信件送到我們家裡來。

 (A) pungent〔'pʌndʒənt〕*adj.* 辛辣的；（言語）尖酸刻薄的
pungent criticism 尖刻的批評

 (B) punctual〔'pʌŋktʃʊəl〕*adj.* 準時的（= *on time*）　　punctuality *n.*

 (C) *express*〔ɪk'sprɛs〕*adj.* 快速的；快遞的　　express delivery 限時專送；快遞

 (D) proficient〔prə'fɪʃənt〕*adj.* 精通的　　be proficient in/at 精通於
proficiency *n.*

 ＊mailman〔'mel,mæn〕*n.* 郵差　　delivery〔dɪ'lɪvərɪ〕*n.* 遞送（郵件）

11. (**A**) It is true that <u>indulging in</u> something to excess, for example reading too much,
can turn it into a vice. 過度<u>沈溺於</u>某事物，如過度閱讀，可能會變成一種惡習。

 (A) *indulge in* 沈溺於（= *indulge oneself in*）

 (B) converge on 集結於；交會在
Crowds of people converged on that scenic spot.
大批人潮集結在那個風景區。

 (C) make a fuss about 小題大作；大驚小怪

 (D) team up with 聯合（= *join together with*）

 ＊*to excess* 過度地　　*turn A into B* 使 A 變成 B　　vice〔vaɪs〕*n.* 惡習

12. (**A**) This is exactly what happened. Take my word for it.

發生的事就是這樣。相信我講的話。

(A) *take one's word for it* 相信某人的話 (= *believe what sb. says*)

(B) hold true for~ 對~適用；對~有效

(C) turn a deaf ear to~ 對~充耳不聞

turn a deaf ear to *one's* advice 對某人的勸告充耳不聞

(D) stick to the point 不離題；講重點 (↔ *be beside the point* 離題)

stick to 遵守 point (pɔɪnt) *n.* 重點

＊exactly (ɪg'zæktlɪ) *adv.* 就是；正是

13. (**D**) Janet can't wear that hat; it will not go with her pink dress.

珍娜不能戴那頂帽子，它不配她粉紅色的洋裝。

(A) come into contact with 與~接觸 (↔ *lose contact with~* 跟~失去聯絡)

(B) do with 應付；處理 (= *cope with* = *handle*)

(C) be through with 完成；結束 (= *be done with* = *be finished with*)

(D) *go with* 配合 (= *match*)；跟~一起去；同意 (= *agree with*)

14. (**B**) A brain trust is a group of experts who serve as consultants on strategy.

智囊團即一群擔任策略顧問的專家。

(A) brainstorming *n.* 腦力激盪 brainstorm *v.*

Let's brainstorm a solution to the problem.

我們來腦力激盪共同想出問題的答案。

(B) *brain trust n.* 智囊團；顧問團

(C) brain drain *n.* 人才外流 brain-drain *v.*

drain (dren) *v.* 逐漸流出；耗盡

(D) brainwashing *n.* 洗腦 brainwash *v.*

＊*serve as* 擔任 consultant (kən'sʌltənt) *n.* 顧問

strategy ('strætədʒɪ) *n.* 策略

15. (**B**) The police plan to crack down on the selling of liquor to minors.

警方打算嚴加取締賣酒給未成年人。

(A) have a word with 和…談話

(B) *crack down on* 嚴加取締；嚴厲處罰

(C) hunt down 追捕；對~窮追不捨

hunt down the terrorists 追捕恐怖分子

(D) pull a face at 對~做鬼臉 (= *make a face at*)

＊*the police* 警方 liquor ('lɪkə) *n.* 酒 (尤指烈酒)

minor ('maɪnə) *n.* 未成年人

TEST 24

Directions: The following questions are incomplete sentences. You are to choose the one word that best completes the sentence.

1. According to the X-ray, your _____ is broken.
   (A) angel   (B) angle
   (C) ankle   (D) anchor   (   )

2. Kiwi fruit's sweet and juicy flesh, which is dotted with many tiny _____ seeds, can be used in salads and desserts.
   (A) edible   (B) invisible
   (C) tangible   (D) audible   (   )

3. Comparison and contrast are often used _____ in advertisements.
   (A) casually   (B) intentionally
   (C) incidentally   (D) tiresomely   (   )

4. It began to rain suddenly and I heard the _____ of thunder in the sky.
   (A) rumbling   (B) mumbling
   (C) tumbling   (D) grumbling   (   )

5. Mr. Bloom is not _____ now, but he will be famous someday.
   (A) magnificent   (B) peculiar
   (C) dominant   (D) prominent   (   )

6. There are many theories, but no _____ about how the earth came into being.
   (A) compassion   (B) combat
   (C) consensus   (D) conquest   (   )

7. We should draw more attention to the protection of intellectual property rights, because the _____ piracy in the recording and publishing industry will lead to higher prices for consumers.
   (A) triumphant   (B) innovative
   (C) amateur   (D) rampant   (   )

8. The church, the largest one along the shore, can hold one thousand
   _____.
   (A) worshippers   (B) peddlers
   (C) sculptors   (D) governors   (   )

9. The price of beer _____ from 50 cents to 4 dollars per liter
   during the summer season.
   (A) separated   (B) ranged
   (C) differed   (D) altered   (   )

10. Although they plant trees in this area every year, the tops of some
    hills are still _____.
    (A) bare   (B) blank
    (C) hollow   (D) vacant   (   )

11. Henry is not able to come to work because he _____ the flu.
    (A) came out with   (B) got down to
    (C) got up to   (D) came down with   (   )

12. The two boys started by _____ at each other. Then they began
    to fight.
    (A) cutting back   (B) fooling around
    (C) making faces   (D) reading over   (   )

13. He's constantly whining about every mishap of his life. Can't he
    just _____?
    (A) knock it off   (B) lose his control
    (C) go through channels (D) hold his breath   (   )

14. Though her parents _____ her musical talent, Helen's piano
    playing is really terrible.
    (A) pour scorn on   (B) heap praise upon
    (C) give vent to   (D) cast light upon   (   )

15. His wife left him. Besides, he has committed a crime and been
    sent to jail. He is really _____.
    (A) in good hands   (B) at loose ends
    (C) in the know   (D) at the end of his rope   (   )

TEST 24 詳解

1. (**C**) According to the X-ray, your <u>ankle</u> is broken.
根據 X 光判斷，你的<u>腳踝</u>斷了。
   (A) angel〔'endʒəl〕 *n.* 天使；美麗而善良的人
   　　 Be an angel and do me a favor. 做個好心人，幫我個忙吧。
   (B) angle〔'æŋgl̩〕 *n.* 角度　　a right angle　直角
   　　 an acute/obtuse angle　銳角/鈍角
   (C) *ankle*〔'æŋkl̩〕 *n.* 腳踝（連接 foot 跟 leg 的部位）
   (D) anchor〔'æŋkɚ〕 *n.* 船錨；（電視新聞節目）主播（= *anchorman*）
   ＊*according to* 根據　　*X-ray* X 光

2. (**A**) Kiwi fruit's sweet and juicy flesh, which is dotted with many tiny <u>edible</u>
seeds, can be used in salads and desserts.
奇異果的果肉甜又多汁，佈滿了許多<u>可以吃的</u>小種子，可用於沙拉和甜點中。
   (A) *edible*〔'ɛdəbl̩〕 *adj.* 可以食用的（↔ inedible 不可以食用的）
   (B) invisible〔ɪn'vɪzəbl̩〕 *adj.* 看不見的（↔ visible 看得見的）
   (C) tangible〔'tændʒəbl̩〕 *adj.* 觸摸得到的；實體的
   　　（↔ intangible 觸摸不到的；無形的）
   (D) audible〔'ɔdəbl̩〕 *adj.* 聽得見的（↔ inaudible 聽不見的）
   ＊kiwi〔'kiwɪ〕 *n.* 奇異果（= *kiwi fruit*）　　juicy〔'dʒusɪ〕 *adj.* 多汁的
   flesh〔flɛʃ〕 *n.* 果肉　　dot〔dɑt〕 *v.* 散佈於　　seed〔sid〕 *n.* 種子
   dessert〔dɪ'zɝt〕 *n.* 甜點

3. (**B**) Comparison and contrast are often used <u>intentionally</u> in advertisements.
比較和對比常被<u>刻意地</u>用在廣告當中。
   (A) casually〔'kæʒʊəlɪ〕 *adv.* 不在意地（↔ *intentionally*）；隨便地
   (B) *intentionally*〔ɪn'tɛnʃənlɪ〕 *adv.* 故意地（= *on purpose*）
   　　 intention *n.* 意圖；目的
   (C) incidentally〔͵ɪnsə'dɛntl̩ɪ〕 *adv.* 附帶地；順便地　　incident *n.* 事件；插曲
   (D) tiresomely〔'taɪrsəmlɪ〕 *adv.* 令人厭倦地　【比較】tired *adj.*（人）感到疲倦的
   ＊comparison〔kəm'pærəsn̩〕 *n.* 比較　　contrast〔'kɑntræst〕 *n.* 對比
   advertisement〔͵ædvɚ'taɪzmənt〕 *n.* 廣告

4. (**A**) It began to rain suddenly and I heard the <u>rumbling</u> of thunder in the sky.
天空突然下起雨，我聽到天際雷聲<u>隆隆作響</u>。
   (A) *rumble*〔'rʌmbl̩〕 *v.*（雷聲、砲聲、肚子）隆隆作響
   (B) mumble〔'mʌmbl̩〕 *v.* 喃喃自語（= *murmur*）
   　　 The old man mumbled to himself. 老人自己喃喃自語。
   (C) tumble〔'tʌmbl̩〕 *v.* 跌倒（= *fall*）；翻滾
   (D) grumble〔'grʌmbl̩〕 *v.* 抱怨 < *about/at/over* >

5. (**D**) Mr. Bloom is not <u>prominent</u> now, but he will be famous someday.
布倫先生現在並不<u>有名</u>，但是他總有一天會出名的。

(A) magnificent〔mæg'nɪfəsn̩t〕*adj.* 壯麗的；宏偉的　　magnificence *n.*
a magnificent view 壯麗的景緻　　a magnificent house 豪宅

(B) peculiar〔pɪ'kjuljɚ〕*adj.* 獨特的；古怪的（= *strange* ）

(C) dominant〔'dɑmənənt〕*adj.* 支配的；（生物）顯性的
dominate *v.* 支配　　the dominant party 多數黨
a dominant character 顯性的特徵

(D) *prominent*〔'prɑmənənt〕*adj.* 出名的（= *well-known* ）；卓越的
（= *outstanding* ）

6. (**C**) There are many theories, but no <u>consensus</u> about how the earth
came into being. 地球是如何形成的，有許多理論，但尚無<u>共識</u>。

(A) compassion〔kəm'pæʃən〕*n.* 同情心；憐憫
compassionate *adj.* 同情的

(B) combat〔'kɑmbæt〕*n. v.* 戰鬥；打鬥
We combated with them for our rights. 我們為自己的權利，與他們戰鬥。

(C) *consensus*〔kən'sɛnsəs〕*n.* 共識　　reach a consensus 達成共識

(D) conquest〔'kɑŋkwɛst〕*n.* 征服　　conquer *v.*

* theory〔'θiərɪ〕*n.* 理論　　*come into being* 形成

7. (**D**) We should draw more attention to the protection of intellectual property rights,
because the <u>rampant</u> piracy in the recording and publishing industry will lead
to higher prices for consumers.
我們應更加注意保護智慧財產權的問題，因為唱片以及出版界<u>猖狂的</u>盜版行為，
將導致消費者付出更高的代價。

(A) triumphant〔traɪ'ʌmfənt〕*adj.* 獲勝的；洋洋得意的　　triumph *n.* 勝利

(B) innovative〔'ɪnəˌvetɪv〕*adj.* 有創意的　　innovate *v.* 革新
innovation *n.* 革新

(C) amateur〔'æməˌt(ʃ)ur〕① *adj.* 業餘的（↔ professional 專業的）
② *n.* 業餘者（↔ professional 專業人士）
She is only an amateur golfer; she is not a professional.
她只是業餘的打高爾夫球的人；她並非專業球員。

(D) *rampant*〔'ræmpənt〕*adj.* （壞事、疾病）猖狂的；（言語）激烈的

* *draw attention to* 注意　　*intellectual property rights* 智慧財產權
piracy〔'paɪrəsɪ〕*n.* 盜版行為　　recording〔rɪ'kɔrdɪŋ〕*n.* 錄音；唱片
publishing〔'pʌblɪʃɪŋ〕*n.* 出版　　industry〔'ɪndəstrɪ〕*n.* 行業
lead to 導致；造成（= *result in* = *cause* ）
consumer〔kən's(j)umɚ〕*n.* 消費者

8. (**A**) The church, the largest one along the shore, can hold one thousand <u>worshippers</u>.
　　這座教堂是岸邊規模最大的一家，可容納一千名<u>信徒</u>。

　　(A) *worship(p)er* ('wɝʃəpɚ) *n.* 崇拜者；信徒　　　worship *v.* 崇拜；做禮拜

　　(B) peddler ('pɛdlɚ) *n.* 小販　　peddle *v.* 沿街叫賣

　　(C) sculptor ('skʌlptɚ) *n.* 雕刻家　　sculpt *v.* 雕刻　　sculpture *n.* 雕像

　　(D) governor ('gʌvənɚ) *n.* (美國) 州長；主管人員　　govern *v.* 管理

　　＊shore (ʃor) *n.* (海、湖、河) 岸　　hold (hold) *v.* 容納

9. (**B**) The price of beer <u>ranged</u> from 50 cents to 4 dollars per liter during
　　the summer season. 夏季啤酒的定價<u>範圍</u>由一公升五毛到四塊都有。

　　(A) separate ('sɛpə,ret) *v.* 分離　　separate A from B 分開 A 與 B

　　(B) *range* (rendʒ) *v.* 分布範圍；涉及；伸展
　　　　range from A to B = range between A and B 分布範圍由 A 至 B

　　(C) differ ('dɪfɚ) *v.* 不同　　differ from～ 跟～不同

　　(D) alter ('ɔltɚ) *v.* 修改；變更 (= *change*)　　alter *one's* clothes 修改衣服

　　＊per (pɚ) *prep.* 每一　　liter ('litɚ) *n.* 公升 (等於 1,000 c.c.)

10. (**A**) Although they plant trees in this area every year, the tops of some hills are still
　　<u>bare</u>. 雖然他們每年都在此區種樹，有些山頂還是<u>光禿禿的</u>。

　　(A) *bare* (bɛr) *adj.* (山) 光禿禿的；(身體) 赤裸的；(事物) 無修飾的
　　　　bare feet 打赤腳　　a bare fact 赤裸裸的事實

　　(B) blank (blæŋk) *adj.* (上頭未寫字而) 空白的；單調的；無表情的
　　　　a blank form 空白表格　　a blank look 表情茫然

　　(C) hollow ('halo) *adj.* 空心的；虛偽的
　　　　a hollow tube 空心的管子　　hollow compliments 虛偽的恭維

　　(D) vacant ('vekənt) *adj.* (未經使用而) 空著的；(座位、職位) 出缺的
　　　　a vacant room 空房　　a vacant position 空缺；職缺

　　＊plant (plænt) *v.* 種植　　top (tap) *n.* (山) 頂

11. (**D**) Henry is not able to come to work because he <u>came down with</u> the flu.
　　亨利<u>罹患</u>流行性感冒，無法來上班。

　　(A) come out with 說出；宣佈 (= *announce*)
　　　　Come out with it. Don't beat about the bush. 說出來吧。別拐彎抹角。

　　(B) get down to 開始做 (= *start*)
　　　　Let's get down to business. 我們來談正經事。

　　(C) get up to 到達；從事
　　　　What is he getting up to? 他到底在幹什麼？

　　(D) *come down with* 罹患

12. (**C**) The two boys started by <u>making faces</u> at each other. Then they began to fight.
兩個男孩開始是<u>互做鬼臉</u>，之後就打了起來。

(A) cut back 縮減 < *on* >　　　cut back on spending 縮減開支

(B) fool around 混日子；遊手好閒 (= *hang around* = *mess around*
= *play around*)

(C) *make a face* 做鬼臉；做出厭惡的表情 < *at* >

(D) read over 瀏覽 (= *read through*)

13. (**A**) He's constantly whining about every mishap of his life. Can't he just
<u>knock it off</u>? 他老是在抱怨人生每一件不幸的事。他不能把<u>嘴閉上</u>嗎？

(A) *knock it off* 住手 (= *stop*)；住嘴 (= *shut up*)

(B) lose *one's* control 失控　　【比較】keep *one's* control 掌控

(C) go through channels 循正當的途徑　　channels〔'tʃænlz〕*n. pl.* 正當的途徑
The officer hadn't gone through channels when accepting the gifts.
這位軍官未循正當的途徑（呈報），就收了禮物。

(D) hold *one's* breath （因恐懼、興奮而）屏息
【比較】lose *one's* breath 喘息；喘不過氣來

＊constantly〔'kɑnstəntlɪ〕*adv.* 總是　　***whine about*** 抱怨
mishap〔mɪs'hæp〕*n.* 不幸

14. (**B**) Though her parents <u>heap praise upon</u> her musical talent, Helen's piano
playing is really terrible.
雖然海倫的父母<u>大力讚揚</u>她的音樂天份，她的鋼琴其實是彈得一蹋糊塗。

(A) pour scorn on/over 輕視；瞧不起 (= *think scorn of*)
scorn〔skɔrn〕*n.* 輕視

(B) *heap praise upon/on* 大力讚揚　　heap〔hip〕*v.* 堆積

(C) give vent to 發洩　　vent〔vɛnt〕*n.* 排氣口
He gave vent to his anger by hitting his wife. 他打老婆以發洩怒氣。

(D) cast light upon/on～ 提供～線索；使～露出一道曙光
(= *throw/shed light upon/on*)

15. (**D**) His wife left him. Besides, he has committed a crime and been sent to jail.
He is really <u>at the end of his rope</u>.
他太太棄他而去。此外，他犯了罪、被送進監獄。他真是<u>山窮水盡</u>。

(A) in good hands 受到良好的照料

(B) at loose ends 無所事事；遊手好閒
He felt himself at loose ends — no job, no prospects.
他感到無所事事 —— 沒工作，無絲毫希望。

(C) in the know 熟悉（機密）；通曉（內情）

(D) *at the end of one's rope* 山窮水盡；窮途末路
＊***commit a crime*** 犯罪　　***be sent to jail*** 被送進監獄；入獄

TEST 25

Directions: The following questions are incomplete sentences. You are to choose the one word that best completes the sentence.

1. A program has been set up to _____ cooperation between the police and the community.
   (A) facilitate
   (B) irritate
   (C) withdraw
   (D) purchase   (   )

2. A _____ of the long report was submitted to the mayor for approval.
   (A) shorthand
   (B) showdown
   (C) schedule
   (D) sketch   (   )

3. Though _____ in New York, he prefers to write about the plain life of small towns.
   (A) raised
   (B) grown
   (C) developed
   (D) cultivated   (   )

4. The doctor told me in order to keep healthy, I should _____ more fat and salt from my diet.
   (A) domesticate
   (B) eliminate
   (C) absorb
   (D) adapt   (   )

5. Some people are fond of graffiti. That's why public bathroom walls are sometimes covered with _____ words and sayings.
   (A) vulgar
   (B) bleak
   (C) populous
   (D) credulous   (   )

6. The enemy have _____ fighting and asked for peace negotiations.
   (A) faded
   (B) pretended
   (C) ceased
   (D) overcome   (   )

7. I must leave now. _____, if you need that book, I'll bring it next time.
   (A) Incidentally
   (B) Accidentally
   (C) Occasionally
   (D) Subsequently   (   )

8. The 2008 Olympic Games turned many parts of Beijing City into a noisy, disjointed construction _____.

(A) zone
(B) phase
(C) elevation
(D) ambiguity ( )

9. Some scholars warned that the demolition of the historic buildings would be _____ to the cultural heritage of this city.

(A) courteous
(B) indispensable
(C) amiable
(D) devastating ( )

10. The pollution problem as well as several other issues is going to be discussed when Congress is in _____ next spring.

(A) assembly
(B) session
(C) recess
(D) conversation ( )

11. We have _____ sugar. Go buy some more.

(A) run out of
(B) have no liking for
(C) put up with
(D) pass out ( )

12. If you _____ all that junk, you will have much more space.

(A) put in order
(B) get along
(C) give in to
(D) get rid of ( )

13. Peter likes to talk and can _____ a conversation with anybody.

(A) put forth
(B) get on with
(C) cut in
(D) strike up ( )

14. She was ashamed to ask me in, for her room was _____.

(A) in a litter
(B) in a liter
(C) at six and seven
(D) in mess ( )

15. Mike _____ his father with a gloomy look until he was out of sight.

(A) looked into
(B) looked over
(C) looked after
(D) looked down upon ( )

TEST 25 詳解

1. (**A**) A program has been set up to <u>facilitate</u> cooperation between the police and the community. 有一個計劃已經成立,用以促進警方和社區之間的合作。

    (A) *facilitate*〔fə'sɪlə,tet〕v. 促進;使(事情)容易(注意:此動詞不可以「人」為受詞)

    (B) irritate〔'ɪrə,tet〕v. 激怒　　irritating *adj.*(事物)令人生氣的
irritated *adj.*(人)生氣的

    (C) withdraw〔wɪð'drɔ〕v. 撤退;收回;取出　　withdrawal *n.*
withdraw troops 撤退軍隊　　withdraw money　(從銀行)領錢出來

    (D) purchase〔'pɝtʃəs〕① v. 購買(= *buy*)　　② n. 購買 < *of* >;購買之物

    * *set up* 成立　　cooperation〔ko,apə'reʃən〕n. 合作
community〔kə'mjunətɪ〕n. 社區

2. (**D**) A <u>sketch</u> of the long report was submitted to the mayor for approval.
這份冗長報告的大綱,被提交給市長等候批准。

    (A) shorthand〔'ʃɔrt,hænd〕n. 速記　　take shorthand 速記下來

    (B) showdown〔'ʃo,daʊn〕n.(撲克牌)攤牌;最後決定階段

    (C) schedule〔'skɛdʒʊl〕n. 時間表;計畫　　on schedule 準時
(↔ *behind schedule* 落後)

    (D) *sketch*〔skɛtʃ〕n. 大綱(= *summary* = *outline*);素描
sketch book 素描本

    * submit〔səb'mɪt〕v. 提交　　mayor〔'meɚ〕n. 市長
approval〔ə'pruvl̩〕n.(正式)承認

3. (**A**) Though (*he was*) <u>raised</u> in New York, he prefers to write about the plain life of small towns. 雖然在紐約長大,他卻偏好描述小城的簡樸生活。

    (A) *raise*〔rez〕v. 撫養(小孩)(= *rear* = *bring up*);飼養(動物);
舉起(東西);提升　　raise a family 撫養一家子
raise the blinds 拉起百葉窗

    (B) grow〔gro〕v. 長大(主詞是人時,無被動,本句可改成 Though he *grew up* in New York, he prefers to write about the plain life of small towns.)

    (C) develop〔dɪ'vɛləp〕v. 發展;培養(興趣等);罹患(疾病);展開(計畫等)
develop good taste 發展好品味　　develop an illness 罹患疾病

    (D) cultivate〔'kʌltə,vet〕v. 栽培(作物);培養(才能;品味等)
cultivation *n.*　　cultivate tomatoes 栽培番茄
cultivate *one's* mind 培養心性

    * plain〔plen〕*adj.* 簡樸的

4. (**B**) The doctor told me in order to keep healthy, I should <u>eliminate</u> more fat and salt from my diet. 醫生告訴我要保持健康，飲食要<u>去除</u>更多的脂肪和鹽份。

    (A) domesticate〔də'mɛstə,ket〕*v.* 馴服（動物）；使（人）開化

        domestic *adj.* 家庭的

    (B) **eliminate**〔ɪ'lɪmə,net〕*v.* 去除　　eliminate A from B　從 B 中去除 A

    (C) absorb〔əb'sɔrb〕*v.* 吸收；使專心

        absorb *oneself* in 專心於（= *be absorbed in* ）

    (D) adapt〔ə'dæpt〕*v.* 改編；使適應

        The play was adapted from a novel. 此劇是由小說改編。

    ＊fat〔fæt〕*n.* 脂肪　　diet〔'daɪət〕*n.* 飲食

5. (**A**) Some people are fond of graffiti. That's why public bathroom walls are sometimes covered with <u>vulgar</u> words and sayings.

有些人喜歡塗鴉。這也是公廁牆壁有時佈滿<u>粗俗</u>的字眼和話語的原因。

    (A) **vulgar**〔'vʌlgɚ〕*adj.* 粗俗的（↔ cultured　有教養的）

    (B) bleak〔blik〕*adj.* 陰冷的（= *cold* ）；荒涼的（= *dreary* ）

    (C) populous〔'pɑpjələs〕*adj.* 人口稠密的（↔ sparse　人口稀少的）

        population *n.* 人口

    (D) credulous〔'krɛdʒələs〕*adj.* 容易相信別人的；容易被騙的　　credit *n.* 信用

    ＊**be fond of** 喜歡　　graffiti〔grə'fitɪ〕*n.* 塗鴉　　saying〔'seɪŋ〕*n.* 話語

6. (**C**) The enemy have <u>ceased</u> fighting and asked for peace negotiations.

敵軍<u>停止</u>作戰，並要求和平談判。

    (A) fade〔fed〕*v.* 逐漸衰退 < *away*/*off*/*out* >；褪色；凋謝（= *wither* ）

        Her beauty faded away year by year. 她的姿色逐年衰退。

    (B) pretend〔prɪ'tɛnd〕*v.* 假裝　　pretense *n.*（= *make-believe* ）

    (C) **cease**〔sis〕*v.* 停止（= *stop* ）　　cease fire 停火

    (D) overcome〔,ovɚ'kʌm〕*v.* 克服（難題）；打敗（敵人）（= *defeat* ）

    ＊**the enemy** 敵軍（可視為單數或複數）　　fighting〔'faɪtɪŋ〕*n.* 戰鬥

    ask for 要求　　negotiation〔nɪ,goʃɪ'eʃən〕*n.* 談判

7. (**A**) I must leave now. <u>Incidentally</u>, if you need that book, I'll bring it next time.

我現在得離開了。<u>順便一提</u>，如果你需要那書，我下次幫你帶來。

    (A) **incidentally**〔,ɪnsə'dɛntl̩ɪ〕*adv.* 順便一提（= *by the way* ）

    (B) accidentally〔,æksə'dɛntl̩ɪ〕*adv.* 偶然地（= *by accident* ）

    (C) occasionally〔ə'keʒənl̩ɪ〕*adv.* 偶爾（= *now and then* = *at times* = *sometimes* ）

    (D) subsequently〔'sʌbsɪ,kwɛntlɪ〕*adv.* 隨後地；後來

        （↔ previously　先前；之前）

8. (**A**) The 2008 Olympic Games turned many parts of Beijing City into a noisy, disjointed construction <u>zone</u>. 2008 年要舉辦的奧林匹克運動大會，已經把北京城許多地方，變成吵雜而混亂的建築<u>區域</u>。

(A) *zone* 〔 zon 〕 *n.* (依照某種目的或特質而劃分的) 區域
  a construction zone 建築區　　 a war zone 交戰地帶
  an earthquake zone 易地震區
(B) phase 〔 fez 〕 *n.* (發展、變化之) 階段；時期 (= *stage*)
  enter into a new phase 進入新階段
(C) elevation 〔ˌɛlə'veʃən〕 *n.* 舉起；高度 (= *height*)；海拔 (= *altitude*)
  elevate *v.* 舉起　　 at an elevation of 1,000 feet 在海拔一千英呎的高度
(D) ambiguity 〔ˌæmbɪ'gjuətɪ〕 *n.* 模稜兩可；曖昧　　 ambiguous *adj.*

* *the Olympic Games* 奧林匹克運動大會
 turn A *into* B 把 A 變成 B (= *change* A *into* B)
 disjointed 〔 dɪs'dʒɔɪntɪd 〕 *adj.* 混亂的；支離破碎的
 construction 〔 kən'strʌkʃən 〕 *n.* 建築

9. (**D**) Some scholars warned that the demolition of the historic buildings would be <u>devastating</u> to the cultural heritage of this city. 有些學者警告，拆除這些歷史性的建築，對本城的文化遺產，將是<u>破壞性的</u>行為。

(A) courteous 〔'kɜtɪəs〕 *adj.* 有禮貌的；慇懃的　　 courtesy *n.* 禮貌；慇懃
(B) indispensable 〔ˌɪndɪ'spɛnsəbḷ〕 *adj.* 不可或缺的；必要的 (= *necessary*)
(C) amiable 〔'emɪəbḷ〕 *adj.* 和藹可親的 (= *agreeable*)；溫柔的 (= *kind*)
(D) *devastating* 〔'dɛvəsˌtetɪŋ〕 *adj.* 破壞性的；使荒廢的　　 devastate *v.* 破壞

* scholar 〔'skɑlə〕 *n.* 學者　　 demolition 〔ˌdɛmə'lɪʃən〕 *n.* 拆除；破壞
 historic 〔 hɪs'tɔrɪk 〕 *adj.* 歷史性的　　 cultural 〔'kʌltʃərəl〕 *adj.* 文化的
 heritage 〔'hɛrətɪdʒ〕 *n.* 遺產

10. (**B**) The pollution problem as well as several other issues is going to be discussed when Congress is in <u>session</u> next spring.
國會來春<u>會期</u>中，將討論污染及其他的問題。

【注意】連接詞 as well as 連接兩個主詞時，動詞單複數與第一個主詞一致。

(A) assembly 〔 ə'sɛmblɪ 〕 *n.* 集合；議會　　 the city assembly 市議會
  assemble *v.*
(B) *session* 〔'sɛʃən〕 *n.* (會議) 開會　　 in session 會期中
(C) recess 〔 rɪ'sɛs 〕 *n.* 休會　　 in recess 休會中
(D) conversation 〔ˌkɑnvə'seʃən〕 *n.* 交談　　 in conversation with~ 跟~交談

* pollution 〔 pə'luʃən 〕 *n.* 污染　　 issue 〔'ɪʃju〕 *n.* 問題
 Congress 〔'kɑngrəs〕 *n.* 國會

11. (**A**) We have <u>run out of</u> sugar. Go buy some more.
我們已經把糖<u>用完</u>了。去買點糖吧。

    (A) ***run out of*** 用完

    (B) have no liking for 不喜歡 (= *do not like*)

    (C) put up with 忍受 (= *endure*)

    (D) pass out 分配；失去知覺

        例：The teacher *passed out* the test papers. (老師分發考卷。)

              If he took one more drink, he would *pass out*.

          (他再多喝一杯就會不醒人事。)

12. (**D**) If you <u>get rid of</u> all that junk, you will have much more space.
你若<u>除掉</u>那一堆垃圾，空間會多出來許多。

    (A) put ~ in order 把 ~ 整理好

    (B) get along 滾開 (= *go away*)

    (C) give away 贈送；頒發；暴露；使露出馬腳

        例：He *gave away* all his money to the orphanage.

            (他所有錢都捐給孤兒院。)

    (D) ***get rid of*** 除掉；拿走

13. (**D**) Peter likes to talk and can <u>strike up</u> a conversation with anybody.
彼得喜歡聊天，碰到什麼人都可以<u>開始</u>聊起來。

    (A) put forth 提出；發揮

    (B) get on with 繼續 (= *continue*)

        例：*Get on with* your job. (繼續做你的工作。)

    (C) cut in 打岔；插嘴 (= *interrupt*)

    (D) ***strike up*** 開始 (= *begin*)

14. (**A**) She was ashamed to ask me in, for her room was <u>in a litter</u>.
她不好意思邀我入內，因為她的房間<u>亂七八糟</u>。

    (A) ***in a litter*** 亂七八糟；雜亂的   (B) liter〔ˈlɪtɚ〕*n.* 公升

    (C) 應改成 at sixes and sevens 「亂七八糟」

    (D) 應改成 in a mess 「亂七八糟」

    ＊litter〔ˈlɪtɚ〕*n.* 雜亂；垃圾；廢物

15. (**C**) Mike <u>looked after</u> his father with a gloomy look until he was out of sight.
邁克面帶憂鬱地<u>目送</u>父親，直到他走遠看不見為止。

    (A) look into 調查；翻閱 (字典)   (B) look over 過目一遍；忽略

    (C) ***look after*** 目送；照顧 (= *take care of* = *see after*)

    (D) look down on/upon 瞧不起 (↔ *look up to* 尊敬)

TEST 26

Directions: The following questions are incomplete sentences. You are to choose the one word that best completes the sentence.

1. I felt _____ to death because I could make nothing of the chairman's speech.
   - (A) fatigued
   - (B) tired
   - (C) exhausted
   - (D) bored   (   )

2. The Minister of Foreign Affairs offered a _____ for settling the border dispute.
   - (A) sake
   - (B) fortune
   - (C) vehicle
   - (D) formula   (   )

3. It is well-known that every citizen in our country is _____ to free medical care.
   - (A) entitled
   - (B) involved
   - (C) provided
   - (D) submitted   (   )

4. North Korean leader Kim Jong-il's nuclear test drew regional condemnation and U.N. _____ backed by China, Kim's long-time supporter.
   - (A) sanctions
   - (B) proliferations
   - (C) dismantlings
   - (D) disarmaments   (   )

5. A man has to make _____ for his old age by putting aside enough money to live on when he is old.
   - (A) supply
   - (B) assurance
   - (C) provision
   - (D) adjustment   (   )

6. Florence played a _____ role during the great artistic period called the Renaissance.
   - (A) temporary
   - (B) significant
   - (C) coherent
   - (D) content   (   )

7. Guests may feel they are not highly _____ if the invitation to a party is given only a couple of days before the party.
   - (A) admired
   - (B) regarded
   - (C) expected
   - (D) worshipped   (   )

8. The newly built theater is _____ enough to accommodate an audience of 2,000 people.
   (A) spacious   (B) sophisticated
   (C) substantial   (D) steady   (   )

9. Tom made an attempt to apologize only to _____ her even more.
   (A) assemble   (B) agitate
   (C) attribute   (D) dismiss   (   )

10. A big suit of armor was hung on the wall, and a corner cupboard, _____ left open, displayed immense treasures of old silver.
    (A) aimlessly   (B) absurdly
    (C) intentionally   (D) diligently   (   )

11. When the engine would not start, the mechanic inspected all its parts to find out what was _____.
    (A) at fault   (B) in trouble
    (C) in difficulties   (D) on the watch   (   )

12. I was speaking to Ann on the phone when suddenly we were _____.
    (A) hung up   (B) hung back
    (C) cut down   (D) cut off   (   )

13. All the information we have collected in relation to that case _____ very little.
    (A) adds up to   (B) makes up for
    (C) comes up with   (D) puts up with   (   )

14. The supervisor hasn't had time so far to get into it _____, but he gave us an idea of his plan.
    (A) at hand   (B) in turn
    (C) in conclusion   (D) at length   (   )

15. Christmas is a Christian holy day usually celebrated on December 25th _____ the birth of Jesus Christ.
    (A) in accordance with   (B) in terms of
    (C) in favor of   (D) in honor of   (   )

TEST 26 詳解

1. (**D**) I felt <u>bored</u> to death because I could make nothing of the chairman's speech.
主席的演說我一點也聽不懂，眞是無聊至極。

(A) fatigued〔fə'tigd〕*adj.* 勞累的　　be fatigued with~　因~而勞累

(B) tired〔taɪrd〕*adj.* 勞累的；厭倦的

　　be tired from/with~　因~而勞累　　be tired of~　厭倦~

(C) exhausted〔ɪg'zɔstɪd〕*adj.* 筋疲力盡的

　　be exhausted from/with~　因~而筋疲力盡

(D) *bored*〔bord〕*adj.* 厭倦的；無聊的　　be bored to death　無聊至極

＊*make nothing of* 完全不了解　　chairman〔'tʃɛrmən〕*n.* 主席

speech〔spitʃ〕*n.* 演說

2. (**D**) The Minister of Foreign Affairs offered a <u>formula</u> for settling the border
dispute. 外交部長提出一份方案，來解決國界的糾紛。

(A) sake〔sek〕*n.* 緣故　　for ~'s sake = for the sake of~　爲了~的緣故

(B) fortune〔'fɔrtʃən〕*n.* 財富；運氣　　make a fortune　發大財

(C) vehicle〔'viɪkḷ〕*n.* 陸上交通工具；車輛

　　transportation vehicles 運輸工具

(D) *formula*〔'fɔrmjələ〕*n.* 方案；公式；準則

　　a math formula　數學公式

＊minister〔'mɪnɪstɚ〕*n.* 部長　　affair〔ə'fɛr〕*n.* 事務

foreign affairs 外交事務　　settle〔'sɛtḷ〕*v.* 解決

border〔'bɔrdɚ〕*n.* 國界　　dispute〔dɪ'spjut〕*n.* 糾紛

3. (**A**) It is well-known that every citizen in our country is <u>entitled</u> to free medical
care. 我國國民都有資格享用免費醫療是人盡皆知的事。

(A) *entitle*〔ɪn'taɪtḷ〕*v.* 使有資格 <*to*>　　be entitled to　有資格享用

(B) involve〔ɪn'vɑlv〕*v.* 牽涉；包含 <*in*>　　be involved in　捲入

(C) provide〔prə'vaɪd〕*v.* 提供 <*with*>

　　be provided with　被提供（用法與 supply 同，見第 5 題）

(D) submit〔səb'mɪt〕*v.* 提出 <*to*>

　　be submitted to　被提交給

＊well-known〔'wɛl'non〕*adj.* 人盡皆知的

citizen〔'sɪtəzṇ〕*n.* 市民　　*medical care* 醫療

4. (**A**) North Korean leader Kim Jong-il's nuclear test drew regional condemnation and U.N. <u>sanctions</u> backed by China, Kim's long-time supporter.

北韓領導人金正日進行核子試爆,招致區域內國家的譴責以及聯合國的<u>制裁</u>,而中國是金正日長期的支持者,也支持這次的制裁。

(A) *sanction* 〔'sæŋkʃən〕 *n.* (對違反法令的) 制裁;批准

apply/take/put economic sanctions against~ 對~實施經濟制裁

lift military sanctions against~ 對~解除軍事制裁

(B) proliferation 〔 proˌlɪfə'reʃən 〕 *n.* 激增 (= *rapid increase*);擴散

proliferation of nuclear weapons 核子武器的擴散

(C) dismantling 〔 dɪs'mæntlɪŋ 〕 *n.* 拆除 (工具、設備等)　　dismantle *v.*

(D) disarmament 〔 dɪs'ɑrməmənt 〕 *n.* 解除武裝;裁軍

arm *v.* 武裝;配備武器　　arms *n. pl.* 武器

disarm *v.* 解除武裝;裁軍

＊*North Korean* 北韓的　　*nuclear test* 核子試爆;核子測試

draw 〔 drɔ 〕 *v.* 招致　　regional 〔'ridʒənl 〕 *adj.* 區域內的

condemnation 〔ˌkɑndɛm'neʃən 〕 *n.* 譴責

U.N. 聯合國 (= *United Nations*)

back 〔 bæk 〕 *v.* 支持　　supporter 〔 sə'portɚ 〕 *n.* 支持者

5. (**C**) A man has to make <u>provision</u> for his old age by putting aside enough money to live on when he is old.

每個人都要儲存足夠金額的錢,以<u>準備</u>老來生活之需。

(A) supply 〔 sə'plaɪ 〕 ① *n.* 供應　② *v.* 供應 (= *provide*)

supply A with B = supply B for/to A 供應 B 給 A

The lake supplies the town *with* water. 此湖供水給這個城鎮。

= The lake supplies water *for/to* the town.

(B) assurance 〔 ə'ʃʊrəns 〕 *n.* 保證 (= *guarantee*);信心 (= *confidence*)

assure *v.*

(C) *provision* 〔 prə'vɪʒən 〕 *n.* ① 準備 (為不可數名詞)

② 食物;糧食 (一定得用複數形)　　provide *v.*

make provision for~ 為~做準備　　run out of provisions 糧食短缺

(D) adjustment 〔 ə'dʒʌstmənt 〕 *n.* 調整;適應

make an adjustment 做調整　　adjust *v.*

＊*put aside* 儲存 (= *save*)　　*live on* ~ 靠~過生活

6. (**B**) Florence played a <u>significant</u> role during the great artistic period called the Renaissance.

佛羅倫斯在偉大的藝術期即文藝復興時，扮演<u>極重要的</u>角色。

(A) temporary〔ˈtɛmpəˌrɛrɪ〕*adj.* 暫時的（↔ permanent 永遠的）

(B) *significant*〔sɪgˈnɪfəkənt〕*adj.* 非常重要的（= *very important*）；顯著的

(C) coherent〔koˈhɪrənt〕*adj.* 有條理的（= *logical*）

　　cohere *v.* 有條理；緊密結合

(D) content〔kənˈtɛnt〕*adj.* 滿足的＜ with ＞（= *satisfied*）

　　content〔ˈkɑntɛnt〕*n.* 內容

　＊Florence〔ˈflɔrəns〕*n.* 佛羅倫斯（位於義大利中部）

　　Renaissance〔ˌrɛnəˈzɑns〕*n.* 文藝復興

7. (**B**) Guests may feel they are not highly <u>regarded</u> if the invitation to a party is given only a couple of days before the party.

如果請帖在宴會前幾天，才發給賓客，客人會覺得沒受到高度<u>重視</u>。

(A) admire〔ədˈmaɪr〕*v.* 讚賞（通常用 greatly 和 deeply 修飾）

(B) *regard*〔rɪˈgɑrd〕*v.* 重視（通常用 highly 修飾）；視為

　　regard…as～　把…視為～

(C) expect〔ɪkˈspɛkt〕*v.* 期待（通常用 much 修飾）

(D) worship〔ˈwɝʃɪp〕*v.* 崇拜（通常用 devoutly「虔誠地」修飾）

　＊invitation〔ˌɪnvəˈteʃən〕*n.* 邀請　　　*a couple of* 數個（= *several*）

8. (**A**) The newly built theater is <u>spacious</u> enough to accommodate an audience of 2,000 people. 新蓋的戲院十分<u>寬敞</u>，足以容納兩千名觀眾。

(A) *spacious*〔ˈspeʃəs〕*adj.* 寬敞的　　　space *n.* 空間

(B) sophisticated〔səˈfɪstəˌketɪd〕*adj.* 複雜的；老練的

　　（= *experienced* = *refined* = *polished*）

(C) substantial〔səbˈstænʃəl〕*adj.* 實質（存在）的；大量的

　　substance *n.* 物質

(D) steady〔ˈstɛdɪ〕*adj.* 穩定（不變）的；可靠的

　　go steady　（男女）固定交往

　　Slow but steady wins the race.【諺】慢而穩者獲勝。

　＊accommodate〔əˈkɑməˌdet〕*v.* 容納

　　audience〔ˈɔdɪəns〕*n.*（一群）觀眾；聽眾

9. (**B**) Tom made an attempt to apologize only to <u>agitate</u> her even more.
   湯姆嘗試道歉，卻只是更<u>激怒</u>她。

   (A) assemble〔əˈsɛmbḷ〕*v.* 裝配；集合（= *gather* = *congregate*）
   assembly *n.* 裝配；集合　　assembly line　（工廠）裝配線
   the city assembly　市議會

   (B) *agitate*（ˈædʒəˌtet）*v.* 激怒（= *irritate*）；使心煩
   （= *disturb* = *trouble* = *upset*）

   (C) attribute〔əˈtrɪbjut〕*v.* 歸因於 < *to* >　　attribution　*n.*
   attributable　*adj.*　　attribute…to~　把…歸因於~（= *ascribe*…*to*~）

   (D) dismiss〔dɪsˈmɪs〕*v.* 解散（團體）；解僱（= *fire* = *lay off* = *sack*）
   Class dismissed.　下課。

   ＊attempt〔əˈtɛmpt〕*n.* 嘗試
   apologize〔əˈpɑləˌdʒaɪz〕*v.* 道歉　　***only to*** 卻

10. (**C**) A big suit of armor was hung on the wall, and a corner cupboard, (*which had*
   been) <u>intentionally</u> left open, displayed immense treasures of old silver.
   一套很大的盔甲掛在牆上，而在角落的碗櫥，<u>故意</u>門是
   開著的，裡頭陳列眾多古銀器之類的貴重物品。

   (A) aimlessly（ˈemlɪslɪ）*adv.* 無目標地（= *without aim*）
   aim　*n.* 目標

   (B) absurdly〔əbˈsɝdlɪ〕*adv.* 荒謬地
   （= *ridiculously* = *foolishly*）

   (C) *intentionally*〔ɪnˈtɛnʃənḷɪ〕*adv.* 故意地（= *deliberately*）

   (D) diligently（ˈdɪlədʒəntlɪ）*adv.* 勤勉地

   ＊*a suit of armor*　一套盔甲
   hang〔hæŋ〕*v.* 掛（三態變化為 hang-hung-hung）
   corner（ˈkɔrnɚ）*n.* 角落　　cupboard（ˈkʌbəd）*n.* 碗櫥
   leave〔liv〕*v.* 使~成為某種狀態　　display〔dɪˈsple〕*v.* 陳列
   immense〔ɪˈmɛns〕*adj.* 眾多的；龐大的
   treasure（ˈtrɛʒɚ）*n.* 貴重物品；寶藏
   silver（ˈsɪlvɚ）*n.* 銀器（集合名詞）

11. (**A**) When the engine would not start, the mechanic inspected all its parts to find out what was <u>at fault</u>.

引擎無法發動時，技工檢查所有的零件，想找出<u>故障的</u>部分。

(A) *at fault* 故障的；錯的 (= *wrong*)
(B) in trouble 陷入困境的 (= *in hot water* = *in deep water*)
(C) in difficulties 有困難的 (特指經濟方面) (= *short of money* = *needy*)
　　【比較】with difficulty 千辛萬苦地 (= *difficultly*)
　　(↔ *without difficulty* 毫無困難地)
(D) on the watch 小心警戒 < *for* > (= *on the ball* = *alert* = *watchful*)
　　We should be on the watch for any possible attack from the terrorists.
　　我們要小心警戒任何恐怖分子的攻擊行為。

＊engine (ˈɛndʒən) *n.* 引擎
mechanic (məˈkænɪk) *n.* 技工　　inspect (ɪnˈspɛkt) *v.* 檢查
parts (parts) *n. pl.* 零件 (多用複數形)

12. (**D**) I was speaking to Ann on the phone when suddenly we were <u>cut off</u>.

我跟安講電話時，突然通話被<u>中斷</u>。

(A) hang up 掛電話 (↔ *hold on* 不掛電話)
　　Hold on; don't hang up. 不要掛掉電話。
(B) hang back 抑制 (= *restrain* = *suppress*)；退縮 < *from* >
(C) cut down （量）減少 (= *bring down* = *decrease*)
　　【比較】cut up 切割；剁碎
(D) *cut off* 中斷 (= *break off* = *terminate*)

13. (**A**) All the information we have collected in relation to that case <u>adds up to</u> very little. 我們針對這個案例所能蒐集到的資料，<u>結果是</u>極其有限的。

(A) *add up to* 結果是 (= *turn out to be*)；加起來總合 (= *sum up to*)
(B) make up for 補償 (= *compensate for* = *atone for*)
(C) come up with （人）想到 (點子等)
(D) put up with 忍受 (= *bear* = *endure* = *tolerate*)

＊*in relation to* 有關 (= *regarding* = *concerning* = *about*)
case (kes) *n.* 案例；問題

14. (**D**) The supervisor hasn't had time so far to get into it <u>at length</u>, but he gave us an idea of his plan.

督導至今都沒有空<u>仔細地</u>著手研究這個問題,只給我們計劃大致的構想。

(A) at hand 在手邊 (= *nearby*);即將到來 (= *approaching*)

    ⎰ I always keep the dictionary *at hand.* 我總是把字典放在手邊。
    ⎱ Christmas is (*near/close*) *at hand.* 聖誕節即將到來。

(B) in turn 依順序地

(C) in conclusion 總之 (= *in sum* = *in summary* = *in a word* = *in a nutshell* = *to conclude* = *to sum up*)

(D) *at length* 詳細地;最後 (= *at last* = *finally* = *eventually* = *at the end* = *in the long run*)

    ＊supervisor〔ˌsupɚˈvaɪzɚ〕*n.* 督導;監督者   ***so far*** 至今

    get into 開始;著手

15. (**D**) Christmas is a Christian holy day usually celebrated on December 25th <u>in honor of</u> the birth of Jesus Christ.

聖誕節是基督教的聖日,通常在十二月二十五日這天慶祝,
以<u>紀念</u>耶穌基督的誕生。

(A) in accordance with 按照 (= *according to*)

    accordance〔əˈkɔrdn̩s〕*n.* 一致

(B) in terms of 用~角度 (= *in view of*);按照 (= *according to*)

    He thinks of everything in terms of money.

    他用錢的角度來看待一切事物。

(C) in favor of 支持;贊成 (= *for*)

    【比較】in favor with 得~(某人)寵

    Public opinion is strongly in favor of this project.

    輿論強烈支持這項計劃。

(D) *in honor of* 紀念 (= *in memory of* = *in remembrance of*)

    【比較】in celebration of 慶祝

    ＊Christian〔ˈkrɪstʃən〕*adj.* 基督教的   holy〔ˈholɪ〕*adj.* 神聖的

    celebrate〔ˈsɛləˌbret〕*v.* 慶祝

    Jesus Christ〔ˈdʒizəs ˈkraɪst〕*n.* 耶穌基督

TEST 27

Directions: The following questions are incomplete sentences. You are to choose the one word that best completes the sentence.

1. Too much _____ to X-rays can cause skin burns or other damage to the body.
   - (A) disclosure
   - (B) exhibition
   - (C) contact
   - (D) exposure   (   )

2. Some of the most important concepts in physics _____ their success to these mathematical theories.
   - (A) own
   - (B) owe
   - (C) contribute
   - (D) contemplate   (   )

3. About 1,657 metric tons of smuggled farm _____ were destroyed last year under government efforts to deter smuggling and to stablize Taiwan's agricultural sector.
   - (A) magnitude
   - (B) facility
   - (C) produce
   - (D) supplement   (   )

4. As a defense against air-pollution damage, many plants and animals _____ a substance that absorbs pollutants.
   - (A) relieve
   - (B) release
   - (C) dismiss
   - (D) discard   (   )

5. Applause has been given to "Brokeback Mountain," a movie directed by internationally-acclaimed Taiwanese director Ang Lee, since its _____.
   - (A) premiere
   - (B) primary
   - (C) premise
   - (D) premium   (   )

6. Your improper words will give _____ to doubts concerning your true intentions.
   - (A) rise
   - (B) reason
   - (C) suspicion
   - (D) impulse   (   )

7. He never _____ the fact that he is married.
   - (A) held over
   - (B) held good
   - (C) let on
   - (D) broke into   (   )

8. The news item about the fire was followed by a detailed report made on the _____.
   (A) spot
   (B) spy
   (C) spirit
   (D) spice   (　)

9. One reason for the success of Asian immigrants in the U.S. is that they have taken great _____ to educate their children.
   (A) efforts
   (B) pains
   (C) attempts
   (D) endeavors   (　)

10. The remarkable _____ of life on the Galapagos Islands inspired Charles Darwin to establish his theory of evolution.
    (A) classification
    (B) variety
    (C) density
    (D) diversion   (　)

11. The English language contains a(n) _____ of words which are comparatively rare in ordinary conversation.
    (A) altitude
    (B) latitude
    (C) multitude
    (D) attitude   (　)

12. The match on Saturday was _____ and re-arranged for tonight.
    (A) called down
    (B) rained out
    (C) put down
    (D) knocked out   (　)

13. The employees would _____ when the boss was not around.
    (A) goof off
    (B) wade through
    (C) get lost
    (D) drop a line   (　)

14. My father was furious about my mistake — he shouted at me and didn't _____.
    (A) pull any punches
    (B) pull my leg
    (C) pull his weight
    (D) pull my teeth   (　)

15. He was once a very popular movie star in Hollywood, but recently he has been _____.
    (A) losing his tongue
    (B) losing his touch
    (C) losing his head
    (D) losing his shirt   (　)

TEST 27 詳解

1. (**D**) Too much <u>exposure</u> to X-rays can cause skin burns or other damage to the body. 過度暴露在 X 光下，會造成皮膚灼傷或傷害到身體。
   - (A) disclosure〔dɪsˈkloʒɚ〕*n.* 揭發（秘密等）　　disclose *v.*
   - (B) exhibition〔͵ɛksəˈbɪʃən〕*n.* 展示；展覽會　　exhibit〔ɪgˈzɪbɪt〕*v.*
   - (C) contact〔ˈkɑntækt〕*n.* 接觸 < *with* >　　contact *v.*
   - (D) ***exposure***〔ɪkˈspoʒɚ〕*n.* 暴露 < *to* >；揭發 < *of* >；（底片）張數
     expose *v.*
   - * ***X-ray*** X 光　　burn〔bɝn〕*n.* 灼傷

2. (**B**) Some of the most important concepts in physics <u>owe</u> their success to these mathematical theories. 有些最重要的物理概念，<u>來自於</u>這些數學理論。
   - (A) own〔on〕*v.* 擁有（= *possess*）；承認（事實、罪行等）（= *admit*）
   - (B) ***owe***〔o〕*v.* 由於；將~歸功於 < *to* >　　**owe** A ***to*** B 將 A 歸功於 B
   - (C) contribute〔kənˈtrɪbjut〕*v.* 貢獻 < *to* >　　contribute A to B 貢獻 A 給 B
   - (D) contemplate〔ˈkɑntəm͵plet〕*v.* 注視（= *gaze at*)；沉思（= *think about*)
   - * concept〔ˈkɑnsɛpt〕*n.* 概念　　physics〔ˈfɪzɪks〕*n.* 物理
     mathematical〔͵mæθəˈmætɪk!〕*adj.* 數學的

3. (**C**) About 1,657 metric tons of smuggled farm <u>produce</u> were destroyed last year under government efforts to deter smuggling and to stablize Taiwan's agricultural sector.
   去年大概有 1,657 公噸的走私<u>農產品</u>被毀，因為政府努力要遏止走私，以及穩定台灣的農產部門。
   - (A) magnitude〔ˈmægnə͵tjud〕*n.* 巨大；重要
     the magnitude of the space 宏大的宇宙
   - (B) facility〔fəˈsɪlətɪ〕*n.* 設施（多用複數形）；容易（↔ difficulty 困難）
     public facilities 公共設施　　with facility 容易地（= *with ease*)
   - (C) ***produce***〔ˈprɑd(j)us〕*n.* 農產品（注意：此字為集合名詞。當名詞時，
     重音在前，與當動詞時，唸作〔prəˈdjus〕不同）
   - (D) supplement〔ˈsʌpləmənt〕*n.* 補充；補給品
     vitamin supplements 維他命補充品
   - * ***metric ton*** 公噸　　smuggle〔ˈsmʌg!〕*v.* 走私
     government〔ˈgʌvənmənt〕*n.* 政府　　deter〔dɪˈtɝ〕*v.* 遏止
     stablize〔ˈstæb!͵aɪz〕*v.* 使穩定
     agricultural〔͵ægrɪˈkʌltʃərəl〕*adj.* 農業的
     sector〔ˈsɛktɚ〕*n.* 部門

4. (**B**) As a defense against air-pollution damage, many plants and animals <u>release</u> a substance that absorbs pollutants.

為了抵抗空氣污染的傷害，許多動植物，會<u>釋放</u>一種物質來吸收污染物。

(A) relieve〔rɪ'liv〕*v.* 減輕（ *= ease = alleviate* ）

relieve pain 減輕痛苦

(B) ***release***〔rɪ'lis〕*v.* 釋放；鬆開（ *= loosen* ）

release a prisoner 釋放犯人

(C) dismiss〔dɪs'mɪs〕*v.* 解散；開除（ *= fire = sack* ）

dismiss the class 下課

(D) discard〔dɪs'kɑrd〕*v.* 拋棄（ *= throw out = get rid of* ）

* defense〔dɪ'fɛns〕*n.* 抵抗；防禦 substance〔'sʌbstəns〕*n.* 物質

absorb〔əb'sɔrb , əb'z-〕*v.* 吸收 pollutant〔pə'lutn̩t〕*n.* 污染物

5. (**A**) Applause has been given to "Brokeback Mountain," a movie directed by internationally-acclaimed Taiwanese director Ang Lee, since its <u>premiere</u>.

享譽國際的臺灣導演李安所導的片子「斷背山」，自<u>首演</u>之後，就掌聲不斷。

(A) ***premiere***〔prɪ'mɪr〕*n.* 首演

(B) primary〔'praɪmərɪ〕*n.* (選舉等) 初選

(C) premise〔'prɛmɪs〕*n.* 前提 make a premise 設定前提

major premise 大前提

(D) premium〔'primɪəm〕*n.* 獎金（ *= prize* ）；保險費

put a premium on 高度重視

* applause〔ə'plɔz〕*n.* 喝采；掌聲 direct〔də'rɛkt〕*v.* 導演

acclaim〔ə'klem〕*v.* 稱讚

6. (**A**) Your improper words will give <u>rise</u> to doubts concerning your true intentions.

你用詞不當，會<u>導致</u>別人懷疑你的真正的用意為何。

(A) ***rise***〔raɪz〕*n.* 發生；上升；起床

give rise to 導致（ *= lead to = bring about = result in = cause* ）

(B) reason〔'rizn̩〕*n.* 理由 *< for >* the reason for~ ~的起因

(C) suspicion〔sə'spɪʃən〕*n.* 懷疑 *< of / about >* suspicious *adj.*

arouse suspicion 引起懷疑 under suspicion of~ 涉嫌~

(D) impulse〔'ɪmpʌls〕*n.* 衝動 on (an) impulse 衝動地；不加思索地

impulsive *adj.* 衝動的 impulsive decision 衝動下的決定

* improper〔ɪm'prɑpɚ〕*adj.* 不得當的 word〔wɝd〕*n.* (口說的) 言語

doubt〔daʊt〕*n.* 懷疑 concerning〔kən'sɝnɪŋ〕*prep.* 關於（ *= about* ）

intention〔ɪn'tɛnʃən〕*n.* 用意

7. (**C**) He never <u>let on</u> the fact that he is married.　他從不<u>洩漏</u>自己已婚的事實。

　　(A) hold over　延期 (= *postpone*)

　　　　The meeting was held over till the following week.　會議延至下週舉行。

　　(B) hold good　適用；有效 (= *stand good*)

　　(C) *let on*　洩漏 (秘密等)

　　(D) break into　闖入

　　＊married (ˈmærɪd) *adj.* 已婚的

8. (**A**) The news item about the fire was followed by a detailed report made on the <u>spot</u>.　火災的新聞之後，接著是<u>現場</u>的詳細報導。

　　(A) *spot* (spɑt) *n.* 地點；斑點；痕跡 (= *mark* = *stain*)

　　　　spots and stripes　斑點與條紋

　　(B) spy (spaɪ) ① *n.* 間諜

　　　　be a spy for～　幫～做間諜　　industrial spy　工業間諜

　　　　② *v.* 偵查　　spy on *sth.* 偵查某事

　　(C) spirit (ˈspɪrɪt) *n.* 精神；心情 (= *mood*)

　　　　high/low spirits　心情好/不好

　　　　例：The spirit is willing but the flesh is weak. (心有餘而力不足。)

　　(D) spice (spaɪs) *n.* 香料

　　　　例：Variety is the spice of life. (【諺】變化是人生的香料。)

　　＊item (ˈaɪtəm) *n.* (新聞) 一則

　　　detailed (dɪˈteld) *adj.* 詳細的

9. (**B**) One reason for the success of Asian immigrants in the U.S. is that they have taken great <u>pains</u> to educate their children.

　　在美國，亞裔移民之所以成功的理由之一，是他們對於子女的教育真是不遺餘<u>力</u>。

　　(A) effort (ˈɛfət) *n.* 努力

　　　　make efforts　努力 (= *make an effort*)

　　(B) *pain* (pen) *n.* 費力 (用複數形)；痛苦 (用單數形)

　　　　painful *adj.* 痛苦的　　take pains　費力；努力

　　　　get over the pain　從痛苦恢復

　　(C) attempt (əˈtɛmpt) *n.* 努力嘗試

　　　　make attempts　努力嘗試 (= *make an attempt*)

　　(D) endeavor (ɪnˈdɛvə) *n.* 努力　　make endeavors　努力

　　　　(= *make an endeavor*)

　　＊Asian (ˈeʃən) *adj.* 亞洲的　　immigrant (ˈɪməgrənt) *n.* (從國外移入的) 移民

10. (**B**) The remarkable <u>variety</u> of life on the Galapagos Islands inspired Charles Darwin to establish his theory of evolution.

加拉巴哥群島生物的<u>種類</u>繁多，啓發達爾文寫下他的進化論。

(A) classification〔,klæsəfəˈkeʃən〕 *n.*（郵件、貨物等的）分類；
（生物學）分類法

(B) *variety*〔vəˈraɪətɪ〕 *n.* 多樣性　　a variety of 各式各樣的（= *various*）

(C) density〔ˈdɛnsətɪ〕 *n.* 密度　　dense *adj.* 稠密的

(D) diversion〔dəˈvɝʒən〕 *n.* 轉變；轉向　　diverse *adj.* 不同的；各種的

＊remarkable〔rɪˈmɑrkəbḷ〕 *adj.* 驚人的　　life〔laɪf〕 *n.* 生物（為集合名詞）

the Galapagos Islands 加拉巴哥群島（在南美洲厄瓜多爾西邊的太平洋上）

inspire〔ɪnˈspaɪr〕 *v.* 啓發　　evolution〔,ɛvəˈluʃən〕 *n.* 進化

11. (**C**) The English language contains a <u>multitude</u> of words which are comparatively rare in ordinary conversation.

英文裡有<u>衆多</u>的字彙，在日常對話中比較少會使用到。

(A) altitude〔ˈæltə,tjud〕 *n.* 高度【alt（= *high*）+ itude（*n.*）】

(B) latitude〔ˈlætə,tjud〕 *n.* 緯度【lat（= *wide*）+ itude（*n.*）】
（↔ longitude〔ˈlɑndʒə,tjud〕 *n.* 經度）

(C) *multitude*〔ˈmʌltə,tjud〕 *n.* 衆多　　a multitude of 衆多的

(D) attitude〔ˈætə,tjud〕 *n.* 態度
take/adopt/assume a(n)~attitude 採取~的態度

＊contain〔kənˈten〕 *v.* 包含　　comparatively〔kəmˈpærətɪvlɪ〕 *adv.* 比較地

rare〔rɛr〕 *adj.* 稀有的；少見的　　ordinary〔ˈɔrdṇ,ɛrɪ〕 *adj.* 日常的

12. (**B**) The match on Saturday was <u>rained out</u> and re-arranged for tonight.

禮拜六的比賽<u>因雨延期</u>，重新安排到今晚再比。

(A) call down 嚴厲責備（人）；請求（事物）
He called me down for carelessness. 他嚴厲責備我的疏忽。

(B) *be rained out* （比賽）因雨而中斷延期

(C) put down 放下；寫下；儲存；壓抑
put down your name 寫下你的名字
put down a riot 鎮壓暴動

(D) knock out 擊昏；打敗
He knocked out the challenger in the first round.
他在第一回合就把挑戰者擊昏了。

＊match〔mætʃ〕 *n.* 比賽

13. (**A**) The employees would <u>goof off</u> when the boss was not around.

老闆不在時，員工就偷懶。

(A) *goof off* 偷懶　　goof-off *n.* 懶人

(B) wade through 艱苦度過（困境）

wade through a financial crisis 度過財務危機

(C) get lost 迷路（= *lose oneself* = *lose one's way*）

(D) drop a line 寫（一封短）信　　【比較】draw a line 劃清界線

* employee〔͵ɛmplɔɪˈi〕*n.* 員工

14. (**A**) My father was furious about my mistake — he shouted at me and didn't
<u>pull any punches</u>.

爸爸因為我的過錯而大發雷霆，他對著我吼叫，毫不留情。

(A) *pull* (*one's*) *punches* （拳擊）故意不用力打；【喻】手下留情

(B) pull *one's* leg 愚弄某人（= *make fun of somebody*）

He's not serious; he's only pulling our leg.

他不是說真的；他只是在愚弄我們。

(C) pull *one's* weight 盡本分；盡一己之力

We will succeed in this business if only everyone pulls his weight.

只有人人各盡本分，我們才能在這事業上成功。

(D) pull *one's* teeth 拔牙；【喻】挫其銳氣

* furious〔ˈfjʊrɪəs〕*adj.* 很生氣的　　shout〔ʃaʊt〕*v.* 大吼大叫

15. (**B**) He was once a very popular movie star in Hollywood, but recently he has
been <u>losing his touch</u>.

他曾經是好萊塢紅極一時的明星，近來已<u>魅力不再</u>。

(A) lose *one's* tongue （因吃驚等）說不出話來

tongue〔tʌŋ〕*n.* 口才；舌頭

He had lost his tongue. He found his tongue after being silent for five
minutes. 他說不出話來。他沉默了五分鐘後才再開口。

(B) *lose one's touch* 失去魅力　　【比較】lose touch 失去聯繫

(C) lose *one's* head 失去理智；非常興奮（↔ *keep one's head*）

Don't lose your head during an emergency. 在緊急情況中勿喪失理智。

(D) lose *one's* shirt 一貧如洗；失去一切

【比較】keep *one's* shirt on 保持冷靜

Mark lost his shirt betting on the horses. 馬克賭馬輸得精光。

* once〔wʌns〕*adv.* 曾經；一度　　Hollywood〔ˈhɑlɪ͵wʊd〕*n.* 好萊塢

TEST 28

Directions: The following questions are incomplete sentences. You are to choose the one word that best completes the sentence.

1. During the 1930's the world experienced a severe economic
   _____. Stock prices fell and the jobless rate soared.
   (A) suppression   (B) expression
   (C) depression   (D) impression   ( )

2. As a(n) _____ of women's liberation, she devoted her life to the
   pursuit of women's welfare.
   (A) agent   (B) proponent
   (C) opponent   (D) substitute   ( )

3. The medicine should be able to _____ some of the pain from the
   operation.
   (A) diagnose   (B) appeal
   (C) imply   (D) alleviate   ( )

4. A large _____ of students took part in the Scholastic Ability Test
   that took place on Jan. 22nd & 23rd.
   (A) plenty   (B) amount
   (C) percent   (D) percentage   ( )

5. The pain _____ on. It kept me awake most of the night.
   (A) lingered   (B) lodged
   (C) pioneered   (D) shrugged   ( )

6. China Airlines, now the biggest carrier in Taiwan, said it would
   add a stopover in Abu Dhabi on its Taipei-Vienna _____.
   (A) rotation   (B) root
   (C) routine   (D) route   ( )

7. It's a sad thing in Taiwan that many young couples tend to believe
   divorce is a contemporary _____ for all matrimonial ills.
   (A) panacea   (B) resolve
   (C) projection   (D) allocation   ( )

8. I remember seeing him some years ago, but I don't _____ where it was.
   (A) remind
   (B) reinforce
   (C) recall
   (D) memorize
   (   )

9. Children growing up in _____ areas are far more likely to turn to crime and drug abuse.
   (A) objective
   (B) deprived
   (C) insane
   (D) invincible
   (   )

10. Good plays can provoke tremendous _____ between the actors and the audience.
    (A) interaction
    (B) disguise
    (C) sensation
    (D) speculation
    (   )

11. The speaker _____ his speech by quoting a passage from President John F. Kennedy's inaugural address.
    (A) came to an end
    (B) put an end
    (C) soaked up
    (D) wrapped up
    (   )

12. She wondered if she could spend _____ here so she could learn more about the city.
    (A) sometimes
    (B) some time
    (C) sometime
    (D) some times
    (   )

13. A really powerful speaker can _____ the feelings of the audience to a fever of excitement.
    (A) work out
    (B) work over
    (C) work at
    (D) work up
    (   )

14. He failed to carry out the contract, and now he has to _____ the consequences.
    (A) answer for
    (B) run into
    (C) apply for
    (D) step into
    (   )

15. The boy was supposed to wash the dishes but his mother said she would _____ him _____ if he could finish his assignment before supper.
    (A) let...down
    (B) let...by
    (C) let...off
    (D) let...up
    (   )

TEST 28 詳解

1. (**C**) During the 1930's the world experienced a severe economic <u>depression</u>. Stock prices fell and the jobless rate soared.

在一九三○年代，全世界經歷了一次嚴重的經濟蕭條。股價下跌而失業率狂飆。

    (A) suppression〔səˈprɛʃən〕*n.* 壓抑【sup (= *under*) + press】

        suppress *v.* 壓抑

    (B) expression〔ɪkˈsprɛʃən〕*n.* 表達【ex (= *out*) + press】   express *v.* 表達

    (C) *depression*〔dɪˈprɛʃən〕*n.* 蕭條【de (= *down*) + press】

        depress *v.* 使沮喪；使蕭條

    (D) impression〔ɪmˈprɛʃən〕*n.* 印象【im (= *in*) + press】

        impress *v.* 使印象深刻

    * severe〔səˈvɪr〕*adj.* 嚴重的   economic〔͵ikəˈnɑmɪk〕*adj.* 經濟的

      stock〔stɑk〕*n.* 股票   *jobless rate* 失業率   soar〔sor〕*v.* 高漲；狂飆

2. (**B**) As a <u>proponent</u> of women's liberation, she devoted her life to the pursuit of women's welfare. 身爲婦女解放運動的倡導者，她終生奉獻於追求婦女福利。

    (A) agent〔ˈedʒənt〕*n.* 代辦人；經紀人；原動力

        a real estate agent 不動產經紀人

        agency *n.* 代辦處   a travel agency 旅行社

    (B) *proponent*〔prəˈponənt〕*n.* 倡導者   propose *v.* 提倡

    (C) opponent〔əˈponənt〕*n.* 反對者   oppose *v.* 反對

    (D) substitute〔ˈsʌbstə͵tjut〕① *n.* 代理人；替身 ② *v.* 用～代替

        substitute A for B 用 A 代替 B (= *replace* B *with* A)

    * liberation〔͵lɪbəˈreʃən〕*n.* 解放

      pursuit〔pəˈsut〕*n.* 追求   welfare〔ˈwɛl͵fɛr〕*n.* 福利

3. (**D**) The medicine should <u>alleviate</u> some of the pain from the operation.

這藥物應可減輕手術後的疼痛。

    (A) diagnose〔͵daɪəgˈnos , -ˈnoz〕*v.* (醫生) 診斷   diagnosis〔͵daɪəgˈnosɪs〕*n.*

        The doctor diagnosed his illness as malaria. 醫生診斷他的疾病是瘧疾。

    (B) appeal〔əˈpil〕*v.* 懇求；訴諸；上訴 < *to* >   appeal to *sb.* 懇求某人

        appeal to violence 訴諸於武力   appeal to a higher court 向高等法院上訴

    (C) imply〔ɪmˈplaɪ〕*v.* 暗示   implication *n.*   implied *adj.* 暗示的；含蓄的

    (D) *alleviate*〔əˈlivɪ͵et〕*v.* 減輕 (痛苦等) (= *decrease* = *lessen*)

        alleviation *n.*

    * operation〔͵ɑpəˈreʃən〕*n.* 手術

4. (**D**) A large <u>percentage</u> of students took part in the Scholastic Ability Test that took place on Jan. 22nd & 23rd.
大<u>部分</u>的學生都會參加在一月 22 日、23 日舉行的學科能力測驗。

(A) plenty〔'plɛntɪ〕*n.* 很多　plenty of 很多的（之前不加冠詞 a，故不能選此答案）

(B) amount〔ə'maʊnt〕*n.* 份量

【注意】 amount 形容用「量」計算（不可數）的名詞；number 形容用「數」
計算（可數）的名詞。

如：┌ There's a small *amount* of water. 有少量的水。
　　└ There are a great *number* of flowers. 有很多的花。

(C) percent〔pə'sɛnt〕*n.* 百分之～

(D) *percentage*〔pə'sɛntɪdʒ〕*n.* 百分比

【注意】percent 之前與數字連用；percentage 則與數字以外的形容詞連用。

如：┌ 70 *percent* of students 百分之七十的學生
　　└ a large/small *percentage* of students 很大/小百分比的學生

＊*take part in* 參加　　scholastic〔sko'læstɪk〕*adj.* 學校（教育）的
Scholastic Ability Test 學科能力測驗　　*take place* 舉行

5. (**A**) The pain <u>lingered</u> on. It kept me awake most of the night.
疼痛<u>持續</u>不斷，讓我幾乎徹夜未眠。

(A) *linger*〔'lɪŋgə〕*v.*（病、習慣等）持續；（人）徘徊　　*linger on* 持續不斷

(B) lodge〔ladʒ〕*v.* 住宿　　lodging *n.* 住宿處

(C) pioneer〔‚paɪə'nɪr〕① *v.* 開拓　② *n.* 先驅

(D) shrug〔ʃrʌg〕*v.* 聳聳肩

＊awake〔ə'wek〕*adj.* 清醒的

6. (**D**) China Airlines, now the biggest carrier in Taiwan, said it would add a stopover in Abu Dhabi on its Taipei-Vienna <u>route</u>. 華航，台灣目前最大的航空公司，
宣布在台北飛往維也納的<u>航線</u>中，中途停留阿布達比這個城市。

(A) rotation〔ro'teʃən〕*n.*（以軸為中心的）旋轉；（天體的）自轉
【比較】revolution *n.* 公轉

(B) root〔rut〕*n.*（植物）<u>莖</u>；（東西）根部；（抽象事物）根本
take root 生根；鞏固　　the root of all evil 萬惡的根源

(C) routine〔ru'tin〕*n.* 例行公事；常規

(D) *route*〔rut , raʊt〕*n.* 路線；航線

＊airline〔'ɛr‚laɪn〕*n.* 航空公司　　carrier〔'kærɪə〕*n.* 運輸公司
stopover〔'stap‚ovə〕*n.*（旅途）中途停留處；中途下車處
Abu Dhabi〔'abu'dabɪ〕*n.* 阿布達比（位於阿拉伯聯合大公國）
Vienna〔vɪ'ɛnə〕*n.* 維也納

7. (**A**) It's a sad thing in Taiwan that many young couples tend to believe divorce is a contemporary <u>panacea</u> for all matrimonial ills.

悲哀的是，台灣有許多的年輕夫妻相信，離婚是一劑現代的<u>萬靈丹</u>，可解決所有婚姻上的不幸。

   (A) *panacea* (ˌpænəˈsiə) *n.* 萬靈丹
   (B) resolve (rɪˈzɑlv) ① *n.* 決心 (= *resolution*)
       ② *v.* 下決心 (= *determine*)；溶解
       make a resolve 下決心 (= *make a resolution*)
   (C) projection (prəˈdʒɛkʃən) *n.* 發射；投射；計畫
       project (prəˈdʒɛkt) *v.* 投射；傳達
   (D) allocation (ˌæləˈkeʃən) *n.* 分配；配給量
       allocate (ˈæləˌket) *v.* 分配
   * *tend to* 傾向於；容易去   divorce (dəˈvɔrs) *n.* 離婚
     contemporary (kənˈtɛmpəˌrɛrɪ) *adj.* 現代的
     matrimonial (ˌmætrəˈmonɪəl) *adj.* 婚姻的   ill (ɪl) *n.* 不幸；災難

8. (**C**) I remember seeing him some years ago, but I don't <u>recall</u> where it was.

我記得幾年前看過他，只是不<u>記得</u>地點。

   (A) remind (rɪˈmaɪnd) *v.* 提醒   remind *sb.* of~ 提醒某人~
       (= *remind sb. to V.*)
   (B) reinforce (ˌriɪnˈfors) *v.* 加強；強化   reinforcement *n.*
       reinforce a bridge 鞏固橋樑   reinforce *one's* argument 強化論點
   (C) *recall* (rɪˈkɔl) *v.* 記得 (= *remember*)；（ 有意識地 ）想起
   (D) memorize (ˈmɛməˌraɪz) *v.* 背下來；背誦   memory *n.* 記憶力
   * remember (rɪˈmɛmbɚ) *v.* 記得 (之後加動名詞，表示「記得已做過此事」)

9. (**B**) Children growing up in <u>deprived</u> areas are far more likely to turn to crime and drug abuse.

在<u>貧困</u>區長大的小孩，非常容易犯罪和染上毒癮。

   (A) objective (əbˈdʒɛktɪv) *adj.* 客觀的 (↔ subjective 主觀的)
   (B) *deprived* (dɪˈpraɪvd) *adj.* 貧困的 (= *poor* = *impoverished*)
       deprive *v.* 剝奪；使喪失
   (C) insane (ɪnˈsen) *adj.* 瘋狂的 (= *mad* = *crazy* = *out of one's mind*)
   (D) invincible (ɪnˈvɪnsəbḷ) *adj.* 無敵的；征服不了的 (= *unconquerable*)
   * *be likely to* 容易；可能   *turn to* 從事   crime (kraɪm) *n.* 犯罪
     abuse (əˈbjus) *n.* 濫用   *drug abuse* 吸毒

10. (**A**) Good plays can provoke tremendous <u>interaction</u> between the actors and the audience. 好的戲劇，能激發演員與觀衆之間極大的<u>互動</u>。

(A) *interaction* 〔͵ɪntə'ækʃən 〕*n.* 互動；交互作用 < *between/with* >
    interact *v.*

(B) disguise 〔 dɪs'gaɪz 〕*n. v.* 偽裝　　in disguise 假扮的；偽裝的

(C) sensation 〔 sɛn'seʃən 〕*n.* (五官的) 知覺；轟動 (的事物)

(D) speculation 〔͵spɛkjə'leʃən 〕*n.* (沒有證據的) 推測 < *on/about* >；
    投機 < *in* >

＊provoke 〔 prə'vok 〕*v.* 激發　　tremendous 〔 trɪ'mɛndəs 〕*adj.* 極大的
    audience 〔'ɔdɪəns 〕*n.* 觀衆

11. (**D**) The speaker <u>wrapped up</u> his speech by quoting a passage from President John F. Kennedy's inaugural address.
    演講者引用約翰甘迺迪總統就職演說的一段話，來<u>結束</u>他的演說。

(A) come to an end 結束 (當不及物動詞片語用，如改成及物的用法 bring ~ to
    an end，就可以接受詞)

(B) put an end <u>to</u> 結束 (= *end* = *end off* = *bring an end to* = *bring ~ to an end*
    = *wind up* = *wrap up*)

(C) soak up 吸收 (水分、陽光等)　　soak 〔 sok 〕*v.* 吸收

(D) *wrap up* 結束 (其他用法見選項 (B))

＊quote 〔 kwot 〕*v.* 引用　　passage 〔'pæsɪdʒ 〕*n.* 一段話
    president 〔'prɛzədənt 〕*n.* 總統
    inaugural 〔 ɪn'ɔgjərəl 〕*adj.* 就職的
    inaugural address 就職演說

12. (**B**) She wondered if she could spend <u>some time</u> here so she could learn more about the city.
    她在想是否能花<u>一些時間</u>在這裡逗留，以便多了解這個城市。

(A) sometimes 有時候 (副詞)

(B) *some time* 一段時間 (名詞)

(C) sometime (過去或未來的) 某時 (副詞)
    I will come to call on you sometime next week.
    下禮拜我會找時間來拜訪你。

(D) some times 好幾次 (time 當「次數」解時，才是可數名詞)

＊wonder 〔'wʌndə 〕*v.* 想 (知道)

13. (**D**) A really powerful speaker can <u>work up</u> the feelings of the audience to a fever of excitement.

眞正有說服力的演講者，能<u>激起</u>觀衆的情緒到狂熱的程度。

(A) work out 解決（問題）；計算（數字）；辛苦達成

(B) work over 重新做

例：Whenever I work the sum over, I get a different answer.

（我每次重新計算總數，都得到不同的答案。）

(C) work at 從事；執行；努力於　　work at social reform 從事社會改革

(D) *work up* 激起（情緒）；建立

*powerful〔'pauɚfəl〕*adj.* 有說服力的　　audience〔'ɔdɪəns〕*n.* 觀衆

fever〔'fivɚ〕*n.* 狂熱

14. (**A**) He failed to carry out the contract, and now he has to <u>answer for</u> the consequences. 他無法履行這個契約，所以<u>得爲</u>後果<u>負責</u>。

(A) *answer for* 爲～負責（= *be responsible for* = *take responsibility for*）

(B) run into （東西）互撞；（人）偶然遇見

（= *bump into* = *come across* = *run across*）

(C) apply for 申請；應徵　　apply to 適用於

(D) step into 踩進去；不勞而獲

例：He stepped into a big fortune after his uncle died.

（他在舅舅死後，輕鬆得到一大筆遺產。）

*fail to 未能　　*carry out* 履行　　contract〔'kɑntrækt〕*n.* 契約

consequence〔'kɑnsə,kwɛns〕*n.* 後果

15. (**C**) The boy was supposed to wash the dishes but his mother said she would <u>let</u> him <u>off</u> if he could finish his assignment before supper.

男孩應該要洗碗的，但是媽媽說如果他能在晚餐前寫完作業，就<u>放</u>他<u>一馬</u>。

(A) let～down 使～失望（= *disappoint*）

(B) let～by 讓～通過；忽略（= *overlook*）

例：Let me by.（讓我過。）

He doesn't let errors by.（他不會忽略錯誤。）

(C) *let～off* 從輕發落～；放～一馬 <*from*>

(D) let up 停止；（風雨）停息

例：The rain never let up all night.（雨整夜下個不停。）

*be supposed to 應該　　assignment〔ə'saɪnmənt〕*n.* 作業

supper〔'sʌpɚ〕*n.* 晚餐

TEST 29

Directions: The following questions are incomplete sentences. You are to choose the one word that best completes the sentence.

1. She cut herself when she was _____ a pencil with a knife.
   (A) carving
   (B) felling
   (C) sharpening
   (D) tracing   ( )

2. The sudden rise in the student dropout rate deserves _____.
   (A) advance
   (B) consistency
   (C) notice
   (D) guarantee   ( )

3. In the U.S., Asian-American families tend to be intact and focused on their children's getting ahead _____. And this respect for education pays.
   (A) academically
   (B) suspiciously
   (C) exhaustedly
   (D) permissively   ( )

4. People who live in the city can not enjoy the _____ of calm and peace in the country.
   (A) pomposity
   (B) atmosphere
   (C) adversity
   (D) proponent   ( )

5. We cannot give you a _____ answer now; there are still many uncertainties about this issue.
   (A) familiar
   (B) courteous
   (C) hollow
   (D) definite   ( )

6. I have never heard of the author that you told me about. Maybe he is nothing but a _____ writer.
   (A) minor
   (B) distinguished
   (C) celebrated
   (D) renowned   ( )

7. The long _____ southern San Andreas fault could soon suffer a major earthquake, according to an oceanography researcher.
   (A) hostile
   (B) dormant
   (C) vital
   (D) significant   ( )

8. Several people were missing and hundreds were _____ after torrential rains flooded the villages here.
   - (A) evacuated
   - (B) ejected
   - (C) exempted
   - (D) exhaled
   (　)

9. There must be mutual _____ between husband and wife to maintain a happy marriage.
   - (A) connections
   - (B) consciences
   - (C) confections
   - (D) concessions
   (　)

10. The doctor made a _____ examination of his lungs to see if anything was wrong.
    - (A) transitional
    - (B) chronic
    - (C) thorough
    - (D) concise
    (　)

11. It is only _____ that you get an opportunity like that. You should do your very best to fully utilize it.
    - (A) once in a blue moon
    - (B) here and now
    - (C) in the limelight
    - (D) the second nature
    (　)

12. The government should face up to the situation and try to _____ it.
    - (A) make the best of
    - (B) make room for
    - (C) fall short of
    - (D) look out for
    (　)

13. Students who too obviously _____ their teachers are usually disliked by their classmates.
    - (A) play up to
    - (B) make up for
    - (C) play a joke on
    - (D) pick a hole in
    (　)

14. The drunkard felt dizzy and _____ on the street on his way home.
    - (A) dawned on
    - (B) threw up
    - (C) marked down
    - (D) took off
    (　)

15. His criticism was totally _____, but he thought he was hitting the nail on the head.
    - (A) a white lie
    - (B) down to earth
    - (C) beside the point
    - (D) upside down
    (　)

TEST 29 詳解

1. (**C**) She cut herself when she was <u>sharpening</u> a pencil with a knife.
她用刀子<u>削</u>鉛筆時，割傷自己。

    (A) carve〔karv〕*v.* 雕刻　　carving *n.* 雕刻；雕刻品

    (B) fell〔fɛl〕*v.* 砍伐（= *cut down* ）；打倒（= *knock down* ）

      （注意：「跌倒」fall 的三態變化是 fall-fell-fallen，而「砍伐」fell 的三態是 fell-felled-felled ）

    (C) *sharpen*〔'ʃɑrpən〕*v.* 削尖；使敏銳；使增強

      sharpen *one's* skill 增強技藝

    (D) trace〔tres〕*v.* 追蹤；追溯　　can be traced back to 可追溯到

2. (**C**) The sudden rise in the student dropout rate deserves <u>notice</u>.
學生退學率突然增加，值得<u>注意</u>。

    (A) advance〔əd'væns〕*n. v.* 前進；進步　　in advance 事先

    (B) consistency〔kən'sɪstənsɪ〕*n.* 一致；（液體）濃度　　consistent *adj.*

    (C) *notice*〔'notɪs〕*n.* 注意；通知；公告　　draw/attract notice 引人注意

      without notice 沒有通知；擅自　　put on a notice 貼公告

    (D) guarantee〔ˌgærən'ti〕① *v.* 保證；承諾　② *n.* 保證；保證書；抵押品

  *dropout〔'drɑpˌaʊt〕*n.* 退學　rate〔ret〕*n.* 比率　deserve〔dɪ'zɝv〕*v.* 值得

3. (**A**) In the U.S., Asian-American families tend to be intact and focused on their children's getting ahead <u>academically</u>. And this respect for education pays.
美國的亞裔家庭比較完整，並且致力於讓自己的孩子在<u>學業上</u>名列前茅。
而這種對教育的尊重，確有斬獲。

    (A) *academically*〔ˌækə'dɛmɪklɪ〕*adv.* 學業上地；學術方面地

      academy *n.* 學校；學院

    (B) suspiciously〔sə'spɪʃəslɪ〕*adv.* 懷疑地；不信地　　suspicion *n.*

      suspect *v.*　　on suspicion of~ 涉嫌做~

      suspect *sb.* of *sth.* 懷疑某人做某事

    (C) exhaustedly〔ɪg'zɔstɪdlɪ〕*adv.* 筋疲力盡地

      exhaust *v.* 用盡（體力；資源等）

    (D) permissively〔pɚ'mɪsɪvlɪ〕*adv.* 許可地；寬容地

      permit *v.* 許可　　permission *n.* 許可

  *Asian〔'eʃən〕*adj.* 亞裔的

    intact〔ɪn'tækt〕*adj.* 完整的（此處指家庭完整，少破碎、離異的情況）

    be focused on 專注於；致力於　　*get ahead* 超越；勝過他人

    pay〔pe〕*v.* 產生回報；值得

4. (**B**) People who live in the city can not enjoy the <u>atmosphere</u> of calm and peace in the country.

住在都市裡的人，無法享受鄉間平和與寧靜的氣氛。

(A) pomposity〔pɑm'pɑsətɪ〕 *n.* 自大（= *arrogance*）；擺架子
pompous *adj.*

(B) *atmosphere*〔'ætməs,fɪr〕 *n.* 氣氛；大氣；空氣

(C) adversity〔əd'vɝsətɪ〕 *n.* 不幸；逆境　　adverse *adj.* 不利的；反對的
adversary *n.* 敵人　　Adversity makes men wise. 【諺】逆境增長智慧。

(D) proponent〔prə'ponənt〕 *n.* 贊成者（= *advocate*〔'ædvəkɪt〕 = *supporter*）

＊calm〔kɑm〕 *n.* 平靜　　peace〔pis〕 *n.* 寧靜
country〔'kʌntrɪ〕 *n.* 鄉下

5. (**D**) We cannot give you a <u>definite</u> answer now; there are still many uncertainties about this issue.

我們現在無法給你一個明確的答案；這件事仍存在許多不確定性。

(A) familiar〔fə'mɪljə〕 *adj.* 熟悉的（↔ *unfamiliar*）　　familiarity *n.*
be familiar with 熟悉（↔ *be unfamiliar with*）

(B) courteous〔'kɝtɪəs〕 *adj.* 有禮貌的　　courtesy *n.*

(C) hollow〔'hɑlo〕 *adj.* 中空的（↔ *solid*）；凹陷的（= *sunken*）；
虛偽的（= *insincere*）　　a hollow tree 中空的樹
hollow eyes 凹陷的雙眼　　a hollow compliment 虛偽的讚美

(D) *definite*〔'dɛfənɪt〕 *adj.* 明確的
define *v.* 下定義；界定　　definition *n.* 定義

＊uncertainty〔ʌn'sɝtn̩tɪ〕 *n.* 不確定性　　issue〔'ɪʃjʊ〕 *n.* 事件

6. (**A**) I have never heard of the author that you told me about. Maybe he is nothing but a <u>minor</u> writer.

我從未聽過你說的那位作家，或許他只是一個二流的作家。

(A) *minor*〔'maɪnə〕 *adj.* 較小的；二流的（↔ major 較大的；主要的）
a minor role 小角色（↔ *a major role* 主角）

(B) distinguished〔dɪs'tɪŋgwɪʃt〕 *adj.* 卓越的；高貴的
the distinguished guest 貴賓

(C) celebrated〔'sɛlə,bretɪd〕 *adj.* 著名的（詳見 (D) 選項）

(D) renowned〔rɪ'naʊnd〕 *adj.* 著名的（= *celebrated* = *famed* = *noted*
= *well-known* = *famous*）

＊*hear of* 聽說　　maybe〔'mebɪ〕 *adv.* 可能；也許
author〔'ɔθə〕 *n.* 作家　　*nothing but* 只是（= *only*）

7. (**B**) The long <u>dormant</u> southern San Andreas fault could soon suffer a major earthquake, according to an oceanography researcher.

根據一位海洋學研究人員的預測,長期一直處於<u>休眠狀態的</u>南聖安德瑞斯斷層,很快就會歷經一次強烈的地震。

(A) hostile〔'hɑstḷ〕*adj.* 有敵意的;不良的　　hostility *n.* 敵意
　　hostile country 敵國
　　have/show hostility to(ward)～ 對～懷有敵意

(B) *dormant*〔'dɔrmənt〕*adj.* 睡覺的;休眠的 (↔ active 活躍的)
　　a dormant volcano 休火山 (↔ *an active volcano* 活火山)

(C) vital〔'vaɪtḷ〕*adj.* 生命的;極為重要的
　　vitality *n.* 生命力;活力
　　vital signs 生命跡象 (如呼吸、心跳等)
　　vital importance 極大的重要性

(D) significant〔sɪg'nɪfəkənt〕*adj.* 重要的 (= *important*);意義深遠的
　　significance *n.* 重要性;意義

*fault〔fɔlt〕*n.* (地質學) 斷層　　suffer〔'sʌfɚ〕*v.* 歷經;遭受
　major〔'medʒɚ〕*adj.* 大的　　earthquake〔'ɝθ,kwek〕*n.* 地震
　according to 根據　　oceanography〔,oʃɪən'ɑgrəfɪ〕*n.* 海洋學
　researcher〔'risɝtʃɚ〕*n.* 研究人員

8. (**A**) Several people were missing and hundreds were <u>evacuated</u> after torrential rains flooded villages here.

在豪雨淹沒本區的村莊之後,好幾個人失蹤,幾百位村民被<u>疏散</u>。

(A) *evacuate*〔ɪ'vækjʊ,et〕*v.* 疏散 (人);撤離 (軍隊);撤出 (建築物)
　　evacuation *n.*

(B) eject〔ɪ'dʒɛkt〕*v.* 噴出;排出【e- (= *out*) + ject (= *throw*)】
　　If you push the "eject" button, the CD will be sent out from the machine.
　　你一按「跳出」這個鍵,這片 CD 就會從播放機中被送出來。

(C) exempt〔ɪg'zɛmpt〕*v.* 使免除 (義務、責任等) < *from* >
　　【ex- (= *out*) + empt (= *take*)】
　　He was exempted from military service. 他不必服兵役。

(D) exhale〔ɛks'hel〕*v.* 呼出 (↔ inhale〔ɪn'hel〕*v.* 吸入)
　　【ex- (= *out*) + hale (= *breathe*)】

*missing〔'mɪsɪŋ〕*adj.* 失蹤的
　torrential〔tɔ'rɛnʃəl〕*adj.* 傾盆的;激烈的
　flood〔flʌd〕*v.* 淹沒　　village〔'vɪlɪdʒ〕*n.* 村莊

9. (**D**) There must be mutual <u>concessions</u> between husband and wife to maintain a happy marriage.

夫妻之間必須互相<u>讓步</u>，才能維持快樂的婚姻。

(A) connection〔kə'nɛkʃən〕 *n.* 連接；關係　　connect *v.*

(B) conscience〔'kɑnʃəns〕 *n.* 良心　　【比較】conscious〔'kɑnʃəs〕 *adj.* 有知覺的

(C) confection〔kən'fɛkʃən〕 *n.* 甜點（如糖果、蜜餞等）
　　 cf. confession *n.* 承認；召供

(D) *concession*〔kən'sɛʃən〕 *n.* 讓步
　　 make <u>a concession/concessions</u> to～ 對～讓步

＊mutual〔'mjutʃuəl〕 *adj.* 互相的　　maintain〔men'ten〕 *v.* 維持
　 marriage〔'mærɪdʒ〕 *n.* 婚姻

10. (**C**) The doctor made a <u>thorough</u> examination of his lungs to see if anything was wrong.

醫生對他的肺部做了一個<u>徹底的</u>檢查，看看有沒有問題。

(A) transitional〔træn'zɪʃənḷ〕 *adj.* 過渡的　　transition *n.* 過渡

(B) chronic〔'krɑnɪk〕 *adj.* 慢性的（↔ acute〔ə'kjut〕 *adj.* 急性的）

(C) *thorough*〔'θɝo〕 *adj.* 徹底的（= *complete*）；細心的（= *careful*）
　　 a thorough search 仔細搜查　　a thorough worker 細心的工人

(D) concise〔kən'saɪs〕 *adj.* 精簡的（↔ wordy *adj.* 冗長的；囉唆的）

＊examination〔ɪg,zæmə'neʃən〕 *n.* 檢查
　 lungs〔lʌŋz〕 *n. pl.* 肺（用複數形）

11. (**A**) It is only <u>once in a blue moon</u> that you get an opportunity like that. You should do your very best to fully utilize it.

要得到像這種機會真是<u>千載難逢</u>。你應該盡力而為，充分利用這個機會。

(A) *once in a blue moon* 難得的；千載難逢的

(B) here and now 此時此地；立刻（= *at once* = *right away*）
　　 I insist on being paid here and now. 我堅持此時此地就得拿到錢。

(C) in the limelight 引人注目（= *in the spotlight*）
　　 limelight〔'laɪm,laɪt〕 *n.* 石灰燈（以前人們使用有強烈白光的石灰燈，來照明舞台）

(D) the second nature 第二天性（即習慣、毛病等）
　　 Habit is second nature. 【諺】習慣是第二天性。

＊*do one's* (*very*) *best* 盡力而為　　utilize〔'jutḷ,aɪz〕 *v.* 利用

12. (**A**) The government should face up to the situation and try to <u>make the best of</u> it.
　　　政府必須面對這個狀況，並想辦法儘量減低損失或不良影響。
　　　(A) *make the best of it* 儘量減低損失或不良影響
　　　　　make the best of 善用；儘量利用
　　　(B) make room for 讓位給
　　　　　Please make room for the elderly. 請讓座給長者。
　　　(C) fall short of 不足；未達到（標準等）(= *come short of*)
　　　(D) look out for 小心；警戒 (= *watch out for* = *be on the alert for*)
　　　＊*face up to* 面對　　situation〔,sɪtʃu'eʃən〕*n.* 狀況

13. (**A**) Students who too obviously <u>play up to</u> their teachers are usually disliked by
　　　their classmates.
　　　很明顯在巴結老師的學生，同學們通常都不太喜歡。
　　　(A) *play up to* 巴結；奉承 (= *flatter* = *butter up*)
　　　(B) make up for 補償 (= *compensate for* = *make amends for*)
　　　(C) play a joke on 惡作劇 (= *play a trick on*)
　　　(D) pick a hole in 挑毛病 (= *pick holes in*)
　　　＊obviously〔'abvɪəslɪ〕*adv.* 明顯地　　dislike〔dɪs'laɪk〕*v.* 不喜歡

14. (**B**) The drunkard felt dizzy and <u>threw up</u> on the street on his way home.
　　　醉漢感到一陣暈眩，在回家路上當街嘔吐。
　　　(A) dawn on~ 使~明白；使~想到 (= *dawn upon*)
　　　　　It dawned on me that I had left the oven on. 我想到我爐子還沒關火。
　　　(B) *throw up* 嘔吐
　　　(C) mark down 記下來 (= *write down*)；調降價錢 (= *lower*)
　　　(D) take off 拿走；動身；脫掉（衣、鞋、飾品等）(↔ *put on*)；
　　　　　（飛機）起飛 (↔ land 降落)
　　　＊drunkard〔'drʌŋkəd〕*n.* 醉漢　　dizzy〔'dɪzɪ〕*adj.* 暈眩的

15. (**C**) His criticism was totally <u>beside the point</u>, but he thought he was hitting the
　　　nail on the head. 他的評論完全離題，他還以為自己所言一針見血。
　　　(A) a white lie 善意的謊言
　　　(B) down to earth 實際的；實事求是的 (= *practical*)
　　　(C) *beside the point* 離題的 (↔ *to the point*)
　　　(D) upside down 顛倒地；混亂地
　　　　　He turned everything upside down. 他把每一件事都弄得亂七八糟。
　　　＊criticism〔'krɪtə,sɪzm〕*n.* 批評　　*hit the nail on the head* （說話）一針見血

TEST 30

Directions: The following questions are incomplete sentences. You are to choose the one word that best completes the sentence.

1. Universal Studios has become a major tourist spot in southern California, drawing millions of tourists _____.
   (A) mournfully
   (B) inquisitively
   (C) annually
   (D) perpetually
   (　)

2. Los Angeles is often _____ as the prototype of the big city in the world.
   (A) overlooked
   (B) separated
   (C) referred
   (D) cited
   (　)

3. They _____ the play by laughing at the sad parts and crying noisily over the jokes.
   (A) complimented
   (B) disrupted
   (C) originated
   (D) envied
   (　)

4. He feels so _____ because he just lost his job a couple of weeks ago.
   (A) melancholy
   (B) insincere
   (C) absolute
   (D) unpredictable
   (　)

5. Jazz survived the neglect of the age to become America's one _____ contribution to the world's music.
   (A) respectful
   (B) triumphant
   (C) candid
   (D) commercial
   (　)

6. With 100 billion neurons and a huge number of connections, the brain is a system _____ with variables.
   (A) burdened
   (B) refilled
   (C) loaded
   (D) filed
   (　)

7. Thanksgiving is America's _____ of festivals celebrating the harvest season.
   (A) version
   (B) verse
   (C) vase
   (D) vice
   (　)

8. Put simply, intelligence is the ability to successfully perform
   _____ operations.
   (A) organic   (B) corporate
   (C) mental   (D) physical   ( )

9. His behavior has been so _____ lately that everybody wonders if
   he is actually out of his mind.
   (A) pitiful   (B) fierce
   (C) urgent   (D) bizarre   ( )

10. The government said it had just foiled a huge terrorist _____ and
    arrested 25 young Muslims on suspicion of involvement.
    (A) plot   (B) formula
    (C) trap   (D) seizure   ( )

11. His works _____ from others'. He is an excellent writer.
    (A) take off   (B) cheer up
    (C) stand out   (D) come to   ( )

12. The band sounded terrible because the instruments were _____.
    (A) out of touch   (B) out of tune
    (C) out of business   (D) out of shape   ( )

13. _____ two of the cards at a time and see if they match.
    (A) Turn over   (B) Lay off
    (C) Back up   (D) Let up   ( )

14. _____ being blond and pretty, she was smart and helpful.
    (A) In addition   (B) Apart from
    (C) Away from   (D) Beside   ( )

15. Would you please _____ the cigarette? I can't stand the smoke
    here.
    (A) put out   (B) carry out
    (C) make out   (D) run out   ( )

TEST 30 詳解

1. (**C**) Universal Studios has become a major tourist spot in southern California, drawing millions of tourists <u>annually</u>.
環球影城已變成南加州主要的觀光景點，<u>每年</u>吸引幾百萬的觀光客前來。

    (A) mournfully〔'mɔrnfəlɪ〕 *adv.* 悲哀地   mourn *v.* 哀悼

    (B) inquisitively〔ɪn'kwɪzətɪvlɪ〕 *adv.* 好管閒事地；好奇地 (= *curiously*)
        inquire *v.* 詢問

    (C) *annually*〔'ænjʊəlɪ〕 *adv.* 每年地   annual leave 年假
        annual ring （樹木）年輪

    (D) perpetually〔pɚ'pɛtʃʊəlɪ〕 *adv.* 永遠地 (= *forever* = *for good*
        = *for ever and ever*)

    ＊Universal Studios 環球影城 (位於加州洛杉磯市的郊區)
    major〔'medʒɚ〕 *adj.* 主要的   ***tourist spot*** 觀光景點
    California〔ˌkælə'fɔrnjə〕 *n.* (美國) 加州   draw〔drɔ〕 *v.* 吸引

2. (**D**) Los Angeles is often <u>cited</u> as the prototype of the big city in the world.
洛杉磯常被<u>列舉</u>為世界上大都會之典範。

    (A) overlook〔ˌovɚ'lʊk〕 *v.* 俯瞰；忽略 (= *neglect* = *ignore*)；放過 (過失)
        (= *excuse*)

    (B) separate〔'sɛpə,ret〕 *v.* 分開；隔離   separate A from B 分開 A 與 B

    (C) refer〔rɪ'fɝ〕 *v.* 談到；引用
        refer *to* A as B 認為 A 是 B (注意要加 to)

    (D) *cite*〔saɪt〕 *v.* 列舉；引用   cite A as B 列舉 A 是 B

    ＊Los Angeles〔lɔs'ændʒələs〕 *n.* 洛杉磯   prototype〔'protə,taɪp〕 *n.* 典範

3. (**B**) They <u>disrupted</u> the play by laughing at the sad parts and crying noisily over the jokes. 他們在悲傷的情節大笑，在好笑的地方大哭，<u>使這齣戲一片混亂</u>。

    (A) compliment〔'kɑmpləmənt〕 *v. n.* 稱讚 (= *praise*)
        【比較】complement *v. n.* 補充
        compliment *sb.* = pay/make a compliment to *sb.* 稱讚某人

    (B) *disrupt*〔dɪs'rʌpt〕 *v.* 使混亂；使解散   disruption *n.*

    (C) originate〔ə'rɪdʒə,net〕 *v.* 起源 < *from/in/with* >   origin *n.* 起源
        original *adj.* 最早的

    (D) envy〔'ɛnvɪ〕 *v. n.* 忌妒；羨慕   envy *sb.* for *sth.* 羨慕某人某事

    ＊play〔ple〕 *n.* 戲劇   noisily〔'nɔɪzɪlɪ〕 *adv.* 大聲地

4. (**A**) He feels so <u>melancholy</u> because he just lost his job a couple of weeks ago.
他感到非常憂鬱，因為他幾週前剛失業。

(A) *melancholy* (ˈmɛlənˌkɑlɪ) *adj.* 憂鬱的 (= *depressed* = *gloomy* = *moody*
= *blue*)

(B) insincere (ˌɪnsɪnˈsɪr) *adj.* 不誠懇的 (↔ *sincere*)　　insincerity *n.*

(C) absolute (ˈæbsəˌlut) *adj.* 完全的 (↔ partial 部分的)；絕對的
(↔ relative 相對的)

(D) unpredictable (ˌʌnprɪˈdɪktəbḷ) *adj.* 無法預測的 (↔ *predictable*)

**a couple of* 數個 (= *a few*)

5. (**B**) Jazz survived the neglect of the age to become America's one <u>triumphant</u>
contribution to the world's music.
爵士樂經歷長期的忽視，終於成為美國對全世界音樂，一項輝煌的貢獻。

(A) respectful (rɪˈspɛktfəl) *adj.* (對別人) 尊敬的

【比較】respectable *adj.* 值得人尊敬的

He is a *respectable* person; I'm *respectful* to him.

他很值得尊敬；我很尊敬他。

(B) *triumphant* (traɪˈʌmfənt) *adj.* 勝利的；得意洋洋的；輝煌的

triumph *n.* 勝利

(C) candid (ˈkændɪd) *adj.* 坦白的 (= *frank* = *plain* = *outspoken*)

(D) commercial (kəˈmɝʃəl) *adj.* 商業 (化) 的；營利的

commerce *n.* 商業

**jazz (dʒæz) *n.* 爵士樂　　survive (səˈvaɪv) *v.* 經歷~ (還存在)

neglect (nɪˈglɛkt) *n.* 忽視　　age (edʒ) *n.* 長時間

contribution (ˌkɑntrəˈbjuʃən) *n.* 貢獻

6. (**C**) With 100 billion neurons and a huge number of connections, the brain is a
system <u>loaded</u> with variables.
內含一千億個神經細胞及大量的連線，腦系統中充滿各種變數。

(A) burden (ˈbɝdṇ) *v.* 使負擔　　be burdened with 揹負~ (重擔)

(B) refill (riˈfɪl) *v.* 再裝滿 (飲料等)

Please refill my coke. 請幫我的可樂續杯。

(C) *load* (lod) *v.* 裝載；(車船) 載貨　　be loaded with 裝滿了~ (內容物)

(D) file (faɪl) *v.* 將~歸檔　　file a document 將文件歸檔

**billion (ˈbɪljən) *n.* 十億　　neuron (ˈnjurɑn) *n.* 神經細胞

a huge number of 大量的　　connection (kəˈnɛkʃən) *n.* 連接 (之物)

variable (ˈvɛrɪəbḷ) *n.* 變數

7. (**A**) Thanksgiving is America's <u>version</u> of festivals celebrating the harvest season.
感恩節是美國<u>版</u>的慶豐收節日。

(A) *version*〔'vɜʃən , 'vɜʒən〕*n.* 版本；
（從個人立場、見解來發表的）說法；變化型
the Chinese version of the Bible　聖經的中文版
Give me your version of what happened.
告訴我對發生之事你的見解爲何。

(B) verse〔vɜs〕*n.* 詩（= *poetry*）；韻文（↔ prose〔proz〕*n.* 散文）

(C) vase〔ves〕*n.* 花瓶；裝飾用的水甕　　【比較】vas〔væs〕*n.* 血管；導管

(D) vice〔vaɪs〕*n.* 罪惡；（制度上的）缺陷　virtue and vice　善與惡
vicious〔'vɪʃəs〕*adj.* 罪惡的　vicious circle　惡性循環

　*Thanksgiving〔,θæŋks'gɪvɪŋ〕*n.* 感恩節（十一月的第四個禮拜四）
festival〔'fɛstəvḷ〕*n.* 節日　celebrate〔'sɛlə,bret〕*v.* 慶祝
harvest〔'hɑrvɪst〕*n.* 收割；收穫　season〔'sizṇ〕*n.* 時節；季節

8. (**C**) Put simply, intelligence is the ability to successfully perform <u>mental</u> operations.
簡單地說，智慧就是順利達成<u>智力</u>運作的能力。

(A) organic〔ɔr'gænɪk〕*adj.* 有機的（↔ *inorganic*）；器官的
organic matter　有機物

(B) corporate〔'kɔrpərɪt〕*adj.* 公司的　corporation　*n.* 公司

(C) *mental*〔'mɛntḷ〕*adj.* 智力的；精神的　　【比較】metal〔'mɛtḷ〕*n.* 金屬
mental arithmetic　心算　mental disorder　精神錯亂

(D) physical〔'fɪzɪkḷ〕*adj.* 身體的；（相對於精神而言）物質的
physical checkup　身體檢查　the physical world　物質世界

　put simply 簡單地說（= *to put it simply*）
intelligence〔ɪn'tɛlədʒəns〕*n.* 智慧　perform〔pə'fɔrm〕*v.* 實行
operation〔,ɑpə'reʃən〕*n.* 運作

9. (**D**) His behavior has been so <u>bizarre</u> lately that everybody wonders if he is
actually out of his mind.
他最近行爲<u>詭異</u>，大家都懷疑他是否真的瘋了。

(A) pitiful〔'pɪtɪfəl〕*adj.* 可憐的；悲慘的（= *miserable*）　pity　*n.*

(B) fierce〔fɪrs〕*adj.* 兇猛的；激烈的　fierce competition　激烈的競爭

(C) urgent〔'ɜdʒənt〕*adj.* 迫切的　urge　*v.* 迫使

(D) *bizarre*〔bɪ'zɑr〕*adj.* 詭異的；奇怪的　　【比較】bazaar　*n.* 市集；商店街

　*behavior〔bɪ'hevjə〕*n.* 行爲　*out of* one's *mind* 發瘋（= *crazy*）

10. (**A**) The government said it had just foiled a huge terrorist <u>plot</u> and arrested 25 young Muslims on suspicion of involvement.

政府說他們剛破獲一項龐大的恐怖主義<u>陰謀</u>，並逮捕了二十五位涉嫌捲入此陰謀的年輕回教徒。

    (A) ***plot*** ﹝ plɑt ﹞ *n.* 陰謀；策劃

        frame/hatch/lay a plot against~　策劃陰謀不利於~

        a bomb plot　一項炸彈陰謀　　　a murder plot　一項謀殺陰謀

    (B) formula ﹝ˈfɔrmjələ﹞ *n.* 固定的說法；老套；（數學、化學）方程式

        formulate　*v.*

    (C) trap ﹝ træp ﹞ ① *n.* 陷阱；（騙人的）圈套　　② *v.* 設下圈套；欺騙

        lay/set a trap　設下圈套　　　walk/fall into a trap　陷入圈套中

    (D) seizure ﹝ˈsiʒɚ﹞ *n.* 捕捉；查封；（疾病的）發作　　seize *v.* 捕捉；抓到

        the seizure of *one's* property　查封某人的財產

        a heart seizure　心臟病發作

    ＊government ﹝ˈgʌvɚnmənt﹞ *n.* 政府　　foil ﹝ fɔɪl ﹞ *v.* 使挫敗；使未能得逞

    terrorist ﹝ˈtɛrərɪst﹞ *adj.* 恐怖主義的；恐怖份子的　　arrest ﹝ əˈrɛst ﹞ *v.* 逮捕

    Muslim ﹝ˈmʌzlɪm , ˈmus-﹞ *n.* 回教徒　　suspicion ﹝ səˈspɪʃən ﹞ *n.* 嫌疑

    on suspicion of 涉嫌　　involvement ﹝ ɪnˈvɑlvmənt ﹞ *n.* 捲入

11. (**C**) His works <u>stand out</u> from others'. He is an excellent writer.

他的作品比其他人的<u>傑出</u>。他是優秀的作家。

    (A) take off　① (*vt.*) 脫掉（衣、帽等）

           ② (*vi.*)（人）動身；（飛機）起飛　　　takeoff *n.* 起飛

    (B) cheer up　使高興；振作起來　（＝ *keep one's spirits up*）

    (C) ***stand out***　傑出　　　outstanding *adj.* 傑出的

    (D) come to　甦醒過來　（＝ *come to oneself* ＝ *come to one's senses* ＝ *revive*）

    ＊works ﹝ wɝks ﹞ *n. pl.*（文學、藝術的）作品

12. (**B**) The band sounded terrible because the instruments were <u>out of tune</u>.

樂隊的聲音糟透了，因為樂器<u>音調不準</u>。

    (A) out of touch　失去聯絡（↔ *in touch* 保持聯繫）

    (B) ***out of tune*** 音調不準（↔ *in tune* 音調準確）

    (C) out of business 停止營業　　*cf.* in business　經商

    (D) out of shape　身體不健康（↔ *in shape* 身體健康）

    ＊(musical) instrument ﹝ˈɪnstrəmənt﹞ *n.* 樂器

13. (**A**) <u>Turn over</u> two of the cards at a time and see if they match.
把其中兩張牌一次<u>翻轉</u>過來看看是否成對。

(A) *turn over* 翻轉 (= *turn upside down* = *invert*)

(B) lay off 解雇 (= *fire* = *sack*)

(C) back up 支持 (= *stand by* = *side with* = *stand up for* = *take part with* = *support*)

(D) let up 雨勢減弱
We can go out when the rain lets up. 雨勢一減,我們就可出門。

* *at a time* 一次 　　 match〔mætʃ〕*v.* 花色配合;成對

14. (**B**) <u>Apart from</u> being blond and pretty, she was smart and helpful.
她<u>除了</u>膚白金髮和美麗<u>之外</u>,還很聰明樂於助人。

(A) in addition 此外 (副詞)

(B) *apart from* 除~之外還有 (介系詞)
(= *besides* = *in addition to* = *aside from*)

(C) away from 遠離

(D) beside 在旁邊 (介系詞)

* blond〔blɑnd〕*adj.* 膚白金髮的

15. (**A**) Would you please <u>put out</u> the cigarette? I can't stand the smoke here.
拜託你把香煙<u>弄熄</u>好嗎?我受不了煙味。

(A) *put out* 熄滅 (= *extinguish*)

(B) carry out 實現 (= *carry/put ~ into practice* = *put ~ into effect*)

(C) make out 瞭解 (= *figure out* = *understand*);分辨;進展

(D) run out 用完 (= *be used up*)
Their food will soon run out. 他們的食物快用完了。

* stand〔stænd〕*v.* 忍受

TEST 31

Directions: The following questions are incomplete sentences. You are to choose the one word that best completes the sentence.

1. We managed to catch a _____ of Queen Elizabeth as the procession passed.

   (A) view   (B) glance

   (C) sign   (D) glimpse   ( )

2. The two secrets to living longer are regular exercise and _____ from worry.

   (A) freedom   (B) motion

   (C) favor   (D) process   ( )

3. Her white dress _____ the redness of her sunburned arms.

   (A) lightened   (B) affirmed

   (C) encouraged   (D) emphasized   ( )

4. If you go to Scotland, you may see people in Highland _____.

   (A) costume   (B) parcel

   (C) bundle   (D) custom   ( )

5. Tell me what happened at the end of the love story. Don't keep me in _____.

   (A) suspense   (B) memory

   (C) mystery   (D) permission   ( )

6. Grandfathers are usually _____ to their grandchildren even when they make mistakes.

   (A) cruel   (B) benevolent

   (C) ambitious   (D) dash   ( )

7. She _____ when she heard the bad news about her boyfriend's sudden death.

   (A) trembled   (B) hailed

   (C) acclaimed   (D) sowed   ( )

8. The car accident left a(n) _____ scar on his face. He has been upset since then.
   - (A) forever
   - (B) eternal
   - (C) everlasting
   - (D) permanent   (   )

9. If he wants to be a great baseball player, the first thing he should do is _____ his skills.
   - (A) realize
   - (B) progress
   - (C) increase
   - (D) sharpen   (   )

10. Japan made a(n) _____ to Korea aimed at increasing trade between the two countries.
    - (A) dissent
    - (B) exception
    - (C) proposal
    - (D) companion   (   )

11. This mission is pretty tedious. I would like to _____ as soon as possible.
    - (A) think it over
    - (B) begin all over again
    - (C) get it over with
    - (D) take it out   (   )

12. To enter this military base, you must have a _____.
    - (A) remit
    - (B) submit
    - (C) limit
    - (D) permit   (   )

13. The convenience store's _____ tape enabled the police to catch the robber in an hour.
    - (A) souvenir
    - (B) surveillance
    - (C) surcharge
    - (D) surfeit   (   )

14. If help does not come, we must _____ to the end.
    - (A) bear
    - (B) endeavor
    - (C) retain
    - (D) strain   (   )

15. There is a lot of _____ between the host and audience in TV call-in shows.
    - (A) do's and don'ts
    - (B) p's and q's
    - (C) give-and-take
    - (D) hide-and-seek   (   )

TEST 31 詳解

1. (**D**) We managed to catch a <u>glimpse</u> of Queen Elizabeth as the procession passed.
當隊伍經過的時候，我們設法要<u>看伊麗莎白女皇一眼</u>。
   - (A) view〔vju〕*n.* 視野；景色　　a distant view 遠景
   - (B) glance〔glæns〕*n.* 匆匆的一看
     cast / throw a glance at~ 對~匆匆看一眼
   - (C) sign〔saɪn〕*n.* 信號　　a safety sign 安全駕駛標誌
   - (D) *glimpse*〔glɪmps〕*n.* 看一眼　　***catch a glimpse of*~** 對~看一眼
   - * manage〔'mænɪdʒ〕*v.* 設法　　procession〔prə'sɛʃən〕*n.* 隊伍

2. (**A**) The two secrets to living longer are regular exercise and <u>freedom</u> from worry. 長壽的兩個秘訣，就是規律地運動以及<u>免於</u>煩惱。
   - (A) *freedom*〔'fridəm〕*n.* 自由；免除　　freedom from care 無憂無慮
     例：He had freedom to do what he liked. 他有想做什麼就做什麼的自由。
   - (B) motion〔'moʃən〕*n.* 提案　　adopt a motion 採納一項提案
   - (C) favor〔'fevɚ〕*n.* 好意；恩惠　　ask a favor of *sb.* 請某人幫忙
   - (D) process〔'prɑsɛs〕*n.* 過程　　the process of history 歷史的演進
   - * regular〔'rɛgjələ〕*adj.* 規律的

3. (**D**) Her white dress <u>emphasized</u> the redness of her sunburned arms.
她的白色衣服<u>突顯出</u>她曬紅的手臂。
   - (A) lighten〔'laɪtn̩〕*v.* 照亮
   - (B) affirm〔ə'fɝm〕*v.* 斷言　　affirmable〔ə'fɝməbl̩〕*adj.* 可斷言的
   - (C) encourage〔ɪn'kɝɪdʒ〕*v.* 鼓勵　　encouraging〔ɪn'kɝɪdʒɪŋ〕*adj.* 鼓勵的
   - (D) *emphasize*〔'ɛmfə,saɪz〕*v.* 突顯；強調　　emphasis〔'ɛmfəsɪs〕*n.* 強調
     例：He emphasized the necessity of taking strong measures.
     他強調採取強硬手段的必要性。
   - * sunburned〔'sʌn,bɝnd〕*adj.* 曬黑的

4. (**A**) If you go to Scotland, you may see people in Highland <u>costume</u>.
如果你去蘇格蘭，你可以看到人們穿著蘇格蘭高地<u>服裝</u>。
   - (A) *costume*〔'kɑstjum〕*n.* 服裝　　a street costume 外出服
     a hunting costume 獵裝　　the national costume of India 印度的民族服裝
   - (B) parcel〔'pɑrsl̩〕*n.* 包裹；小包　　by parcels 一點一點地
   - (C) bundle〔'bʌndl̩〕*n.* 束；包　　a bundle of clothes 一包衣服
   - (D) custom〔'kʌstəm〕*n.* 習慣；風俗　　keep up the custom 保持風俗
   - * Highland〔'haɪlənd〕*adj.* 蘇格蘭高地的

5. (**A**) Tell me what happened at the end of the love story. Don't keep me in suspense.

告訴我那個愛情故事最後發生了什麼事情。不要讓我懸疑緊張。

(A) *suspense* 〔 sə'spɛns 〕 *n.* 懸疑；掛念

hold *one's* judgement in suspense 遲遲不作判決

例：The story kept me in suspense until the end.

那個故事讓我懸疑緊張直到結束。

(B) memory 〔'mɛmərɪ〕 *n.* 記憶　　speak from memory 背誦

(C) mystery 〔'mɪstrɪ〕 *n.* 秘密；謎　　mysterious 〔 mɪs'tɪrɪəs 〕 *adj.* 神秘的

(D) permission 〔 pə·'mɪʃən 〕 *n.* 許可　　ask for permission 請求許可

without permission 未經許可　　written permission 許可證

6. (**B**) Grandfathers are usually benevolent to their grandchildren even when they make mistakes.

祖父對待孫子經常是仁慈的，即使當他們犯錯的時候也一樣。

(A) cruel 〔'kruəl〕 *adj.* 殘酷的　　cruelty 〔'kruəltɪ〕 *n.* 殘酷

(B) *benevolent* 〔 bə'nɛvələnt 〕 *adj.* 仁慈的；親切的

benevolent words 親切的話

例：He is benevolent to poor people. 他對窮人很親切。

(C) ambitious 〔 æm'bɪʃəs 〕 *adj.* 有野心的

an ambitious politician 有野心的政治家

(D) dash 〔 dæʃ 〕 *v.* 猛衝；急奔　　dash off 疾書

例：He dashed to catch the last train. 他急奔去趕搭最後一班火車。

* *make mistakes* 犯錯

7. (**A**) She trembled when she heard the bad news about her boyfriend's sudden death. 當她得知她男朋友突然死亡的壞消息的時候，她震驚地發抖。

(A) *tremble* 〔'trɛmbḷ〕 *v.* (因震驚、生病、恐懼) 發抖

tembling 〔'trɛmbḷɪŋ〕 *adj.* 發抖的

例：His hands tremble from drinking too much.

他的手因為喝酒過多而發抖。

(B) hail 〔 hel 〕 *v.* 向～歡呼　　hail from 出身於

例：The crowd hailed the winner. 群眾向獲勝者歡呼。

(C) acclaim 〔 ə'klem 〕 *v.* 稱讚；喝采

acclamation 〔ˌæklə'meʃən 〕 *n.* 稱讚

(D) sow 〔 so 〕 *v.* 播種　　sower 〔'soɚ〕 *n.* 播種者

* *sudden death* 突然死亡

8. (**D**) The car accident left a <u>permanent</u> scar on his face. He has been upset since
then. 那場車禍在他臉上留下<u>永久的</u>疤痕。他從那時候開始就很不高興。
   - (A) forever〔fɚˈɛvɚ〕*adv.* 永久地　　forever and ever 永久（強調説法）
   - (B) eternal〔ɪˈtɝnl〕*adj.* 永恆的；不朽的（形容抽象的概念）
     eternal life 永恆的生命
   - (C) everlasting〔͵ɛvɚˈlæstɪŋ〕*adj.* 不朽的（形容抽象的概念）
     everlasting fame 不朽的名聲
   - (D) ***permanent***〔ˈpɝmənənt〕*adj.* 永久的（通常用於形容實體之物）
     permanent teeth 恆齒
   - * scar〔skɑr〕*n.* 疤；傷痕　　upset〔ʌpˈsɛt〕*adj.* 不高興的

9. (**D**) If he wants to be a great baseball player, the first thing he should do is
<u>sharpen</u> his skills. 如果一個人想要成為偉大的棒球選手，他第一件必須做
的事就是要<u>磨練</u>他的技巧。
   - (A) realize〔ˈriə͵laɪz〕*v.* 了解；領悟　　realizing〔ˈriə͵laɪzɪŋ〕*adj.* 易於了解的
     例：He has not realized his own mistakes. 他還沒有認清自己的錯誤。
   - (B) progress〔prəˈgrɛs〕*v.* 前進；進步　　progression〔prəˈgrɛʃən〕*n.* 前進
     例：The work has not progressed very far. 工作沒有多大的進展。
   - (C) increase〔ɪnˈkris〕*v.* 增加　　increase twofold 增加兩倍
   - (D) ***sharpen***〔ˈʃɑrpən〕*v.* 使銳利；增進　　sharpen *one's* tongue 磨練說話能力
     例：Exercise will sharpen your appetite. 運動會增進你的食慾。

10. (**C**) Japan made a <u>proposal</u> to Korea aimed at increasing trade between the two
countries. 日本對韓國做出一個增加兩國貿易的<u>提案</u>。
   - (A) dissent〔dɪˈsɛnt〕*n.* 反對　　incite dissent 煽動鬧意見分歧
   - (B) exception〔ɪkˈsɛpʃən〕*n.* 例外　　exceptional〔ɪkˈsɛpʃənl〕*adj.* 例外的
   - (C) ***proposal***〔prəˈpozl〕*n.* 提案；建議
     make proposals for peace 提出和平建議
   - (D) companion〔kəmˈpænjən〕*n.* 同伴
     a companion in *one's* misfortune 共患難的同伴

11. (**C**) This mission is pretty tedious. I would like to <u>get it over with</u> as soon as
possible. 這項任務令人覺得非常乏味。我想儘快<u>讓它結束</u>。
   - (A) think it over 仔細考慮
   - (B) begin all over again 全部重新開始
   - (C) ***get it over with*** 讓它結束
   - (D) take it out 把它拿出來
   - * mission〔ˈmɪʃən〕*n.* 任務　　tedious〔ˈtidɪəs〕*adj.* 乏味的

12. (**D**) To enter this military base, you must have a <u>permit</u>.

要進入這個軍事基地，你必須要有<u>許可證</u>。

(A) remit〔rɪˋmɪt〕v. 匯寄　　remit a check 匯寄支票

(B) submit〔səbˋmɪt〕v. 服從　　submission〔səbˋmɪʃən〕n. 服從

(C) limit〔ˋlɪmɪt〕n. 限制　　a speed limit 速度限制

to the utmost limit 到極限

(D) *permit*〔ˋpɝmɪt〕n. 許可證　　a parking permit 停車證

＊military〔ˋmɪləˌtɛrɪ〕*adj.* 軍事的　　***military base*** 軍事基地

13. (**B**) The convenience store's <u>surveillance</u> tape enabled the police to catch the robber in an hour.

那家便利商店的<u>監視</u>錄影帶讓警察能在一個小時內抓到搶匪。

(A) souvenir〔ˌsuvəˋnɪr〕n. 紀念品；特產

(B) *surveillance*〔səˋveləns〕n. 監視；看守

under surveillance 在監視下

(C) surcharge〔ˋsɝˌtʃardʒ〕n. 超載

(D) surfeit〔ˋsɝfɪt〕n. 暴食；過度

a surfeit of commercials 商業廣告的氾濫

＊enable〔ɪnˋebl̩〕v. 使能夠　　robber〔ˋrabɚ〕n. 強盜

14. (**B**) If help does not come, we must <u>endeavor</u> to the end.

假使沒有援助，我們必須<u>努力</u>到最後。

(A) bear〔bɛr〕v. 生育；忍耐　　bear pain 忍受痛苦

(B) *endeavor*〔ɪnˋdɛvɚ〕v. 努力

endeavor to the best of *one's* ability 盡最大的努力

(C) retain〔rɪˋten〕v. 保持；保留　　retainer〔rɪˋtenɚ〕n. 保留物

(D) strain〔stren〕v. 拉緊；繃緊　　strained〔strend〕*adj.* 緊張的

strainer〔ˋstrenɚ〕n. 濾器

15. (**C**) There is a lot of <u>give-and-take</u> between the host and audience in TV call-in shows.

在電視邀請觀眾打電話進來的節目中，主持人和觀眾有很多的<u>意見交換</u>。

(A) do's and don'ts 行為準則

(B) p's and q's　　Mind your p's and q's.【諺】謹慎行事。

(C) *give-and-take*　（言語等）意見的交換

(D) hide-and-seek 捉迷藏

＊call-in〔ˋkɔlˌɪn〕n. 以通電話方式參與的節目

TEST 32

Directions: The following questions are incomplete sentences. You are to choose the one word that best completes the sentence.

1. The _____ snake hissed whenever Harry came near.
   (A) hostile   (B) vulnerable
   (C) appealing   (D) decent   (   )

2. The seven-year-old boy was not allowed to run in the marathon because _____ in the race were required to be over 12 years of age.
   (A) sponsors   (B) participants
   (C) residents   (D) proponents   (   )

3. Anne could tell the new student was from France because she spoke English with a(n) _____.
   (A) interval   (B) accent
   (C) descendant   (D) reputation   (   )

4. The fear of a dentist's drill is _____; no one on the globe is not afraid of it.
   (A) authentic   (B) unbearable
   (C) optional   (D) universal   (   )

5. The use of cameras is _____ forbidden inside the theater because it might interfere with the performance.
   (A) reluctantly   (B) significantly
   (C) strictly   (D) annually   (   )

6. A university _____ wouldn't be as special if everyone could attend university.
   (A) applicant   (B) diploma
   (C) facility   (D) agenda   (   )

7. The patient's condition improved _____ after she began taking the new medication.
   (A) enormously   (B) occasionally
   (C) respectively   (D) strictly   (   )

8. You may turn the knob to _____ the temperature of the water produced by the water heater.
   (A) eliminate
   (B) adjust
   (C) generate
   (D) submit   (   )

9. The future of this company is _____; many of its most talented employees are going into more profitable businesses.
   (A) at odds
   (B) in vain
   (C) at stake
   (D) on end   (   )

10. The changes Liz has made in her diet are _____. She's getting into a healthier eating pattern.
    (A) paying off
    (B) taking over
    (C) getting through
    (D) catching on   (   )

11. People used to _____ from the idea of getting into debt; now with the common use of credit cards, it is widely accepted.
    (A) reckon
    (B) deviate
    (C) recoil
    (D) distinguish   (   )

12. Don't take it seriously; I meant it _____ as a joke.
    (A) scarcely
    (B) merely
    (C) nearly
    (D) uniquely   (   )

13. What is all that _____? It sounds like a tsunami is coming again!
    (A) commotion
    (B) comparison
    (C) companion
    (D) compassion   (   )

14. After several terms of presidency, the Chiang family is _____ respected.
    (A) resentfully
    (B) eminently
    (C) stunningly
    (D) tastefully   (   )

15. Because of the scandal, the vice-president had to resign in _____.
    (A) recession
    (B) acknowledgement
    (C) relief
    (D) disgrace   (   )

TEST 32 詳解

1. (**A**) The <u>hostile</u> snake hissed whenever Harry came near.
   每當他靠近過來的時候，那隻帶<u>有敵意的</u>蛇就會發出嘶嘶聲。

   (A) *hostile* (ˋhɑstḷ) *adj.* 有敵意的　　a hostile army　敵軍
   a hostile country　敵國

   (B) vulnerable (ˋvʌlnərəbḷ) *adj.* 易受攻擊的；脆弱的 (= *fragile*)
   a vulnerable point　弱點

   (C) appealing (əˋpilɪŋ) *adj.* 令人心動的；吸引人的 (= *attractive* = *tempting* = *fascinating*)

   (D) decent (ˋdisṇt) *adj.* 端正的；相當好的
   get decent marks　得到相當好的分數

   * hiss (hɪs) *v.* 發出嘶嘶聲

2. (**B**) The seven-year-old boy was not allowed to run in the marathon because <u>participants</u> in the race were required to be over 12 years of age.
   那個七歲大的小男孩不能參加馬拉松比賽，因為<u>參賽者</u>的年紀必須超過 12 歲。

   (A) sponsor (ˋspɑnsɚ) *n.* 贊助者
   a sponsor for a TV program　電視節目的贊助者

   (B) *participant* (pɚˋtɪsəpənt) *n.* 參加者；參與者　　participate *v.*
   participation *n.*

   (C) resident (ˋrɛzədənt) *n.* 居民 (= *citizen* = *dweller* = *inhabitant*)
   reside *v.* 居住

   (D) proponent (prəˋponənt) *n.* 提議者 (= *broacher*)；支持者 (= *supporter*)

   * marathon (ˋmærə͵θɑn) *n.* 馬拉松
   require (rɪˋkwaɪr) *v.* (命令、規則等) 要求；命令
   12 years of age 十二歲 (= *12 years old*)

3. (**B**) Anne could tell the new student was from France because she spoke English with an <u>accent</u>. 安能夠分辨出那個新同學是從法國來的，因為她的英文有個<u>腔調</u>。

   (A) interval (ˋɪntɚvḷ) *n.* 間隔　　at short intervals　常常
   at long intervals　偶爾

   (B) *accent* (ˋæksɛnt) *n.* (外國的) 口音；腔調；重音
   accentual (ækˋsɛntʃuəl) *adj.* 有重音的

   (C) descendant (dɪˋsɛndənt) *n.* 子孫 (= *offspring* = *posterity* = *seed*)

   (D) reputation (͵rɛpjəˋteʃən) *n.* 名聲；名譽 (= *fame* = *prestige* = *renown*)

   * tell (tɛl) *v.* 辨別；分辨

4. (**D**) The fear of a dentist's drill is <u>universal</u>; no one on the globe is not afraid of it.
大家<u>普遍</u>都會害怕牙醫師的牙鑽；世界上沒有人不怕的。

    (A) authentic〔ɔ'θɛntɪk〕*adj.* 可靠的（= *reliable* = *trustworthy*）；真正的

        （= *genuine* = *downright*）

    (B) unbearable〔ʌn'bɛrəbḷ〕*adj.* 難以忍受的

        unbearable sorrow 難以忍受的悲哀

    (C) optional〔'ɑpʃənḷ〕*adj.* 隨意的（= *free*）；可選擇的；選修的

        （↔ required 必修的）

    (D) *universal*〔ˌjunə'vɝsḷ〕*adj.* 普遍性的（= *general* = *common*）

        a universal rule 一般的法則   a universal truth 普遍的真理

        a universal human weakness 普遍的人性弱點

    ＊dentist〔'dɛntɪst〕*n.* 牙醫   drill〔drɪl〕*n.* 牙鑽   globe〔glob〕*n.* 地球

5. (**C**) The use of cameras is <u>strictly</u> forbidden inside the theater because it might
interfere with the performance.
在戲院裡面<u>嚴格</u>禁止使用照相機，因為使用照相機可能會干擾演出。

    (A) reluctantly〔rɪ'lʌktəntlɪ〕*adv.* 不情願地；勉強地   reluctant *adj.*

        （= *unwilling* = *disinclined*）

    (B) significantly〔sɪg'nɪfəkəntlɪ〕*adv.* 重大地；相當地   significant *adj.*

        （= *critical* = *crucial*）

    (C) *strictly*〔'strɪktlɪ〕*adv.* 嚴格地   strict *adj.*（= *rigid* = *stark* = *sharp*）

    (D) annually〔'ænjʊəlɪ〕*adv.* 每年一次地   annual *adj.*

    ＊forbid〔fə'bɪd〕*v.* 禁止   interfere〔ˌɪntə'fɪr〕*v.*（人、事物）阻礙；干擾

    performance〔pə'fɔrməns〕*n.* 表演；演出

6. (**B**) A university <u>diploma</u> wouldn't be as special if everyone could attend university.
如果每個人都能上大學的話，大學<u>文憑</u>就不再像以前一樣稀奇了。

    (A) applicant〔'æpləkənt〕*n.* 申請人；應徵者

        an applicant for admission to a school 申請入學者

    (B) *diploma*〔dɪ'plomə〕*n.* 學位證書；文憑   receive *one's* diploma 畢業

        diplomacy *n.* 外交；外交手腕   diplomat *n.* 外交官

    (C) facility〔fə'sɪlətɪ〕*n.*（醫院、圖書館等的）設備；設施

        education facilities 教育設施

    (D) agenda〔ə'dʒɛndə〕*n.* 議程；應辦之事

        the first item on the agenda 議程上的第一項

    ＊attend〔ə'tɛnd〕*v.* 上（學、教堂）

7. (**A**) The patient's condition improved <u>enormously</u> after she began taking the new medication.

自從服用新的藥物之後，病人的健康狀況獲得<u>很大的</u>改善。

(A) *enormously* 〔 ɪˈnɔrməslɪ 〕 *adv.* 巨大地；龐大地　　enormous *adj.*
(= *huge* = *titanic*)

(B) occasionally 〔 əˈkeʒənəlɪ 〕 *adv.* 偶爾；有時 (= *at times* = *at long intervals* = *on occasion*)

(C) respectively 〔 rɪˈspɛktɪvlɪ 〕 *adv.* 個別地；各自地　　respectably 可敬地
respectfully 恭敬地

(D) strictly 〔ˈstrɪktlɪ 〕 *adv.* 嚴格地 (= *rigidly* = *rigorously* = *severely* = *starkly*)
strict *adj.*

* patient 〔ˈpeʃənt 〕 *n.* 病人　　condition 〔 kənˈdɪʃən 〕 *n.* 健康狀況
medication 〔͵mɛdɪˈkeʃən 〕 *n.* 藥物

8. (**B**) You may turn the knob to <u>adjust</u> the temperature of the water produced by the water heater.

要<u>調整</u>由熱水器加熱後的水溫，你可以轉一下把手就可以了。

(A) eliminate 〔 ɪˈlɪmə͵net 〕 *v.* 去除　　eliminate sex barriers 消除男女的差別

(B) *adjust* 〔 əˈdʒʌst 〕 *v.* 調節；調整　　adjust color on a TV 調整電視的色彩
adjust *one's* tie in a mirror 照鏡子調整領帶　　adjust a clock 調整時鐘

(C) generate 〔ˈdʒɛnə͵ret 〕 *v.* 產生；引起 (= *create* = *cause* = *produce*)
generation *n.* 一代

(D) submit 〔 səbˈmɪt 〕 *v.* 服從 (= *follow* = *obey* = *comply*)；提出

* knob 〔 nɑb 〕 *n.* 球形開關；把手　　temperature 〔ˈtɛmpərətʃə 〕 *n.* 溫度
heater 〔ˈhitə 〕 *n.* 加熱器　　*water heater* 自動熱水器

9. (**C**) The future of this company is <u>at stake</u>; many of its most talented employees are going into more profitable businesses.

這家公司的未來<u>岌岌可危</u>，許多最有才幹的員工，紛紛出走到其他公司行號。

(A) at odds 爭吵　　odds 〔 ɑdz 〕 *n. pl.* (給予弱者的) 有利條件

(B) in vain 徒勞無功　　vain 〔 ven 〕 *adj.* 徒勞的 (= *futile*)

(C) *at stake* 岌岌可危的　　stake 〔 stek 〕 *n.* 賭注；利害關係

(D) on end 豎起；直立著
make *one's* hair stand on end 使某人 (因恐怖等) 毛髮豎立

* talented 〔ˈtæləntɪd 〕 *adj.* 有才能的　　employee 〔͵ɛmplɔɪˈi 〕 *n.* 員工
profitable 〔ˈprɑfɪtəb!〕 *adj.* 有利的；賺錢的

10. (**A**) The changes Liz has made in her diet are <u>paying off</u>. She's getting into a healthier eating pattern.

麗茲在飲食上面做的改變逐漸有了回報。她開始有了更健康的飲食模式。

(A) *pay off* 回報；（事業、計畫等）順利進行；（債務等）償清
(= *repay* = *discharge* = *wipe out*)

(B) take over 接替；接收
The building was taken over by the army. 該房屋被軍隊接收。

(C) get through 穿越；（電話等）接通；通過（考試等）；完成
get through college 大學畢業

(D) catch on 風行 (= *prevail*)；明白；領會 (= *understand* = *realize* = *comprehend*)

* diet ('daɪət) *n.* 飲食　　**get into** 開始

11. (**C**) People used to <u>recoil</u> from the idea of getting into debt; now with the common use of credit cards, it is widely accepted.

以前借錢的觀念使得人們退卻，現在因為信用卡的普遍使用，這個觀念就被廣泛地接受了。

(A) reckon ('rɛkən) *v.* 計算
reckoning ('rɛkənɪŋ) *n.* 帳單　　reckon the cost of the trip 計算旅費
reckoner ('rɛkənɚ) *n.* 計算表

(B) deviate ('divɪ‚et) *v.* 偏離；背離　　deviation (‚divɪ'eʃən) *n.* 偏差
deviate from the rule 違背原則
deviate to minor issues 偏離到次要問題

(C) *recoil* (rɪ'kɔɪl) *v.* 退卻　　recoilless (rɪ'kɔɪllɪs) *adj.* 無後座力的
例：They recoiled from such radical ideas.
　　那樣偏激的想法使他們望而生畏。

(D) distinguish (dɪ'stɪŋgwɪʃ) *v.* 辨別
distinguishable (dɪ'stɪŋgwɪʃəbl̩) *adj.* 可區別的
distinguished (dɪ'stɪŋgwɪʃt) *adj.* 卓越的
distinguishing (dɪ'stɪŋgwɪʃɪŋ) *adj.* 特殊的
例：It is too hard to distinguish him from his brother.
　　要分辨他和他哥哥是困難的。

* debt (dɛt) *n.* 債務　　**get into debt** 負債；借錢
accept (ək'sɛpt) *v.* 接受

12. (**B**) Don't take it seriously; I meant it <u>merely</u> as a joke.
不要太認眞，我<u>只是</u>在開玩笑而已。

(A) scarcely〔'skɛrslɪ〕*adv.* 幾乎沒有
scarce〔skɛrs〕*adj.* 稀有的；不足的
例：At first he was so astonished that he scarcely knew what to say.
起初他驚訝得幾乎不知道要說什麼才好。

(B) *merely*〔'mɪrlɪ〕*adv.* 單單；僅僅　　mere *adj.*
例：She is merely a child. 她只是個小孩。

(C) nearly〔'nɪrlɪ〕*adv.* 幾乎；差不多　　near *adj.*
例：We are nearly at the top of the hill.
我們差不多到了山頂上。

(D) uniquely〔ju'niklɪ〕*adv.* 獨特地　　unique *adj.*

＊seriously〔'sɪrɪəslɪ〕*adv.* 認眞地　　joke〔dʒok〕*n.* 玩笑

13. (**A**) What is all that <u>commotion</u>? It sounds like a tsunami is coming again!
到底在<u>騷動</u>什麼？聽起來好像海嘯又來了！

(A) *commotion*〔kə'moʃən〕*n.* 騷動
make a commotion about nothing 無理取鬧
be in commotion 在動盪中　　create a commotion 引起騷動
例：They were awakened by the commotion in the street.
他們被街上的騷動吵醒了。

(B) comparison〔kəm'pærəsn̩〕*n.* 比較；對照
compare〔kəm'pɛr〕*v.* 比較
on careful comparison 仔細比較之下
by comparison 比較起來
例：In comparison with most first novels hers shows considerable polish.
跟大多數的處女作比較起來，她的作品顯得相當精練。

(C) companion〔kəm'pænjən〕*n.* 夥伴
a companion for life 終生伴侶

(D) compassion〔kəm'pæʃən〕*n.* 同情心
have compassion on～ 對～寄予同情

＊tsunami〔tsu'nɑmɪ〕*n.* 海嘯

14. (**B**) After several terms of presidency, the Chiang family is <u>eminently</u> respected.
在當了好幾任的總統之後，蔣家<u>大大地</u>受到尊重。

    (A) resentfully〔rɪˈzɛntfəlɪ〕*adv.* 憎恨地   resentful *adj.*

    (B) *eminently*〔ˈɛmənəntlɪ〕*adv.* 大大地；顯著地   eminent *adj.*

    (C) stunningly〔ˈstʌnɪŋlɪ〕*adv.* 令人讚嘆地   stunning *adj.*

    (D) tastefully〔ˈtestfəlɪ〕*adv.* 精緻地；美味地   tasteful *adj.*

    ＊term〔tɝm〕*n.* 任期   presidency〔ˈprɛzədənsɪ〕*n.* 總統的職位

    respect〔rɪˈspɛkt〕*v.* 尊重

15. (**D**) Because of the scandal, the vice-president had to resign in <u>disgrace</u>.
因為那個醜聞，副總統必須<u>不名譽地</u>辭職。

    (A) recession〔rɪˈsɛʃən〕*n.* (暫時的) 蕭條

        recess〔rɪˈsɛs〕*n.* (短暫的) 休息

        a severe recession 嚴重的不景氣

        recover from a recession 景氣復甦

    (B) acknowledgement〔əkˈnɑlɪdʒmənt〕*n.* 承認；自白

        acknowledge〔əkˈnɑlɪdʒ〕*v.* 承認

        in acknowledgement of 藉以感謝

        bow *one's* acknowledgements of 表示感謝頻頻鞠躬

    (C) relief〔rɪˈlif〕*n.* 減輕；救濟

        obtain relief from pain 疼痛消除

        give a sigh of relief 寬慰地舒一口氣   relief of old people 救濟老人

        例：Hearing the news, he breathed a sigh of relief.

            一聽到消息，他如釋重負地鬆一口氣。

    (D) *disgrace*〔dɪsˈgres〕*n.* 不名譽   disgraceful *adj.*

        bring disgrace on *one's* family 玷污某人的家門

        fall into disgrace 失去寵愛

        例：The divorce was a disgrace to the royal family.

            該離婚案件對皇家來說是不名譽的事。

    ＊scandal〔ˈskændl̩〕*n.* 醜聞   vice〔vaɪs〕*adj.* 副的

    resign〔rɪˈzaɪn〕*v.* 辭職

TEST 33

Directions: The following questions are incomplete sentences. You are to choose the one word that best completes the sentence.

1. Greek archaeologists _____ an ancient Macedonian city in the foothills of Mount Olympus have uncovered a 2,600-meter defensive wall.
   - (A) constructing
   - (B) terminating
   - (C) exploiting
   - (D) excavating
   ( )

2. A market survey _____ by the Consumers' Foundation showed that some seven percent of lipsticks sold in Taipei contain heavy metals such as cadmium and lead.
   - (A) experimented
   - (B) explored
   - (C) investigated
   - (D) conducted
   ( )

3. In a wild _____, that reporter claimed that the company had gone bankrupt. In fact, it was merely suffering a small financial problem.
   - (A) estimation
   - (B) exaggeration
   - (C) evaluation
   - (D) calculation
   ( )

4. Since she tends to be _____ of her promises, you had better not take her words seriously.
   - (A) characteristic
   - (B) suggestive
   - (C) oblivious
   - (D) indicative
   ( )

5. In the meeting, the resolution was _____ accepted by the board of directors. They agreed to a man.
   - (A) miraculously
   - (B) incredibly
   - (C) simultaneously
   - (D) unanimously
   ( )

6. He questioned the _____ of those figures since they were not issued by reputable scholars and experts.
   - (A) validity
   - (B) complexity
   - (C) ambiguity
   - (D) guarantee
   ( )

7. One of the _____ of smoking is that smokers are in grave danger of contracting lung cancer.
   - (A) profits
   - (B) advantages
   - (C) dividends
   - (D) hazards
   ( )

8. She only gave me a _____ description of what happened here yesterday.
   (A) vague   (B) skeptical
   (C) vivid   (D) distinct   (   )

9. In the government-organized campaign to vote on an image to represent Taiwan internationally, glove puppetry has _____ as the top choice of the people.
   (A) condemned   (B) acclaimed
   (C) applauded   (D) emerged   (   )

10. Health officials and farm workers in protective clothing _____ hundreds of thousands of chickens in western India, hoping to prevent the spread of the deadly H5N1 bird flu virus.
    (A) cultivated   (B) slaughtered
    (C) reproduced   (D) migrated   (   )

11. Travel to the moon may become _____ in the near future. Its possibility will enable many rich men to realize their dream of space travel.
    (A) critical   (B) feasible
    (C) threatening (D) apparent   (   )

12. You are more _____ to injury if you exercise infrequently.
    (A) liable   (B) justified
    (C) flawless (D) worthy   (   )

13. The new sexual harassment law has taken effect. Those who violate the law will _____ punishment including fines and jail terms.
    (A) be discriminated against (B) be subject to
    (C) devote themselves to   (D) hold responsible for   (   )

14. His conduct has been entirely _____. He has a clear conscience.
    (A) in the dark   (B) on the horizon
    (C) aboveboard   (D) into his shell   (   )

15. The mayor acted _____ the law in every way.
    (A) at the cost of   (B) in accordance with
    (C) at the core of   (D) in terms of   (   )

TEST 33 詳解

1. (**D**) Greek archaeologists <u>excavating</u> an ancient Macedonian city in the foothills of Mount Olympus have uncovered a 2,600-meter defensive wall.

希臘考古學家在奧林帕斯山丘上，<u>挖掘</u>出古馬其頓城，並讓兩千六百公尺高的防禦城牆重現於世。

(A) construct (kən'strʌkt) v. 組合；構成；建造
construct a sentence 造句

(B) terminate ('tɜmə,net) v. 終止 (= end = cease = expire = close)
termination n.

(C) exploit (ɪk'splɔɪt) v. 開發；利用　　exploit a mine 開礦
exploit an opportunity 利用機會

(D) *excavate* ('ɛkskə,vet) v. 發掘；挖出（被埋的東西）(= *unearth*)
excavation n.

* archaeologist (,ɑrkɪ'ɑlədʒɪst) n. 考古學家
Macedonian (,mæsə'donɪən) adj. 馬其頓的
foothill ('fʊt,hɪl) n. 山丘　　uncover (ʌn'kʌvə) v. 揭發
defensive (dɪ'fɛnsɪv) adj. 防禦的

2. (**D**) A market survey <u>conducted</u> by the Consumers' Foundation showed that some seven percent of lipsticks sold in Taipei contain heavy metals such as cadmium and lead.

一份由消費者文敎基金會所<u>做</u>的研究指出，在台北地區販售的口紅，大約有百分之七，含有像鎘以及鉛的重金屬。

(A) experiment (ɪk'spɛrəmənt) v. 做實驗
experiment with electricity 用電做實驗

(B) explore (ɪk'splor) v. 探測；調查　　explorer n. 探險家

(C) investigate (ɪn'vɛstə,get) v. 調查；研究　　investigation n.
investigator n. 調查員

(D) *conduct* (kən'dʌkt) v. 處理；經營；管理
conduct ('kɑndʌkt) n. 行爲；經營

* *Consumers' Foundation* 消費者文敎基金會
lipstick ('lɪp,stɪk) n. 口紅
cadmium ('kædmɪəm) n. 鎘　　lead (lɛd) n. 鉛

3. (**B**) In a wild <u>exaggeration</u>, that reporter claimed that the company had gone bankrupt. In fact, it was merely suffering a small financial problem.

眞是<u>誇張</u>到荒謬的境界，那個記者說這家公司已經破產了。事實上，他們只不過是遭遇一個小小的財務問題而已。

    (A) estimation〔͵ɛstə'meʃən〕*n.* (價值等的) 判斷 (= *evaluation*)
        estimate *v.* 估計

    (B) *exaggeration*〔ɪg͵zædʒə'reʃən〕*n.* 誇張 (= *overstatement* = *puffiness*)
        exaggerate *v.* 誇大

    (C) evaluation〔ɪ͵vælju'eʃən〕*n.* 評價 (= *estimation*)   evaluate *v.* 評估

    (D) calculation〔͵kælkjə'leʃən〕*n.* 計算；推測   calculate *v.* 計算

    ＊wild〔waɪld〕*adj.* 荒謬的；毫無根據的
      claim〔klem〕*v.* 主張；宣稱
      bankrupt〔'bæŋkrʌpt〕*adj.* 破產的   suffer〔'sʌfɚ〕*v.* 遭受
      financial〔fə'nænʃəl〕*adj.* 財務的

4. (**C**) Since she tends to be <u>oblivious</u> of her promises, you had better not take her words seriously.

旣然她有忘記諾言的傾向，你最好不要太在意她的話。

    (A) characteristic〔͵kærɪktə'rɪstɪk〕*adj.* 獨特的   *n.* 特質；特色
      character *n.* 性格；氣質

    (B) suggestive〔səg'dʒɛstɪv〕*adj.* 暗示性的
      a suggestive comment 富於暗示性的評論

    (C) *oblivious*〔ə'blɪvɪəs〕*adj.* 健忘的
      be oblivious of *one's* promise 忘記諾言

    (D) indicative〔ɪn'dɪkətɪv〕*adj.* 指示 (表示、暗示) 的
      indicative of contempt 表示輕視

    ＊tend〔tɛnd〕*v.* 有～的傾向   ***had better*** 最好～
      take〔tek〕*v.* 看待 (某事)

5. (**D**) In the meeting, the resolution was <u>unanimously</u> accepted by the board of directors. They agreed to a man.

會議中，董事會<u>一致</u>通過這個決議案，沒有人持不同意見。

    (A) miraculously〔mə'rækjələslɪ〕*adv.* 奇蹟般地
      miraculous *adj.*   miracle *n.* 奇蹟

    (B) incredibly〔ɪn'krɛdəblɪ〕*adv.* 難以置信地
      incredible *adj.*   incredibility *n.*

(C) simultaneously〔͵saɪml̩'tenɪəslɪ〕*adv.* 同時發生地

simultaneous *adj.*　simultaneity *n.*

(D) *unanimously*〔ju'nænəməslɪ〕*adv.* 全體一致地

consensus〔kən'sɛnsəs〕*n.* 意見一致

＊resolution〔͵rɛzə'luʃən〕*n.* 決議案

a board of directors 董事會　　*to a man* 全體一致

6.（ **A** ）He questioned the <u>validity</u> of those figures, since they were not issued by reputable scholars and experts.

因為這些數字並非經由聲望高的學者和專家所公布出來的，因此他質疑其<u>有效性</u>。

(A) *validity*〔və'lɪdətɪ〕*n.* 正當；合法性

the term of validity 有效期限

(B) complexity〔kəm'plɛksətɪ〕*n.* 複雜；複雜的事物

complex〔'kɑmplɛks〕*n.* 複合體；合成物

(C) ambiguity〔͵æmbɪ'gjuətɪ〕*n.* 模稜兩可；曖昧的措辭

ambiguous *adj.* 模稜兩可的

(D) guarantee〔͵gærən'ti〕*n. v.* 保證；約定；保證人

guaranty〔'gærəntɪ〕*n.* 擔保；保證書

＊figures〔'fɪgjəz〕*n. pl.* 數字　　issue〔'ɪʃu〕*v.* 發出

reputable〔'rɛpjətəbl̩〕*adj.* 有聲望的

7.（ **D** ）One of the <u>hazards</u> of smoking is that smokers are in grave danger of contracting lung cancer.

抽煙其中的<u>風險</u>之一就是，有感染肺癌的高度危險性。

(A) profit〔'prɑfɪt〕*n.*（金錢上的）盈利（= *benefit* ）

net profit 淨利　　gross profit 毛利

(B) advantage〔əd'væntɪdʒ〕*n.* 利益（= *benefit* ）；優點

advantageous *adj.* 有益的

(C) dividend〔'dɪvə͵dɛnd〕*n.*（股票、保險的）利息；紅利

a high dividend 高額股息

(D) *hazard*〔'hæzəd〕*n.* 危險（= *danger* = *peril* = *risk* = *jeopardy* ）；風險

＊grave〔grev〕*adj.* 重大的　　*in danger of* 陷入～的危險

contract〔kən'trækt〕*v.* 感染

8. (**A**) She only gave me a <u>vague</u> description of what happened here yesterday.
對於昨天這裡發生的事情,她只給了我一個<u>模糊的</u>敘述。

(A) *vague*〔veg〕*adj.*(語言、觀念、感情等)不明確的;模糊的(↔ *distinct*)

(B) skeptical〔'skɛptɪkl̩〕*adj.* 懷疑的;多疑的
a skeptical person 多疑的人

(C) vivid〔'vɪvɪd〕*adj.* 生動的;(色彩)鮮明的(↔ *dull*)
a vivid description 生動的敘述

(D) distinct〔dɪ'stɪŋkt〕*adj.* 明確的(↔ *vague*);不同的
a distinct difference 明顯的差異

＊description〔dɪ'skrɪpʃən〕*n.* 敘述;說明

9. (**D**) In the government-organized campaign to vote on an image to represent
Taiwan internationally, glove puppetry has <u>emerged</u> as the top choice of
the people. 政府辦了一個為投票選出,代表台灣在國際間形象的宣傳活動,
在該活動中,布袋戲木偶<u>脫穎而出</u>。

(A) condemn〔kən'dɛm〕*v.* 譴責;強烈責難(= *blame*)
condemn war as evil 譴責戰爭為罪惡

(B) acclaim〔ə'klem〕*v.* 讚揚
acclaim *sb.* as a great actor 讚揚某人是個偉大的演員

(C) applaud〔ə'plɔd〕*v.* 鼓掌;喝采;稱讚
applaud *sb.'s* courage 稱讚某人的勇氣

(D) *emerge*〔ɪ'mɝdʒ〕*v.* 出現　　emergence *n.*　　emergency *n.* 緊急

＊campaign〔kæm'pen〕*n.* 宣傳活動　　vote〔vot〕*v.* 投票
glove puppetry 布袋戲木偶

10. (**B**) Health officials and farm workers in protective clothing <u>slaughtered</u>
hundreds of thousands of chickens in western India, hoping to prevent
the spread of the deadly H5N1 bird flu virus.
身穿防護衣的衛生局官員和農夫,在西印度<u>屠殺</u>數十萬計的雞隻,希望此
舉能防止致命的 H5N1 禽流感病毒的散播。

(A) cultivate〔'kʌltə,vet〕*v.* 耕作;培養(= *develop*)
cultivate a field 耕田

(B) *slaughter*〔'slɔtɚ〕*v.* 屠殺(動物);殘殺(人)
slaughterhouse 屠宰場

(C) reproduce〔,riprə'djus〕*v.* 重生;繁殖　　produce *v.* 製造

(D) migrate〔'maɪgret〕*v.* 定期性移居；遷移

　　migratory *adj.* 移居的　　　migration *n.*

＊health〔hɛlθ〕*n.* 衛生　　official〔ə'fɪʃəl〕*n.* 官員

　　health official 衛生局官員

　　deadly〔'dɛdlɪ〕*adj.* 致命的　　*bird flu* 禽流感

11.(**B**) Travel to the moon may become <u>feasible</u> in the near future.　Its possibility
will enable many rich men to realize their dream of space travel.
在不久的將來，眞的有可能<u>可以</u>到月球上去旅行，而這將使得許多有錢人得
以實現太空旅行的夢想。

　(A) critical〔'krɪtɪk!〕*adj.* 危急的；重要的

　　　(= *crucial* = *essential* = *decisive* = *grave*)

　(B) *feasible*〔'fizəb!〕*adj.* 可實行的；好像有道理的

　　　a feasible plan 可實行的計畫

　(C) threatening〔'θrɛtn̩ɪŋ〕*adj.* 恐嚇的；威脅的

　　　threaten *v.*　　a threatening letter 恐嚇信

　(D) apparent〔ə'pærənt〕*adj.* 明顯的 (= *evident*)；顯然的；表面上的

　　　appear *v.* 出現

　＊enable〔ɪn'eb!〕*v.* 使能夠

　　realize〔'rɪə,laɪz〕*v.* 實現　　*space travel* 太空旅行

12.(**A**) You are more <u>liable</u> to injury if you exercise infrequently.
如果你不常運動，就比較<u>可能</u>會受傷。

　(A) *liable*〔'laɪəb!〕*adj.* 可能受…影響的 <*to*>；應負責的 <*for*>

　　　be liable to injury 容易受傷

　　　be liable for all damage 應負起一切損壞賠償的責任

　(B) justified〔'jʌstə,faɪd〕*adj.* 正當的；理所當然的

　　　justify〔'jʌstə,faɪ〕*v.* 為 (某人的言行等) 辯護；使成為正當

　(C) flawless〔'flɔlɪs〕*adj.* 完美的；無瑕疵的 (= *perfect* = *faultless*)

　　　flaw *n.* 瑕疵

　(D) worthy〔'wɜðɪ〕*adj.* 值得的；合適的

　　　be worthy of the name 名副其實

　＊injury〔'ɪndʒərɪ〕*n.* 傷害

　　infrequently〔ɪn'frikwəntlɪ〕*adv.* 不常

13. (**B**) The new sexual harassment law has taken effect. Those who violate the law will be subject to punishment including fines and jail terms.

新性騷擾防治法已經生效。觸犯此法的人，將須接受徒刑以及易科罰金的判罰。

(A) discriminate against　歧視

(B) *be subject to*　該服從

(C) devote *oneself* to　專心致力於

(D) hold responsible for　為～負責任

＊harassment〔həˈræsmənt〕*n.* 騷擾

sexual harassment law 性騷擾防治法　　*take effect* 生效

violate〔ˈvaɪəˌlet〕*v.* 違反　　fine〔faɪn〕*n.* 罰鍰；罰金

14. (**C**) His conduct has been entirely aboveboard. He has a clear conscience.

他的行為一直都是光明磊落的。他有清白的良心。

(A) in the dark　在黑暗中；偷偷地；全然不知

(B) on the horizon　在地平線上；即將發生

(C) *aboveboard*〔əˈbʌvˈbord〕*adj.* 光明磊落的；光明正大的

(D) into *one's* shell　自我封閉地

＊entirely〔ɪnˈtaɪrlɪ〕*adv.* 完全地；全然地

conscience〔ˈkɑnʃəns〕*n.* 良心；道德

15. (**B**) The mayor acted in accordance with the law in every way.

這個市長一切都遵照法律行動。

(A) at the cost of　以…為代價

(B) *in accordance with*　依照

(C) at the core of　在～的核心

(D) in terms of　以～的觀點（角度）

＊mayor〔ˈmeɚ〕*n.* 市長　　act〔ækt〕*v.* 行動

way〔we〕*n.* 方面

TEST 34

Directions: The following questions are incomplete sentences. You are to choose the one word that best completes the sentence.

1. At a(n) _____ of more than 3,952 meters, the summit of Jade Mountain is the highest point in Taiwan.
   (A) capacity   (B) altitude
   (C) measure   (D) estimation   (   )

2. In September of 2005, the world's newest Disney _____ park opened in Hong Kong. So far, millions of visitors have been drawn to this special place.
   (A) fancy   (B) fairy
   (C) theme   (D) cartoon   (   )

3. The Taipei District Court _____ the 26-year-old "rice bomber" to seven and a half years in jail plus a fine of NT$100,000.
   (A) judged   (B) executed
   (C) committed   (D) sentenced   (   )

4. That politician is such an _____ speaker that he can win his voters' support by talking black into white.
   (A) eloquent   (B) insincere
   (C) imaginative   (D) encouraging   (   )

5. The 10-year-old educational reform program leaves much to be _____. It should be improved upon on a large scale.
   (A) expected   (B) recommended
   (C) desired   (D) debated   (   )

6. Because of weather abnormalities, the weather is still _____ hot even in November.
   (A) immaturely   (B) virtually
   (C) freezingly   (D) unbearably   (   )

7. An institution that provides vocational training for the ____ disabled was recently accused of exploiting its employees by paying them less than minimum wage.
   (A) individually   (B) emotionally
   (C) physically   (D) skillfully   (   )

8. The surest way to success is to _____ ourselves of every minute of time that we may have at our disposal.
   (A) account (B) benefit
   (C) avail (D) propose ( )

9. To prevent _____ birds from spreading avian flu in Taiwan, the Department of Health urges the public to maintain good hygiene, wash their hands and avoid uncooked meat and eggs.
   (A) emigrant (B) suspicious
   (C) immigrant (D) infectious ( )

10. Although they departed at different times, they arrived almost _____ at the destination. Neither of them arrived early or late.
    (A) punctually (B) simultaneously
    (C) amazingly (D) successfully ( )

11. To be qualified for graduation, a college student should earn enough _____ by taking required or optional courses.
    (A) diplomas (B) certificates
    (C) licenses (D) credits ( )

12. According to the Consumer's Foundation, _____ chopsticks were found to contain traces of sulfur dioxide and some of the chopsticks wrappers contained lead.
    (A) disposable (B) expensive
    (C) plastic (D) sanitary ( )

13. He was elected chairman three times in a row. His _____ victories were due to his generous character and political strategy.
    (A) eventual (B) financial
    (C) admirable (D) successive ( )

14. The Directorate General of Telecommunications has allowed mobile phone users to keep their phone numbers when _____ carriers. This convenience enables them to change carriers as they please.
    (A) commuting (B) switching
    (C) communicating (D) registering ( )

15. September 28th is Teacher's Day, which is celebrated to _____ the birth of Confucius.
    (A) commemorate (B) symbolize
    (C) memorize (D) demonstrate ( )

TEST 34 詳解

1. (**B**) At an <u>altitude</u> of more than 3,952 meters, the summit of Jade Mountain is the highest point in Taiwan.

玉山山頂的高度超過 3,952 公尺，是台灣的最高點。

(A) capacity〔kə'pæsətɪ〕*n.* 容量；才能

a man of great capacity 能力很強的人

(B) *altitude*〔'æltə,tjud〕*n.* 高度 (= *height*)　　altitude sickness 高空病

(C) measure〔'mɛʒɚ〕*n.* 測量　　measure of capacity 容量

by measure 根據測量

(D) estimation〔,ɛstə'meʃən〕*n.* 判斷；評價　　in my estimation 根據我的判斷

* meter〔'mitɚ〕*n.* 公尺　　summit〔'sʌmɪt〕*n.* 山頂　　jade〔dʒed〕*n.* 玉

2. (**C**) In September of 2005, the world's newest Disney <u>theme</u> park opened in Hong Kong. So far, millions of visitors have been drawn to this special place.

2005 年 9 月，世界上最新的迪士尼主題樂園在香港開幕了。到目前為止，已經吸引了好幾百萬個遊客到這個特別的地方來。

(A) fancy〔'fænsɪ〕*n.* 幻想；喜歡　　flights of fancy 幻想的飛翔

(B) fairy〔'fɛrɪ〕*n.* 小仙子　　fairy tale 童話故事 (= *fable*)　　fairyland 仙境

(C) *theme*〔θim〕*n.* 主題 (= *subject*)　　theme song 主題曲

theme park 主題樂園

(D) cartoon〔kɑr'tun〕*n.* 卡通影片；連載漫畫

cartoonist〔kɑr'tunɪst〕*n.* 漫畫家

* *so far* 到目前為止　　draw〔drɔ〕*v.* 吸引（注意力、顧客等）

3. (**D**) The Taipei District Court <u>sentenced</u> the 26-year-old "rice bomber" to seven and a half years in jail plus a fine of NT\$100,000. 台北地方法院對 26 歲的白米炸彈客判處七年半的徒刑，併科罰金新台幣十萬元。

(A) judge〔dʒʌdʒ〕*v.* 審理；判決　　judge a case 審理案件

judge *sb.* guilty 判決某人有罪

(B) execute〔'ɛksɪ,kjut〕*v.* 執行；處死（人）　　execute a command 執行命令

(C) commit〔kə'mɪt〕*v.* 犯（罪、過錯等）；承諾　　commit a crime 犯罪

(D) *sentence*〔'sɛntəns〕*v.* 宣判（刑罰）　　*n.* 刑罰　　a life sentence 無期徒刑

* district〔'dɪstrɪkt〕*n.* 地區　　court〔kort〕*n.* 法院

the Taipei District Court 台北地方法院

bomber〔'bɑmɚ〕*n.* 炸彈客　　*rice bomber* 白米炸彈客

plus〔plʌs〕*prep.* 加上；外加　　fine〔faɪn〕*n.* 罰款；罰鍰

4. (**A**) That politician is such an <u>eloquent</u> speaker that he can win his voters'
support by talking black into white.
那位政客真是個<u>雄辯</u>專家，能把黑的說成白的，也因此贏得選民的支持。

(A) *eloquent* (ˈɛləkwənt) *adj.* 雄辯的；善辯的　　*an eloquent speaker* 雄辯家
(B) insincere (ˌɪnsɪnˈsɪr) *adj.* 不誠實的；虛偽的
an insincere compliment 虛偽的恭維
(C) imaginative (ɪˈmædʒəˌnetɪv) *adj.* 想像的
imaginary (ɪˈmædʒəˌnɛrɪ) *adj.* 假想的
(D) encouraging (ɪnˈkɜɪdʒɪŋ) *adj.* 激勵的；鼓勵的
encourage (ɪnˈkɜɪdʒ) *v.* 鼓勵

＊politician (ˌpɑləˈtɪʃən) *n.* 政治家　　voter (ˈvotɚ) *n.* 選民
talk black into white 把黑的說成白的

5. (**C**) The 10-year-old educational reform program leaves much to be <u>desired</u>.
It should be improved upon on a large scale.
這個進行十年的教改計畫，有不少<u>需要改善</u>的地方。它需要大規模地檢討改進。

(A) expect (ɪkˈspɛkt) *v.* 預期；期待 (= *anticipate*)　　expectation *n.*
(B) recommend (ˌrɛkəˈmɛnd) *v.* 推薦　　recommendation *n.*
recommendatory *adj.*
(C) *desire* (dɪˈzaɪr) *v.* (強烈地) 希望
leave much to be desired 有不少需要改善之處
例：It leaves nothing to be desired. 它完全沒有缺點。
(D) debate (dɪˈbet) *v.* 辯論；討論 (= *argue* = *dispute* = *contend*)
debate an issue 討論議題

＊reform (rɪˈfɔrm) *v.* 改革　　improve (ɪmˈpruv) *v.* 改進
on a large scale 大規模地

6. (**D**) Because of weather abnormalities, the weather is still <u>unbearably</u> hot even in
November. 因為天氣異常的緣故，即使到了十一月，天氣還是<u>難以忍受的</u>熱。

(A) immaturely (ˌɪməˈtjʊrlɪ) *adv.* 不成熟地　　immature *adj.*
immaturity *n.*
(B) virtually (ˈvɜtʃʊəlɪ) *adv.* 事實上；實際上 (= *practically* = *actually*
= *effectually*)
(C) freezingly (ˈfrizɪŋlɪ) *adv.* 冷凍地；嚴寒地　　freeze *v.* 結冰
freezing *adj.*
(D) *unbearably* (ʌnˈbɛrəblɪ) *adv.* 難以忍受地　　bear (bɛr) *v.* 忍受
(= *endure* = *stand*)

＊abnormality (ˌæbnɔrˈmælətɪ) *n.* 異常；反常

7. (**C**) An institution that provides vocational training for the <u>physically</u> disabled was recently accused of exploiting its employees by paying them less than minimum wage.

那個提供<u>身障人士</u>職業訓練的機構，最近被告發剝削勞工，因其給付之薪資低於最低工資。

(A) individually (͵ɪndəˋvɪdʒʊəlɪ) *adv.* 個別地
　　individual *n.* 個人　*adj.* 個別的

(B) emotionally (ɪˋmoʃənəlɪ) *adv.* 多愁善感地；情緒地
　　emotional *adj.*　　emotion *n.* 情緒

(C) *physically* (ˋfɪzɪkəlɪ) *adv.* 身體地
　　physically disabled 身障的；殘障的

(D) skillfully (ˋskɪlfəlɪ) *adv.* 熟練地；擅長地
　　skillful *adj.* (= *skilled*)　　skill *n.* 技巧

* institution (͵ɪnstəˋtjuʃən) *n.* 機構
　vocational (voˋkeʃənḷ) *adj.* 職業上的
　disabled (dɪsˋeblḍ) *adj.* 殘障的
　accuse (əˋkjuz) *v.* 控告　　exploit (ɪkˋsplɔɪt) *v.* 剝削
　minimum (ˋmɪnəməm) *adj.* 最低的　　wage (wedʒ) *n.* 工資

8. (**C**) The surest way to success is to <u>avail</u> ourselves of every minute of time that we may have at our disposal.

要成功最穩當的方法就是，盡可能地<u>利用</u>我們可以運用的每一分鐘。

(A) account (əˋkaʊnt) *v.* 說明；負責
　　account for *one's* absence　說明某人缺席原因

(B) benefit (ˋbɛnəfɪt) *v.* 有益於
　　例：The fresh air will benefit you. 新鮮空氣對你有益。

(C) *avail* (əˋvel) *v.* 有用；有幫助
　　avail *oneself of* 利用 (= *make use of*)
　　available (əˋveləbḷ) *adj.* 可利用的
　　例：We should avail ourselves of this opportunity.
　　　　我們應該好好利用這個機會。

(D) propose (prəˋpoz) *v.* 建議；計畫；求婚
　　propose an attack　計畫攻擊

* surest (ˋʃʊrɪst) *adj.* 最穩當的　　disposal (dɪˋspozḷ) *n.* 處置
　at *one's* ***disposal*** 隨某人自由處置

9. (**D**) To prevent <u>infectious</u> birds from spreading avian flu in Taiwan, the Department of Health urges the public to maintain good hygiene, wash their hands and avoid uncooked meat and eggs.

為了預防<u>有傳染性的</u>鳥類在台灣引發禽流感，衛生署強烈呼籲國人，要保持良好衛生，洗手，避免食用未經烹煮的肉和蛋。

(A) emigrant〔ˈɛməgrənt〕*adj.*（向他國）移居的　　emigrate *v.*　　emigration *n.*

(B) suspicious〔səˈspɪʃəs〕*adj.* 懷疑的

(C) immigrant〔ˈɪməgrənt〕*adj.*（由外國）移入的　　immigrate *v.*

immigration *n.*

(D) *infectious*〔ɪnˈfɛkʃəs〕*adj.* 傳染性的；有感染性的

an infectious disease 傳染病

* *avian flu* 禽流感（= *bird flu*）　　*the Department of Health* 衛生署

urge〔ɝdʒ〕*v.* 力勸；強調　　hygiene〔ˈhaɪdʒin〕*n.* 衛生

uncooked〔ʌnˈkʊkt〕*adj.* 未煮的；生的

10. (**B**) Although they departed at different times, they arrived almost <u>simultaneously</u> at the destination. Neither of them arrived early or late.

雖然他們不同時間出發，但是幾乎<u>同時</u>到達目的地。沒有人早到或晚到。

(A) punctually〔ˈpʌŋktʃʊəlɪ〕*adv.* 準時地　　punctual *adj.*　　punctuality *n.*

(B) *simultaneously*〔ˌsaɪmlˈtenɪəslɪ〕*adv.* 同時地　　simultaneous *adj.*

simultaneity *n.*

(C) amazingly〔əˈmezɪŋlɪ〕*adv.* 令人驚訝地；絕頂地　　amazing *adj.*

amaze *v.* 使驚訝

(D) successfully〔səkˈsɛsfəlɪ〕*adv.* 成功地

successful *adj.*　　success *n.*

* depart〔dɪˈpart〕*v.* 出發　　destination〔ˌdɛstəˈneʃən〕*n.* 目的地

11. (**D**) To be qualified for graduation, a college student should earn enough <u>credits</u> by taking required or optional courses.

為了能夠合格畢業，大學生應該在必修或選修課程上取得足夠的<u>學分</u>。

(A) diploma〔dɪˈplomə〕*n.* 文憑　　receive *one's* diploma 獲得執照；畢業

(B) certificate〔səˈtɪfəkɪt〕*n.* 證明書　　a birth certificate 出生證明

(C) license〔ˈlaɪsn̩s〕*n.* 許可證；執照　　a driver's license 駕照

license plate 牌照

(D) *credit*〔ˈkrɛdɪt〕*n.* 學分　　*earn enough credits* 取得足夠的學分

* qualified〔ˈkwɑləˌfaɪd〕*adj.* 合格的　　earn〔ɝn〕*v.* 獲得

required〔rɪˈkwaɪrd〕*adj.* 必修的　　optional〔ˈɑpʃən̩l〕*adj.* 選修的

12. (**A**) According to the Consumer's Foundation, <u>disposable</u> chopsticks were found to contain traces of sulfur dioxide and some of the chopsticks wrappers contained lead.

根據消費者文教基金會指出，<u>免洗筷</u>被發現含有少量的二氧化硫，而且有些筷子的包裝物含鉛。

(A) *disposable*〔dɪˈspozəbl̩〕*adj.* 用完即丟的
disposable diapers 用完即丟的紙尿布

(B) expensive〔ɪkˈspɛnsɪv〕*adj.* 昂貴的（↔ *inexpensive*）
an expensive dress 昂貴的女裝

(C) plastic〔ˈplæstɪk〕*adj.* 塑膠的；不自然的　a plastic toy 塑膠玩具
a plastic smile 強笑

(D) sanitary〔ˈsænəˌtɛrɪ〕*adj.* 衛生的；保健的（↔ *insanitary*）
sanitary fittings 保健設備

* *the Consumer's Foundation* 消費者文教基金會
chopsticks〔ˈtʃɑpstɪks〕*n. pl.* 筷子
trace〔tres〕*n.* 少量　　sulfur〔ˈsʌlfɚ〕*n.* 硫
dioxide〔daɪˈɑksaɪd〕*n.* 二氧化物
wrapper〔ˈræpɚ〕*n.* 包裝物　　lead〔lɛd〕*n.* 鉛

13. (**D**) He was elected chairman three times in a row. His <u>successive</u> victories were due to his generous character and political strategy.

他連續三次當選主席。他能<u>連續</u>順利當選是因為他慷慨的個性以及政治策略。

(A) eventual〔ɪˈvɛntʃuəl〕*adj.* 最終的（= *final* = *endmost* = *ultimate*）
eventually *adv.*

(B) financial〔fəˈnænʃəl〕*adj.* 財務的　　financial ability 財力
a financial crisis 財務危機

(C) admirable〔ˈædmərəbl̩〕*adj.* 值得稱讚的；出色的
an admirable essay 出色的小品文

(D) *successive*〔səkˈsɛsɪv〕*adj.* 連續的
例：It rained two successive days. 連續下了兩天雨。

* elect〔ɪˈlɛkt〕*v.* 選舉　　chairman〔ˈtʃɛrmən〕*n.* 主席
in a row 連續地　　victory〔ˈvɪktrɪ〕*n.* 勝利
due to 因為　　generous〔ˈdʒɛnərəs〕*adj.* 慷慨的
strategy〔ˈstrætədʒɪ〕*n.* 策略

14. (**B**) The Directorate General of Telecommunications has allowed mobile phone users to keep their phone numbers when <u>switching</u> carriers. This convenience enables them to change carriers as they please.

電信總局允許手機用戶，在<u>更換</u>電信業者時不必換門號。這個便利性使得用戶可以更換自己喜歡的業者。

(A) commute〔kə'mjut〕v. 折算；通勤
commute dollars to yen 把美金換成日圓

(B) *switch*〔swɪtʃ〕v. 開、關（電源、收音機）；轉變
switch the subject 轉變話題

(C) communicate〔kə'mjunə,ket〕v. 傳達；溝通
communication *n.*　communicative *adj.*

(D) register〔'rɛdʒɪstə〕v. 登記；註冊；將（郵件等）掛號
register a letter 寄掛號信

＊ *the Directorate General of Telecommunications* 電信總局
mobile phone 行動電話　　carrier〔'kærɪə〕*n.* 運輸業者
please〔pliz〕v. 高興；喜歡

15. (**A**) September 28th is Teacher's Day, which is celebrated to <u>commemorate</u> the birth of Confucius.

9 月 28 日教師節，是為了<u>紀念</u>孔子的生日而設立的。

(A) *commemorate*〔kə'mɛmə,ret〕v.（以祝詞或儀式等）紀念；祝賀
commemoration *n.*

(B) symbolize〔'sɪmbḷ,aɪz〕v. 象徵
例：A lily symbolizes purity. 百合花象徵純潔。

(C) memorize〔'mɛmə,raɪz〕v. 記憶；背誦　　memorization *n.*

(D) demonstrate〔'dɛmən,stret〕v. 證明；示範　　demonstration *n.*

＊celebrate〔'sɛlə,bret〕v. 舉行
Confucius〔kən'fjuʃəs〕*n.* 孔子

TEST 35

Directions: The following questions are incomplete sentences. You are to choose the one word that best completes the sentence.

1. Those who act on _____ tend to make more mistakes and feel regretful afterwards.
   (A) institution
   (B) intelligence
   (C) impatience
   (D) impulse   (   )

2. Machines have changed society _____. It's doubtful that we will voluntarily return to the days when we used our muscles to do most of our work.
   (A) irrevocably
   (B) flexibly
   (C) tentatively
   (D) influentially   (   )

3. One look at today's best-selling books and popular magazines will demonstrate America's _____ with physical appearance.
   (A) precept
   (B) preconception
   (C) precedence
   (D) preoccupation   (   )

4. Tight-fitting jeans that _____ a thin, youthful appearance are the fashion of the day.
   (A) appreciate
   (B) accentuate
   (C) alleviate
   (D) associate   (   )

5. In order to predict whether an idea will become part of our daily lives, it's important to know if the idea is technologically and economically _____.
   (A) formidable
   (B) forcible
   (C) feasible
   (D) flammable   (   )

6. She gave _____ directions about the way the rug should be cleaned.
   (A) brisk
   (B) opaque
   (C) explicit
   (D) transient   (   )

7. She expressed her strong determination that nothing could _____ her to give up her career as a teacher.
   (A) reduce
   (B) deduce
   (C) seduce
   (D) induce   (   )

8. By turning this knob to the right you can _____ the sound from the radio.
   (A) enlarge   (B) amplify
   (C) reinforce   (D) intensify   ( )

9. A _____ official is one who is irresponsible in his work.
   (A) slack   (B) monotonous
   (C) demure   (D) acquiescent   ( )

10. My grandfather, a retired worker, often _____ the past with a feeling of longing and respect.
   (A) contrives   (B) considers
   (C) ejects   (D) contemplates   ( )

11. When I told him the strange news, he gaped at me in _____.
   (A) solitude   (B) modification
   (C) bewilderment   (D) embarrassment   ( )

12. His health condition was _____ by his early release from the hospital.
   (A) resented   (B) disregarded
   (C) mobilized   (D) aggravated   ( )

13. In Middle Eastern countries, life is often greatly _____ by war.
   (A) excluded   (B) stabilized
   (C) perplexed   (D) dominated   ( )

14. The children looked _____ since the final exam was over.
   (A) ill-spent   (B) lighthearted
   (C) back-alley   (D) full-fledged   ( )

15. To stay in good shape, you need to exercise _____ and regularly.
   (A) moderately   (B) increasingly
   (C) mockingly   (D) evidently   ( )

TEST 35 詳解

1. (**D**) Those who act on <u>impulse</u> tend to make more mistakes and feel regretful afterwards.

做事情衝動的人，容易犯比較多的錯誤，而且以後會後悔。

(A) institution (ˌɪnstəˈtjuʃən) *n.* 學會；協會
a charitable institution 慈善機構

(B) intelligence (ɪnˈtɛlədʒəns) *n.* 智能　　intelligent *adj.*
human intelligence 人的智能

(C) impatience (ɪmˈpeʃəns) *n.* 沒耐心 (↔ patience (ˈpeʃəns) *n.* 耐心)
with impatience 焦急地　　impatient *adj.* (↔ *patient*)

(D) *impulse* (ˈɪmpʌls) *n.* 衝動
under the impulse of curiosity 在好奇心的驅使之下
on the impulse of the moment 因一時的衝動
a man of impulse 易衝動的人

* regretful (rɪˈgrɛtfəl) *adj.* 後悔的；遺憾的
afterwards (ˈæftəwədz) *adv.* 後來

2. (**A**) Machines have changed society <u>irrevocably</u>. It's doubtful that we will voluntarily return to the days when we used our muscles to do most of our work.

機器改變了社會，而且已經<u>無法挽回</u>。我們不太可能自願回到以前，大多用人力做事的日子。

(A) *irrevocably* (ɪˈrɛvəkəblɪ) *adv.* 不能挽回地　　irrevocable *adj.*

(B) flexibly (ˈflɛksəblɪ) *adv.* 有彈性地
flexibility (ˌflɛksəˈbɪlətɪ) *n.* 彈性

(C) tentatively (ˈtɛntətɪvlɪ) *adv.* 暫時地 (= *temporarily*)
tentative *adj.*

(D) influentially (ˌɪnfluˈɛnʃəlɪ) *adv.* 有影響力地　　influential *adj.*
influence *v. n.*

* doubtful (ˈdautfəl) *adj.* 懷疑的
voluntarily (ˈvɑlənˌtɛrəlɪ) *adv.* 自願地；自動地

3. (**D**) One look at today's best-selling books and popular magazines will
   demonstrate America's <u>preoccupation</u> with physical appearance.
   看一下今日的暢銷書和流行雜誌，就可以證明美國熱中於身體的外觀。

   (A) precept ('prisɛpt) *n.* 教誨
       Example is better than precept.【諺】身教勝於言教。
   (B) preconception (,prikən'sɛpʃən) *n.* 事先考慮；預料　　preconceive *v.*
   (C) precedence (prɪ'sidn̩s) *n.* (時間、順序等) 在前　　precedent *adj.*
   (D) ***preoccupation*** (pri,ɑkjə'peʃən) *n.* 全神貫注；熱中　　preoccupy *v.*
       preoccupied *adj.*

   * best-selling ('bɛst'sɛlɪŋ) *adj.* 暢銷的 (書、作者等)
     demonstrate ('dɛmən,stret) *v.* 證明　　physical ('fɪzɪkl̩) *adj.* 身體的
     appearance (ə'pɪrəns) *n.* 外觀

4. (**B**) Tight-fitting jeans that <u>accentuate</u> a thin, youthful appearance are the fashion
   of the day.
   可以強調出苗條、年輕外觀的緊身牛仔褲，是現代的潮流。

   (A) appreciate (ə'priʃɪ,et) *v.* 感激；欣賞　　appreciation *n.*
       appreciative *adj.*
   (B) ***accentuate*** (æk'sɛntʃu,et) *v.* 強調　　accentuation *n.*
   (C) alleviate (ə'livɪ,et) *v.* 減輕；緩和　　alleviation *n.*　　alleviative *adj.*
   (D) associate (ə'soʃɪ,et) *v.* 將 (人、物等) 聯想在一起；聯合
       association *n.*

   * tight-fitting ('taɪt'fɪtɪŋ) *adj.* 緊身的　　***the day*** 現代

5. (**C**) In order to predict whether an idea will become part of our daily lives, it's
   important to know if the idea is technologically and economically <u>feasible</u>.
   為了要預知一個構想，是否會成為我們日常生活的一部分，了解它在技術和經
   濟上的可行性是重要的。

   (A) formidable ('fɔrmɪdəbl̩) *adj.* 可怕的；艱鉅的
       a formidable enemy　難以對付的敵人
   (B) forcible ('forsəbl̩) *adj.* 強制性的　　a forcible entry　非法侵入
   (C) ***feasible*** ('fizəbl̩) *adj.* 行得通的 (= *workable*)
       a feasible plan　可實行的計畫
   (D) flammable ('flæməbl̩) *adj.* 易燃的 (= *inflammable*)　　flame *n.* 火焰

   * predict (prɪ'dɪkt) *v.* 預測

6. (**C**) She gave <u>explicit</u> directions about the way the rug should be cleaned.
地毯該如何清理的方式，她做了很<u>清楚的</u>說明。

(A) brisk〔brɪsk〕*adj.* 輕快的　　a brisk walker 步履輕快的人
at a brisk pace 用輕快的腳步

(B) opaque〔oˈpek〕*adj.* 不透明的；不清楚的　　opaquely *adv.*

(C) *explicit*〔ɪkˈsplɪsɪt〕*adj.* 清楚的（= *clear* = *well-defined*）
explicitly *adv.*

(D) transient〔ˈtrænʃənt〕*adj.* 瞬間的；一時的
a transient emotion 一時的感情

* direction〔dəˈrɛkʃən〕*n.* 說明；指示　　rug〔rʌg〕*n.* 地毯

7. (**D**) She expressed her strong determination that nothing could <u>induce</u> her to give up her career as a teacher.
她表達了她強烈的決心，沒有任何事可以<u>引誘</u>她，放棄當老師這個職業。

(A) reduce〔rɪˈdjus〕*v.* 減低　　reduce expenses 削減開銷
reduce production 降低生產

(B) deduce〔dɪˈdjus〕*v.* 演繹；推斷（= *infer*）（↔ induce〔ɪnˈdjus〕*v.* 歸納）

(C) seduce〔sɪˈdjus〕*v.* 誤導；勾引
seductive〔sɪˈdʌktɪv〕*adj.* 誘惑的；迷人的

(D) *induce*〔ɪnˈdjus〕*v.* 引誘；歸納（↔ deduce〔dɪˈdjus〕*v.* 演繹）
inducement *n.*

* determination〔dɪˌtɜməˈneʃən〕*n.* 決心

8. (**B**) By turning this knob to the right you can <u>amplify</u> the sound from the radio.
把開關向右轉，你就可以把收音機的聲音<u>調大</u>。

(A) enlarge〔ɪnˈlɑrdʒ〕*v.*（實際物體的）擴大
enlarge a photograph 放大照片

(B) *amplify*〔ˈæmpləˌfaɪ〕*v.*（聲音的）擴大；詳述
amplify a statement 詳述該項說明

(C) reinforce〔ˌriɪnˈfors〕*v.* 加強；增強（= *intensify*）
reinforce a bridge 加固橋樑

(D) intensify〔ɪnˈtɛnsəˌfaɪ〕*v.* 加強；增強（= *reinforce*）　　intension *n.*

* knob〔nɑb〕*n.* 球形開關（把手）

9. (**A**) A <u>slack</u> official is one who is irresponsible in his work.
  <u>怠慢的</u>官員，對自己的工作不負責。

  (A) *slack* ﹝ slæk ﹞ *adj.* 怠慢的；鬆懈的
    slack law control　鬆懈的法律控制

  (B) monotonous ﹝ mə'natn̩əs ﹞ *adj.* 單調的；呆板的
    monotonous work　呆板的工作

  (C) demure ﹝ dɪ'mjʊr ﹞ *adj.* 害羞的；靦腆的（ = *chary = bashful* ）

  (D) acquiescent ﹝ ˌækwɪ'ɛsn̩t ﹞ *adj.* 默許的；默認的　　acquiescently *adv.*

  ＊ irresponsible ﹝ ˌɪrɪ'spɑnsəbl̩ ﹞ *adj.* 不負責任的

10. (**D**) My grandfather, a retired worker, often <u>contemplates</u> the past with a feeling of longing and respect.
  我爺爺是個退休的員工，經常用嚮往和尊敬的心情<u>緬懷</u>過去。

  (A) contrive ﹝ kən'traɪv ﹞ *v.* 發明；策劃
    contrive a way of escape　策劃逃亡的方式

  (B) consider ﹝ kən'sɪdə ﹞ *v.* 考慮　　consideration *n.*
    considerate ﹝ kən'sɪdərɪt ﹞ *adj.* 體貼的

  (C) eject ﹝ ɪ'dʒɛkt ﹞ *v.* 放逐；噴出　　ejection *n.*
    ejector ﹝ ɪ'dʒɛktə ﹞ *n.* 放射器；放逐者

  (D) *contemplate* ﹝ 'kɑntəmˌplet ﹞ *v.* 緬懷；熟慮
    contemplate an action　慎重考慮一個行動

  ＊ longing ﹝ 'lɔŋɪŋ ﹞ *n.* 嚮往

11. (**C**) When I told him the strange news, he gaped at me in <u>bewilderment</u>.
  當我告訴他這個怪異的新聞時，他<u>不知所措</u>地張嘴望著我。

  (A) solitude ﹝ 'sɑləˌtud ﹞ *n.* 孤單　　live in solitude　孤單地生活

  (B) modification ﹝ ˌmɑdəfə'keʃən ﹞ *n.* 修正
    modify ﹝ 'mɑdəˌfaɪ ﹞ *v.* 修正；調整

  (C) *bewilderment* ﹝ bɪ'wɪldəmənt ﹞ *n.* 迷惑；張惶失措
    bewilder ﹝ bɪ'wɪldə ﹞ *v.* 使慌亂

  (D) embarrassment ﹝ ɪm'bærəsmənt ﹞ *n.* 困窘　　embarrassed *adj.* 困窘的

  ＊ gape ﹝ gep ﹞ *v.* （因驚訝或讚許而）張口

12. (**D**) His health condition was <u>aggravated</u> by his early release from the hospital.
由於提早出院，他的健康狀況因此惡化。

(A) resent〔rɪ'zɛnt〕v. 憎恨　　resentment〔rɪ'zɛntmənt〕n. 憎恨
例：He resented the cutting remark.
他聽了那種尖酸刻薄的話很氣憤。

(B) disregard〔͵dɪsrɪ'gɑrd〕v. 忽視
disregard for human rights 忽視人權
例：They disregarded my objections to the proposal.
他們忽視我對該提案的異議。

(C) mobilize〔'mobl͵aɪz〕v. 動員　　mobilization n.
mobility〔mo'bɪlətɪ〕n. 機動性

(D) *aggravate*〔'ægrə͵vet〕v. 使惡化　　aggravation n.
例：His bad temper was aggravated by a headache.
他的壞脾氣因爲頭痛而變本加厲。

*condition〔kən'dɪʃən〕n. 狀況　　release〔rɪ'lis〕n. 釋放
release from the hospital 出院

13. (**D**) In Middle Eastern countries, life is often greatly <u>dominated</u> by war.
在中東國家，生活通常由戰爭來主導。

(A) exclude〔ɪk'sklud〕v. 拒絕（排除）～在外　　exclusion n.
exclusive〔ɪk'sklusɪv〕adj. 獨占性的；排他性的　　exclusively adv.

(B) stabilize〔'stebl͵aɪz〕v. 穩定；安定　　stable adj.
stabilization n.　　stabilizer〔'stebl͵aɪzɚ〕n. 穩定器

(C) perplex〔pɚ'plɛks〕v. 使困惑　　perplexing adj.
例：The question perplexed him. 這個問題使他困惑。

(D) *dominate*〔'dɑmə͵net〕v. 支配；操控
dominant〔'dɑmənənt〕adj. 支配的
domination〔͵dɑmə'neʃən〕n. 統治；支配
dominator〔'dɑmə͵netɚ〕n. 統治者
例：A man of strong will often dominates others.
意志堅強的人經常支配他人。

Middle Eastern 中東的

14. (**B**) The children looked <u>lighthearted</u> since the final exam was over.

因爲期末考已經結束了，小孩們看起來很<u>快活</u>。

(A) ill-spent〔'ɪl'spɛnt〕*adj.* 花費不當的

例：Drunkenness and the ill-spent wage-packet are still hardly known.

酗酒以及胡亂花費工資的情形至今還鮮爲人知。

(B) *lighthearted*〔'laɪt'hɑrtɪd〕*adj.* 快活的

lightheartedness *n.* lightheartedly *adv.*

(C) back-alley〔'bæk'ælɪ〕*adj.* 邊邊的；卑劣的

back-alley gossip 流言蜚語

(D) full-fledged〔'fʊl'flɛdʒd〕*adj.* 發育齊全的；有充分資格的

例：After one's internship, one becomes a full-fledged physician.

經過實習醫生的階段，就能成爲完全合格的醫生。

15. (**A**) To stay in good shape, you need to exercise <u>moderately</u> and regularly.

爲了要保持好身材，你需要<u>適度</u>以及規律地運動。

(A) *moderately*〔'mɑdərɪtlɪ〕*adv.* 適度地　　moderate *adj.*

(B) increasingly〔ɪn'krisɪŋlɪ〕*adv.* 逐漸地

increasing *adj.* 愈來愈多的

(C) mockingly〔'mɑkɪŋlɪ〕*adv.* 嘲弄地　　mock〔mɑk〕*v.* 嘲弄

(D) evidently〔'ɛvədəntlɪ〕*adv.* 顯然地　　evident *adj.*

＊stay in good shape 保持好身材

regularly〔'rɛgjələlɪ〕*adv.* 規律地

TEST 36

Directions: The following questions are incomplete sentences. You are to choose the one word that best completes the sentence.

1. Scientists suggest the explosion caused by a comet hitting the Earth's surface may be an important cause of the dinosaurs' _____.
   (A) distinction   (B) extinction
   (C) expiration   (D) malfunction   (   )

2. An organized framework of concepts is important for further learning and thinking. Graphic representations of conceptual relationships may be useful both for teaching and for _____ learning.
   (A) assessable   (B) assuming
   (C) assembly   (D) assortative   (   )

3. This hotel can _____ two thousand people.
   (A) accommodate   (B) accumulate
   (C) accomplish   (D) accelerate   (   )

4. Thomas Edison's _____ led to many inventions.
   (A) ingenuity   (B) indignation
   (C) idiosyncrasy   (D) incredulity   (   )

5. A great deal of preparation usually _____ moving from one place to another.
   (A) succeeds   (B) precedes
   (C) predicts   (D) proscribes   (   )

6. It has been generally acknowledged that advertisements are made to stimulate _____.
   (A) assumption   (B) redemption
   (C) resumption   (D) consumption   (   )

7. Many games are _____; for example, they attempt to model some real-life problem or situation.
   (A) assimilation   (B) simultaneous
   (C) semiotic   (D) simulations   (   )

8. Are you one of those women who feel that lipstick is one of the
_____ of life?
(A) essays   (B) essentials
(C) estates   (D) accesses   (   )

9. Many college teachers are now using methods of learning evaluation
that are more _____ related to later uses of learning than to
conventional tests.
(A) alternatively   (B) atheistically
(C) artistically   (D) authentically   (   )

10. There is a simple mathematical truism that, when a person uses
several selection criteria, each will have some _____.
(A) vainglory   (B) validity
(C) variety   (D) vapidity   (   )

11. Being _____ to the drug, the child reacted to it by going into
convulsions.
(A) allergic   (B) responsible
(C) representative   (D) symbolic   (   )

12. I like living here; the climate is very _____ to my health.
(A) conjunctive   (B) persuasive
(C) congenial   (D) persistent   (   )

13. You'll have your own office soon, but _____, you'll have to
share mine.
(A) for safety's sake   (B) up front
(C) for the time being   (D) from now on   (   )

14. With so many guests present, I'm afraid this little food is not
enough to _____.
(A) go around   (B) set forth
(C) move down   (D) bring forth   (   )

15. With skillful diplomacy, this country stays _____ with its many
strong neighbors.
(A) on account   (B) on good terms
(C) under control   (D) in conflict   (   )

TEST 36 詳解

1. (**B**) Scientists suggest the explosion caused by a comet hitting the Earth's surface may be an important cause of the dinosaurs' <u>extinction</u>.
科學家指出，由彗星撞擊地球表面所引發的爆炸，可能是造成恐龍滅絕的重要原因之一。

(A) distinction〔dɪ'stɪŋkʃən〕*n.* 區別　　distinct *adj.* 不同的
distinctive〔dɪ'stɪŋktɪv〕*adj.* 獨特的

(B) *extinction*〔ɪk'stɪŋkʃən〕*n.* 滅絕　　extinct *adj.* 絕種的

(C) expiration〔ˌɛkspə'reʃən〕*n.* 呼氣
(↔ inspiration〔ˌɪnspə'reʃən〕*n.* 吸氣)
expire *v.* (↔ inspire〔ɪn'spaɪr〕*v.* 吸氣)

(D) malfunction〔ˌmæl'fʌŋkʃən〕*n.* 機能故障
a malfunction of a generator　發電機故障

* explosion〔ɪk'sploʒən〕*n.* 爆炸　　comet〔'kɑmɪt〕*n.* 彗星
surface〔'sɝfɪs〕*n.* 表面

2. (**A**) An organized framework of concepts is important for further learning and thinking. Graphic representations of conceptual relationships may be useful both for teaching and for <u>assessable</u> learning.
對於進一步的學習和思考而言，有組織的概念架構是重要的。使用圖解表示概念關係，對於教學和<u>評估</u>學習都可能有幫助。

(A) *assessable*〔ə'sɛsəbḷ〕*adj.* 評估的　　assess〔ə'sɛs〕*v.* 評估
assessment *n.* 評估

(B) assuming〔ə'sumɪŋ〕*adj.* 傲慢的 (= *arrogant*)
(↔ humble〔'hʌmbḷ〕*adj.* 謙虛的)

(C) assembly〔ə'sɛmblɪ〕*n.* 集會；裝配
assemble *v.* 集合；裝配

(D) assortative〔ə'sɔrtətɪv〕*adj.* 相配的 (= *assortive*)
assort〔ə'sɔrt〕*v.* 相配

* organized〔'ɔrgən,aɪzd〕*adj.* 有組織的
framework〔'frem,wɝk〕*n.* 架構
graphic〔'græfɪk〕*adj.* 圖解的
representation〔ˌrɛprɪzɛn'teʃən〕*n.* 表示；表現

3. (**A**) This hotel can <u>accommodate</u> two thousand people.
這家旅館可以<u>容納</u>二千人。

    (A) *accommodate* ﹝ ə'kɑmə‚det ﹞ *v.* 容納；裝載

        accommodating *adj.* 樂於助人的

        accommodation *n.* (旅館、船的) 住宿設備

    (B) accumulate ﹝ ə'kjumjə‚let ﹞ *v.* (長期地) 累積；堆積   accumulation *n.*

    (C) accomplish ﹝ ə'kɑmplɪʃ ﹞ *v.* 達成；完成   accomplishment *n.*

        accomplished *adj.*   accomplish a task 完成任務

    (D) accelerate ﹝ æk'sɛlə‚ret ﹞ *v.* 加速 (↔ decelerate ﹝ di'sɛlə‚ret ﹞ *v.* 減速)

        accelerate a car 加快車速

        accelerate economic recovery 加快經濟復甦

4. (**A**) Thomas Edison's <u>ingenuity</u> led to many inventions.
湯瑪士愛迪生的<u>發明才能</u>，讓他創造出許多發明。

    (A) *ingenuity* ﹝ ‚ɪndʒə'nuətɪ ﹞ *n.* 發明的才能；智巧

        display ingenuity 展現智巧   exercise ingenuity 運用智慧

        (= *use one's ingenuity*)

    (B) indignation ﹝ ‚ɪndɪg'neʃən ﹞ *n.* 憤怒；憤慨

        righteous indignation 義憤

    (C) idiosyncrasy ﹝ ‚ɪdɪə'sɪnkrəsɪ ﹞ *n.* (個人特有的) 特質；癖好

        idiosyncratic *adj.*

    (D) incredulity ﹝ ‚ɪnkrə'dulətɪ ﹞ *n.* 不輕信；深疑   incredulous *adj.*

    ＊ invention ﹝ ɪn'vɛnʃən ﹞ *n.* 發明

5. (**B**) A great deal of preparation usually <u>precedes</u> moving from one place to
another. 當要從一個地方搬到另一個地方的時候，經常<u>先前</u>需要很多的準備。

    (A) succeed ﹝ sək'sid ﹞ *v.* 成功 (↔ fail ﹝ fel ﹞ *v.* 失敗)

        success ﹝ sək'sɛs ﹞ *n.* 成功

    (B) *precede* ﹝ pri'sid ﹞ *v.* 在～之前發生

        precedence ﹝ prɪ'sidn̩s ﹞ *n.* (時間、順序等) 在前

        precedent ﹝ prɪ'sidn̩t ﹞ *adj.* 在前的

        precedential ﹝ ‚prɛsə'dɛnʃəl ﹞ *adj.* 有先例的

    (C) predict ﹝ prɪ'dɪkt ﹞ *v.* 預測 (= *foretell*)   predictable *adj.* 可預測的

    (D) proscribe ﹝ pro'skaɪb ﹞ *v.* 置 (人) 於法律保護之外；褫奪～公權

        proscription *n.*

    ＊ *a great deal of* 許多的

6. (**D**) It has been generally acknowledged that advertisements are made to stimulate <u>consumption</u>.
一般大家都知道，廣告製作是爲了刺激<u>消費</u>。
   (A) assumption〔ə'sʌmpʃən〕*n.*（無確實根據的）假定
   assume *v.*　　assumptive *adj.*
   (B) redemption〔rɪ'dɛmpʃən〕*n.* 贖回；救贖
   redeem〔rɪ'dim〕*v.*　　redemptive *adj.* 償還的
   (C) resumption〔rɪ'zʌmpʃən〕*n.*（中斷之後的）再開始　　resume *v.*
   (D) *consumption*〔kən'sʌmpʃən〕*n.* 消費
   （↔ production〔prə'dʌkʃən〕*n.* 製造；生產）
   consume *v.*　　consumption duty 消費稅
   consumption goods 消費品
   * acknowledge〔ək'nɑlɪdʒ〕*v.* 承認　　stimulate〔'stɪmjə,let〕*v.* 刺激；鼓舞

7. (**D**) Many games are <u>simulations</u>; for example, they attempt to model some real-life problem or situation.
很多遊戲是<u>模擬</u>遊戲；舉個例子來說，它們試圖仿造眞實生活中的問題或狀況。
   (A) assimilation〔ə,sɪml'eʃən〕*n.* 消化；吸收　　assimilate *v.*　　assimilative *adj.*
   (B) simultaneous〔,saɪml'tenɪəs〕*adj.* 同時發生的
   simultaneous interpretation 同步口譯
   (C) semiotic〔,simɪ'ɑtɪk〕*adj.* 符號學的　　semiotics *n.* 符號學
   (D) *simulation*〔,sɪmjə'leʃən〕*n.* 模擬；僞裝　　simulate〔'sɪmjə,let〕*v.* 模擬
   simulative〔,sɪmjə'letɪv〕*adj.* 僞裝的　　simulator〔'sɪmjə,letɚ〕*n.* 模擬訓練
   * attempt〔ə'tɛmpt〕*v.* 試圖　　model〔'mɑdl〕*v.* 仿造
   real-life〔'ril'laɪf〕*adj.* 眞實生活的

8. (**B**) Are you one of those women who feel that lipstick is one of the <u>essentials</u> of life? 有些女人認爲口紅是生活<u>必需品</u>，妳也是其中之一嗎？
   (A) essay〔'ɛse〕*n.* 文章；散文　　essay question 問答題
   essay test 問答題測驗
   (B) *essentials*〔ə'sɛnʃəlz〕*n. pl.* 基本必要的東西
   the essentials of astronomy 天文學基礎　　essential *adj.* 重要的
   essentiality〔ɪ,sɛnʃɪ'ælətɪ〕*n.* 必要性；本質
   (C) estate〔ə'stet〕*n.* 地產；社區　　buy an estate 購置地產
   a housing estate 住宅地區　　landed estate 不動產（= *real estate*）
   personal estate 動產　　estate tax 遺產稅
   (D) access〔'æksɛs〕*n.* 通路；入口（= *entrance*；*approach*）
   * lipstick〔'lɪp,stɪk〕*n.* 口紅

9. (**D**) Many college teachers are now using methods of learning evaluation that are more <u>authentically</u> related to later uses of learning than to conventional tests.

許多大學教授現在使用學習評估的方法，該方法比起傳統的考試，與日後學習的運用，更<u>確實</u>有關聯。

(A) alternatively〔ɔl'tɜnətɪvlɪ〕*adv.* 兩者選一個地　　alternative *adj.*

(B) atheistically〔ˌeθɪ'ɪstɪkəlɪ〕*adv.* 無神論者地
atheistical *adj.* (= *atheistic*)

(C) artistically〔ɑr'tɪstɪklɪ〕*adv.* 藝術地；美術地　　artistic *adj.*

(D) *authentically*〔ɔ'θɛntɪklɪ〕*adv.* 眞正地；確實地
authentic *adj.*　　authenticate〔ɔ'θɛntɪˌket〕*v.* 證明
authenticity〔ˌɔθɛn'tɪsətɪ〕*n.* 可靠性

* evaluation〔ɪˌvæljʊ'eʃən〕*n.* 評估
conventional〔kən'vɛnʃənḷ〕*adj.* 傳統的

10. (**B**) There is a simple mathematical truism that, when a person uses several selection criteria, each will have some <u>validity</u>.

有個簡單的數學眞理是這樣的，當一個人使用好幾個挑選標準的時候，每一個標準都<u>有效</u>。

(A) vainglory〔ven'glorɪ〕*n.* 自負；虛榮
vainglorious *adj.*　　vaingloriously *adv.*

(B) *validity*〔və'lɪdətɪ〕*n.* 有效；正當　　the term of validity 有效期間
validate〔'væləˌdet〕*v.* 使有效　　valid *adj.*
validation〔ˌvælə'deʃən〕*n.* 批准；認可

(C) variety〔və'raɪətɪ〕*n.* 多樣性　　variety store 雜貨店
a life full of variety 富於變化的人生
a variety of opinions 多樣化的意見

(D) vapidity〔væ'pɪdətɪ〕*n.* 乏味
vapid〔'væpɪd〕*adj.* 乏味的　　vapidly *adv.*

* truism〔'truɪzəm〕*n.* 眞理
criterion〔kraɪ'tɪrɪən〕*n.* 標準 (複數形為 criteria 或 criterions)

11. (**A**) Being <u>allergic</u> to the drug, the child reacted to it by going into convulsions.
   由於對此種藥物<u>過敏</u>，這個小孩起了痙攣的反應。

   (A) ***allergic*** 〔 ə'lɜdʒɪk 〕 *adj.* 過敏的   an allergic disease 過敏性疾病

   (B) responsible 〔 rɪ'spɑnsəbḷ 〕 *adj.* 負責任的   responsibility *n.*
      responsibly *adv.*   hold a person responsible for~ 使某人負~責任

   (C) representative 〔 ͵rɛprɪ'zɛntətɪv 〕 *adj.* 代理的
      the representative chamber 議院

   (D) symbolic 〔 sɪm'bɑlɪk 〕 *adj.* 象徵性的   a symbolic meaning 象徵性的意義

   ＊drug 〔 drʌg 〕 *n.* 藥；藥品   convulsions 〔 kən'vʌlʃənz 〕 *n. pl.* 痙攣

12. (**C**) I like living here; the climate is very <u>congenial</u> to my health.
   我喜歡住在這裡，這裡的氣候很<u>適合</u>我的健康。

   (A) conjunctive 〔 kən'dʒʌŋktɪv 〕 *adj.* 結合的
      conjunction 〔 kən'dʒʌŋkʃən 〕 *n.* 連接詞

   (B) persuasive 〔 pɚ'swesɪv 〕 *adj.* 有說服力的   persuade 〔 pɚ'swed 〕 *v.* 說服

   (C) ***congenial*** 〔 kən'dʒinjəl 〕 *adj.* 適於（健康、趣味等）的
      congeniality 〔 kən͵dʒinɪ'ælətɪ 〕 *n.*

      例：Congenial co-workers help dispel office tedium.
          興味相投的同事有助於消除辦公室的沉悶。

   (D) persistent 〔 pɚ'zɪstənt 〕 *adj.* 固執的；百折不撓的
      persistent efforts 百折不撓的努力

   ＊climate 〔 'klaɪmɪt 〕 *n.* 氣候

13. (**C**) You'll have your own office soon, but <u>for the time being</u>, you'll have to share mine.
   你很快就有自己的辦公室了，但是<u>目前</u>你要先跟我共用一間。

   (A) for safety's sake 為了安全起見   sake 〔 sek 〕 *n.* 緣故

   (B) up front 非常地坦誠
      例：Be more up front with me. 對我再坦誠一點吧。

   (C) ***for the time being*** 目前
      例：The baby is asleep for the time being. 那個嬰兒目前睡著了。
          She is staying with her aunt for the time being.
          她目前住在她姨媽那邊。

   (D) from now on 從現在開始

14. (**A**) With so many guests present, I'm afraid this little food is not enough to
<u>go about</u>.

有這麼多的客人出席，我擔心這麼少的食物會<u>不夠分配給大家</u>。

(A) *go around* 流傳；蔓延；(食物) 足夠分配給每一個人

例：There is a lot of flu going about just now. 目前流感猖獗。

(B) set forth 發表；宣佈

(C) move down 降級；(地位等) 降低

例：The department store moved from first in gross sales down to third.

那家百貨公司的營業總額從第一位掉到第三位。

(D) bring forth 引起；提出

例：April showers bring forth May flowers. 四月雨帶來五月花。

＊present (′prɛzn̩t) *adj.* 出席的

15. (**B**) With skillful diplomacy, this country stays <u>on good terms</u> with its many
strong neighbors.

因為有高超的外交手腕，這個國家得以和許多強盛的鄰國<u>維持良好的關係</u>。

(A) on account 作為暫付款或訂金

money paid on account 部分支付的款項

(B) *on good terms* 維持良好的關係　　terms (tɝmz) *n. pl.* 關係；地位

be on ~ terms with *sb.* 跟某人維持 ~ 的關係

例：They are on friendly terms. 他們關係友好。

(C) under control 在控制之下

keep temper under control 克制著不發脾氣

(D) in conflict 與 ~ 衝突的

例：His statements are in conflict with his actions.

他的言行不一致。

＊skillful (′skɪlfəl) *adj.* 高超的；巧妙的

diplomacy (dɪ′ploməsɪ) *n.* 外交手腕；外交

TEST 37

Directions: The following questions are incomplete sentences. You are to choose the one word that best completes the sentence.

1. The volume of such drugs as cocaine, morphine and heroin in Taiwan has registered a significant _____ in the last three years.
   (A) surprise   (B) decline
   (C) status   (D) threat   (   )

2. The chef in this Western restaurant is so _____ that he can use local ingredients to make foreign foods and flavor the dishes to make locals accept them.
   (A) conservative   (B) revolutionary
   (C) ingenious   (D) informative   (   )

3. Caught in a downpour without an umbrella at hand, he got home _____ wet.
   (A) boiling   (B) soaking
   (C) scorching   (D) penetrating   (   )

4. After getting my first job, I had a new _____ on life and looked at things in a new light.
   (A) phenomenon   (B) episode
   (C) perspective   (D) barrier   (   )

5. The Shaolin Temple, located in China, is _____ for its expert training in martial arts.
   (A) legendary   (B) solitary
   (C) superstitious   (D) ambiguous   (   )

6. Tens of thousands of Hong Kong protesters raised candles in the air and sang solemn songs on June 4 as they marked the 16th _____ of China's bloody crackdown on the Tiananmen Square pro-democracy demonstrations.
   (A) conference   (B) tournament
   (C) anniversary   (D) triumph   (   )

7. Steve Fossett, the pilot who flew the airplane Globalflyer around the world solo, without ever stopping or refueling, _____ his achievement to the endeavors of the aviation engineer Burt Rutan.
   (A) launched   (B) attributed
   (C) focused   (D) assumed   (   )

8. With so many people out of work at present, the ruling party needs
   to be _____ to the problem of unemployment.
   (A) surrendered   (B) awakened
   (C) reminded   (D) investigated   (   )

9. When he said that he was "living in hope," he meant that _____
   because he lives in a town called Hope.
   (A) symbolically   (B) virtually
   (C) literally   (D) similarly   (   )

10. Even though her knee was hurting a little, Maria hiked to the top of
    the mountain in a(n) _____ short time.
    (A) gradually   (B) painfully
    (C) exceptionally   (D) unfortunately   (   )

11. When you are talking to people, look them _____ in the eye so
    that you can know whether they are listening to you.
    (A) extra   (B) halfway
    (C) straight   (D) somehow   (   )

12. Some physicians and social workers say mental illness _____ in
    family suicide-homicides, but they say societal changes are also
    important factors.
    (A) plays a big role   (B) has a lot to do
    (C) makes both ends meet (D) comes back to life (   )

13. Guard well your personal data. If you don't, _____ you may
    lose your credit standing, for someone may use the data to do
    something bad.
    (A) in no case   (B) in no way
    (C) up and down   (D) the chances are   (   )

14. The latest medical report on smoking tells us that cigarettes are
    harming us in more ways than we ever imagined and that, _____
    making us blind, anxious, and very sick, they are also killing us.
    (A) instead of   (B) in order to
    (C) in addition to   (D) with the help of   (   )

15. My sister happens to dislike hiking. I, _____, go hiking with my
    friends almost every weekend.
    (A) on the run   (B) in other words
    (C) at the same time (D) on the other hand   (   )

TEST 37 詳解

1. (**B**) The volume of such drugs as cocaine, morphine and heroin in Taiwan has registered a significant <u>decline</u> in the last three years.
   在台灣，過去三年內，像古柯鹼、嗎啡以及海洛因這類的毒品，顯示出已大幅<u>減少</u>。

   (A) surprise〔sə'praɪz〕*n.* 驚訝
   (B) *decline*〔dɪ'klaɪn〕*n.* 下降；衰退；減少
   (C) status〔'stetəs〕*n.* 地位（= *position*）；狀態（= *condition*）
       social status 社會地位
   (D) threat〔θrɛt〕*n.* 威脅　　threaten〔'θrɛtn̩〕*v.* 威脅
       threatening〔'θrɛtn̩ɪŋ〕*adj.* 脅迫的

   * volume〔'vɑljəm〕*n.* 量　　drug〔drʌg〕*n.* 藥物；毒品
   cocaine〔ko'ken〕*n.* 古柯鹼
   morphine〔'mɔrfin〕*n.* 嗎啡　　heroin〔'hɛroˌɪn〕*n.* 海洛因
   register〔'rɛdʒɪstə〕*v.* 顯示
   significant〔sɪg'nɪfəkənt〕*adj.* 相當大的；顯著的

2. (**C**) The chef in this Western restaurant is so <u>ingenious</u> that he can use local ingredients to make foreign foods and flavor the dishes to make locals accept them.
   這家西方餐廳的主廚很有<u>獨創才能</u>，他可以運用本地的食材做出外國食物，並且在菜餚上加以調味，讓當地人接受這些菜。

   (A) conservative〔kən'sɝvətɪv〕*adj.* 保守的
       （↔ progressive〔prə'grɛsɪv〕*adj.* 革新的；進步的）
   (B) revolutionary〔ˌrɛvə'luʃənˌɛrɪ〕*adj.* 革命的；革命性的
       revolution〔ˌrɛvə'luʃən〕*n.* 革命
   (C) *ingenious*〔ɪn'dʒinjəs〕*adj.* 獨創的（= *inventive*）
       ingeniously *adv.*
   (D) informative〔ɪn'fɔrmətɪv〕*adj.* 提供知識的；有教育性的

   * chef〔ʃɛf〕*n.*（餐館的）主廚　　Western〔'wɛstən〕*adj.* 西方的
   local〔'lokl̩〕*adj.* 當地的　　*n.* 當地人
   ingredient〔ɪn'gridɪənt〕*n.* 原料　　flavor〔'flevə〕*v.* 給～調味
   dish〔dɪʃ〕*n.* 菜餚

3. (**B**) Caught in a downpour without an umbrella at hand, he got home <u>soaking</u> wet.
他遇到傾盆大雨，而且又沒有雨傘在手邊，所以他<u>全身溼透地</u>回家。

(A) boiling (ˈbɔɪlɪŋ) *adj.* 沸騰的　　boiling hot　酷熱的
boiling point　沸點

(B) *soaking* (ˈsokɪŋ) *adj.* 溼透的　　a soaking downpour　豪雨
get soaking wet　全身溼透

(C) scorching (ˈskɔrtʃɪŋ) *adj.* 酷熱的　　scorching heat　酷暑
scorching hot　熱得快燒起來

(D) penetrating (ˈpɛnəˌtretɪŋ) *adj.* 貫穿的　　penetrate (ˈpɛnəˌtret) *v.* 貫穿

＊*be caught in* 遇到　　downpour (ˈdaʊnˌpor) *n.* 傾盆大雨
at hand 在手邊

4. (**C**) After getting my first job, I had a new <u>perspective</u> on life and looked at things in a new light.
獲得第一份工作後，我對人生有新的<u>看法</u>，並且以新的觀點看待事情。

(A) phenomenon (fəˈnɑməˌnɑn) *n.* 現象（複數形為 phenomena）

(B) episode (ˈɛpəˌsod) *n.*（小說等）一回；一集
episodic (ˌɛpəˈsɑdɪk) *adj.* 插曲般的；短暫的

(C) *perspective* (pəˈspɛktɪv) *n.* 看法　　in perspective　目光正確地

(D) barrier (ˈbærɪə) *n.* 障礙；隔閡；剪票口
a language barrier　語言障礙

＊light (laɪt) *n.* 觀點；看法　　*in a new light* 持新的觀點

5. (**A**) The Shaolin Temple, located in China, is <u>legendary</u> for its expert training in martial arts.
坐落於中國的少林寺，<u>以其專門的武術訓練為傳奇</u>。

(A) *legendary* (ˈlɛdʒəndˌɛrɪ) *adj.* 傳奇的　　legend (ˈlɛdʒənd) *n.* 傳奇

(B) solitary (ˈsɑləˌtɛrɪ) *adj.* 孤獨的　　solitude *n.* 孤獨

(C) superstitious (ˌsupəˈstɪʃəs) *adj.* 迷信的
superstition (ˌsupəˈstɪʃən) *n.* 迷信

(D) ambiguous (æmˈbɪgjʊəs) *adj.* 含糊的
ambiguity (ˌæmbɪˈgjuətɪ) *n.* 模稜兩可的話

＊*Shaolin Temple* 少林寺　　locate (loˈket) *v.* 使坐落於
expert (ˈɛkspɜt) *adj.* 專門的
martial (ˈmɑrʃəl) *adj.* 軍事的　　*martial arts* 武術

6. (**C**) Tens of thousands of Hong Kong protesters raised candles in the air and sang solemn songs on June 4 as they marked the 16th <u>anniversary</u> of China's bloody crackdown on the Tiananmen Square pro-democracy demonstrations.

在六月四日，數以萬計的香港抗議民眾把蠟燭舉在空中，並且唱著莊嚴的歌曲，突顯中國在天安門廣場，血腥鎮壓倡導民主示威運動十六週年紀念。

(A) conference ('kɑnfərəns) *n.* 會議 (= *meeting*)
conference call 電話會議

(B) tournament ('tɜnəmənt) *n.* 錦標賽 (= *tourney* ; *contest*)

(C) *anniversary* (,ænə'vɜsərɪ) *n.* 週年紀念 (日)
adj. 週年的；週年紀念的

(D) triumph ('traɪəmf) *n.* (大) 勝利
triumphant (traɪ'ʌmfənt) *adj.* 勝利的

＊*tens of thousands of* 數以萬計的
protester (pro'tɛstə) *n.* 抗議者
solemn ('sɑləm) *adj.* 莊嚴的　　mark (mɑrk) *v.* 標明
crackdown ('kræk,daʊn) *n.* 鎮壓　　***Tiananmen Square*** 天安門廣場
pro-democracy ('prodɪ'mɑkrəsɪ) *adj.* 倡導民主的
demonstration (,dɛmən'streʃən) *n.* 示威運動

7. (**B**) Steve Fossett, the pilot who flew the airplane Globalflyer around the world solo, without ever stopping or refueling, <u>attributed</u> his achievement to the endeavors of the aviation engineer Burt Rutan.

飛行員史蒂夫佛塞特駕駛「地球飛行號」單獨環繞地球，途中始終沒有停留或補給燃料，他將這項成就歸因於航空工程師伯特魯丹的努力。

(A) launch (lɔntʃ) *v.* 發射；發動；開始　　launch an attack 發動攻擊

(B) *attribute* (ə'trɪbjut) *v.* 歸因於 (= *ascribe*)
attribute A *to* B 把 A 歸因於 B　　attribution (,ætrə'bjuʃən) *n.* 歸因

(C) focus ('fokəs) *v.* 專注；集中 (= *concentrate*)　　focus on 集中於

(D) assume (ə'sjum) *v.* 假定；認為

＊pilot ('paɪlət) *n.* 飛行員　　solo ('solo) *adv.* 單獨地
refuel (ri'fjuəl) *v.* 補給燃料　　endeavor (ɪn'dɛvə) *n.* 努力
aviation (,evɪ'eʃən) *n.* 航空

8. (**B**) With so many people out of work at present, the ruling party needs to be <u>awakened</u> to the problem of unemployment.

由於目前有這麼多的人沒有工作，執政黨應該意識到失業的問題。

(A) surrender〔sə'rɛndə〕*v.* 投降（= *capitulate*）
　　surrender *oneself* to 向（警方等）自首
(B) *awaken*〔ə'wekən〕*v.* 使意識到（= *awake*）　　be awakened to 意識到
(C) remind〔rɪ'maɪnd〕*v.* 提醒　　reminder〔rɪ'maɪndə〕*n.* 提醒之人或物
(D) investigate〔ɪn'vɛstə‚get〕*v.* 調查（= *explore*; *examine*）
　　investigation *n.*

＊*out of work* 沒有工作　　*at present* 目前
　ruling〔'rulɪŋ〕*adj.* 統治的　　*ruling party* 執政黨
　unemployment〔‚ʌnɪm'plɔɪmənt〕*n.* 失業

9. (**C**) When he said that he was "living in hope," he meant that literally because he lives in a town called Hope. 當他說他「住在希望裡」，他指的是字面上的意思，因為他住在一個名為希望的城鎮。
(A) symbolically〔sɪm'bɑlɪklɪ〕*adv.* 象徵性地
　　symbolical *adj.* 象徵性的（= *symbolic*）　　symbol *n.* 象徵
　　symbolize〔'sɪmbl‚aɪz〕*v.* 象徵
(B) virtually〔'vɝtʃʊəlɪ〕*adv.* 實際上（= *actually* = *practically* = *substantially*）
(C) *literally*〔'lɪtərəlɪ〕*adv.* 照字面意思地　　translate literally 直譯
　　take a person literally 照字面意思解釋某人的話
(D) similarly〔'sɪməlɚlɪ〕*adv.* 類似地　　similar *adj.*
　　similarity〔‚sɪmə'lærətɪ〕*n.* 相似之處

10. (**C**) Even though her knee was hurting a little, Maria hiked to the top of the mountain in an exceptionally short time.
雖然膝蓋有一點痛，瑪麗亞仍然以非常短的時間走到山頂。
(A) gradually〔'grædʒʊəlɪ〕*adv.* 逐漸地（= *increasingly*）
(B) painfully〔'penfəlɪ〕*adv.* 痛苦地　　painful *adj.*
　　pain *n.*（精神上、身體上的）痛苦
(C) *exceptionally*〔ɪk'sɛpʃənl̩ɪ〕*adv.* 非常地；特別地
　　（= *unusually*; *extraordinarily*; *remarkably*）
(D) unfortunately〔ʌn'fɔrtʃənɪtlɪ〕*adv.* 不幸地（= *unluckily*）
　　【↔ fortunately〔'fɔrtʃənɪtlɪ〕*adv.* 幸運地（= *luckily*）】

11. (**C**) When you are talking to people, look them straight in the eye so that you can know whether they are listening to you.
當你跟人說話的時候，要直視他們的眼睛，這樣你才能知道他們是否在聽你說話。

(A) extra〔'ɛkstrə〕*adv.* 格外地；額外地

　　try extra hard 格外努力　　an extra train 加班車

　　an extra job 副業　　an extra edition 特刊

(B) halfway〔'hæf'we〕*adv.* 中途地

　　meet a person halfway 與某人妥協

　　meet trouble halfway 自尋煩惱

(C) *straight*〔stret〕*adv.* 直直地　　*adj.* 直的

　　shoot straight 瞄準射擊　　sit up straight 坐直

　　a straight line 直線　　a straight road 直直的道路

　　straight thinking 有條理的思考　　straight speech 直言

　　keep straight on 一直繼續下去

(D) somehow〔'sʌm,haʊ〕*adv.* 設法；不知道爲什麼

　　例：Somehow I must find her. 我必須設法找到她。

12. (**A**) Some physicians and social workers say mental illness <u>plays a big role</u> in family suicide-homicides, but they say societal changes are also important factors. 有些醫生和社工說，精神疾病是造成家庭殺人後自殺案件的<u>主因</u>，但是他們說社會的改變也是重要的因素。

(A) *play a big role* 扮演重要的角色　　role〔rol〕*n.* 角色

(B) have a lot to do 和～有很大的關係

　　have nothing to do with 和～沒有關係

(C) make (both) ends meet 使收支平衡

　　例：We are having trouble making ends meet.

　　　　我們在爲收支平衡而傷腦筋。

(D) come back to life 甦醒過來

　　例：The boy came back to life again. 那個男孩恢復了知覺。

＊physician〔fə'zɪʃən〕*n.* 內科醫師　　*mental illness* 精神疾病

　suicide〔'suə,saɪd〕*n.* 自殺　　homicide〔'hɑmə,saɪd〕*n.* 殺人行爲

　suicide-homicide 殺人後自殺　　factor〔'fæktə〕*n.* 因素

13. (**D**) Guard well your personal data. If you don't, <u>the chances are</u> you may lose your credit standing, for someone may use the data to do something bad. 保護好你的個人資料。如果沒有保護好的話，<u>恐怕</u>你就會失去你的信用，因爲有人可能會用你的資料去做壞事。

(A) in no case 在任何情況下絕不　　case〔kes〕n. 情況

　　例：You should in no case forget it. 在任何情況下你都不能忘記那件事。

(B) in no way 絕不　　例：I am in no way to blame. 我一點也沒錯。

(C) up and down 上上下下地　　jump up and down 上下地跳

(D) *the chances are* 恐怕；或許

　　例：The chances are he has got there. 恐怕他已經到那裡了。

＊guard〔gɑrd〕v. 保護　　standing〔'stændɪŋ〕n. 名聲；地位

14. (**C**) The latest medical report on smoking tells us that cigarettes are harming us in more ways than we ever imagined and that, <u>in addition to</u> making us blind, anxious, and very sick, they are also killing us.

最近的醫學報導指出，香煙傷害我們的層面遠超過想像，<u>除了</u>讓我們失明、焦慮，以及病得很重<u>之外</u>，也會致人於死。

(A) instead of 而不是

　　例：Let's learn English instead of French. 我們來學英文，不要學法文。

(B) in order to 為了

　　例：She has gone to England in order to improve her English.

　　　　為了要改善她的英文，她已經去英國了。

(C) *in addition to* 除了～之外

(D) with the help of 在～的幫助下

＊latest〔'letɪst〕adj. 最新的　　imagine〔ɪ'mædʒɪn〕v. 想像

anxious〔'æŋkʃəs〕adj. 焦慮的

15. (**D**) My sister happens to dislike hiking. I, <u>on the other hand</u>, go hiking with my friends almost every weekend. 我妹妹碰巧不喜歡健行，我<u>正好相反</u>，幾乎每個週末都跟我朋友一起去健行。

(A) on the run 忙個不停

　　例：Mom has been on the run all week preparing for Tom's wedding.

　　　　媽媽整個禮拜都在為湯姆的婚禮忙個不停。

(B) in other words 換句話說

(C) at the same time 同時

(D) *on the other hand* 反過來說；另一方面

　　例：Food was abundant, but on the other hand, water was running short.

　　　　食物很充足，但是反過來說，水卻短缺。

＊*happen to* 碰巧　　hike〔haɪk〕v. 健行

TEST 38

Directions: The following questions are incomplete sentences. You are to choose the one word that best completes the sentence.

1. The explosive popularity of cell phones has brought about a _____ in human communication. The great change has made modern life more convenient and enjoyable.
   (A) privacy   (B) commodity
   (C) revolution   (D) phenomenon   (   )

2. Education should be a right, not a _____. People from all walks of life should have equal opportunity to receive education regardless of age and sex.
   (A) heritage   (B) diploma
   (C) certificate   (D) privilege   (   )

3. The car accident was a tragedy. How did it _____?
   (A) come about   (B) come around
   (C) come off   (D) come over   (   )

4. The girl often _____ her back pain to get sympathy. In fact, it was not as serious as she described.
   (A) interpreted   (B) transported
   (C) transformed   (D) exaggerated   (   )

5. Washington has urged that the Israeli soldiers held hostage be _____ by Lebanon. Once they are set free, there is the possibility of a ceasefire.
   (A) distributed   (B) released
   (C) imprisoned   (D) restrained   (   )

6. I will expect you at seven thirty; _____, it's an informal dinner.
   (A) by the way   (B) by all means
   (C) by and by   (D) by accident   (   )

7. What with economic depression and what with individual financial difficulty, many jobless people in Taiwan have _____ ended their lives.
   (A) gloriously   (B) sufficiently
   (C) hopelessly   (D) exclusively   (   )

8. Giant pandas are _____ to China. Taken away from their habitats, they have great difficulty surviving.
   (A) indigenous
   (B) crucial
   (C) impoverished
   (D) superstitious
   (   )

9. Shakespeare's poems and plays are mandatory for those who major in English literature. All English majors are _____ to study them.
   (A) acquired
   (B) inquired
   (C) acquainted
   (D) required
   (   )

10. The invention of new drugs and the advance of medical technology have greatly _____ people's lives. People are able to live longer than before.
    (A) prompted
    (B) prolonged
    (C) declined
    (D) contributed
    (   )

11. J.K. Rowling is a novelist who specializes in _____. Her famous novels have been widely published all over the world and adapted into a series of films.
    (A) distinction
    (B) mystery
    (C) exploration
    (D) fantasy
    (   )

12. During the dinner time, Hank _____ his notes so he would remember them for the exam.
    (A) ran into
    (B) ran over
    (C) ran out of
    (D) ran off
    (   )

13. The diligent young girl owes her success to many people, her father _____.
    (A) after all
    (B) in particular
    (C) by chance
    (D) on purpose
    (   )

14. Recently a weather front sent temperatures _____ in California. The high temperatures that smashed records across the state resulted in many deaths.
    (A) operating
    (B) hovering
    (C) soaring
    (D) lowering
    (   )

15. Hagen was late for this family gathering _____ the traffic congestion.
    (A) on account of
    (B) in spite of
    (C) apart from
    (D) in accordance with
    (   )

TEST 38 詳解

1. (**C**) The explosive popularity of cell phones has brought about a <u>revolution</u> in human communication. The great change has made modern life more convenient and enjoyable.

手機快速的流行，導致人類通訊的<u>革命</u>。這重大的改變，使得現代生活更加便利與舒適。

    (A) privacy ('praɪvəsɪ) *n.* 隱私   in privacy 私下   live in privacy 隱居

    (B) commodity (kə'madətɪ) *n.* 商品 (= *goods* = *merchandise*)

        price of commodities 物價

    (C) *revolution* (ˌrɛvə'luʃən) *n.* 革命；公轉 (↔ rotation 自轉)

        revolutionary *adj.* 改革的

    (D) phenomenon (fə'namə,nan) *n.* 現象；傑出的人

        a child phenomenon 神童

    * explosive (ɪk'splosɪv) *adj.* 急劇的   popularity (ˌpapjə'lærətɪ) *n.* 流行

    bring about 導致   enjoyable (ɪn'dʒɔɪəbḷ) *adj.* 愉悅的

2. (**D**) Education should be a right, not a <u>privilege</u>. People from all walks of life should have equal opportunity to receive education regardless of age and sex.

教育應該是人民的權利，而不是<u>特權</u>。各行各業的人，不分年紀和性別，都應該有同等的機會可以接受教育。

    (A) heritage ('hɛrətɪdʒ) *n.* 世襲祖產；遺產 (= *bequest* = *legacy*)

        a cultural heritage 文化遺產

    (B) diploma (dɪ'plomə) *n.* 文憑   receive *one's* diploma 獲得文憑；畢業

    (C) certificate (sə'tɪfəkɪt) *n.* 證明書   a birth certificate 出生證明

        a medical certificate 診斷書

    (D) *privilege* ('prɪvḷɪdʒ) *n.* 特權

        the privilege of citizenship 公民權   privileged *adj.* 有特權的

    * *all walks of life* 各行各業的人   *regardless of* 不拘；不分

3. (**A**) The car accident was a tragedy. How did it <u>come about</u>?

那場車禍是個悲劇。怎麼<u>發生</u>的？

    (A) *come about* 發生 (= *take place* = *occur* = *happen*)

    (B) come around 恢復知覺 (= *revive*)；恢復健康

    (C) come off 舉行；成功；脫落

    (D) come over 順便到訪

    * tragedy ('trædʒədɪ) *n.* 悲劇

4.(**D**) The girl often <u>exaggerated</u> her back pain to get sympathy. In fact, it was not as serious as she described.

那個女孩通常會<u>誇張</u>她的背痛來搏得同情。事實上，情況並不像她所描述的那麼嚴重。

(A) interpret〔ɪn'tɜprɪt〕*v.* 解釋；口譯　　interpretation *n.*
interpreter *n.* 說明者；翻譯者

(B) transport〔træns'port〕*v.* 運送　　transportation *n.* 交通工具；運輸

(C) transform〔træns'fɔrm〕*v.* 改變（= *change* = *alter* = *convert*）
transformation *n.*

(D) *exaggerate*〔ɪg'zædʒəˌret〕*v.* 誇張（= *magnify*）
exaggerated *adj.* 誇張的

* sympathy〔'sɪmpəθɪ〕*n.* 同情　　describe〔dɪ'skraɪb〕*v.* 描述

5.(**B**) Washington has urged that the Israeli soldiers held hostage be <u>released</u> by Lebanon. Once they are set free, there is the possibility of a ceasefire.

華盛頓主張，黎巴嫩應該<u>釋放</u>被挾持當人質的以色列軍人。一旦人質被釋放，才有可能停戰。

(A) distribute〔dɪ'strɪbjut〕*v.* 分配；分發（= *allocate*）
distribution *n.*

(B) *release*〔rɪ'lis〕*v.* 釋放（= *discharge* = *liberate*）；發售
release a new single　發售新單曲

(C) imprison〔ɪm'prɪzn̩〕*v.* 關入牢獄　　imprisonment *n.* 監禁；下獄

(D) restrain〔rɪ'stren〕*v.* 抑制（= *abstain from* = *refrain from* = *inhibit*）；
限制（= *limit* = *constrict*）

* urge〔ɜdʒ〕*v.* 主張　　hostage〔'hɑstɪdʒ〕*n.* 人質
hold hostage 扣留當人質　　*set free* 釋放
ceasefire〔'sis'faɪr〕*n.* 停火；停戰

6.(**A**) I will expect you at seven thirty; <u>by the way</u>, it's an informal dinner.

我七點半的時候等你來；<u>順便一提</u>，這不是正式晚餐。

(A) *by the way* 順便一提

(B) by all means 務必；當然（= *on all accounts*）

(C) by and by 不久（= *shortly* = *soon*）

(D) by accident 意外地（= *accidentally*）

* expect〔ɪk'spɛkt〕*v.* 期盼（～要來的事）
informal〔ɪn'fɔrməl〕*adj.* 非正式的

7. (**C**) What with economic depression and what with individual financial difficulty, many jobless people in Taiwan have <u>hopelessly</u> ended their lives.

有人因爲經濟不景氣，有人因爲個人財務困難，台灣很多失業的人，<u>絕望地</u>結束自己的生命。

(A) gloriously〔'glorɪəslɪ〕 *adv.* 光榮地；輝煌地　　glorious *adj.* 光榮的
glorify *v.* 歌頌；讚揚

(B) sufficiently〔sə'fɪʃəntlɪ〕 *adv.* 充分地 (= *adequately* = *aplenty* = *plentifully*)

(C) *hopelessly*〔'hoplɪslɪ〕 *adv.* 絕望地 (= *desperately* = *despairingly*)

(D) exclusively〔ɪk'sklusɪvlɪ〕 *adv.* 專門地；獨佔性地　　exclusive *adj.*

* *what with ~ and what with*⋯ 一則因 ~ 一則因⋯
depression〔dɪ'prɛʃən〕 *n.* 蕭條；沮喪
jobless〔'dʒɑblɪs〕 *adj.* 失業的；待業的　　*end one's life* 結束生命

8. (**A**) Giant pandas are <u>indigenous</u> to China. Taken away from their habitats, they have great difficulty surviving.

大貓熊<u>原產於</u>中國。如果牠們離開原棲息地，將會很難存活。

(A) *indigenous*〔ɪn'dɪdʒənəs〕 *adj.* 原產的 (= *native*) < *to* > (↔ *exotic* 外來的)

(B) crucial〔'kruʃəl〕 *adj.* 極重要的 (= *critical* = *cardinal* = *vital*)
a crucial moment 關鍵時刻

(C) impoverished〔ɪm'pɑvərɪʃt〕 *adj.* 窮困的 (= *poor* = *needy*)

(D) superstitious〔͵supə'stɪʃəs〕 *adj.* 迷信的　　superstition *n.*

* habitat〔'hæbə͵tæt〕 *n.* 原產地；棲息地
have difficulty (*in*) + *V-ing* 難以 ~

9. (**D**) Shakespeare's poems and plays are mandatory for those who major in English literature. All English majors are <u>required</u> to study them.

對於主修英國文學的人而言，莎士比亞的詩和戲劇是必修的。主修英文的人都<u>必須讀</u>。

(A) acquire〔ə'kwaɪr〕 *v.* 獲得 (= *obtain*)

(B) inquire〔ɪn'kwaɪr〕 *v.* 詢問 (= *ask*)

(C) acquaint〔ə'kwent〕 *v.* 使認識；使了解
be acquainted with 認識　　acquaintance *n.* 認識的人

(D) *require*〔rɪ'kwaɪr〕 *v.* 要求　　*be required to* 必須

* play〔ple〕 *n.* 戲劇
mandatory〔'mændə͵torɪ〕 *adj.* 義務性的；必須的
major〔'medʒɚ〕 *v.* 主修 < *in* > *n.* 主修學生

10. (**B**) The invention of new drugs and the advance of medical technology have greatly <u>prolonged</u> people's lives. People are able to live longer than before.

新開發的藥品以及醫療科技的進步，使人類的壽命延長許多。人類可以活得比以前久。

(A) prompt〔prɑmpt〕v. 促使（ = make = send ） adj. 迅速的；即時的

(B) *prolong*〔prə'lɔŋ〕v. 延長（ = extend ）
   prolonged adj. 延長的　　prolongation n.

(C) decline〔dɪ'klaɪn〕v. 拒絕（ = refuse = reject ）
   declining adj. 傾斜的；衰退的

(D) contribute〔kən'trɪbjut〕v. 捐助；貢獻
   contributor n. 捐獻者　　contributive adj. 有貢獻的

*advance〔əd'væns〕n. 進步　　greatly〔'gretlɪ〕adv. 大大地
   enable〔ɪn'ebḷ〕v. 使能夠

11. (**D**) J.K. Rowling is a novelist who specializes in <u>fantasy</u>. Her famous novels have been widely published all over the world and adapted into a series of films.

J.K. Rowling 是專門寫幻想文學作品的小說家。她的作品在全世界廣為發行，也被改編成一系列的電影。

(A) distinction〔dɪ'stɪŋkʃən〕n. 卓越；著名
   a writer of distinction 著名的作家

(B) mystery〔'mɪstərɪ〕n. 秘密；神秘
   make a mystery of 隱瞞　　mysterious adj.

(C) exploration〔,ɛksplə'reʃən〕n. 探勘；探險
   explore v.　　explorer n. 探險家

(D) *fantasy*〔'fæntəsɪ〕n. 幻想；幻想的文學作品
   fantastic adj. 幻想的；絕佳的

*novelist〔'nɑvḷɪst〕n. 小說家　　*specialize in* 專攻　　publish〔'pʌblɪʃ〕v. 出版
   all over the world 全世界（ = around the world = worldwide ）
   adapt〔ə'dæpt〕v. 改編　　series〔'sɪrɪz〕n. 一系列

12. (**B**) During the dinner time, Hank <u>ran over</u> his notes so he would remember them for the exam.

晚餐的時候，漢克複習他的筆記來準備考試。

(A) run into 撞上（ = bump into ）；偶遇

(B) *run over* 複習（ = go over = review ）

(C) run out of 用完（ = deplete = exhaust ）

(D) run off 逃跑（ = escape = flee ）

13. (**B**) The diligent young girl owes her success to many people, her father <u>in</u> <u>particular</u>.

這個勤奮的年輕女孩，把她的成功歸功於很多人，<u>特別</u>是她父親。

(A) after all　畢竟

(B) *in particular*　特別地；尤其

(C) by chance　偶然地

(D) on purpose　故意地

＊diligent〔ˈdɪlədʒənt〕*adj.* 勤奮的　　*owe* A *to* B 把 A 歸功於 B

14. (**C**) Recently a weather front sent temperatures <u>soaring</u> in California. The high temperatures that smashed records across the state resulted in many deaths. 最近，一道鋒面使得加州的氣溫**飆**高。這次打破全國記錄的高溫，造成多人喪生。

(A) operate〔ˈɑpəˌret〕*v.* 運作；經營　　operation *n.*
　　operate a school　經營學校

(B) hover〔ˈhʌvɚ〕*v.* 盤旋；徘徊（= *lurk* = *digress* = *wander*）
　　hover about　徘徊不定

(C) *soar*〔sor〕*v.* 高飛；高漲
　　例：Prices have soared. 物價高漲。

(D) lower〔ˈloɚ〕*v.* 降低　　lower the blood pressure　降低血壓

＊front〔frʌnt〕*n.* 鋒面　　*weather front* 鋒面
send〔sɛnd〕*v.*（迫）使　　smash〔smæʃ〕*v.* 打破
smash records 破紀錄　　*result in* 造成

15. (**A**) Hagen was late for this family gathering <u>on account of</u> the traffic congestion.

<u>由於</u>塞車，哈根來不及參加家庭聚會。

(A) *on account of*　由於（= *as a result of* = *because of* = *owing to* = *due to*）

(B) in spite of　儘管（= *despite*）　　in spite of *oneself* 不知不覺地

(C) apart from　除了～以外

(D) in accordance with　根據

＊gathering〔ˈgæðərɪŋ〕*n.* 聚會
congestion〔kənˈdʒɛstʃən〕*n.* 阻塞

TEST 39

Directions: The following questions are incomplete sentences. You are to choose the one word that best completes the sentence.

1. Several friends of his felt _____ to give something as an act of charity.
   (A) similar   (B) tend
   (C) intend   (D) obliged   (   )

2. I hate to be the one to _____ him, but as the director of this film, I have to choose the most qualified actor for the role.
   (A) disengage   (B) disillusion
   (C) disclose   (D) dismantle   (   )

3. The _____ among the world's scientists is that global warming will have a big impact on our environment.
   (A) tendency   (B) essence
   (C) distinction   (D) consensus   (   )

4. I'd be _____ if someone told me that I'm incapable of performing my present job well.
   (A) outlawed   (B) depleted
   (C) mortified   (D) speculated   (   )

5. Linda _____, "How can I finish the report within three days when you ask me to do so many other jobs at the same time?"
   (A) chirped   (B) beamed
   (C) growled   (D) giggled   (   )

6. He is a _____ who has repeatedly cheated some old retired people of their money.
   (A) swindler   (B) slander
   (C) sleuth   (D) scavenger   (   )

7. His hair was _____ and filthy.
   (A) untidy   (B) treacherous
   (C) unraveled   (D) screwed   (   )

8. The _____ of our winning several medals in the Olympic Games
   are becoming brighter.
   (A) aspects   (B) expects
   (C) prospects   (D) suspects   ( )

9. The boss is _____ because his staff didn't consult him on an
   important decision.
   (A) imposing   (B) indignant
   (C) inhibited   (D) impervious   ( )

10. You might run that comb through your hair so you will look _____.
    (A) plausible   (B) insurmountable
    (C) accessible   (D) presentable   ( )

11. The strong hurricane caused great destruction in the U.S., and the
    President tried to find out who was truly _____ for the severe
    losses in New Orleans.
    (A) at fault   (B) in service
    (C) on line   (D) by law   ( )

12. The magic tricks _____ were quite successful and the audience
    went crazy for the magician who performed the show.
    (A) out of the question (B) in no sense
    (C) on the whole   (D) by no means   ( )

13. The president of the company believes that good quality work is the
    key to success. Therefore, anyone who does a good job, _____,
    shall be needed in the company.
    (A) off and on   (B) up and down
    (C) back and forth   (D) for better or worse   ( )

14. In recent years, a lot of traditional ways of doing things have
    _____ new ones.
    (A) had a way of   (B) found a way of
    (C) given way to   (D) changed the way of   ( )

15. Emily lost her dog, and it was a great blow to her. She spent so
    much time _____ the grief.
    (A) putting out   (B) coming across
    (C) getting over   (D) going around   ( )

TEST 39 詳解

1. (**D**) Several friends of his felt <u>obliged</u> to give something as an act of charity.
   他的幾個朋友，<u>不得不</u>捐些東西做慈善。
   (A) similar〔'sɪmələ〕 *adj.* 相似的（↔ dissimilar 不相似的）
      similar tastes 相似的嗜好
   (B) tend〔tɛnd〕 *v.* 有～的傾向；留意　　tendency〔'tɛndənsɪ〕 *n.* 傾向；趨勢
   (C) intend〔ɪn'tɛnd〕 *v.* 意圖；打算（ = *plan* = *purpose* ）
      intended〔ɪn'tɛndɪd〕 *adj.* 有企圖的
   (D) *obliged*〔ə'blaɪdʒd〕 *adj.* 不得不的；（為某人、事情等）感恩的
      obligation *n.* 責任；義務
   * *an act of ~* ～的行為　　charity〔'tʃærətɪ〕 *n.* 慈善（心）
      an act of charity 慈善的行為

2. (**B**) I hate to be the one to <u>disillusion</u> him, but as the director of this film, I have
   to choose the most qualified actor for the role. 我很不想當那個<u>讓他理想破滅</u>
   的人，但身為這部影片的導演，我必須挑選出最適合這個角色的演員。
   (A) disengage〔,dɪsɪn'gedʒ〕 *v.* 解開；使解除（義務、束縛等）
      engage *v.* 從事；參與
   (B) *disillusion*〔,dɪsɪ'luʒən〕 *v.* 使理想破滅　　disillusionment *n.*
      illusion *n.* 幻覺；幻想
   (C) disclose〔dɪs'kloz〕 *v.* 暴露；洩露（ = *unlock* = *reveal* = *leak out* ）
      disclosure *n.*
   (D) dismantle〔dɪs'mæntḷ〕 *v.* 分解；拆除　　mantle *v.* 覆蓋；裏住
   * director〔də'rɛktə〕 *n.* 導演；指揮者
      qualified〔'kwɑlə,faɪd〕 *adj.* 合格的；適任的　　role〔rol〕 *n.* （演員的）角色

3. (**D**) The <u>consensus</u> among the world's scientists is that global warming will have
   a big impact on our environment.
   全世界的科學家<u>一致同意</u>，全球暖化會對我們的環境造成很大的衝擊。
   (A) tendency〔'tɛndənsɪ〕 *n.* 傾向；趨勢　　tend *v.* 有～的傾向；留意
   (B) essence〔'ɛsṇs〕 *n.* 本質；精華　　vanilla essence 香草精
      essential *adj.* 重要的
   (C) distinction〔dɪ'stɪŋkʃən〕 *n.* 區別；差別　　distinctive *adj.* 獨特的；顯著的
   (D) *consensus*〔kən'sɛnsəs〕 *n.* 一致；全體的意見
      a national consensus 全國一致的意見
   * global〔'globḷ〕 *adj.* 全球的　　*global warming* 全球暖化
      impact〔'ɪmpækt〕 *n.* 衝擊

4. (**C**) I'd be <u>mortified</u> if someone told me that I'm incapable of performing my
present job well.
假如有人告訴我，我沒有能力把我目前的工作做好的話，我會感到羞辱。

(A) outlaw〔'aʊt,lɔ〕 v. 禁止　　n. 不法之徒
outlaw drunk driving　禁止酒醉駕駛

(B) deplete〔dɪ'plit〕 v. 用盡（力量、資源等）（= *exhaust*）
depletion n. 枯竭

(C) *mortify*〔'mɔrtə,faɪ〕 v. 使感到羞辱　　mortification　羞辱
mortifying adj. 感到羞辱的

(D) speculate〔'spɛkjə,let〕 v. 推測；思索　　speculative adj. 推理的

∗ incapable〔ɪn'kepəbl̩〕 adj. 不能的；無能的
perform〔pə'fɔrm〕 v. 執行；實行
present〔'prɛznt̩〕 adj. 目前的；當前的

5. (**C**) Linda <u>growled</u>, "How can I finish the report within three days when you
ask me to do so many other jobs at the same time?"
琳達<u>生氣地說</u>：「你要我做完這個報告，又要我一次做這麼多其他的事情，
這怎麼可能？」

(A) chirp〔tʃɝp〕 v. 吱喳地叫；以尖銳聲講話
chirpy adj. 吱喳叫的；快活的

(B) beam〔bim〕 v. 發出光；以微笑表示（喜悅等）
beaming adj. 發光的；喜悅的

(C) *growl*〔graʊl〕 v.（人）生氣地說；怒罵；（動物）咆哮
growling adj. 吼叫的；發牢騷的

(D) giggle〔'gɪgl̩〕 v. 吃吃地笑　　giggling adj. 吃吃地笑的

6. (**A**) He is a <u>swindler</u> who has repeatedly cheated some old retired people of
their money.
他是個<u>騙子</u>，一直不斷地騙取一些退休老人的錢。

(A) *swindler*〔'swɪndlə〕 n. 詐騙者；騙子（= *liar* = *cheater*）
swindle v. 詐騙　　n. 詐欺

(B) slander〔'slændə〕 n. v. 誹謗；中傷　　slanderer n. 誹謗者
slender adj. 苗條的

(C) sleuth〔sluθ〕 n.【口語】刑警；偵探（= *sleuthhound*）

(D) scavenger〔'skævɪndʒə〕 n. 吃腐肉的動物（如禿鷹、胡狼等）；撿破爛者
scavenge v. 撿破爛

∗ repeatedly〔rɪ'pitɪdlɪ〕 adv. 反覆地；再三地
cheat〔tʃit〕 v. 騙取（= *defraud*）　　retired〔rɪ'taɪrd〕 adj. 退休的

7. (**A**) His hair was <u>untidy</u> and filthy.

他的頭髮又<u>亂</u>又髒。

(A) *untidy* ﹝ ʌn'taɪdɪ ﹞ *adj.* 亂七八糟的；不修邊幅的

an untidy kitchen 亂七八糟的廚房

a long and untidy beard 長而亂的鬍子

untidily *adv.* untidiness *n.*

(B) treacherous ﹝'trɛtʃərəs ﹞ *adj.* 叛逆的；不忠的；不可靠的

a treacherous action 叛逆行為

a treacherous memory 不可靠的記憶

treacherous ice 看似堅固，實為易碎的冰

(C) unraveled ﹝ ʌn'rævl̩d ﹞ *adj.* 解開的

ravel *v.* 使糾結；使錯綜複雜

(D) screwed ﹝ skrud ﹞ *adj.* 以螺絲釘固定的；【俚】被騙的

screw *v.* 以螺絲釘固定 *n.* 螺絲釘 screw cap 螺絲帽

screwdriver 螺絲起子；柳橙汁雞尾酒（由伏特加酒和柳橙汁調和而成）

＊filthy ﹝'fɪlθɪ ﹞ *adj.* 污穢的；髒的

8. (**C**) The <u>prospects</u> of our winning several medals in the Olympic Games are becoming brighter.

我們要在奧運會中奪得幾面獎牌的<u>期望</u>，變得越來越有希望了。

(A) aspect ﹝'æspɛkt ﹞ *n.* 形勢；局面 (= *phase*)；觀點

(= *viewpoint* = *point of view* = *angle*)

(B) expect ﹝ ɪk'spɛkt ﹞ *v.* 預期；期待 expectancy *n.* 期待

expectant *adj.* 盼望的

(C) *prospect* ﹝'prɑspɛkt ﹞ *n.* 預期；期待；希望

a prospect of recovery 復原的希望

(D) suspect ﹝'sʌspɛkt ﹞ *n.* 嫌疑犯 *adj.* 令人懷疑的

a murder suspect 殺人兇嫌

rather suspect evidence 相當可疑的證據

suspect ﹝ sə'spɛkt ﹞ *v.* 懷疑

＊*the Olympic Games* 奧林匹克運動會 medal ﹝'mɛdl̩ ﹞ *n.* 獎牌

brighter ﹝'braɪtɚ ﹞ *adj.* 更有希望的；更光明的

9. (**B**) The boss is <u>indignant</u> because his staff didn't consult him on an important decision.

老闆非常<u>氣憤</u>，因為他的員工在做重要決定之前沒跟他商量。

(A) imposing〔ɪmˈpozɪŋ〕*adj.* 給人深刻印象的；顯眼的
an imposing presence 相貌堂堂
imposingly *adv.*　　impose *v.* 將（意見等）強加於（人）

(B) *indignant*〔ɪnˈdɪgnənt〕*adj.* 氣憤的；憤慨的　　indignation *n.* 氣憤

(C) inhibited〔ɪnˈhɪbɪtɪd〕*adj.* 被抑制的；拘謹的
an inhibited person 拘謹的人

(D) impervious〔ɪmˈpɝvɪəs〕*adj.* 不透（水、空氣等）的
imperviously *adv.*　　imperviousness *n.*
a fabric impervious to water 不透水的布

＊staff〔stæf〕*n.* 職員；工作人員　　consult〔kənˈsʌlt〕*v.* 請教；查閱

10. (**D**) You might run that comb through your hair so you will look <u>presentable</u>.

你應該用梳子梳一下頭髮，這樣看起來會比較<u>體面</u>。

(A) plausible〔ˈplɔzəbḷ〕*adj.* 似真實的；好像有道理的
a plausible excuse 好像有道理的藉口

(B) insurmountable〔͵ɪnsɚˈmaʊntəbḷ〕*adj.* （障礙等）難以克服的
surmountable 可以克服的

(C) accessible〔ækˈsɛsəbḷ〕*adj.* （地點、人等）易接近的；容易到達的
access *n.* 接近；進入

(D) *presentable*〔prɪˈzɛntəbḷ〕*adj.* 體面的
make *oneself* presentable （為了見人而）整裝

＊run〔rʌn〕*v.* 將（線、針頭、梳子等）穿過；插入
comb〔kom〕*n.* 梳子

11. (**A**) The strong hurricane caused great destruction in the U.S., and the President tried to find out who was truly <u>at fault</u> for the severe losses in New Orleans.

這個強烈颶風在美國造成嚴重破壞，而總統試圖要找出，誰是真正<u>該負責</u>紐奧良嚴重損失的人。

(A) *at fault* 有過失；該受責備　　(B) in service 使用中；服役中

(C) on line 在線上；連線中　　(D) by law 根據法律

＊hurricane〔ˈhɝ͵ken〕*n.* 颶風（尤指西印度群島附近的大旋風，美國一向為這種颶風取女性名字）
destruction〔dɪˈstrʌkʃən〕*n.* 破壞　　severe〔səˈvɪr〕*adj.* 嚴重的
New Orleans 紐奧良（位於美國路易斯安納州東南部，密西西比河畔的港市）

12. (**C**) The magic tricks <u>on the whole</u> were quite successful and the audience was crazy about the magician who performed the show.

<u>整體而言</u>，這次的魔術表演大受歡迎。觀眾對於演出的魔術師為之瘋狂。

(A) out of the question 不可能　　out of question 無疑地 (= *beyond question*)

(B) in no sense 絕不（是）

例：He is in no sense normal. 他絕對不是正常的。

(C) *on the whole* 整體而言

例：On the whole I think you did a great job.

整體而言，我覺得你做得不錯。

(D) by no means 絕不　　by all means 必定；一定

* *magic tricks* 魔術表演　　audience (ˈɔdɪəns) *n.* 觀眾

erazy (ˈkrezɪ) *adj.* 狂熱的；很喜歡的

magician (məˈdʒɪʃən) *n.* 魔術師　　perform (pɚˈfɔrm) *v.* 表演

13. (**D**) The president of the company believes that good quality work is the key to success. Therefore, anyone who does a good job, <u>for better or worse</u>, shall be needed in the company. 這家公司的總裁相信，優良的工作品質是成功的秘訣。因此，表現好的人，<u>無論如何</u>都是這家公司所需的人才。

(A) off and on 斷斷續續地　　　　(B) up and down 上上下下地

(C) back and forth 來回地

(D) *for better or worse* 不管好壞；無論如何

* president (ˈprɛzədənt) *n.* 總裁；董事長　　quality (ˈkwɑlətɪ) *n.* 品質；素質

key (ki) *n.* （成功的）秘訣　　therefore (ˈðɛr,for) *adv.* 因此

14. (**C**) In recent years, a lot of traditional ways of doing things have <u>given way to</u> new ones. 近年來，許多傳統做事的方法，已經<u>被</u>新方法<u>取代</u>了。

(A) have a way of 有～的方式　　(B) find a way of 找到～的方法

(C) *give way to* 向～屈服；被～取代　(D) change the way of 改變～的方式

* recent (ˈrisn̩t) *adj.* 最近的　　traditional (trəˈdɪʃən!̩) *adj.* 傳統的

15. (**C**) Emily lost her dog, and it was a great blow to her. She spent so much time <u>getting over</u> the grief.

愛蜜莉受到失去愛狗的重大打擊。她花了很多時間才<u>從悲傷中恢復過來</u>。

(A) put out 熄滅　　　　　　　　(B) come across 偶然遇到

(C) *get over* 自～中恢復　　　　　(D) go around 足夠分配

* blow (blo) *n.* 打擊　　grief (grif) *n.* 悲傷

TEST 40

Directions: The following questions are incomplete sentences. You are to choose the one word that best completes the sentence.

1. Zack got hit with a broken bottle and needed seven _____ in his forehead.
   - (A) stings
   - (B) scars
   - (C) strokes
   - (D) stitches
   - (   )

2. We chased after the thief, but he instantly _____ into the crowd.
   - (A) extended
   - (B) vanished
   - (C) bumped
   - (D) strolled
   - (   )

3. Kelly's opinion of Taipei has _____ changed. She used to dislike it, but now it's her favorite city in the world.
   - (A) radically
   - (B) partially
   - (C) casually
   - (D) barely
   - (   )

4. Chris has German blood because his _____ were from Germany.
   - (A) mentors
   - (B) counterparts
   - (C) rivals
   - (D) ancestors
   - (   )

5. The boutique is _____ closed for redecoration. It will re-open on December 10.
   - (A) temporarily
   - (B) annually
   - (C) ultimately
   - (D) eventually
   - (   )

6. Please _____ the items you'd like by placing a check next to them.
   - (A) specify
   - (B) generate
   - (C) utter
   - (D) abuse
   - (   )

7. Rubber is a _____ substance. It can be bent easily without breaking.
   - (A) fragile
   - (B) fertile
   - (C) flexible
   - (D) fragrant
   - (   )

8. Because of their _____ sense of smell, rescue dogs can find people trapped in debris.
   (A) keen
   (B) elaborate
   (C) desperate
   (D) bitter   ( )

9. The old lady is very nosy and always shows _____ about everything her neighbors are doing.
   (A) impatience
   (B) curiosity
   (C) prejudice
   (D) modesty   ( )

10. Tokyo is a very modern city because large _____ of the city were demolished and reconstructed during the 20th century.
    (A) proponents
    (B) portions
    (C) proceeds
    (D) perspectives   ( )

11. He wrote the song in memory of his daughter, who died in an accident. It well _____ how he felt about her tragic death.
    (A) withstood
    (B) reflected
    (C) undertook
    (D) dominated   ( )

12. Katie apparently had a(n) _____ to the medicine. Her face immediately started to swell after she took it.
    (A) addiction
    (B) illusion
    (C) reaction
    (D) tendency   ( )

13. It's hard not to take it personally when someone says something _____ about your family.
    (A) negative
    (B) appropriate
    (C) crucial
    (D) remote   ( )

14. Renee is in the _____ in her profession. Few of her colleagues are female.
    (A) priority
    (B) minority
    (C) authority
    (D) majority   ( )

15. A _____ to prevent theft is to keep your doors locked.
    (A) rule of thumb
    (B) role model
    (C) stumbling block
    (D) blessing in disguise   ( )

TEST 40 詳解

1. (**D**) Zack got hit with a broken bottle and needed seven <u>stitches</u> in his forehead.
查克的前額被一個破掉的瓶子打到，並且需要縫七針。

(A) sting〔stɪŋ〕*n.*（昆蟲的）針；（植物的）刺；諷刺
the sting of *one's* tongue 刻薄話

(B) scar〔skɑr〕*n.*（割傷、燙傷等的）疤；（傢俱的）刮痕
a scar on the table 桌上的刮痕

(C) stroke〔strok〕*n.* 打；打擊；（中風等的）發作   have a stroke 患中風

(D) *stitch*〔stɪtʃ〕*n.*（縫衣、刺繡等的）一針
put a stitch in a garment 把衣服縫一縫
A stitch in time saves nine.【諺】及時縫一針，省掉將來縫九針。

* bottle〔'bɑtḷ〕*n.*（瓶口細小的）瓶子   forehead〔'fɔr,hɛd〕*n.* 前額

2. (**B**) We chased after the thief, but he instantly <u>vanished</u> into the crowd.
我們追捕那個小偷，但他馬上就消失在人群中。

(A) extend〔ɪk'stɛnd〕*v.* 擴大（= *expand*）；延伸（= *stretch*）   extension *n.*

(B) *vanish*〔'vænɪʃ〕*v.*（在眼前的東西突然）消失（= *disappear*）

(C) bump〔bʌmp〕*v.* 碰；撞   bump into 意外碰到
bump up 抬高（物價、工資等）

(D) stroll〔strol〕*v.*（在某處）溜達；閒逛；巡迴演出
strolling *adj.* 巡迴演出的

* chase〔tʃes〕*v.* 追趕；追捕   instantly〔'ɪnstəntlɪ〕*adv.* 立即地；立刻地

3. (**A**) Kelly's opinion of Taipei has <u>radically</u> changed. She used to dislike it, but
now it's her favorite city in the world.
凱莉對於台北的看法已經徹底地改變。她以前討厭台北，但現在卻反而變成是
她世界上最喜歡的城市。

(A) *radically*〔'rædɪkḷɪ〕*adv.* 徹底地（= *thoroughly* = *completely* = *utterly*
= *totally* = *entirely*）；激進地（= *progressively*）；基本地（= *basically*
= *fundamentally*）

(B) partially〔'pɑrʃəlɪ〕*adv.* 部分地（= *partly*）；不公平地
judge partially 不公平地審判

(C) casually〔'kædʒəlɪ〕*adv.* 偶然地（= *accidentally* = *contingently*）；
意料之外地

(D) barely〔'bɛrlɪ〕*adv.* 幾乎不（= *hardly* = *scarcely*）

* opinion〔ə'pɪnjən〕*n.* 意見；看法（= *point of view* = *viewpoint*）
used to 以前   dislike〔dɪs'laɪk〕*v.* 不喜歡；討厭（= *hate* = *abominate*）

4. (**D**) Chris has German blood because his <u>ancestors</u> were from Germany.
克里斯有德國血統，因爲他的<u>祖先</u>來自德國。

(A) mentor（'mɛntɚ）*n.* 優秀的領導者；良師（源自於希臘故事中，奧地修斯之子的良師：曼托）

(B) counterpart（'kaʊntɚ,pɑrt）*n.* 相對物；對照物

(C) rival（'raɪvl̩）*n.* 競爭對手　　without rival 無可匹敵
a rival in love 情敵

(D) *ancestor*（'ænsɛstɚ）*n.* 祖先（= *forefathers*）
ancestry *n.*（集合稱）祖先

* German（'dʒɝmən）*adj.* 德國的　　blood（blʌd）*n.* 血統；血緣
Germany（'dʒɝmənɪ）*n.* 德國

5. (**A**) The boutique is <u>temporarily</u> closed for redecoration. It will re-open on December 10.
這家精品店因重新裝潢而<u>暫停</u>營業。十二月十日會重新開幕。

(A) *temporarily*（'tɛmpə,rɛrəlɪ）*adv.* 暫時地；短暫地
（↔ permanently　永久地）

(B) annually（'ænjʊəlɪ）*adv.* 一年一次地　　annual *adj.*

(C) ultimately（'ʌltəmɪtlɪ）*adv.* 最後地（= *finally* = *eventually* = *at last* = *at length*）；終極地

(D) eventually（ɪ'vɛntʃʊəlɪ）*adv.* 最後（= *finally* = *ultimately* = *at last* = *in the end*）

* boutique（bu'tik）*n.* 專賣流行服飾、高級用品等的小時裝店
redecoration（,ridɛkə'reʃən）*n.* 重新裝潢

6. (**A**) Please <u>specify</u> the items you'd like by placing a check next to them.
請<u>逐一</u>在你想要的樣品旁邊打個勾。

(A) *specify*（'spɛsə,faɪ）*v.* 逐一明示；詳述
specific（spɪ'sɪfɪk）*adj.* 具體的；明確的

(B) generate（'dʒɛnə,ret）*v.* 產生；引起（= *create* = *produce*）

(C) utter（'ʌtɚ）*v.* 自口中發出（聲音、言語、嘆息等）　　*adj.* 徹底的
utter darkness 漆黑

(D) abuse（ə'bjuz）*v.* 濫用（特權、地位、才能等）
abuse *one's* authority 濫用職權

* item（'aɪtəm）*n.* 項目；品目　　place（ples）*v.* 放置
check（tʃɛk）*n.* 查核的記號

7. (**C**) Rubber is a <u>flexible</u> substance. It can be bent easily without breaking.
橡皮是個<u>有彈性的</u>物質。它很容易折彎而不會斷。

   (A) fragile〔'frædʒəl〕*adj.* 脆弱的；虛弱的（= *flimsy*）
      fragile health 虛弱的體質

   (B) fertile〔'fɝtl̩〕*adj.* 肥沃的；豐饒的（↔ *infertile*）
      fertile land 肥沃的土地

   (C) *flexible*〔'flɛksəbl̩〕*adj.* 有彈性的（= *elastic* = *rubbery*）
      flexible hours 自由的時間

   (D) fragrant〔'fregrənt〕*adj.* 有香味的；芬芳的   fragrantly *adv.*
      fragrance *n.*

   * rubber〔'rʌbɚ〕*n.* 橡皮   substance〔'sʌbstəns〕*n.* 物質
    bend〔bɛnd〕*v.* 使彎曲

8. (**A**) Because of their <u>keen</u> sense of smell, rescue dogs can find people trapped
in debris. 由於救難犬有很<u>敏銳的</u>嗅覺，他們可以很快地找到受困在瓦礫碎片
堆中的受難者。

   (A) *keen*〔kin〕*adj.*（視覺、聽覺等）敏銳的（= *fine*）
      a keen sense of hearing 敏銳的聽覺

   (B) elaborate〔ɪ'læbərɪt〕*adj.* 精巧的；精緻的
      （= *exquisite* = *delicate*）

   (C) desperate〔'dɛspərɪt〕*adj.* 非常渴望的（= *anxious*）；絕望的
      （= *despairing* = *heartbroken*）

   (D) bitter〔'bɪtɚ〕*adj.* 苦味的；難受的；嚴酷的
      a bitter winter 嚴冬   bitterness *n.*

   * sense〔sɛns〕*n.* 感覺   *sense of smell* 嗅覺
    rescue〔'rɛskju〕*adj.* 營救的   *rescue dog* 救難犬
    trap〔træp〕*v.* 使困住   debris〔də'bri〕*n.* 碎片；瓦礫

9. (**B**) The old lady is very nosy and always shows <u>curiosity</u> about everything her
neighbors are doing. 那位老太太很喜歡問東問西的，對於街坊鄰居在做什
麼事情，她總是充滿了<u>好奇心</u>。

   (A) impatience〔ɪm'peʃəns〕*n.* 不耐煩
      with impatience 不耐煩地   patience *n.* 耐心

   (B) *curiosity*〔‚kjʊrɪ'ɑsətɪ〕*n.* 好奇（心）
      out of curiosity 出於好奇   curious *adj.* 好奇的

   (C) prejudice〔'prɛdʒədɪs〕*n.* 偏見（= *bias*）；歧視
      racial prejudice 種族歧視

   (D) modesty〔'mɑdəstɪ〕*n.* 謙遜；謙虛   modest *adj.*（= *humble*）

   * nosy〔'nozɪ〕*adj.* 好問東問西的；愛探聽的

10. (**B**) Tokyo is a very modern city because large <u>portions</u> of the city were demolished and reconstructed during the 20th century.
東京是個非常現代的城市，因爲該市的建築有很大的<u>部分</u>在二十世紀期間，經過破壞以及重建過。

(A) proponent (prə'ponənt) *n.* 提議者；支持者 (= *backer* = *supporter* = *upholder*)

(B) *portion* ('pɔrʃən) *n.* 部分 (= *part* = *proportion* = *section*)

(C) proceeds ('prosidz) *n. pl.* 營收額　　net proceeds 淨收入
(prə'sid) *v.* 著手進行

(D) perspective (pɚ'spɛktɪv) *n.* 洞察力；遠景；展望
a fine perspective　一幅美麗的遠景

∗ demolish (dɪ'mɑlɪʃ) *v.* 破壞
reconstruct (,rikən'strʌkt) *v.* (於破壞之後) 重建

11. (**B**) He wrote the song in memory of his daughter, who died in an accident. It well <u>reflected</u> how he felt about her tragic death.　他的女兒在一場意外中過世了，他寫了這首歌紀念她。對於他女兒不幸喪生的傷感，在這首歌中<u>表露無遺</u>。

(A) withstand (wɪθ'stænd) *v.* 抵抗 (= *oppose*)
【大家站在一起，表示要並肩「抵抗」】

(B) *reflect* (rɪ'flɛkt) *v.* 反映；顯示；流露 (= *display* = *communicate* = *demonstrate*)

(C) undertake (,ʌndɚ'tek) *v.* 承擔 (工作、責任、義務等)
【站在底下拿東西，表示「承擔」】

(D) dominate ('dɑmə,net) *v.* 支配；控制 (= *control* = *command* = *rule* = *govern*)

∗ *in memory of* 紀念　　tragic ('trædʒɪk) *adj.* 悲劇的；悲慘的

12. (**C**) Katie apparently had a <u>reaction</u> to the medicine. Her face immediately started to swell after she took it.
凱蒂似乎是對該藥物起<u>反應</u>。吃了藥之後，她的臉馬上開始腫脹。

(A) addiction (ə'dɪkʃən) *n.* 上癮　　addictive *adj.* 習慣性的
addicted *adj.* 上癮的

(B) illusion (ɪ'luʒən) *n.* 幻覺 (= *hallucination*)；錯覺；錯誤的想法
illusory *adj.* 錯覺的

(C) *reaction* (rɪ'ækʃən) *n.* 反應 (= *response*)

(D) tendency ('tɛndənsɪ) *n.* 趨勢 (= *trend* = *current* = *inclination*)；性向

∗ apparently (ə'pærəntlɪ) *adv.* 似乎
immediately (ɪ'midɪɪtlɪ) *adv.* 立刻
swell (swɛl) *v.* 膨脹；(手、腳、臉、腹等) 腫起來

13. (**A**) It's hard not to take it personally when someone says something <u>negative</u> about your family.

當有人對你家批評一些<u>負面的</u>話，很難不把它想成是別人在做人身攻擊。

(A) *negative* (ˈnɛgətɪv) *adj.* 否定的 (↔ *affirmative*)；負面的 (↔ *positive*)

(B) appropriate (əˈproprɪˌet) *adj.* 適切的 (= *fit* = *apt* = *proper*)
appropriate words 適當的話

(C) crucial (ˈkruʃəl) *adj.* 極重要的 (= *critical* = *cardinal* = *significant* = *vital* = *key*)

(D) remote (rɪˈmot) *adj.* 遙遠的　　a remote place 遙遠的地方
remote control 遙控

* take (tek) *v.* 把…認為
personally (ˈpɜsn̩lɪ) *adv.* 就本人而言；做為攻擊個人地
take it personally 做人身攻擊

14. (**B**) Renee is in the <u>minority</u> in her profession. Few of her colleagues are female.

蕾妮在她工作的行業中算是<u>少數</u>。她的同事當中很少有女性。

(A) priority (praɪˈɔrətɪ) *n.* (時間、順序上的) 先；優先權 (= *preference*)

(B) *minority* (maɪˈnɔrətɪ) *n.* 少數 (↔ *majority*)
minority leader 少數黨領袖

(C) authority (əˈθɔrətɪ) *n.* 權威；權限；權威人士
authorities *n. pl.* 官方；當局

(D) majority (məˈdʒɔrətɪ) *n.* 大多數 (↔ *minority*) (指整體時當單數用；
指全部個體時當複數用)

* profession (prəˈfɛʃən) *n.* 職業；同業
colleague (ˈkɑlig) *n.* 同事 (= *co-worker*)

15. (**A**) A <u>rule of thumb</u> to prevent theft is to keep your doors locked.

就<u>經驗法則</u>來看，把門關好可以防止竊盜案的發生。

(A) *rule of thumb* 根據經驗而不根據理論的做法；經驗之談；經驗法則
thumb (θʌm) *n.* 大拇指

(B) role model 榜樣角色；模範　　role (rol) *n.* 角色
model (ˈmɑdl̩) *n.* 模範

(C) stumbling block 絆腳石　　stumble *v.* 絆倒
block (blɑk) *n.* 木塊；石塊

(D) a blessing in disguise 塞翁失馬，焉知非福
blessing (ˈblɛsɪŋ) *n.* 幸福　　disguise (dɪsˈgaɪz) *n.* 偽裝

* prevent (prɪˈvɛnt) *v.* 防止　　theft (θɛft) *n.* 竊盜行為

高中 7000 字測驗題庫
40 Tests of The Most Used
English Vocabulary 7000 Words

售價：180 元

主　　編 / 劉　毅
發 行 所 / 學習出版有限公司　　　☎ (02) 2704-5525
郵 撥 帳 號 / 05127272 學習出版社帳戶
登 記 證 / 局版台業 2179 號
印 刷 所 / 裕強彩色印刷有限公司
台 北 門 市 / 台北市許昌街 17 號 6F　☎ (02) 2331-4060
台灣總經銷 / 紅螞蟻圖書有限公司　　☎ (02) 2795-3656
本公司網址 / www.learnbook.com.tw
電 子 郵 件 / learnbook0928@gmail.com

2024 年 1 月 1 日新修訂

4713269382126

高三同學要如何準備「升大學考試」

　　考前該如何準備「學測」呢？「劉毅英文」的同學很簡單，只要熟讀每次的模考試題就行了。每一份試題都在7000字範圍內，就不必再背7000字了，從後面往前複習，越後面越重要，一定要把最後10份試題唸得滾瓜爛熟。根據以往的經驗，詞彙題絕對不會超出7000字範圍。每年題型變化不大，只要針對下面幾個大題準備即可。

準備「詞彙題」最佳資料：

背了再背，背到滾瓜爛熟，讓背單字變成樂趣。

　　考前不斷地做模擬試題就對了！

你做的題目愈多，分數就愈高。不要忘記，每次參加模考前，都要背單字、背自己所喜歡的作文。考壞不難過，勇往直前，必可得高分！

練習「模擬試題」，可參考「學習出版公司」最新出版的「7000字學測試題詳解」。我們試題的特色是：
①以「高中常用7000字」為範圍。②經過外籍專家多次校對，不會學錯。③每份試題都有詳細解答，對錯答案均有明確交待。

「克漏字」如何答題

　　第二大題綜合測驗（即「克漏字」），不是考句意，就是考簡單的文法。當四個選項都不相同時，就是考句意，就沒有文法的問題；當四個選項單字相同、字群排列不同時，就是考文法，此時就要注意到文法的分析，大多是考連接詞、分詞構句、時態等。「克漏字」是考生最弱的一環，你難，別人也難，只要考前利用這種答題技巧，勤加練習，就容易勝過別人。

準備「綜合測驗」（克漏字）可參考「學習出版公司」最新出版的「7000字克漏字詳解」。

本書特色：

1. 取材自大規模考試，英雄所見略同。
2. 不超出7000字範圍，不會做白工。
3. 每個句子都有文法分析。一目了然。
4. 對錯答案都有明確交待，列出生字，不用查字典。
5. 經過「劉毅英文」同學實際考過，效果極佳。

「文意選填」答題技巧

　　在做「文意選填」的時候，一定要冷靜。你要記住，一個空格一個答案，如果你不知道該選哪個才好，不妨先把詞性正確的選項挑出來，如介詞後面一定是名詞，選項裡面只有兩個名詞，再用刪去法，把不可能的選項刪掉。也要特別注意時間的掌控，已經用過的選項就劃掉，以免重複考慮，浪費時間。

準備「文意選填」，可參考「學習出版公司」最新出版的「7000字文意選填詳解」。

特色與「7000字克漏字詳解」相同，不超出7000字的範圍，有詳細解答。

「閱讀測驗」的答題祕訣

① 尋找關鍵字——整篇文章中,最重要就是第一句和最後一句,第一句稱為主題句,最後一句稱為結尾句。每段的第一句和最後一句,第二重要,是該段落的主題句和結尾句。從「主題句」和「結尾句」中,找出相同的關鍵字,就是文章的重點。因為美國人從小被訓練,寫作文要注重主題句,他們給學生一個題目後,要求主題句和結尾句都必須有關鍵字。

② 先看題目、劃線、找出答案、標題號——考試的時候,先把閱讀測驗題目瀏覽一遍,在文章中掃瞄和題幹中相同的關鍵字,把和題目相關的句子,用線畫起來,便可一目了然。通常一句話只會考一題,你畫了線以後,再標上題號,接下來,你找其他題目的答案,就會更快了。

③ 碰到難的單字不要害怕,往往在文章的其他地方,會出現同義字,因為寫文章的人不喜歡重覆,所以才會有難的單字。

④ 如果閱測內容已經知道,像時事等,你就可以直接做答了。

準備「閱讀測驗」,可參考「學習出版公司」最新出版的「7000字閱讀測驗詳解」,本書不超出7000字範圍,每個句子都有文法分析,對錯答案都有明確交待,單字註明級數,不需要再查字典。

「中翻英」如何準備

可參考劉毅老師的「英文翻譯句型講座實況DVD」,以及「文法句型180」和「翻譯句型800」。考前不停地練習中翻英,翻完之後,要給外籍老師改。翻譯題做得越多,越熟練。

「英文作文」怎樣寫才能得高分？

① 字體要寫整齊，最好是印刷體，工工整整，不要塗改。

② 文章不可離題，尤其是每段的第一句和最後一句，最好要有題目所說的關鍵字。

③ 不要全部用簡單句，句子最好要有各種變化，單句、複句、合句、形容詞片語、分詞構句等，混合使用。

④ 不要忘記多使用轉承語，像*at present*（現在），*generally speaking*（一般說來），*in other words*（換句話說），*in particular*（特別地），*all in all*（總而言之）等。

⑤ 拿到考題，最好先寫作文，很多同學考試時，作文來不及寫，吃虧很大。但是，如果看到作文題目不會寫，就先寫測驗題，這個時候，可將題目中作文可使用的單字、成語圈起來，寫作文時就有東西寫了。但千萬記住，絕對不可以抄考卷中的句子，一旦被發現，就會以零分計算。

⑥ 試卷有規定標題，就要寫標題。記住，每段一開始，要內縮5或7個字母。

⑦ 可多引用諺語或名言，並注意標點符號的使用。文章中有各種標點符號，會使文章變得更美。

⑧ 整體的美觀也很重要，段落的最後一行字數不能太少，也不能太多。段落的字數要平均分配，不能第一段只有一、兩句，第二段一大堆。第一段可以比第二段少一點。

準備「英文作文」，可參考「學習出版公司」出版的：